D1489763

# HORROR

2006

## THE BEST OF THE YEAR
### 2006 EDITION

# HORROR
## THE BEST OF THE YEAR
### 2006 EDITION

EDITED BY
JOHN GREGORY BETANCOURT
& SEAN WALLACE

PRIME BOOKS

# HORROR: THE BEST OF THE YEAR 2006 EDITION

Distributed by Diamond Book Distributors.

Prime Book, an imprint of Wildside Press
9710 Traville Gateway Dr. #234
Rockville MD 20850
www.prime-books.com

First Prime Books printing: April 2006

10 9 8 7 6 5 4 3 2 1

Printed in Canada.

*For Kim and Jennifer*

# CONTENTS

# INTRODUCTION

Welcome to a brand-new anthology series, devoted to the best in modern horror — the first since Karl Edward Wagner's *The Year's Best Horror* ended its run back in 1993. It is a companion volume to *Fantasy: The Best of the Year* and *Science Fiction: The Best of the Year* (edited by Rich Horton, from the same publisher).

For this volume, we looked at literally hundreds of short stories from magazines both small and large, single-author collections, original anthologies, and more. There were only two criteria: the stories had to be truly great, and they must have been published in the calendar year of 2005.

As always, many horror stories appear first in magazines, and 2005 was no different. Print publications such as *Apex, Cemetery Dance, Flesh & Blood, Inhuman, Interzone, The Magazine of Fantasy & Science Fiction, Postscripts, Weird Tales*, and many more published interesting work by new and established authors. Often the line between fantasy, suspense, and horror blurred, making stories difficult to classify. When in doubt, we fell back on the "horror is what I mean when I point at it" definition. Be your own judge.

Relatively few new magazines launched in 2005. Bill Schafer's Subterranean Press published two issues of *Subterranean Magazine*, with an impressive line-up of contributors, including Charles De Lint, Harlan Ellison, Joe Hill, Caitlin Kiernan, Joe Lansdale, Peter Crowther, and many more.

The only other major magazine change was the purchase of *Weird Tales*, "The Unique Magazine," by Wildside Press, with John Gregory Betancourt rejoining the editorial team of George Scithers and Darrell Schweitzer. The first issue under Wildside Press included the first William F. Nolan serial in the magazine's history, plus new fiction from old-time greats Jack Williamson and Clark Ashton Smith (a recently unearthed treasure). Many more changes are expected.

Online venues continued to issue quality short fiction as well, including *Chizine, Fortean Bureau*, and *Son and Foe*. However, the online horror community lost one major fiction source when the

Sci-Fi Channel closed down the fiction portion of its web site at the end of 2005. Over the years, *SciFiction* published a steady stream of high-quality fantasy, science fiction, and horror (many of which were picked up for previous years' "Best of" volumes), under the editorial direction of Ellen Datlow. We are hopeful she will find a new editorial home soon.

Anthologies are another mainstay of the horror field. 2005 saw several major releases, including *Dark Delicacies*, edited by Del Howison and Jeff Gelb; *Don't Turn Out the Lights*, edited by Stephen Jones; *Fourbodings*, edited by Peter Crowther; *Outsiders*, edited by Nancy Holder and Nancy Kilpatrick; and *Taverns of the Dead*, edited by Kealan Patrick Burke. Each had at least a few standout stories, and deciding which to include often proved difficult.

Another source of horror short fiction is book publishers. Short novels—or novellas—are appearing as slim standalone books with increasing regularity. Perhaps it's hard for writers to place such works with magazines or anthologies due to their lengths. However, one standout worthy of your attention—too long to include in this volume, though we would have liked to—was Joe Hill's "Voluntary Committal" from Subterranean Press. Seek out a copy; you won't be disappointed.

And speaking of Joe Hill (who is represented in this volume with "The Cape"), his short story collection *20th Century Ghosts* from PS Publishing was one of the finest collections of the year. It heralds the arrival of a top new talent. The other standout collection of 2005 was Holly Phillips' *In the Palace of Repose*, singled out by many reviewers as a top debut. Holly Phillips is in this volume with "The Other Grace," which originally appeared in her collection. The other major collection of the year was *Haunted* by Chuck Palahniuk, which we highly recommend.

From Joe R. Lansdale to Clive Barker, from Jack Cady to Ramsey Campbell—in this volume you will find many of the greats of modern horror with newer voices such as Laird Barron, Jeff VanderMeer, Nick Mamatas, and many others. So sit back, put up your feet, and enjoy some of the best horror stories of the year!

—John Gregory Betancourt
& Sean Wallace

# HORROR
## THE BEST OF THE YEAR

# THE SHADOWS, KITH AND KIN

## *Joe R. Lansdale*

*". . . and the soul, resenting its lot, flies groaningly to the shades."*
— The Æneid, by Virgil

There are no leaves left on the trees, and the limbs are weighted with ice and bending low. Many of them have broken and fallen across the drive. Beyond the drive, down where it and the road meet, where the bar ditch is, there is a brown savage run of water.

It is early afternoon, but already it is growing dark, and the fifth week of the storm raves on. I have never seen such a storm of wind and ice and rain, not here in the South, and only once before have I been in a cold storm bad enough to force me to lock myself tight in my home.

So many things were different then, during that first storm.

No better. But different.

On this day while I sit by my window, looking out at what the great, white, wet storm has done to my world, I feel at first confused, and finally elated.

The storm. The ice. The rain. All of it. It's the sign I was waiting for.

I thought for a moment of my wife, her hair so blond it was almost white as the ice that hung in the trees, and I thought of her parents, white-headed too, but white with age, not dye, and of our little dog, Constance, not white at all, but all brown and black with traces of tan; a rat terrier mixed with all other blends of dog you might imagine.

I thought of all of them. I looked at my watch. There wasn't really any reason to. I had no place to go, and no way to go if I did. Besides, the battery in my watch had been dead for almost a month.

Once, when I was a boy, just before nightfall, I was out hunting with my father, out where the bayou water gets deep and runs between the twisted trunks and low-hanging limbs of water-loving trees; out there where the frogs bleat and jump and the sun don't hardly shine.

We were hunting for hogs. Then out of the brush came a man, running. He was dressed in striped clothes and he had on very thin shoes. He saw us and the dogs that were gathered about us, blue-ticks, long-eared and dripping spit from their jaws; he turned and broke and ran with a scream.

A few minutes later, the sheriff and three of his deputies came beating their way through the brush, their shirts stained with sweat, their laces red with heat.

My father watched all of this with a kind of hard-edged cool, and the sheriff, a man dad knew, said, "There's a man escaped off the chain gang, Hirem. He run through here. Did you see him?"

My father said that we had, and the sheriff said, "Will those dogs track him?"

"I want them to they will," my father said, and he called the dogs over to where the convict had been, where his footprints in the mud were filling slowly with water, and he pushed the dogs heads down toward these shoe prints one at a time, and said, "Sic him," and away the hounds went.

We ran after them then, me and my dad and all these fat cops who huffed and puffed out long before we did, and finally we came upon the man, tired, leaning against a tree with one hand, his other holding his business while he urinated on the bark. He had been defeated some time back, and now he was waiting for rescue, probably thinking it would have been best to have not run at all.

But the dogs, they had decided by private conference that this man was as good as any hog, and they came down on him like heat-seeking missiles. Hit him hard, knocked him down. I turned to my father, who could call them up and make them stop, no matter what the situation, but he did not call.

The dogs tore at the man, and I wanted to turn away, but did not. I looked at my father and his eyes were alight and his lips dripped spit; he reminded me of the hounds.

The dogs ripped and growled and savaged, and then the fat sheriff and his fat deputies stumbled into view, and when one of the deputies saw what had been done to the man, he doubled over and let go of whatever grease-fried goodness he had poked into his mouth earlier that day.

The sheriff and the other deputy stopped and stared, and the sheriff said, "My God," and turned away, and the deputy said, "Stop them, Hirem. Stop them. They done done it to him. Stop them."

My father called the dogs back, their muzzles dark and dripping. They sat in a row behind him, like sentries. The man, what had been a man, the convict, he lay all about the base of the tree, as did the rags that had once been his clothes.

Later, we learned the convict had been on the chain gang for cashing hot checks.

Time keeps on slipping, slipping. . . . Wasn't that a song?

As day comes I sleep, then awake when night arrives. The sky has cleared and the moon has come out, and it is merely cold now. Pulling on my coat, I go out on the porch and sniff the air, and the air is like a meat slicer to the brain, so sharp it gives me a headache. I have never known cold like that.

I can see the yard close up. Ice has sheened all over my world, all across the ground, up in the trees, and the sky is like a black velvet backdrop, the stars like sharp shards of blue ice clinging to it.

I leave the porch light on, go inside, return to my chair by the window, burp. The air is filled with the aroma of my last meal, canned ravioli, eaten cold.

I take off my coat and hang it on the back of the chair.

Has it happened yet, or is it yet to happen.

Time, it just keep on slippin', slippin', yeah, it do.

I nod in the chair, and when I snap awake from a deep nod, there is snow blowing across the yard and the moon is gone and there is only the porch light to brighten it up.

But, in spite of the cold, I know they are out there.

The cold, the heat, nothing bothers them.

They are out there.

They came to me first on a dark night several months back, with no snow and no rain and no cold, but a dark night without clouds and plenty of heat in the air, a real humid night, sticky like dirty undershorts. I awoke and sat up in bed and the yard light was shining thinly through our window. I turned to look at my wife lying there beside me, her very blond hair silver in that light. I looked at her for a long time, then got up and went into the living room. Our little dog, who made her bed by the front door, came over and sniffed me, and I bent to pet her. She took to this for a minute, then found her spot by the door again, lay down.

Finally I turned out the yard light and went out on the porch. In my underwear. No one could see me, not with all our trees, and if they could see me, I didn't care.

I sat in a deck chair and looked at the night, and thought about the job I didn't have and how my wife had been talking of divorce, and how my in-laws resented our living with them, and I thought too of how every time I did a thing I failed, and dramatically at that. I felt strange and empty and lost.

While I watched the night, the darkness split apart and some of it came up on the porch, walking. Heavy steps full of all the world's shadow.

I was frightened, but I didn't move. Couldn't move. The shadow, which looked like a tar-covered human shape, trudged heavily across the porch until it stood over me, looking down. When I looked up, trembling, I saw there was no face, just darkness, thick as chocolate custard. It bent low and placed hand shapes on the sides of my chair and brought its faceless face close to mine, breathed on me, a hot languid breath that made me ill.

"You are almost one of us," it said, then turned, and slowly moved along the porch and down the steps and right back into the shadows. The darkness, thick as a wall, thinned and split, and absorbed my visitor; then the shadows rustled away in all directions like startled bats. I heard a dry crackling leaf sound amongst the trees.

My God, I thought. There had been a crowd of them.

Out there.

Waiting.

Watching.

Shadows.

And one of them had spoken to me.

Lying in bed later that night I held up my hand and found that what intrigued me most were not the fingers, but the darkness between them. It was a thin darkness, made weak by light, but it was darkness and it seemed more a part of me than the flesh.

I turned and looked at my sleeping wife.

I said, "I am one of them. Almost."

*       *       *

I remember all this as I sit in my chair and the storm rages outside, blowing snow and swirling little twirls of water that in turn become ice. I remember all this, holding up my hand again to look.

The shadows between my fingers are no longer thin.

They are dark.

They have connection to flesh.

They are me.

Four flashes. Four snaps.

The deed is done.

I wait in the chair by the window.

No one comes.

As I suspected.

The shadows were right.

They come to me nightly now. They never enter the house. Perhaps they cannot.

But out on the porch, there they gather. More than one now. And they flutter tight around me and I can smell them, and it is a smell like nothing I have smelled before. It is dark and empty and mildewed and old and dead and dry.

It smells like home.

Who are the shadows?

They are all of those who are like me.

They are the empty congregation. The faceless ones. The failures.

The sad, empty folk who wander through life and walk beside you and never get so much as a glance; nerds like me who live inside their heads and imagine winning the lottery and scoring the girls and walking tall. But instead, we stand short and bald and angry, our hands in our pockets, holding not money but our limp balls.

Real life is a drudge.

No one but another loser like myself can understand that.

Except for the shadows, for they are the ones like me. They are the losers and the lost, and they understand and they never do judge.

They are of my flesh, or, to be more precise, I am of their shadow.

They accept me for who I am.

They know what must be done, and gradually they reveal it to me.
The shadows.
I am one of them.
Well, almost.

My wife, my in-laws, every human being who walks this earth, underrates me.

There are things I can do.

I can play computer games, and I can win at them. I have created my own characters. They are unlike humans. They are better than humans. They are the potential that is inside me and will never be.

Oh, and I can do some other things as well. I didn't mention all the things I can do well. In spite of what my family thinks of me. I can do a number of things that they don't appreciate, but should.

I can make a very good chocolate milk shake. My wife knows this, but she won't admit it. She used to say so. Now she does not. She has closed up to me. Internally. Externally.

Battened down hatches, inwardly and outwardly.

Below. In her fine little galley, that hatch is tightly sealed.

But there is another thing I do well.

I can really shoot a gun.

My father, between beatings, he taught me that. It was the only time when we were happy together. When we held the guns.

Down in the basement I have a trunk.

Inside the trunk are guns.

Lots of them.

Rifles and shotguns and revolvers and automatics.

I have collected them over the years.

One of the rifles belongs to my father-in-law.

There is lots of ammunition.

Sometimes, during the day, if I can't sleep, while my wife is at work and my in-laws are about their retirement, golf, which consists of golf and more golf, I sit down there and clean the guns and load them and repack them in the crate. I do it carefully, slowly, like foreplay. And when I finish my hands smell like gun oil. I rub my hands against my face and under my nose, the odor of the oil like some kind of musk.

But now, with the ice and the cold and the dark, with us frozen in and with no place to go, I clean them at night. Not during the day while they are gone.

I clean them at night.

In the dark.

After I visit with the shadows.

My friends.

All the dark ones, gathered from all over the world, past and present.

Gathered out there in my yard — my wife's parents' yard — waiting on me.

Waiting for me to be one with them, waiting on me to join them.

The only club that has ever wanted me.

They are many of those shadows, and I know who they are now. I know it on the day I take the duct tape and use it to seal the doors to my wife's bedroom, to my parents-in-laws bedroom.

The dog is with my wife.

I can no longer sleep in our bed.

My wife, like the others, has begun to smell.

The tape keeps some of the stench out.

I pour cologne all over the carpet.

It helps.

Some.

How it happened:

One night I went out and sat and the shadows came up on the porch in such numbers there was only darkness around me and in me, and I was like something scared, but somehow happy, down deep in a big black sack held by hands that love me.

Yet, simultaneously, I was free.

I could feel them touching me, breathing on me. And I knew, then, that it was time.

Down in the basement, I opened the trunk, took out a well-oiled hunting rifle, I went upstairs and did it quick. My wife first. She never awoke. Beneath her head, on the pillow, in the moonlight, there was a spreading blossom the color of gun oil.

My father-in-law heard the shot, met me at their bedroom door, pulling on his robe. One shot. Then another for my mother-in-law who sat up in her bed, her face hidden in shadow — but a different shadow. Not one of my friends, one made purely by an absence of light, and not an absence of being.

The dog bit me.
I guess it was the noise.
I shot the dog too.
I didn't want her to be lonely.
Who would care for him?

I pulled my father-in-law into his bed with his wife and pulled the covers to their chins. My wife is tucked in too, the covers over her head. I put our little dog, Constance, beside her.

How long ago was the good deed done?

I can't tell.

I think, strangely, of my father-in-law. He always wore a hat. He thought it strange that men no longer wore hats. When he was growing up in the forties and fifties, men wore hats.

He told me that many times.

He wore hats. Men wore hats, and it was odd to him that they no longer did, and to him the men without hats were manless.

He looked at me then. Hatless. Looked me up and down. Not only was I hatless in his eyes, I was manless.

Manless?

Is that a word?

The wind howls and the night is bright and the shadows twist and the moon gives them light to dance by.

They are many and they are one, and I am almost one of them.

One day I could not sleep and sat up all day. I had taken to the couch at first, in the living room, but in time the stench from behind the taped doors seeped out and it was strong. I made a pallet in the kitchen and pulled all the curtains tight and slept the day away, rose at night and roamed and watched the shadows from the windows or out on the porch. The stench was less then, at night, and out on the porch I couldn't smell it at all.

The phone has rung many times and there are messages from relatives. Asking about the storm. If we are okay.

I consider calling to tell them we are.

But I have no voice for anyone anymore. My vocal cords are hollow and my body is full of dark.

The storm has blown away and in a small matter of time people will come to find out how we are doing. It is daybreak and no car could possibly get up our long drive, not way out here in the country like we are, but the ice is starting to melt.

Can't sleep.

Can't eat.

Thirsty all the time.

Have masturbated till I hurt.

Strange, but by nightfall the ice started to slip away and all the whiteness was gone and the air, though chill, was not as cold, and the shadows gathered on the welcome mat, and now they have slipped inside, like envelopes pushed beneath the bottom of the door.

They join me.

They comfort me.

I oil my guns.

Late night, early morning, depends on how you look at it. The guns are well oiled and there is no ice anywhere. The night is as clear as my mind is now.

I pull the trunk upstairs and drag it out on the porch toward the truck. It's heavy, but I manage it into the back of the pickup. Then I remember there's a dolly in the garage.

My father-in-law's dolly.

"This damn dolly will move anything," he used to say. "Anything."

I get the dolly, load it up, stick in a few tools from the garage, start the truck and roll on out.

I flunked out of college.

Couldn't pass the test.

I'm supposed to be smart.

My mother told me when I was young that I was a genius.

There had been tests.

But I couldn't seem to finish anything.

Dropped out of high school. Took the GED eventually. Didn't score high there either, but did pass. Barely.

What kind of genius is that?

Finally got into college, four years later than everyone else.

Couldn't cut it. Just couldn't hold anything in my head. Too stuffed up there, as if Kleenex had been packed inside.

My history teacher, he told me: "Son, perhaps you should consider a trade."

I drive along campus. My mind is clear, like the night. The campus clock tower is very sharp against the darkness, lit up at the top and all around. A giant phallus punching up at the moon.

It is easy to drive right up to the tower and unload the gun trunk onto the dolly.

My father-in-law was right.

This dolly is amazing.

And my head, so clear. No Kleenex.

And the shadows, thick and plenty, are with me.

Rolling the dolly, a crowbar from the collection of tools stuffed in my belt, I proceed to the front of the tower. I'm wearing a jumpsuit. Gray Workman's uniform. For a while I worked for the janitorial department on campus. My attempt at a trade.

They fired me for reading in the janitor's closet.

But I still have the jumpsuit.

The foyer is open, but the elevators are locked.

I pull the dolly upstairs.

It is a chore, a bump at a time, but the dolly straps hold the trunk and I can hear the guns rattling inside, like they want to get out.

By the time I reach the top I'm sweating, feeling weak. I have no idea how long it has taken, but some time, I'm sure. The shadows have been with me, encouraging me.

Thank you, I tell them.

The door at the top of the clock tower is locked.

I take out my burglar's key The crowbar. Go to work.

It's easy.

On the other side of the door I use the dolly itself to push up under the door handle, and it freezes the door. It'll take some work to shake that loose.

There's one more flight inside the tower.

I have to drag the trunk of guns.

Hard work. The rope handle on the crate snaps and the guns

slide all the way back down.

I push them up.

I almost think I can't make it. The trunk is so heavy. So many guns. And all that sweet ammunition.

Finally to the top, shoving with my shoulder, bending my legs all the way.

The door up there is not locked, the one that leads outside to the runway around the clock tower.

I walk out, leaving the trunk. I walk all around the tower and look down at all the small things there.

Soon the light will come, and so will the people.

Turning, I look up at the huge clock hands. Four o'clock.

I hope time does not slip. I do not want to find myself at home by the window, looking out.

The shadows.

They flutter.

They twist.

The runway is full of them, thick as all the world's lost ones. Thick as all the world's hopeless. Thick, thick, thick, and thicker yet to be. When I join them.

There is one fine spot at the corner tower. That is where I should begin.

I place a rifle there, the one I used to put my family and dog to sleep.

I place rifles all around the tower.

I will probably run from one station to the other.

The shadows make suggestions.

All good, of course.

I put a revolver in my belt.

I put a shotgun near the entrance to the runway hidden behind the edge of the tower, in a little outcrop of artful bricks. It tucks in there nicely.

There are huge flowerpots stuffed with ferns all about the runway I stick pistols in the pots.

When I finish, I look at the clock again.

An hour has passed.

\*       \*       \*

Back home in my chair, looking out the window at the dying night. Back home in my chair, the smell of my family growing familiar, like a shirt worn too many days in a row.

Like the one I have on. Like the thick coat I wear.

I look out the window and it is not the window, but the little split in the runway barrier. There are splits all around the runway walk.

I turn to study the place I have chosen and find myself looking out the window at home, and as I stare, the window melts and so does the house.

The smell.

That does not go with the window and the house.

The smell stays with me.

The shadows are way too close, I am nearly smothered. I can hardly breathe.

Light cracks along the top of the tower and falls through the campus trees and runs along the ground like spilt warm honey.

I clutch my coat together, pull it tight. It is very cold. I can hardly feel my legs.

I get up and walk about the runway twice, checking on all my guns.

Well oiled. Fully loaded.

Full of hot lead announcements.

Telegram: STOP. You're dead STOP.

Back at my spot, the one from which I will begin, I can see movement. The day has started, I poke the rifle through the break in the barrier and bead down on a tall man walking across campus.

I could take him easy.

But I do not.

Wait, say the shadows. Wait until the little world below is full.

The hands on the clock are loud when they move, they sound like the machinery I can hear in my head. Creaking and clanking and moving along.

The air has turned surprisingly warm.

I feel so hot in my jacket.

I take it off.

I am sweating.

The day has come but the shadows stay with me.

True friends are like that. They don't desert you.

Its nice to have true friends.

It's nice to have with me the ones who love me.

It's nice to not be judged.

It's nice to know I know what to do and the shadows know too, and we are all the better for it.

The campus is alive.

People swim across the concrete walks like minnows in the narrows.

Minnows everywhere in their new sharp clothes, ready to take their tests and do their papers and meet each other so they might screw. All of them, with futures.

But I am the future-stealing machine.

I remember once, when I was a child, I went fishing with minnows. Stuck them on the hooks and dropped them in the wet.

When the day was done, I had caught nothing. I violated the fisherman's code. I did not pour the remaining minnows into the water to give them their freedom. I poured them on the ground.

And stomped them.

I was in control.

A young, beautiful girl, probably eighteen, tall like a model, walking like a dream across the campus. The light is on her hair and it looks very blond, like my wife's.

I draw a bead.

The shadows gather. They whisper. They touch. They show me their faces.

They have faces now.

Simple faces.

Like mine.

I trace my eye down the length of the barrel.

Without me really knowing it, the gun snaps sharp in the morning light.

The young woman falls amidst a burst of what looks like plum jelly.

The minnows flutter. The minnows flee.

But there are so many and they are panicked. Like they have been poured on the ground to squirm and gasp in the dry.

I begin to fire. Shot after shot after shot.

Each snap of the rifle a stomp of my foot.

Down they go.

Squashed.

I have no hat, father-in-law, and I am full of manliness.

The day goes up hot. Who would have thunk?

I have moved from one end of the tower to the other, I have dropped many of them.

The cops have come.

I have dropped many of them.

I hear noise in the tower.

I think they shook the dolly loose.

The door to the runway bursts open.

A lady cop steps through. My first shot takes her in the throat. But she snaps one off at about the same time. A revolver shot. It hits next to me where I crouch low against the runway wall.

Another cop comes through the door. I fire and miss.

My first miss.

He fires. I feel something hot inside my shoulder.

I find that I am slipping down, my back against the runway wall. I can't hold the rifle. I try to drag the pistol from my belt, but can't. My arm is dead. The other one, well, it's no good either. The shot has cut something apart inside of me. The strings to my limbs. My puppet won't work.

Another cop appears. He has a shotgun. He leans over me. His teeth are gritted and his eyes are wet.

And just as he fires, the shadows say:

Now, you are one of us.

# THE SOULS OF DROWNING MOUNTAIN[1]

## *Jack Cady*

Mountains in eastern Kentucky have names: Black Mountain, Mingo Mountain, Hangar Mountain, Booger Mountain, and, among a thousand others, Drowning Mountain which rises above a hollow where sits Minnie's Beer Store. Both mountain and store carry tales, and I'll tell but one. It says too much, maybe, about folks helpless beyond all help, and angry as sullen fires. There will be however, some satisfying murders.

When I first saw Drowning Mountain these many years ago I was "full of piss and vinegar" as old folks used to say. Thought I knew it all. Had knocked off four years of military duty, then worked my way through college. Took a job with a government agency that was partly in the business of welfare, and partly in sanctimonious advice. My assignment was a railroad town in southeast Kentucky.

I'd seen my share of bad stuff in the bars of Gloucester and in Boston's Scollay Square. I'd seen green water over the flying bridge of a cutter. I'd seen fire at sea. I'd dealt with the dead and dying; figured I could handle whatever came.

The day I arrived trains hooted, ladies gossiped in summer heat while fanning themselves on front porches. They stayed away from town. Hatred, downtown, boiled along the streets like ball lightning. It dawned on me that I was the only man in sight who wasn't wearing a pistol.

"We're in the middle of a coal war," my new boss told me. "Keep your head down and stay polite." His name was Bobby Joe and he was from around there. He'd done army time. Rail-skinny, shrewd as a razor back, but smiling. After the army time he'd come back to

---

1  This story is in memory of Andy Strunk, coal miner of Gatliff, Kentucky.

the hills. Almost everybody from the hills returns sooner or later.

Bobby Joe assigned me a secretary named Sarah Jane, also from around there. She called me Mister James, not Jim, and we did not warm toward each other for weeks and weeks. Sarah Jane was thirtyish, overweight, pale beneath tan freckles, wore frumpish house dresses, and there was nothing about her that would make any preacher claim her a candidate for heaven. She knew her job front and back. I admired her, but didn't understand her anger.

There seemed no end to everybody's anger. My experience with middlewest small towns and large eastern cities meant nothing. I understood ghettos, poverty, welfare, rich bastards, cops, especially rich bastards and cops.

Yet, nothing matched up. There wasn't a kitty-cat's-chance in a dog pound that I could understand Minnie's Beer Store or Drowning Mountain.

"Walk easy," Bobby Joe told me. He spoke slow and southern, but in complete control. "If you bust ass you're courting trouble." He kept me on a short leash for two months. I warmed a chair behind a desk and talked to old men and tired women.

Then Bobby Joe turned me over to a field rep named Tip. We visited small towns, took hardship-claims and gave advice. We visited people who were shut in. When we drove along thin and rutted sideroads we changed from white shirts to chambray shirts, because men in white shirts looked like revenue agents. Men in white shirts got shot.

What thoughts came to pass? These: This is not real. No one lives this way. This place is straight out of medieval times.

Tip was from around there. He looked more like a hill farmer than a government agent. Lank, with longish hair, thin mouth. He could talk tough as barbed wire, and yet the old people we dealt with were crazy about him. "Tell you about Drowning Mountain," he said one day. "Maybe you'll understand why I'm pissed-off ninety percent of the time."

We were outside of Manchester, Kentucky, scouting around the top of a ridge called Pigeon's Roost. Huge broadleaf trees covered the hillside, tangles of bramble, little wisps of smoke on a hot summer day. Smoke, probably from stills.

Tip had a way of explaining the world by telling stories. "Didn't used to be called Drowning Mountain," he told me. "But it sure as sweet-Jesus earned its name."

Even today, all these years later, it breaks my heart to think of it. I'll condense what Tip said.

These mountains are limestone with seams of coal. Sometimes the seam goes straight into the mountain, but not often. It usually angles in and the coal shaft follows one or more seams. Those shafts are propped with timbers, and generally slate lies above the coal. Take out the coal, slate falls, even sometimes, when propped.

Because the limestone is porous there's always ground water. In those days, when miners hit a narrow seam they sometimes had to lie on their backs in the water, underground and between rock, pushing shovels backward over their shoulders to draw out loose coal that had been blasted. In mining camps, even little boys knew how to set a charge of dynamite.

Were these men screwed? You bet they were. Mine owners used up men worse than bad generals killing their own armies. Coal camps were the kinds of hells that made chain gangs look like a vacation. Men actually did owe their souls to the company store. Even if men had enough imagination to leave town they had no money. They were paid in scrip. Plus, they didn't know any better. Lots of those men had gone into the mines at age twelve.

So, in a coal camp, way, way back in World War I, they had driven a shaft deep into the heart of the mountain. When the seams played out the shaft was abandoned. Twenty-six years later, no one remembered the shaft was there. The coal company opened a seam on the other side of the mountain. The seam drove in on much the same angle as the old shaft because of a fracture in the rock.

Miners blasted their way in, propped the slate, drove deeper, and deeper; and on a fatal day blasted through to the old, forgotten shaft, which had filled with ground water. Seven men died that day, drowning in darkness in the middle of a mountain.

"Ah, no," I told Tip.

"Helluva note," he said. "Makes you sorta sick, don't it?" Tip was the kind of guy, who if he had been a preacher, would have been a good one. He would not have been hellfire, only tough and kind.

"The reason I tell the story," he said, "is because next week we go to Drowning Mountain."

It was a miserable weekend. The office closed. Nothing to do except keep my head down and wait. The town sat in a dry county. Each election, preachers and bootleggers went to the polls and kept it dry. A wet county was just next door and Tennessee was not all that far off, but there was nothing going on in those directions. I hung out at the drugstore, slurped coffee, listened to gossip.

The main rich bastard in town was named Sims. He ramrodded a coal corporation. Sims was one of those sanitary pieces of crap that wear summer suits and carry perfumed hankies as they walk across the faces of dying men.

Sims' chief armament was a guy named Pook. Pook had the reputation of a real nut-buster. Pook was an actual killer with at least two murders notched to his gun. Gossip said the sheriff was afraid of him.

The two showed up Sunday afternoon, walking Main Street like they owned it. Sims said, "howdy," or even, "howdy, neighbor" to grim-faced men who stepped aside to let him pass. Sims had a bald spot, a sizeable gut, and dainty little feet. He seemed cheery. He had jowls like a pig, and a sneer that could push people backward. On Sunday afternoon he went into the bank. The banker came down and opened up just for him.

Pook stood outside the bank. He looked like Godzilla with a haircut. Or a better description, maybe: he looked like a storm trooper, but with a .45 automatic on his hip, not a Mauser. People didn't talk to him. Pook couldn't out-sneer Sims, but his look told folks that he figured them for dog-dump. When Sims came from the bank the two cruised town in a new Cadillac, snubbing everybody; the Cadillac black and shiny.

On Monday morning Sarah Jane tsked. "You take it slow, now," she told me. "Jim."

It was the first time she ever called me anything but mister.

Bobby Joe talked to Tip, real quiet. Both men looked serious.

"What's the war about?" I asked Tip. We left the office and headed for Drowning Mountain.

"The usual," he told me. "Wages, mechanization, it's pitiful." He kind of hunched over the steering wheel. He kept a low profile in the hills. His car was a beat-up Ford made before WWII. "The men only know one kind of work, and there's no other work. They strike in order to go back into the hole at a bit higher pay, which is like asking to jump smack into hell." He paused. "And there's something worse. Stripping."

I'd heard about it. Strip mining was coming into fashion. It destroyed whole mountains. Strip mining made 6000-foot mountains into smoking piles of rubble. Trees gone. Not a stick of vegetation.

Only broken rock. Sulfuric acid rose in the air and washed in the streams. Strip mines were profitable because they needed a few machine operators, but no miners.

"There's something else," Tip told me. "Before we get to Minnie's I gotta prepare you." Even though he was the guy in charge, he looked off-guard and hesitant.

"You might meet some people," he told me, "who you won't know, and maybe I won't either, if they're dead or alive. If you want to stay happy take it for granted. Don't try to study it out. Don't back away."

"Why? Come to think of it, Why and What?"

"Dead or alive, all these folks have is each other. They stick together. There's talk of stripping the mountain."

"Sims?"

"Not all rich men are crap, and not all crap-heads are rich. But, yep. Sims." Tip actually looked relieved . . . probably because I didn't make a deal out of that "dead or alive" business. I'd come to trust Tip, and if he said don't figure on something, it seemed best not to figure. What he said made no sense. For me, it was wait and see.

"I got more to tell," he said. "There's a history."

He explained that Minnie's Beer Store sat in an abandoned coal camp. Old men were sparsely scattered in cabins along the sides of the hills. Most were widowers, but some had young wives because there were no young men for girls to marry. The young men had gone away, some to the Army, some to other coal camps.

Miners, back then, were more spirits than real by age forty. They moved slow as cold molasses because of black lung, silicosis, violent arthritis. Their hair, if they had any, was white and their faces were black. Coal dust gets under the skin. It doesn't even go away in the grave. When bones become dust, they are still tainted with coal.

"So much anger," Tip murmured. "They're furious about being screwed, but most of them don't know how much they're screwed. They don't know how to fight back. So, they're really furious about not knowing." He slowed the car, making a point. "That dead and alive business. It happened at least once before, and it happened during a coal war."

As we approached, rusting rails ran beside a road of thin macadam once laid by the coal company. The hills were covered with hardwood trees, and here at the end of August a little spot of yellow, leaves changing color, appeared amid stands of green. The narrow road was rutted now. Most of the railroad had been torn away and sold for scrap.

"This is the day when government checks arrive." Tip seemed talking to himself. "Things might get pretty lively."

"How can that happen?" It was an honest question. I didn't see how anything could get very lively. We were, approximately, forty miles from nowhere.

"These folks live off the land. They trap small game. Sometimes they have to dig roots." Tip was always in control, but he was angry. "Every month we send each of them a lousy thirty-two bucks. Minnie runs a tab. She cashes their checks. The pay up their owes, mostly for canned goods and liniment. Then they buy a pack of factory-made cigarettes, called tight-rolls, and drink. One day a month they get to act like men who don't scratch roots and roll tobacco in newsprint. Around here, that's the main and only use of a beer joint."

Electric lines from earlier days still ran into the hollow, but not to all the cabins. Here and there shelves of rock hovered above what looked like shallow caves. "The people dig out coal for heat," Tip told me. "At least the people who are not too old."

When we turned off the road and up a rutted lane to Minnie's Beer Store, Tip came off the gas. We coasted to a stop. "It looks," he said, "like we got ourselves a goddamn uprising."

The store stood two stories, ramshackle and unpainted. It leaned a little. Upstairs windows had old bed sheets for curtains. Downstairs windows were naked as wind off the mountain. Not much could be seen through the windows because men stood outside the store, blocking the view.

One man packed a silly old over-and-under, a two barrel combination of .22 rifle and .410 shotgun. He pointed it at another man who knelt like in prayer. A half dozen other men stood around, watched, like people stuck in church with the sermon boring. Everybody except the kneeling man wore faded patches on faded clothes. The only man who looked fully alive was the man who knelt. The rest of the men were old and tired. They seemed wispy.

"You are more'n'likely gonna see a shooting," Tip said, "For God's sake keep your mouth shut." He climbed from the Ford. Slammed the door. Knelt like he checked a tire, knelt real easy like he had all the time in the world. He kind of tsked, scratched himself behind the ear, then turned and ambled toward the men like nothing was going on.

"Shitfire, Tom," he said to the man with the gun, "if you shoot the undertaker who's gonna plant him?"

The kneeling man looked about to faint. He dressed in city clothes. His shoes had once been polished. His eyes were wide and scary. Black hair dangled wet over a sweaty forehead. "Tip," he said, "they got it all wrong."

"They probably don't," Tip told him. He turned to me. "This is what comes from too damn much government. The minute we started paying a death benefit, funeral prices went up to match the benefit."

"T'aint that," Tom said. His arm trembled as he held the gun. It looked like the thing would go off just from his shaking. His hair was pure white, his face with black circles around green eyes . . . green but dulled . . . lots of Scots-Irish blood in these hills. Tom seemed feeble, but not at all nervous. "We got graveyard problems," he told Tip.

"Might be fun," Tip said, and sounded droll, "to park him inside. Sweat him a little. You can always shoot him later."

"If you wasn't Tip," Tom said, "I reckon I wouldn't listen." To the kneeling undertaker he said, "Remove your ass. Inside."

I hope to never again see what I saw in Minnie's store. What I heard, I can handle, and tell about. What I smelled was like sweet perfume, the kind that rises from corpses just before they begin to stink. What I saw . . .

A congregation of weary men, white-haired with faces dark, especially around eyes and noses where coal dust painted faces into masks. Eyes, some brilliant, some flat and dull and deathlike, stared at us from the rings of blackness. Here and there a man wheezed. Others sat quiet, and if they breathed no one could hear. The silent ones seemed to have brighter eyes than the ones who drew breath.

Minnie, rail-skinny, gray-haired and sharp of face, stood behind a bar made of plain boards. Behind her, shelves held chewing tobacco, plus some tobacco leaves, little cans of deviled ham, little cans of sardines. There were a few grocery items plus small bottles of aspirin and some patent medicines. Beer coolers ran beneath the shelves.

When the undertaker came inside he stopped, even though he had a gun in his back. He went wild-eyed, gasped, and literally fell into the nearest chair. He was worth watching, but there was lots else to see so I just listened to him gasp.

"Don't you dare do any shootin' in here," Minnie told Tom. "It makes a mess and it brings the law." Her voice sounded lots nicer than she looked, because she looked like fifty years of hard times. Her oversize man's shirt made her seem small, like a boy. Her worn jeans bagged. Her graying hair was done in a bun. Her voice sounded alert in the surrounding tiredness.

"Now me," Tip drawled, "I drink whilst on duty." He grinned at Minnie. She looked at me. Tip nodded. Minnie pulled two bottles. The undertaker still gasped, like maybe he would die for want of air.

Tip straddled a chair and looked to Tom. "I ain't come across a good story in a dog's age. Lemme hear it . . ." He got interrupted.

The undertaker's teeth began to chatter. He kept gasping. Finally, he looked toward one of the sitting men. "Ezekiel, I done buried you."

"And did a piss poor job," Zeke said. Amber eyes flashed like a man alive and angry. Zeke's voice was more like a dry rustle than an actual voice. The rustle did not sound kind. In fact, just the opposite.

Somebody chuckled, but not friendly. Nothing else happened. The undertaker kept gasping. Tom told his story.

"He buried my brother," Tom said. "Buried Ezra. Cheaper coffin than he promised. Coffin got loose. Dropped into the grave, instead of lowered. Cracked open, and Ezra looking at the sky." Tom reached to where he'd leaned the over-and-under. "This bastard threw dirt in Ezra's face, and cussed him."

I couldn't tell whether Tom was dead or alive. He looked mostly alive, and his eyes didn't shine like Zeke's.

"This shootin'-business reminds me," a man said to Minnie. "Give me two cartridges. Might could get a deer."

30-30 cartridges, it turned out, cost thirty-five cents apiece.

"Maybe you wanta wait," Tip said. "Near as I can figure, Ezra might drop in here any minute."

The undertaker was as close to insanity as any man I've ever seen. He hunched in his chair, and when he wasn't gasping for air he sobbed. His face was complete torment. He had badly made false teeth, shiny, but too big and clunky for his face. He whispered to another man. "Why you here, Bill? You're buried."

"The way you laid me out wan't comfortable," Bill said. His voice was a dry whisper. "It ain't right a man's gotta be dead and not comfortable." Bill's eyes were not green, but sharp and glowing blue.

"Preacher," Tip said to another man, "I done heard you'd gone to glory."

"I can't figure it," the preacher whispered. He was a small man. Probably a lay preacher, self-ordained. He wore a frayed, black suit, and his white hair hung to his shoulders. His eyes glowed soft and gray. "Something's goin' on," he whispered. "Maybe the Baptists hogged it all. Might be there's no glory left."

Stillness. From outside a raven chuckled. A cow lowed, a dog barked. It was so quiet I could hear the bubbling of a distant stream that seemed to answer the raven. A way, way off in the distance, maybe two or three mountains to the west, a light plane hummed.

"I reckon," Tom said, like he was talking to himself, "My brother Ezra is out there somewheres and about his own business. Goin' it alone. He had that reputation."

"This all happened once before," Minnie said. "You boys recall that big gom-up durin' the war."

"What gom-up?" Tip sounded just as businesslike and sensible as if he were sitting back at the office. I worked at taking his advice about not studying things. Nobody else seemed troubled. Except, of course, the undertaker.

"When we had those drownings," Minnie said, "it was the same time the company cut wages. Those boys walked out of the hole. People swore they saw 'em. Then the tipple burned. The mine office burned. The company store burned. Rail cars burned. Nary a coal car got loaded for three months. Then those boys disappeared into the forest. People swore they saw 'em." She looked at all of the men, some alive, some dead. "Looks like nobody was lying."

"Which means," Tip said in the direction of Tom and the preacher, "that you gents have been called back to do a hand of work. Instead of going off half-cocked, let's wait it out. I reckon something's about to happen."

What happened was Sims and his pet goon, Pook.

A man lounging in the open doorway looked toward the road. In a voice so tired it quavered he said, "Cadillac car a-coming." He sounded discouraged and beaten. To the preacher he said, "Better get to prayin', for what-dog-good it's gonna do."

Sun sat high but westering. The shadow of Drowning Mountain reached into the hollow and across the road. The Cadillac ran so smooth that nothing could be heard, save the bump of its tires in ruts and potholes. Men stirred, uneasy. "Never to be let alone, never free," someone whispered, ". . . not in this life 'ner any other." The voice filled with sadness.

Pook got from the car first. He came into Minnie's place, looked around, turned back toward the Cadillac. He must have given a signal. Sims got out and stepped toward us. He moved dainty on little feet, and his summer suit was clean as his car. When he spoke his voice was soft. "Very well, Pook. I'll be but a minute." He ignored everyone except Pook. Then he turned to Tip. "Still kneeling, are we," he said to Tip. "Still hugging the poor and unwashed. Were I you, I'd vote Democrat."

"Were I you," Tip told him, "I'd take a bath. Wash off a little-a that snot."

"Watch that mouth." Pook stirred. His hand dropped toward the .45.

"You watch yours," Tip told Pook. "When you threaten me, you threaten my uncle Sammy. Unc will get riled."

"They were about to shoot me." The undertaker's voice quavered like a scared baby. "I gotta get a ride to town."

"You probably got a shootin' comin'." Pook sounded real comfortable.

"He probably does." Sims looked at Pook. "But he's the only one around who handles paupers. The company needs him."

"Get in the car," Pook told the undertaker. "Back seat. Don't drip no sweat."

The undertaker didn't run. He scampered.

"Goddamit, Tip." Tom had his dander up, green eyes coming almost as alive as eyes of the dead.

"Could be I was wrong," Tip murmured, "or maybe not. It's never no trouble to shoot a fella if you give it forethought."

Except for Tip, there wasn't a man in the place who wasn't brow-beat. I exclude myself, since half of what went on breezed right past me. The death smell wasn't quite as strong, or maybe my nose got used to it. There was one woman there, though, and brow-beat she wasn't.

"This is my place," she said to Sims, "and you ain't welcome. Speak your piece and get the hell out." She glanced toward the preacher. "You'll forgive the cuss."

"Yes and no," Sims said pleasantly. "You own the building."

"And the land," Minnie said, "bought fair and square from the company, deed an' all. Twenty bucks a month. Paid in full."

"And the land," Sims agreed. "But the company owns the mineral rights."

Tip pulled me to him. Whispered close in my ear. "Things are gonna get real bad. Keep your mouth shut."

"This is a friendly call." Sims kind-of purred. "Trying to help folks out. You'll be wanting to move. Next month I got machinery coming in."

"Gonna strip," someone whispered.

"My cabin's on that mountain. My woman's buried up there." A man's voice broke.

Pook chuckled. Sims tried to look sad. "Maybe move the grave," he said. "Nothing I can do. It's the company. The company calls the shots."

"Not exactly true," Tip said. "Why are you doing this?"

"Those seams are hardly touched," Sims told Tip. "That mountain has been a curse." He looked toward Minnie. "One month." He turned and walked to his car. Pook followed, but walking kind of sideways so as to cover his back.

Silence. The whir of the Cadillac's starter. The engine purred like an echo of Sim's voice. The car pulled away. Somewhere toward the back of Minnie's place came a dry sob. Men sat stunned, old, tired.

"Give yourselves a minute to breathe," Tip said real quiet. "Those of you with breath. Those without are called back for something."

Silence in the room was as deep as silence outside. No raven, no dog barking, no light plane buzzing. With the shadow of Drowning Mountain reaching across the hollow there should have been a breeze, but not a sound. Not a leaf stirring.

Then, a crack, like doom riding horseback and striking flame from the hooves. I sat straight up. Looked around. Never saw so many happy faces. I tried to place the sound. It was like a three-inch-fifty cannon going off. Sharp. Eardrum buster.

"How in the world," Tip said real pleased and casual, "are me and Jim ever gonna get back to town?"

"Five-stick shot sure'n God's wrath." The preacher looked about to start a sermon.

"That Ezra," Tom said. "By God, Ezra had the nerve to done it. Waste of dynamite. A three-stick would been a-plenty."

Someone laughed out loud. "What do you figger the law will do to Ezra. Kill him?" This, while everybody headed outside to take a look.

The Cadillac, what little was left of it, lay on its back beside a chunk of road that was no longer there. The car was a shiny hunk of black, twisted metal. A body in a summer suit lay sprawled among the weeds, another body big as Godzilla lay without a head, and there were scattered pieces of what had once been an undertaker. Blood stains mixed with burn stains on roadside weeds.

"That Ezra," Minnie said, ". . . now Ezra was always best at setting a shot. He held that reputation."

"Tunneled under the road. Set his charge. Ran his wires to the detonator, and hid on the hill. When the car driv across the charge, he shot those boys straight to hell." The preacher sounded apologetic. "I can't find it in my heart to pray for 'em."

"And now we're gonna catch hell." Tom looked to Tip. "We're gonna get the law."

"Don't give it a first thought," Tip told him. "I got it covered." He turned to the preacher. "Pretty plain why you boys were called back."

A man whispered. The whisper sounded faint, but pleased. He spoke to the preacher. "I reckon brother Sims and his lot feel sorta surprised. They got no experience at being dead." The voice turned mean. "I expect we should show 'em some things. Sort of introduce them around."

"I got a goodly number of things to demonstrate." Another whisper. The whisper sounded most unpleasant.

"I purely agree," the preacher whispered, "an' may The Lord have mercy on my sinful way."

Down by the road an old man limped off the hill. He wore a black burial suit of the cheap kind furnished to the poor. He stood looking at the broken car and broken bodies. Then he scratched his head and looked like a man who figured he had wasted dynamite. Then he looked toward Minnie's.

"That Ezra," Tom said. "I expect you boys better get down there before he has all the fun."

When those who were called-back walked to the road, the crowd in front of Minnie's store thinned. We trooped inside. When screaming and torment went on down there, it was not for the living to know or understand.

"Anybody got a peavey?" Tip looked to Minnie. "Me and Jim have got to fix that road a little."

We borrowed the peavey and used it to crack out sleepers from the broken rail bed. For two hours we tossed sleepers into the torn spot of road. With the sun back of the mountain, the old Ford limped across. We made it back to town considerably after dark.

Next day Bobby Joe pulled Tip off to one side. The two men talked, looked toward me. Sarah Jane looked toward me. Lots of questions on faces. Not much said. It seemed clear I was not on trial.

When the sheriff showed up he pulled me and Tip into Bobby Joe's office. He wasn't much of a sheriff.

"Lord only knows who done it," Tip told him. "I can't say who did, but can say who didn't."

"Could-of been someone from town," I mentioned. "But I'm new around here. You might say I didn't see anything except a well-used Cadillac."

When the sheriff left it was clear I'd passed my test. Sarah Jane was lots more friendly. Bobby Joe said that maybe, in a couple months, I could go into the field alone.

"Will those dead stay dead?" I asked Tip once we cleared out of the office.

"Can't imagine that they won't."

"And those alive?"

"They are not off the hook," Tip told me. "You kill a bastard like Sims and ten more just like him come to the funeral."

It fell out that Tip was wrong. The coal company turned the show over to a man wise in the ways of the hills. He wasn't a bit nicer than Sims, but lots smarter. He figured it more economic to strip some other mountain.

I worked out of that office for two more years, then got transferred to Cincinnati. It took all of those two years, a long, long time, for the old men of Drowning Mountain to repair that road. I'm told that they sang church songs as they worked.

# THE OTHER GRACE

## *Holly Phillips*

### I.

As if she dreamed she were walking, and wakes, and is still walking. Hot feet in heavy shoes. Dust and gravel. The side of a road. A car goes by. There is a ditch, a playing field, a mower. A car goes by. Exhaust and the fresh sap of cut grass. Blue sky. A car goes by. Mosaic without pattern. Dream, except she has awakened and the dream surrounds her. Walking. Her arms are full of books. She stops.

The boy beside her says, "What?"

She hadn't realized. She looks. A face, bristle-cut hair. He makes no more sense than the rest. Sensation without sense. Suspended in the fragmentary world.

The boy beside her says, "Are you all right?"

She gasps. She has forgotten to breathe. She is not all right, but she does not know the word to say — She does not know.

"Grace?" The boy takes her arm. "You look like you're going to faint."

His hand is hot.

"Grace?" he says again.

Is that her name?

"Grace?"

She does not know.

A car pulls up beside them. An open car full of boys. The driver calls out, "Hey, Will! We're going to Georgie's for a malted before practice. Did you want to come with?"

The boy with his hand on her arm says, "Ted, can you give us a lift? I don't think Grace's feeling so good."

"Sure, we can make room."

A boy climbs from the back to the front. A car drives around the convertible and honks its horn. The mower in the field chatters and grumbles, close. The boy with his hand on her arm steers her. The boys in the car watch.

"Come on, Grace. Get in."

There is no sense. She doesn't know. The world has come apart and she is being pushed — pushed —

"Grace! What the hell's the matter with you?"

She twists free. Books scatter in the dirt. A bright blue cover slides into the ditch. The boy reaches. She runs.

Running, it is as if she dreams, and, dreaming, cannot wake.

## II.

The heat broke with a rainstorm near dawn. The gully where she hid grew slick with mud. It stank. The rain was cold. Her hair, stiff and sticky with something, became tangled when she tried to push it off her face. The rain ran through it into her mouth and tasted of chemicals. The fear that shackled her loosened with the discomfort. She got to her feet and climbed through garbage-strewn bushes to the street. There was a streetlight, some houses across the way. She didn't know what to do, but she was tired enough to be calm and calm enough to know she should do something. She asked herself where she lived but received no answer. How is memory supposed to work? As if some muscle in her head had gone to sleep. How does the body know how to move?

She said aloud, "I don't know who I am." Just to prove she knew the words. Just to prove the words made sense. They did, but there was no sense behind the sense. Behind the facade of reason, only nothing.

The rain matted her hair to her shoulders.

The police found her before the day was fully light, a black and white patrol car that slid past her and stopped. Fear broke through again, but the two men wrapped her up in a blanket and drove her away. Her skin felt strange inside the wet clothes inside the dry blanket. She wondered if it was strange because she had never felt it before, or strange because she couldn't remember feeling it before. But she hadn't noticed feeling dry before, so that was probably normal. People didn't normally get wet and then wrap themselves in blankets.

Did they?

A delicate structure of logic that collapsed when the driver stopped the car at the hospital. She knew what that was, the same way she had known what the police car was, but there was no reassurance in the knowledge. She didn't know what was supposed to happen. A policeman pried her out of the back seat and handed her like a package to a man and a woman in white clothes. They were strong and they barricaded her with their arms. The woman said soothing things, but they gave her no ground to stand on. She heard herself gasp for air.

They levered her up onto a high bed and a doctor came. He was a tired-looking man with neat dark hair and smudges under his brown eyes. He shone a pen light into her eyes and pushed his fingers through the sticky mess of her hair to probe her scalp. It stung when he pulled on a tangle.

He said, "So what's your name, sweetheart?"

She had to reach for her breath. In. Out. In. Out.

"Sweetheart?" He touched her chin so she would look at his eyes. "Do you understand what I'm asking you?"

In. Out. Her body made two false starts before the nod came.

"What's your name?"

The tension in her body spat out in jerks and twitches whenever she moved. She shook her head and the fear seemed to expand, stretching her skin. Other people were watching, a couple of women, a younger man. Nurses, her mind said. Intern.

"I'm not crazy," she said. Gasped. On a breath.

"Okay, sweetheart," the doctor said. He turned his head and spoke to one of the nurses, who parted the curtain around the bed and left. He turned back. "Do you remember what your name is?"

"No." Gasp.

"That's all right. Take it easy. You're doing fine." He peeled the blanket away from her and pulled at her arms. She had them locked tight against her chest. He moved slowly and carefully, but he was strong. "Let me take a look here, sweetheart. We have to make sure you aren't hurt anywhere."

"Not. I'm not."

"Okay. Let's just make sure." He smoothed his hand up the inside of her left arm, and then her right. His skin was dry and warm. The other nurse came over to unlace her shoes. She pulled her knees close and tucked in her arms. The fear was huge and threatened to escape. The nurse who had left came back and said something about a family, with a little steel dish in her hand. There was a needle in the dish. The doctor and the other nurse were pulling at her limbs. If they untied her the fear would get loose. She tried to tell them that, but they didn't listen. Maybe she couldn't get the words out. There were three of them pulling now. She pulled back. The needle was out of the dish. Someone screamed.

A face at the curtain stared in.

The needle was in her arm and a huge relief was drowning her. She had seen that face before. The boy beside her on the road. She remembered. She remembered.

She was gone.

## III.

It was a slow awakening, nothing like the walking dream at all. She was so warm and limp in the bed she could hardly feel her legs and arms. In her easy breathing she could feel the soreness of — of the fear — It felt very distant. A fold of sheet lay against her throat, and after a while it began to feel heavy, a pressure instead of a touch. Somewhere rubber wheels squeaked, voices talked. There was light beyond her eyelids. She lifted her hand to push the sheet away and her wrist was caught short.

Fear took a step closer.

She opened her eyes and rolled her head and saw thick brown leather padded with sheepskin. Buckles, a strap, a metal rail. Both her wrists were bound. She turned her head to look at the other one — fear a little closer still — but there was a boy beside the bed, on a chair looking worried. The boy who'd been by her on the road.

"I remember you," she said. Sleep was thick in her throat. She coughed it clear.

Relief washed over the boy's face like a wave. He would be handsome when he was older, with his knobby nose and big jaw. His blue eyes were innocent under the harsh buzz of brown hair.

She said, "You're the boy by the road."

Relief crashed and died. "Don't you — you don't — remember. Before that."

The sheet on her throat bothered her. She went to push it away and her wrist was caught. "Why am I — What are these for?"

His face pinched, discomfort added to worry. Embarrassment. Shame? "You fought. Before. The doctors."

"I was scared." Her breath left her on a sigh. She looked at the ceiling a while, then the boy. "I'm supposed to know you, aren't I?"

Pain now. She was awed at how clear his face was. He said, muffling the words, "I'm your brother. Willis. Will."

"And I'm, you called me, Grace."

"Grandma's name." He put his elbows on his knees and looked at the floor. His brow was wrinkled, his skin red on pale. When he leaned over like that his face was cut in half by the metal rail on her bed. She tried to sit up but the wrist cuffs grabbed her again.

"Could you undo these for me, please?"

He looked anguished. She felt sorry for him. It was a struggle but with a shove from her legs she sat up after all. The cotton hospital gown she wore slipped off one shoulder. The air was cool. Blushing, the boy — Willis — got up and pulled the gown decent again. He even tied it behind her neck, his touch cool and tentative on her skin.

"Thanks," she said.

He sat and tugged at his fingers.

"I don't think I'm crazy," she told him. "I just can't remember."

"But how — What happened?" He peered at her from under his wrinkled brow, then looked down. "They kept asking, the doctors, about drugs. Did you ever do any drugs, or did you ever drink at school. They said there wasn't anything on the X-ray. They even called the school."

The straps were long enough that she could stretch her fingers within half an inch of the other cuff. That, she decided, was an unnecessary tease. "Did I?"

"What?"

"Take drugs."

"No. I don't know." Then he gave an angry shrug. "No. It's stupid. You didn't even — You don't even like beer."

She bent over to scratch her nose. When she straightened her matted hair fell over her face, and throwing it back made her dizzy. She squeezed her eyes shut, then open, and watched the black spots fade.

He said, "What was it like?"

"It was like waking up."

He thought about that. "I've never seen anyone look so scared."

"Well," she said, "it was scary."

He reached through the metal rails and unbuckled the cuff on her wrist.

"Thanks," she said, and unbuckled the other one. The leather was supple and dark from use.

"I should go tell them you're awake." He got up and headed for the door, then paused to tap his fingers on the foot rail. "You going to be okay, do you think?"

She shrugged and scratched her wrist. The left one had a plastic strip around it, and the cuff had pressed it into her skin.

"I'll go tell them," the boy said, and he left. Willis. Her brother Will.

She wasn't sure she believed it.

The parents looked like real people. Neither beautiful nor ugly, neither young nor old, they were tired and sad and holding themselves up inside. The mother had a graceful form and a rumpled dress with coffee-cream butterflies, black hair in a pony tail and lines and folds around her pretty blue eyes. The father looked a lot like Willis, older and craggier, with a nose crooked as well as knobbed at the bridge, and gray-brown hair cut nearly as short. He wore a blue striped shirt with short sleeves, buttons, and a collar. She could feel their need.

The mother said in a small voice, "How are you feeling, sweetheart?"

The father eyed the unbuckled restraints, then looked at her face and tried to pretend he hadn't noticed.

She said, "All right."

They stood by her bed looking at her and away. They took turns in a fashion that made them seem like a couple, a pair. She tried to use that recognition to open a door onto more, but it didn't come.

"We were awfully worried about you, Grace," the mother said. The father gave her a look that suggested that was something they weren't supposed to say. The mother's blue eyes filled with tears that didn't fall.

The father's eyes were gray. Willis' eyes were blue.

She wondered what color her eyes were.

Fear was inside her again, and a sudden loneliness, her heart locked inside her throat. Her hands pulled blanket and sheet over her lap and burrowed beneath them.

"You don't remember us at all, do you?" the mother whispered.

"I'm sorry," she whispered back.

The father put his arm around the mother's shoulders. Someone outside knocked on the door. The father said, "The doctors need to take a look at you, Grace. We told them we wouldn't be long."

The mother wiped at her eyes and said, "We just had to say hello. So you'd know we were here. So you'd know you're not alone."

"Okay," she said.

Then the doctor came in.

He wasn't the one from before. So far, Willis was the only person who had reappeared. This doctor was older, with a stiff brush of gray hair and eyebrows as black as his glasses frames. He noticed the undone restraints, but then he noticed everything, her eyes, her hands, the way she sat with her knees pulled up tight.

"Don't be nervous." He sat in the chair Willis had used. "I'm just going to ask you a few questions." He lifted the clipboard in his hand. It was thick with papers. "Do you know what a neurologist is?"

"A brain," she cleared her throat, "a brain doctor."

"Right." His eyes noticed her again. "Well, these questions I'm going to ask you are going to help me find out what's happening inside your skull. Okay?"

There were tests first. Follow the light with your eyes, stand on one foot, squeeze my fingers. A stick that scraped the soles of her feet. Standing she felt sick and sluggish from the drugs, and cold, but she didn't fall over or try to run. The doctor nodded to himself as he wrote on his clipboard. Then he flipped the page over and the questions began. Where was she, who was the prime minister, what was the year, what was the thing she would look at to know what the date was, what grade was she in, what town was she in, what time did his watch say and was it a.m. or p.m. and how did she know? And a dozen more, a hundred more, and a hundred more after that. Mapping out the limits of what she didn't know. The size of the blank space was terrifying. She knew she was in a hospital, she knew what a calendar was, and she knew it was two in the afternoon because of the light coming through the window, but beyond that was formlessness. Groping in fog, except that again she had the sensation that the part of her brain that was supposed to do the groping was asleep, or missing, or dead. How do you find a memory when you don't know what it is you are looking for, or even how to look?

When the questions finally stopped and he was writing again, she sat in her bed and hugged the fear inside her.

He finished a note and looked at her again. "You can relax, Grace, you're doing just fine."

This was so obviously untrue she smiled.

He leaned toward her. "Tell me the first thing you remember."

"Walking. I was walking, by the road. I had books. Willis, my brother, was there."

"Did you know who he was?"

"No."

"Did you know who you were?"

She shook her head.

"How did you know you didn't know who you were?" He gave a little smile to show he knew how absurd that question sounded.

"He called me Grace. And I didn't know. If that was my name." She was holding the fear in so hard the words escaped in jerks.

"What happened next?"

"I ran. Away."

"Why did you run?"

"I was scared." Almost whispering now.

"Let's go back for a minute, Grace. Tell me about when you were walking by the road. When did you notice something was wrong?"

"I didn't notice. I woke up."

"It felt like you were asleep?"

"Like I was dreaming. Like I dreamed. That I was walking. And then I woke up. And I was walking. And nothing made sense."

"What didn't make sense?"

"Everything. The world. Me."

"You're doing fine, Grace. How didn't it make sense?"

"It was all — pictures and sounds and — smells and — it was all in pieces — everything — was around — me — crowding — in pieces —"

"All right, Grace."

"— it didn't make sense —"

"That's good, Grace, you don't have to —"

"— nothing made sense —"

"— say any more." The doctor stood and put his hand on her shoulder. "Try to breathe, Grace. Take some deep breaths. That's a good girl."

The fear was tying knots in her body. He went to the door and she was glad because she wanted him to leave her alone. If she could just be alone she could wrestle the fear back again. But then he returned, and a nurse was behind him, and she had a needle in her hand.

"No!" She lunged for the end of the bed. Hands grabbed. She threw herself against them. "I'm not crazy!" And free. She put her hands out, her back to the wall. "Please, I'm not crazy, I'm just scared, please, please, I'm just scared —"

"Grace. We know you're scared. This will help." The doctor stopped and put his hands in the air.

But the nurse stepped forward, and she had the needle.

"No! It makes it like before it's like drowning and I can't wake up I want to wake up pleasepleaseplease —"

The nurse took her arm. She pulled free. The doctor was there too. She fought. The door was open. She couldn't get through.

"I'm just scared I'm just scared please —"

The needle like a bee punch in the arm.

Outside, the mother and the father. Willis. Staring.

Looking as scared as she was.

Before she was gone.

## IV.

It was June and the air was balmy. Grace couldn't believe how sweet and warm it was. Maddy had brought a summer dress for her to wear, and the light cotton felt so much like a hospital gown she had to check what she was wearing a couple of times. Before they'd left the room, Maddy had taken a pair of tiny nail scissors out of her purse and used them ceremoniously to cut the plastic identification strip off of Grace's wrist. She put the scissors and hospital bracelet in her purse, then pushed Grace's hair back from her face, a self-conscious caress.

"Well, don't you look fine," she had said.

Grace had offered a smile, but she couldn't help looking at the door. Maddy had taken the hint. They'd run the gauntlet of cheerful nurses and candy-stripers, Maddy profuse in her thanks, and now they were outside and the air was warm, like milk and honey against Grace's skin.

The sun was bright, too, glaring off the chrome wings of Nat's new blue Ford. Nat was behind the wheel and he started the engine when he saw Grace and Maddy come out of the hospital door. Willis opened the rear door and held it for them like an overanxious doorman.

"Why, thank you, sir," Maddy said. She climbed in after Grace and told Willis, "Ride up front with your father, Will. Us ladies are going to travel in style."

Willis grinned and slammed the door, and in a minute he was in his seat and they were off. Everything felt strange to Grace. Too big, too bright, too fast. Of course it wasn't the first time she'd ridden in a car, but it might as well have been. She looked at Maddy, at the unaccustomed smile lightening the older woman's face, and thought that Maddy and Nat were bringing their newborn daughter home and they didn't even know.

Of course they knew Grace's memory was still gone. The doctors had confirmed it, as if Grace's word wasn't good enough on its own, but they could not explain how a girl could walk down the street and lose her memory as casually as she might have lost a button off her shirt. Grace didn't need their explanations. She looked in her parents' eyes and saw them see a stranger, and knew that one girl had died walking down the street that day, and another had been born to take her place. But it would have been cruel to say it. She had swallowed the pills and endured the tests, and when the doctors finally decided to release her she had smiled and tried to be glad.

And she was glad. In the back seat of the big new car, with soft air rushing in the windows and the view outside growing greener and greener as they left the town center behind, she was glad.

If only Maddy and Nat and Willis would stop waiting for her to wake up and remember who she was supposed to be.

Nat pulled into a driveway and she got out and looked up at the house. It was a handsome frame building with a wraparound porch, new but with an old-fashioned look. It was finished with white siding, and the upper windows had diamond panes. Everyone was looking at her.

"It's very nice," she said.

In the hall Maddy said bravely, "Will, why don't you show Grace to her room? And I'll start getting lunch."

Willis started up the stairs without looking at Grace. She followed him, her hand careful on the banister. Drugs still washed around in her system and she'd been a long time in bed. Also, Maddy and Nat were watching. They would take her back to the hospital at the first sign of trouble, she knew. She kept her eyes on the risers. The banister was smooth with polish under her hand.

Willis stood in the upper hall flanked by doors. She stopped at the top of the stairs. Willis watched her as if waiting for her to perform. The doors were all closed.

"Which one is mine?"

Willis shifted his weight. "I thought maybe —"

"I think you're supposed to make the miraculous recovery before you leave the hospital."

His face grew red. "I thought maybe you'd have, like, an instinct. Even if you didn't. You know. Remember."

"What am I? Your science fair project?" Grace went to the nearest door and opened it. Bathroom. Blue and yellow. Pretty. She closed the door. "Too bad I'm not a white mouse." She moved across the hall and reached for the doorknob.

"That's my room." A blurt, almost hostile. "Yours is at the end, across from Mom and Dad."

"I don't even know if you do science fair projects." She opened the door he pointed at. A room with two windows overlooking the back yard. The floor was wood like the rest of the house so far, but there was a large pink and white rug covering most of it. The walls were busy with posters and snapshots of people. The bed had a pink coverlet and a great many pillows. The poster on the wall at its head was of a sulky young man with blue jeans and hair elaborately combed.

"I did this year. It looks good on college applications."

"Mice and mazes?" Grace went to a window and looked out. The yard was fenced, green grass and a pair of big willows drooping leaves to the ground.

"A suspension bridge. I made it with coat hangers and electrical wire. You thought it was dumb."

"Did it work?"

"Yes."

"So you're an engineer."

"I'm going to be." He said it as if he expected her to challenge his ambitions.

She perched on the windowsill. "Is that what Nat is? An engineer?"

Willis went from defensive to stricken. "Dad's an architect. He designed this house."

"Oh."

He took a breath. He had never quite entered the room. "Did you want me to show you where the kitchen is?"

"I'll give you a yell if I get lost."

"Okay." He hesitated. "You know Mom's making lunch."

"I was there when she said it."

"Right. I just — Right." He was going.

She was abruptly sorry for her coldness. "Wait. Willis, who is that?" She nodded at the sulky young man over the bed.

Willis looked suddenly tired. "James Dean. The actor. You cried when he died."

"Did I?" She made a face.

"I'll see you downstairs."

"Okay."

He went.

It was a nice enough room, she thought. An improvement over the hospital room. There was a desk under the other window and a dressing table with a mirror by the closet door. The mirror was half obscured by photographs taped around the frame. She bent over to look at them and saw her face, thin and pale, framed in loose brown hair. Tired blue eyes. The same eyes looked out at her from a dozen snapshots. The same face, rounder and dimpled with smiles. The same hair elaborately waved. She remembered the feel of wet hair matted with rain and chemicals and grimaced. So did the face in the mirror. She sat on the stool. The other Grace watched her, frozen in smiles, frozen in the past. Grace felt a wash of cold sweep over her, raising goosebumps and a shudder, and she pulled down all the pictures off the mirror. She stuck them together with their tape and shoved them in a drawer.

### V.

She was sitting on the back porch trying to decide if she should feel guilty for being bored. She had been "home" for a week. That was how she thought of it, self-consciously: "home." She supposed it really was the only home she had, but the other people who called it that had expectations so much higher than her own. Compared to what they thought she should be, she was a transient. A guest. Is a guest with a crippled brain who is usurping the place of the lost beloved child allowed to feel bored? This was what she was pondering when the screen door opened and the girl came hesitantly outside.

"Hi, Grace," she said. She was a small rounded girl with brown hair curled stiffly out above her shoulders. Her eyes had expectations too.

Grace said, "I guess I'm supposed to know you. I'm sorry."

"It's Felicia?" The girl tried not to look hurt. She smiled gamely. "We were best friends? I mean, I am your best friend." She came and sat on the top step by Grace's side. "How are you feeling?"

"Fine."

"I'm sorry I didn't come see you in the hospital. I wanted to? But your mom said probably I'd better not."

"That's all right."

"So." Felicia had a charm bracelet that she spun around her wrist. It made a pretty sound. "I'm glad you're feeling better?"

"I feel fine. They just let me out when they decided they couldn't fix me."

Felicia tried to smile without meeting Grace's eyes, then let the smile die. It was clear she didn't know how to respond. Grace was sorry for being unkind, but she couldn't think of anything else to say. She didn't feel up to the responsibility of kindness. The screen door slapped open and Maddy came out with two glasses on a tray.

"I thought you girls might like some iced tea," she said.

As if she'd been on the other side of the screen waiting for her cue, Grace thought. Probably she had been.

"Thanks, Mrs. Elliot," Felicia said, her voice a gush of relief.

Grace took her glass off the tray. "Thank you."

"You're welcome." Maddy paused at the door. "Felicia, did you tell Grace yet about the junior prom? I'm sure she'd like to hear how it went."

"Oh! Sure!" Having been fed her lines the girl was buoyant. Maddy went in, but Grace thought she could sense her hovering by the door, listening to Felicia prattle on about who had danced with whom, who hadn't danced at all. Who had broken up and who was going steady. "And Ted Branner didn't even go, and Lucy told me that he had told her brother Mick that he was going to ask you to go steady!" She turned her face to Grace, and there was such a look on it — of laughter, of pleasurable envy, of pride at bearing News — that Grace had to turn away to hide the hurt. Felicia was talking about the other Grace. She was talking to the other Grace.

Felicia fell silent, turning her iced tea in her hands. The charms on her bracelet tinkled against the glass. She said, "Well. I don't want to tire you out."

"It was nice of you to come."

"Well sure! I mean, of course. I'm just sorry I couldn't, you know, come before?"

Grace stood up and put on a smile. Felicia got up as well.

"Okay. Well. I'll see you later. Okay?"

"Good-bye."

Felicia turned at the screen door to give an absurd little wave. Her bracelet chimed. Then she was gone.

Grace wandered onto the lawn to finish her tea in the sunshine. It was good. Nothing in the hospital had been hot and bright, or cold, or sweet. The grass was prickly springy soft to her naked feet. She stood in the sun until she was nearly sweating, and then she went inside.

Maddy was in the kitchen making another pot of iced tea. She said, "That was nice of Felicia to stop by."

Grace took her glass to the sink and filled it with cold water. "Didn't you ask her to come?"

Maddy cut a round slice off a lemon. "She had asked me to let her know when a good time to visit would be." She cut another slice. "She wanted to come see you in the hospital."

"I know. She said." Grace used the dish cloth to wash around the glass rim.

Maddy dropped slices of lemon into the pitcher. "I thought the prom sounded nice, didn't you?"

Grace rinsed the glass again and set it in the drainer. Then she stood at Maddy's side. "You know I'm not going to remember, don't you?"

Maddy was picking mint leaves off a supple red stem. The kitchen smelled of mint and lemon and tea steam.

"You know it doesn't matter who I talk to or where I go. Those memories are gone."

"You don't know that." Maddy went on plucking leaves. "The doctors said you might still —"

"The doctors don't know. They don't know anything."

"I am not giving up on my daughter." Maddy dropped the mint and grasped Grace's hands. Her fingers were cool and damp, her eyes bright with tears. "I am not giving up on you, Grace, and don't you give up either."

"You already have given up." Grace twisted free. "You gave up before you even started. Why can't you let me be who I am now? I don't want to try to be her. I can't be her! I don't know who she was!"

Maddy's face suffused with pity.

She took down everything in the room. Posters, snapshots, everything. There was no room in the closet crowded with clothes, so she shoved it all under the bed. Then she rolled up the rug and shoved that under too. Then the coverlet. The stuffed bear on the dresser. The china clown on the desk. Everything. Out of sight. Gone.

## VI.

The pills for sleeping stood on the table by her bed. The other pills, the heavy tranquilizers in case she panicked, were in the medicine cabinet in Nat and Maddy's en suite. As far as Grace was concerned, they could stay there. She didn't want the sleeping pills either, but Maddy was already upset at what Grace had done to her room. So the pill bottle sat by the lamp, and Grace sat on the windowsill looking out. It was late. A moth drifted in the open casement and wheeled about the light, throwing shadows across the pinholed walls. The willows in the back yard netted the light of streetlamps, reduced it to the spark of deepwater fish even as the leaves breathed a watery sigh. A cricket chirped.

After a while Grace got up and opened the drawer of the night stand, dropped the pills in, and slid it closed. She switched off the light. In the dark she could hear the moth whispering its wings against the lampshade, pat-patter hush. She curled up on the cotton blanket, her arm folded beneath her head, and listened. Patter-pat flick. Poor little moth, lured into nothing. Flut, flut, sigh. The windows became two rectangles of lessened darkness, and gradually, gradually, the first swell of presence began to make itself felt. As if the paper beings exiled under the bed breathed awareness into the room. Grace's body lay as if asleep, but her eyes were fixed open. And against the slowly developing gray of the nearer window a shape revealed itself. A figure, a shadow, the shadow of a girl.

The other Grace.

They stared at each other through the darkness, the dead girl and the live, until Grace on the bed could hardly stand it. She wanted to speak, to move, even just to blink, but she could not. Her body was a stolen thing, unwilling to stir at her command. She felt she could not even breathe. As the other Grace watched, dark shadow against the stars. Timeless moment, small piece of forever. And then the body breathed.

In a convulsive uncoiling, she lunged for the bedside lamp. Numb stupid hands clutched, pressed the switch, knocked over the base. Light flared, glaring off the bare walls, throwing her shadow huge up to the ceiling as it fell. Then the lamp hit the floor, the light bulb burst, and for a frozen moment she was blind.

The door to the hallway swung open.

"Grace?" Nat's hand swept the wall, found the switch to the ceiling fixture. Light sprang out again. "Honey, are you all right?"

She could only stare at him. His hair was too short to be tousled, but his eyes were bleary in the late-night brightness. He wore a white T-shirt and blue pajama bottoms. He sat by her on the bed and put his arm around her shoulders.

"What's up, sleepy head? Did you have a bad dream?"

He was a hot and solid comfort, but he wasn't hers. She propped her head against her knees a moment, then nodded.

"You want to tell me about it?"

She shook her head. He shifted, and she guessed he was looking at the fallen lamp. Then he gave her a squeeze.

"I'll tell you what. I'm going to get you a glass of water. And then I'm going to clean up that glass so's you don't cut your feet when you get up in the morning."

He seemed to want a response so she nodded.

"You'll be all right if I leave you for a minute?"

She nodded again. He gave her another squeeze.

"Hang in there, kiddo." He got up and went into the hall, and through the open door she heard him say, "Okay, Will. Just a nightmare. You go on back to bed."

Then Maddy murmured something from their room, and Grace realized they had all been sleeping with their doors open.

Listening for her.

## VII.

She felt like an experiment turned inside out. If the mouse escapes, how do the scientists react? She buckled her sandals sitting on the front step.

There was a hopscotch chalked on the sidewalk. She had gone from 9 to 3 when she heard Willis' big feet pounding the pavement behind her. It was Saturday and he had been studying for his final exams while Nat mowed the back lawn. She could hear the mower growl from here.

Willis caught up. "Hey. Where you going?"

"For a walk."

"Anywhere in particular?"

"How should I know?"

"Mind if I come along?"

She shrugged. They crossed the street in silence. Then Willis said, "You know, if it makes you feel any better, you're still as much of a jerk as you used to be."

She looked up at him through narrowed eyes, then laughed. "Thanks."

But that only disconcerted him. He shoved his hands in the pockets of his jeans and slouched along at her side. If he stood up straight he was almost as tall as Nat.

"You know, I wasn't planning on running away."

"Sure, I know." He shrugged. "I just thought you could use some company."

"I guess I know what you thought."

He tucked his shoulders up around his ears.

They crossed another side street. The road they were on began to curve.

"Do you want to go to the park?" Willis said.

"Okay." She followed him around a corner. A bulwark of trees ended that street two blocks away. "You aren't going to fail your exams because of this, are you?"

"Because of walking to the park?" His voice went incredulous. "I'm not that dumb."

"You know what I mean."

"I'm not that dumb."

It was almost stuffy under the big trees, the vegetation green and moist from a morning's sprinkling. Willis seemed to have a destination in mind. She trailed him through the trees and across a stretch of grass and daisies to the park's farther side. There was a baseball diamond there with a little league game in progress. The yells of small boys tagged after them down the grassy bank of a ravine, where a stream crooked its way around big gray boulders. Willis scrambled on top of one of these and sat. Grace followed suit. The stone was rough and warm under her hands and bare legs. The air musical with water. The sunlight dappled. Grace propped her arms on her knees and watched the stream curl around their rock. It curled, and curled, and curled.

"Thanks," she said eventually. "This is good."

"You used to come here a lot."

She didn't know what to say to that.

After another long pause, Willis said, "You know, Mom doesn't mean to upset you. She's just trying to help."

"Is anything secret in your family?"

Your family hung in the air between them. Willis plowed bravely through. "She just wants you —"

"— the way I was. Not the way I am."

"And how is that, Grace?" He was tense. Intense. "You don't say anything to anyone. You don't do anything. How are we supposed to want you like that? It's like you're just, you're locked inside your head and you won't, you don't want to let anyone else —" He broke off. There were some people coming up the beaten path above the stream.

Young men, boys Willis' age. Six of them. They saw Willis and Grace and bumped one another to a stop.

"Hey you guys," one of them said, a tall skinny blond boy.

"Hi," Willis shortly said.

Grace said nothing.

"Hi, Grace," the same boy said.

"Hi," she said.

She doesn't know who you are, one of the other boys whispered too loud.

She doesn't even know who she is, someone else whispered back.

"Shut. Up." The blond boy glared at his gang, then shrugged and tried a grin. "They're just morons. Ignore them."

One of the whisperers shoved him in the back. The other one said, "Come on you guys. We're gonna be late." There was a general movement up the path.

The blond boy watched the rest of them go, then turned to Willis. "We were getting together a game after the kids are done. Did you want to come up? We could use another infielder."

For the first time Grace noticed the glove he carried. Baseball, she thought. Why remember what that was, and not that Willis played? It made her sick sometimes. She turned back to the stream.

"No, thanks," Willis said. "I still have to study for physics."

"Yeah, I was at it all morning. But you go cra — I mean, you can't study, you know. All day long."

"You go," Grace said under her breath.

"I guess I won't," Willis said to the blond boy.

"Okay," said the blond boy. "Well, I'll see you around, Will."

"Sure," Willis said.

"Hey, it was nice seeing you, Grace. I'm glad you're feeling better."

She turned her head and waved, squinting as if against the sun so she wouldn't have to see his eyes. He gave a half-finished wave in return and started up the path.

"That was Ted," Willis said.

"You should have gone."

"Don't have my glove. Anyway, I should get back to the books." He stood. "Are you coming?"

She got to her feet.

"He used to have kind of a crush on —"

"Willis." She closed her eyes. Swallowed. "Please?"

He ducked his head and started up the trail.

## VIII.

She had gotten into the habit of clearing the table after supper. While the other three talked amongst themselves, she could come and go, separate, silent, permitted. Maddy used good china, and the plates weighed satisfactorily in the hand. That night Willis excused himself early to get back to his books. While Grace scraped green beans into the bin she heard Nat say to Maddy, "You have to admit, that makes a nice change at least."

"What do you mean?" Maddy asked.

"Housework and homework with no arguments."

There was a strange pause. Grace stood with the clean plate in one hand, a silver fork in the other, listening. Maddy spoke so low she had to strain to hear her:

"How can you joke? Nathan, how can you possibly joke about this?"

"Maddy."

"After everything —"

"You know I didn't mean —"

"— she's been through —"

"Maddy. Now come on."

"Everything we've been through!"

"Maddy, she'll hear you."

A chair scraped. Grace looked at the door to the dining room. The kitchen was lit only by the small bulb above the stove, and the figure in the doorway was silhouetted by the brighter light beyond.

She thought it was Maddy at first. But as her sight darkened about the edges and bees began to sing inside her ears, she heard Maddy's feet running on the stairs, and she knew who it was.

The other Grace.

The other Grace wanted to come home.

The plate broke in three upon the floor, and then she

## IX.

woke in the pink bed. Yellow sunlight slipped through green willow leaves to swim across the emptied walls. She remembered taking the posters down, remembered the hospital, the roadside, the kitchen. The other Grace was gone. She was herself still. Or was it again? She got up, the floor smooth and distinct beneath her bare feet, and found yesterday's clothes atop the vanity table. They were folded neatly but still wrinkled, still with the tiny grass ends clinging to the cotton shirt from when she had lain on the lawn while Maddy fixed dinner, pork chops, new potatoes, green beans that had scattered as significant as a constellation behind the moon of the broken plate —

So. Herself, still. But for how long?

How long?

## X.

The neurologist ordered more X-rays. Willis graduated with college acceptances already in hand. Summer ripened into something hot, fragrant, and slow. And eventually, after too many careful weeks, Nat and Maddy and Willis all went back to sleeping with their bedroom doors closed.

Grace realized, as she eased the front door shut behind her, that she had not been outside at night since the night she'd spent in the rain, the first night she could remember. It was more frightening than she had anticipated — she was closer than she had thought to that wet and nameless girl — but it was liberating, too. She was free of the expectations she could not live up to, the needs she could not fulfill. Free to be herself, a girl who was no longer haunted by the lost, no longer — she shivered, rubbed her bare arms in the warm, streetlighted midnight air — no longer haunting the family who could not admit they had lost the girl whose ghost she was. So: freedom, she thought. Life.

Willis had taken her on tours of the town and countryside since school had ended. Cruising in Nat's new blue Ford with the radio to fill the silence, or even better, to give them something to squabble over like any brother and any sister — Grace felt a pang of disloyalty as she walked the route Willis had often taken, skirting the park and turning onto the broad avenue that led to the highway. But of course they were not brother and sister, not really, and those July rides had been for Willis what they had been for Grace: an opportunity and an excuse to escape Maddy's watchfulness, Nat's wistful concern. They were waiting, all of them, even Willis, waiting for the other Grace to return. Waiting for the false Grace, herself, to disappear.

So she was disappearing. Let them stop waiting, let them get on with their lives. Let her get on with hers. The other Grace could come tomorrow, next week, next year. She could come right now, in the next step, as Grace crossed under the blinking red lights of the deserted downtown street, but Grace would not hold herself in readiness. She was not an empty vessel waiting to be filled. She was going to invent the new Grace so completely, fill herself so full with herself that she would never be crowded into non-existence like the other Grace had been.

The way was much longer on foot. There were whole blocks she had forgotten, or never noticed; the neighborhoods that had breezed by under the Ford's wheels, bright, busy, prosperous in the sunlight, were empty and grim, steel grilles over windows and doors, the sidewalk cracked and seeming too wide. She was frightened in the dark, exposed under the streetlamps, rabbit-like before the headlights of the few passing cars. She remembered the black-and-white that had picked her up that night, the first night, and walked warily, watching for the shadows of recessed doors. Her calves ached by the time she reached the on-ramp, and the light-headedness of fatigue gave her something new to worry about.

The aging night grew cool. The highway folded itself into a wood of tall, leafy trees. The smell was delicious, of sap and earth and hidden water, familiar as a dream. Grace shared the verge with bold raccoons and other creatures she only glimpsed in their retreat. Traffic was rare.

At the first gray hint of dawn, she came upon a roadside rest stop. There was a gravel lot, cinderblock toilets, a caged light over a payphone on the wall. A hundred moths swooned into the electric light and clung, exhausted, to the wall all around. Grace went into the toilet to drink cold water from the tap. And there she was in the mirror above the sink, her tan faded to yellow by the ugly light, her blue eyes shaded by fatigue.

Maddy's blue eyes. She turned away from the mirror, and the thought.

A picnic table had been crowded between trees at the edge of the lot. Grace groped her way onto the table top, and although she had only meant to rest until her legs stopped hurting and the sun was up, she lay down and fell instantly asleep.

XI.

Sunlight on her face. Birdsong. A car went by. She sat up, stiff, catching herself on her elbow when her arm sagged. Eyes hot, legs stiff, throat dry. A car went by. Her first thought, as always, was not what happens now, but what happened last. The dark highway, the animals, the fear.

Maddy's wet hands gripping her own.

She rubbed her palms over her face, then sat sleepily, her forearms folded on her knees. There was not much to look at: the highway behind her, the cinderblock building before her and the green trees beyond. A car went by. She thought vaguely about where she was going — somewhere, anywhere, she had thought in Nat and Maddy's house — but her future was blanker even than her past. She tried to imagine adventure, tried to imagine herself competent and brave, but other images kept intruding, her memory so sparse that they leapt out complete and shining. Nat in his pajamas sweeping up broken glass. Maddy slicing lemons. Willis driving Nat's car, working neat's-foot oil into a new glove, walking beside her on the way home from the park —

A car went by.

And suddenly, the fear that had been plaguing her for so long, the terror of losing herself to the self that had been lost, or to a whole other self different from either, reversed itself: a mirror-reflected fear no less grievous than the other.

For she imagined walking down some street somewhere, anywhere, walking, dreaming of walking, waking to find herself still walking — and no one there beside her to ask her if she was all right.

No one there to call her by her name.

A car went by.

Eventually, after a long, long pause balanced between one fear and the other, Grace levered herself to her feet and walked, limping with a cramp in one calf, to the payphone on the cinderblock wall.

# SITTING TENANT

## *Nicholas Royle*

Mark and Elinore had been in the rented house six months. But it felt more like twelve. All that time they'd been househunting, and while they'd hoped to find somewhere before Christmas, the end of February was now only days away. They were going to have to carry on living in a place that was too small even for them, never mind the kids. Meanwhile, their stuff was stuck in a bunch of containers in a warehouse two hundred miles away. Every day, while Elinore was out at work, Mark cruised the estate agents in the village. He knew everybody's name and they knew his, but that didn't make houses come on to the market any faster. If people weren't looking to move, familiarity with the estate agents was pretty much irrelevant. Not that one or two weren't quite friendly and hadn't gone out of their way to make sure he heard about houses that sounded like the kind of thing they were looking for. Up their street, so to speak. But they were always too small. Or too modern. Or too expensive. Or there was no off-street parking. Or the garden was overlooked, or too poky, or it faced north, which made you wonder why they'd gone to the trouble of building a conservatory. A waste of good glass.

The estate agents didn't help, in fact, with their wide-angle photographs that made back yards look like National Parks, and their brochures so full of spin they fanned out on the coffee table all by themselves. "The house is adjacent to Fog Lane Park." Really? When you get there, you see there's actually another house between the park and the house you're viewing. "The house is adjacent to Marie Louise Gardens." Can it be true? No, it's not, it's across the street.

"Look at this," Mark said to Elinore over breakfast. "'The garden has a southerly aspect.' You know what that means."

"I imagine it faces east. Where do they get the nerve?"

"They've got it all sewn up."

"Stitched up more like," said Elinore, getting to her feet. "I'm going to be late."

In the other room, the kids were bickering. Thomas was winding up Caitlin, just for a change. Mark swore and got to his feet. He went in the other room and shouted at them, laid the law down. Thomas answered back and Mark felt a sudden, almost uncontrollable compulsion to belt him. Instead he returned to the kitchen, where Elinore was lowering her cereal bowl into the sink.

"I wish you wouldn't shout at them so much," she said.

"They don't take any notice otherwise."

"You're turning into your father."

"Whom you never met. All you know about him is what I've told you."

"Yeah, well. Exactly. I've got to go. I'm late."

He watched her cross the tiny kitchen, grinding her teeth. The stress, the frustration, the endless series of disappointments. It was getting to her.

Mark heard her shout goodbye before the front door closed behind her. He poured the rest of his coffee down the sink. It was time to finish getting the kids ready.

Mark had work to do, but he couldn't concentrate, and as there was no deadline he could let it slide. Instead, he walked around the neighbourhood. Looking for private For Sale signs, or boards belonging to out-of-town auction houses that otherwise flew under his radar. All the regular estate agents could be monitored in the village or on the internet, but now and again things came and went, and Mark didn't want to miss them. Like the big house on Old Broadway opposite Tony Wilson's ex-gaff. Sold at auction in Wilmslow. Still, north-facing garden.

As he wandered towards Withington, he wondered again whether they should leaflet the streets they liked. He and Elinore had discussed it. He'd even written the letter and run off fifty copies, which they'd signed, but then Elinore had had second thoughts.

"What if it pisses off the estate agents?" she'd asked. "If we get no response and have to fall back on the estate agents and someone's shown them our letter? Won't it alienate them?"

"You really think they'd give a shit?"

"Is it worth the risk?"

Mark had let it go. He didn't like arguing with Elinore. She was better at it. She always won.

He turned left just before the Christie Hospital, where half his family, his mother and father included, had fought and lost their battles with cancer. There were a few good roads around the Christie — big Victorian and Edwardian family homes, some of which had managed to avoid being butchered by developers — but he wasn't sure he wanted that constant reminder of his mortality on his doorstep.

"Didn't your folks live round here at some point?" Elinore asked him that night once the kids were in bed and they were preparing dinner.

"Yeah, I've got all the addresses written down somewhere. God knows where. Prices were reasonable then, even round here. Pass me that steamer."

"Before or after they broke up? Don't overdo the vegetables for once."

"After. Can you imagine a single person finding a place in Didsbury now? Anything with its own front door, I mean. If you want your veg raw, by the way, eat them straight from the pack. I'm cooking mine."

"It's just odd that you go to the trouble of using the steamer but then cook them to death. As a rough guide, by the time they're the colour of pond water, they're about ready for the bin. They only need a couple of minutes."

Mark glared at her and dropped the steamer in the sink.

"Cook your own fucking dinner. I'm going out."

Later, the argument not so much forgotten as cautiously accommodated, Mark and Elinore lay in bed reading. His and hers. Sunday's sports pages and a glossy interiors magazine. But it was Mark flicking through the latter and Elinore's nose that was buried in the broadsheets.

"Look at that those colours," he said, pointing to a vivid living room.

"Too bright," she said, with a glance.

"Yeah. So, how did Rochdale get on then?" he asked.

"Er, they, er . . . drew. I'm just fascinated by all these places that were just names when we lived in London, and now they seem real. You know, now that we live here."

"I wouldn't get all dewy-eyed about Rochdale," he said. "But we can go and see them play if you like." He turned over and nuzzled into her cheek. "Let's have a look. Leigh RMI v Accrington Stanley.

There's a fixture to set the heart racing. Just say the word and I'll book two tickets."

"What about the kids?" she said, smiling.

"Well, all right, four tickets."

He took the paper out of her hands and let it slide on to the floor. Elinore's dressing gown was lying on the bed. He unthreaded the cord and used it to tie her right hand to the bedstead.

"This wasn't as straightforward before," Mark said.

"No?" she said, grinding her pubic bone against his.

"Well, our bed, which of course we miss so very much because it's so very, very comfortable, much more comfortable than this one, has nothing up here you can tie anything to."

"Still, it's the one thing I'm most looking forward to getting out of storage when we finally find a house."

"Me too. But for the time being we have to make the most of what we've got."

He reached for his own dressing gown and liberated its cord, which he used to secure Elinore's left hand, then he pulled the quilt back and straddled her legs. She pressed her head back into the pillow, closing her eyes. He leaned over and started kissing her.

Mark received a text from one of the agents in the village. Four-bed Cheshire semi, good-sized garden, even a study. Worth looking at, he thought, checking the map to see where it was. A little further up Wilmslow Road than might have been ideal, but they were getting sick of waiting. They'd started looking at places they might have not bothered with six months earlier.

He called the agent and made an appointment.

He looked again at the map. The name of the road was familiar and he couldn't work out why. They hadn't looked at a house there. There hadn't even been a house for sale there while they'd been looking, as far as he could remember. Nor had he been down the road on one of his walks. It was a cul-de-sac.

They liked it. They liked it enough to see it a second time, and the second time they liked it even more.

"Do you know much about the neighbours?" Mark asked the estate agent who had accompanied them.

"Absentee landlords," the young woman replied. "The house is rented out. Some of the time it's empty. Look, have a think. Take your time. I'll just be outside."

She left them to it.

"We'll have to move fast if we don't want to lose it," Mark said to Elinore.

"Yes, but, Mark, we have to make sure it's the right place," she reminded him.

"Remember the house on Alan Road?"

"The one with the funny pillar in the middle of the converted loft?"

"And the lovely little outbuildings, yes."

"So?"

"It's gone. We looked at it twice and still had it in the back of our minds, and now it's gone. You can't hang about in this game." He shielded his eyes against the sun. "I like this place. It feels good."

By now they were standing in the back garden. It wasn't a bad size.

Mark had remembered why the name of the street was familiar, but he hadn't told Elinore. She'd only say he was letting his heart rule his head.

"There are outbuildings here," she said. "Well, an outhouse."

"It looks recent. Relatively, I mean."

They looked up at what the details described as the "rear elevation."

Would they or wouldn't they?

She had to be the one to say it.

"Shall we?" she asked him.

"What do you think?"

"I think we should."

And so they did.

The first night in the new house, Mark bathed the children. He washed Caitlin's hair, then sat her on a chair in the middle of her new bedroom to dry it. He stood behind her with the hairdryer like a hairdresser.

"Are you going anywhere nice this year, Madam?" he asked her, pulling a brush through her velvety hair.

"Daddy, don't be silly. I'm not going anywhere," she answered him firmly.

Being in the new place didn't begin to feel weird until the kids were finally in bed. Up to that point, Mark and Elinore had hardly had a moment to draw breath.

"They're excited being in a new place," Elinore said.

"I'm excited about having our stuff back," Mark said. "Look at it all."

He pointed at the endless boxes that were still packed with CDs, DVDs, videos and books.

"I feel a bit overwhelmed," Elinore admitted.

"It'll be fine. A day or two to unpack and it'll begin to feel like home."

He thought about telling her what he'd remembered, about the road, but didn't. There'd be a moment and he'd recognise it when it came.

"Still," she said. "We've unpacked the important things. Like the telly."

He looked at her. She was smiling.

"Well, yeah. I thought it was important."

"I can't believe you managed to get cable sorted out on the first day."

"I can hardly believe it myself."

"So what's on? Have we got a paper?"

He passed her the *Evening News* and she studied the schedules.

He looked at the boxes. Yes, there was a lot to do, but this was what they had wanted, and they'd got it, so now things would start to get better again. A new beginning. It was what they needed.

He heard a knocking. One of the kids, perhaps. They were probably still awake.

"What was that?" Elinore asked.

He looked at her, faintly annoyed that she'd thought it worth mentioning. That it had been allowed to disturb their evening. He turned to stare at the blank screen of the TV.

"I don't know. One of the kids."

"I don't think so. Maybe it was someone at the door."

"It wasn't anyone at the door."

"One of us should go and see."

He looked at Elinore again. Her legs tucked up on the settee. Glass of Shiraz on the stripped floor just within reach. So what? She was the one who went out to work. Stressful job, proper salary. He stayed at home, worked the odd freelance graphic design commission, picked up the kids from school.

He got up and walked into the hall. He could see through the stained glass that there was no one at the door. The only noise from upstairs was the low murmur of the children's tape machines. He wandered into the front room. No furniture, just stacks and stacks of boxes separated by narrow aisles. He felt like a giant walking into Manhattan.

The knocking could have been coming from anywhere.

He looked out of the window. Their car was parked in the drive. That was a novelty. A house with a drive. He moved into the bay window and looked down the street, wondering which house had been his father's. It could have been this one, but it could just as easily have been any one of the others. He hadn't been able to find the list of old addresses his mother had helped him compile. Possibly it was at the bottom of one of the boxes behind him. Maybe, maybe not. He felt a stab of regret that he had not been closer to his father, that he had never really known him. He hoped his son wouldn't make the same mistake with him.

On cue, he heard a voice floating down from the top of the stairs.

"Mummy . . . Daddy."

"I'll go, Elinore," he said as he passed the living room on his way to the stairs.

He found both Thomas and Caitlin sitting side by side on the top step.

"What's the matter?" he asked, resting when he was on a level with them.

"We can hear noises."

"It's just the house," he said. "We're in a strange house. There are bound to be new noises, things you didn't hear in the old house. This house is older, for a start, so it creaks a bit more, like an old man. Can you hear my back when I bend down? Can you hear it creak? That's all you can hear. The creaky old bones of the new house."

"Daddy, I thought you said it was an old house," Caitlin remarked.

"Yes, well." He ruffled her hair.

"I'm hungry," said Thomas.

"I want some milk," Caitlin added.

"Come on, back to bed. I'll tuck you up. Chop chop." He clapped his hands and they ran off giggling.

\*        \*        \*

The following morning, with Elinore at work and the children already taken to school, Mark put a load of washing on and stood looking out of the kitchen window. It occurred to him that they didn't have a washing line and there was no sign of one outside.

He turned and looked at the boxes in the hall. They could wait. He got his jacket and keyed in the code to set the alarm. As he was pulling the front door to, he heard a knocking sound similar to the noise he and Elinore had heard the night before. He hesitated for a moment, his hand on the door. Investigating it would mean resetting the alarm. He decided against it and closed the door. Having done so, he bent down and peered through the letter box, but, once the alarm had stopped beeping, all he could hear were the normal sounds of an old house settling.

The village was quiet. It was still early. Out of curiosity, he checked the windows of the estate agents. He was surprised to see the Alan Road house back on the market.

"There are a couple of outbuildings in the back garden," the agent told him.

"Yes, I know. I viewed the house."

"Well, apparently, it was all set to go through and at the last minute they discovered the outbuildings actually belonged to the house next door."

"Oh. You'd think someone would have spotted that earlier."

"It's not as unusual as you might think," she said. "Things change hands over the years. People forget. It was in the deeds."

"I see."

A couple of doors down was the hardware shop, where Mark asked about a washing line. The man produced one from a shelf. Mark picked it up. He liked the feel of the cool plastic on his skin.

"I'll take two, please."

He walked back up Wilmslow Road, passed by buses of every colour all operating the same route but charging different fares. He remembered when he was growing up in Altrincham, the buses were all orange and white, and a small yellow square ticket that would take you all the way to Piccadilly cost you 2p.

When he got home, he put one of the washing lines up in the back garden and took the other one up to their bedroom. He opened his bedside drawer and dropped it in.

*       *       *

Mark spent the rest of the short day, until it was time to pick up the kids, unpacking boxes. Then they all played together in the back garden. He was lying on his back on the lawn with both children climbing on top of him when Elinore came home. Playfully he pushed them off and went to pour her a glass of wine, and crack open a beer.

They sat with their drinks at the end of the garden while the children played with a ball.

"Have you heard that knocking today?" asked Elinore.

"Elinore, behold the idyllic scene. Don't spoil it." He regarded her with exasperation. "No, I haven't heard it."

"OK. I was only asking."

But they heard it that night.

"Maybe it's the neighbours," Mark suggested, turning down the sound on the TV.

"Didn't the agent say the house was empty?"

"Look, darling, we've finally got a lovely house. And we're surrounded by all our own stuff again. We should be able to relax now. Don't worry about a little noise."

Elinore stared at the TV, grinding her teeth.

"Will you put up that mirror in the hall tomorrow?" she said at last.

"Whatever you want. I want us to be happy here."

In the morning, Mark found himself up a ladder in the hall with a drill, a pocketful of Rawl plugs and a mouthful of language.

"Fucking Rawl plugs. Fucking stupid bastard Rawl plugs."

The wall was like a slab of Emmental. Each hole had a Rawl plug either sticking out of it or jammed so far in it was equally useless.

Mark got down off the ladder and called Elinore on his mobile.

"It doesn't seem to matter what size Rawl plug I use, what size drill bit and what size screw, it's completely impossible to match them up. It's a fucking nightmare."

"Calm down, sweetheart. It's only a bit of DIY. You're only putting a mirror up."

"It's quite a big mirror. Hang on. There's someone knocking. I've got to go."

"Let's speak later."

He opened the front door, but there was no one there.

"Fuck."

Mark scratched his head. He went round the house checking in every cupboard, behind all the doors, for a dangling coathanger or loose hinge. He shone a torch in the darkest corners of the cellar and climbed up into the eaves, but found nothing that might be the source of the noise. In the end, putting the mirror up began to seem like light relief, so he got back up the ladder and drilled another hole. He slotted the Rawl plug in very slowly and with great care. It still didn't go in all the way, so he pulled the hammer out of his belt and gave it a whack.

The Rawl plug disappeared into the hole, which itself suddenly expanded dramatically as a section of plaster collapsed and fell inside.

Mark swore.

A cold draught wafted out of the hole.

Mark moved his body closer to the wall and put his eye to the hole.

It was too dark to see anything. He got the torch and, with the plaster around the edge of the hole crumbling beneath his touch, pointed its feeble beam into the darkness within.

Mark looked back at the hole from the other side. It was bigger now. A lot bigger. Big enough to climb through.

He was in a room. Not a big room, maybe eight foot by twelve. In the middle of the room was a chair, a standard wooden kitchen chair. And on the chair were the remains of a young woman.

He knew it was a woman because of the jewellery. Simple, inexpensive pieces. A ring, a necklace. Her wrists were tied to the chair behind her back with a length of grimy plastic-coated washing line. It was evident the room had been sealed a long time ago. Years rather than months.

Shock made Mark's entire body shake as he circled the chair. His face had become cold. He put a hand up to his cheeks. They were wet. He knelt in a corner of the room, his torch beam picking out the dead girl's skull, while he chewed the inside of his mouth.

He forced himself to have another close look, in case there were any obvious sign of how she had met her death. There wasn't. He couldn't stop himself imagining scenarios. The girl tied to the chair in the middle of the room. A man behind her, perhaps holding a hood that he would force over her head. Maybe he would have circled her like Mark had just done. If she was conscious, she might have pleaded for her life. He might have hit her. He might have crouched down in the corner and cried.

Mark fixed up the hole in the wall as best he could, using bits and pieces left lying around in the cellar. Then he hung the mirror over it. He was successful on his first fresh attempt with the drill and Rawl plugs.

He still had a couple of hours before it would be time to get the kids from school. He sat in the back garden, thinking. The outhouse, he realised, had been added to conceal the presence of the hidden room from anyone using the garden. He remembered what the estate agent had told him about the house on Alan Road. How the ownership of the outbuildings there had become confused over time. Perhaps that was how this room had remained hidden for so long. No one had compared the layout of rooms on the ground floor with that on the first floor and seen that there was a room missing. Or perhaps they had and merely assumed it belonged to the house next door, an anomaly of the Cheshire semi's irregular design.

The bedroom above the hidden room was Caitlin's. He gripped himself as he remembered sitting her on a chair in the middle of the room to dry her hair. He would have to swop with her and make that room his studio. She wouldn't complain when offered the bigger room on the second floor with skylights and a sloping ceiling.

That night, once the kids had gone to bed, Mark and Elinore sat in front of the TV with a takeaway.

Mark had not managed to find the list of his father's old addresses. He'd looked, half-heartedly, in a couple of boxes, then abandoned the search.

"I want you to be happy here," Mark said, during the ads.

"We will be," said Elinore, with a little smile.

"It's you and the children I'm thinking about," he said quietly. "I don't want anything to go wrong."

He looked at the wall and thought about what was on the other side of it. He thought about what he'd done, or rather hadn't done, and whether it was the right thing. He didn't feel he'd had a choice. He listened throughout the evening, but didn't hear the knocking sound again.

# THE CAPE

## *Joe Hill*

We were little.

I was the Red Bolt and I went up the dead elm in the corner of our yard to get away from my brother, who wasn't anyone, just himself. He had friends coming over and he wanted me not to exist, but I couldn't help it: I existed.

I had his mask and I said when his friends got there, I was going to reveal his secret identity. He said I was lunchmeat, and stood below, chucking stones at me, but he threw like a girl, and I quickly climbed out of range.

He was too old to play superheroes. It had happened all of a sudden, with no warning. He had spent whole days leading up to Halloween dressed as The Streak, who was so fast the ground melted under his feet as he ran. Then Halloween was over and he didn't want to be a hero anymore. More than that, he wanted everyone to forget he had ever been one, wanted to forget himself, only I wouldn't let him, because I was up in a tree with his mask, and his friends were coming over.

The elm had been dead for years. Whenever it was windy, the gusts sheared off branches and flung them across the lawn. The scaly bark splintered and snapped away under the toes of my sneakers. My brother wasn't inclined to follow — beneath his dignity — and it was intoxicating to escape from him.

At first I climbed without thought, scrambling higher than I ever had before. I went into a kind of tree-climbing trance, getting off on altitude and my own seven-year-old agility. Then I heard my brother shout up that he was ignoring me (sure proof that he wasn't) and I remembered what had sent me up the elm in the first place. I set my eye on a long, horizontal branch, a place where I could sit, dangle my feet, and taunt my brother into a frenzy without fear of repercussions. I swept the cape back over my shoulders and climbed on, with a purpose.

The cape had started life as my lucky blue blanket and had kept me company since I was two. Over the years, the color had faded from a deep, lustrous blue to a tired pigeon gray. My mother had cut it down to cape size and stitched a red felt lightning bolt in the center of it. Also sewn to it was a Marine's patch, one of my father's. It showed the number 9, speared through by a lightning bolt. It had come home from Vietnam in his foot locker. He hadn't come with it. My mother flew the black P.O.W. flag from the front porch, but even then I knew no one was holding my father prisoner.

I put the cape on as soon as I came home from school, sucked on the sateen hem while I watched TV, wiped my mouth with it at the dinner table, and most nights, fell asleep wrapped in it. It pained me to take it off. I felt undressed and vulnerable without it. It was just long enough to make trouble underfoot if I was incautious.

I reached the high branch, threw a leg over and straddled it. If my brother wasn't there to witness what happened next, I wouldn't have believed it myself. Later, I would've told myself it was a panicked fantasy, a delusion that gripped me in a moment of terror and shock.

Nicky was sixteen feet below, glaring up at me and talking about what he was going to do to me when I came down. I held up his mask, a black Lone Ranger thing with holes for the eyes, and waggled it.

"Come and get me, Streak," I said.

"You better be planning to live up there."

"I found streaks in my underwear that smell better than you."

"Okay. Now you're fucking dead," he said. My brother hurled comebacks like he hurled rocks: badly.

"Streak, Streak, Streak," I said, because the name was taunt enough.

I was crawling out along the branch as I chanted. I put my right hand down on the cape, which had slid off my shoulder. The next time I tried to move forward, the cape pulled taut, and unbalanced me. I heard cloth tear. I toppled hard against the branch, scraping my chin, throwing my arms around it. The branch sank beneath me, sprang up, sank again . . . and I heard a crack, a brittle snap that carried sharply in the crisp November air. My brother blanched.

"Eric," he shouted. "Hold on, Eric!"

Why did he tell me to hold on? The branch was breaking — I needed to get off it. Was he too shocked to know that, or did some unconscious part of him want to see me fall? I froze, struggling mentally to unscramble what to do, and in the moment I hesitated, the branch gave way.

My brother leaped back. The broken limb, all five feet of it, hit the ground at his feet and shattered, bark and twigs flying. The sky wheeled above me. My stomach did a nauseating somersault.

It took an instant to register that I wasn't falling. That I was staring out over the yard as if still seated on a high tree branch.

I shot a nervous look at Nicky. He stared back — gaping up at me.

My knees were hitched to my chest. My arms were spread out to either side, as for balance. I floated in the air, nothing holding me up. I wobbled to the right. I rolled to the left. I was an egg that wouldn't quite fall over.

"Eric?" my brother said, his voice weak.

"Nicky?" I said, my voice the same. A breeze wafted through the elm's bare branches, so they clicked and clattered against one another. The cape stirred at my shoulders.

"Come down, Eric," my brother said. "Come down."

I gathered my nerve and forced myself to glance over my knees at the ground directly below. My brother stood holding his arms outstretched to the sky, as if to grab my ankles and pull me down, although he was too far below me and standing too far back from the tree for any hope of that.

Something glittered at the edge of my vision and I lifted my gaze. The cape had been held around my neck by a golden safety pin, hooked through two opposing corners of the blanket. But the pin had ripped right through one of the corners, and hung uselessly from the other. I remembered, then, the tearing sound I had heard as I collapsed on the branch. Nothing was holding the cape on me.

The wind gusted again. The elm groaned. The breeze raced through my hair and snatched the cape off my back. I saw it dance away, as if being jerked along by invisible wires. My support danced away with it. In the next instant, I rolled forward, and the ground came at me in a hideous rush, so quickly there was no time even to scream.

I hit the hard earth, landing atop the shattered branch, which broke into pieces beneath me. One long skewer of wood punctured my chest, just beneath the collarbone. When it healed, it left a shiny scar in the shape of a crescent moon, my most interesting feature. I broke my fibula, pulverized my left kneecap and fractured my skull in two places. I bled from my nose, my mouth, my eyes.

I don't remember the ambulance, although I have heard I never truly lost consciousness. I do remember my brother's white and frightened face bending over mine, while we were still in the yard. My cape was balled up in his fists. He was twisting it, unconsciously, into knots.

If I had any doubts about whether it really happened, they were removed two days later. I was still in the hospital, when my brother tied the cape around his neck and leaped from the top of the front stairs, at home. He fell the whole way, eighteen steps in all, hit the last riser on his face. The hospital was able to place him in the same room with me, but we didn't talk. He spent most of the day with his back turned to me, staring at the wall. I don't know why he wouldn't look at me — maybe he was angry because the cape hadn't worked for him, or angry with himself for thinking it would, or just sick at the thought of how the other kids were going to make fun of him, when they learned he had shattered his face trying to be Superman — but at least I could understand why we didn't talk. His jaw was wired shut. It took six pins and two corrective surgeries to rebuild his face into something like its former appearance.

The cape was gone by the time we both got out of the hospital. My mother told us in the car. She had packed it into the trash and sent it to the dump to be incinerated. There would be no more flying in the Shooter household.

I was a different kid after my accident. My knee throbbed when I did too much walking, when it rained, when it was cold. Bright lights gave me shattering migraines. I had trouble concentrating for long stretches of time, found it difficult to follow a lecture from start to finish, sometimes drifted off into daydreams in the middle of tests. I couldn't run, so I was lousy at sports. I couldn't think, so I was worse at schoolwork.

It was misery to try and keep up with other kids, so I stayed inside after school and read comic books. I couldn't tell you who my favorite hero was. I don't remember any of my favorite stories. I read comics compulsively, without any particular pleasure, or any particular thought, read them only because when I saw one I couldn't not read it. I was in thrall to cheap newsprint, lurid colors and secret identities. The comics had a drug-like hold over me, with their images of men shooting through the sky, shredding the clouds as they passed through them. Reading them felt like life. Everything else was a little out of focus, the volume turned too low, the colors not quite bright enough.

I didn't fly again for over ten years.

I wasn't a collector and if not for my brother, I would've just left my comics in piles. But Nick read them as compulsively as I did, was as much under their spell. For years, he kept them in slippery plastic bags, arranged alphabetically in long white boxes.

Then, one day, when I was fifteen, and Nick was beginning as a senior at Passos High, he came home with a girl, an unheard-of event. He left her in the living room with me, said he wanted to drop his backpack upstairs, and then ran up to our room and threw our comics away, all of them, his and mine, almost eight hundred issues. Dumped them in two big Glad bags and snuck them out back.

I understand why he did it. Dating was hard for Nick. He was insecure about his rebuilt face, which didn't look so bad really. His jaw and chin were maybe a bit too square, the skin stretched too tightly over them, so at times he resembled a caricature of some brooding comic book hero. He was hardly The Elephant Man, although there was something terrible about his pinched attempts to smile, the way it seemed to pain him to move his lips and show his white, strong, Clark-Kent-straight false teeth. He was always looking at himself in the mirror, searching for some sign of disfigurement, for the flaw that made others avoid his company. He wasn't easy at being around girls. I had been in more relationships, and was three years younger. With all that against him, he couldn't afford to be uncool too. Our comics had to go.

Her name was Angie. She was my age, a transfer student, too new at school to know my brother was a dud. She smelled of patchouli and wore a hand-knit cap in the red-gold-and-green of the Jamaican flag. We had an English class together and she recognized me. There was a test on Lord of the Flies the next day. I asked what she thought of the book, and she said she hadn't finished it yet, and I said I'd help her study if she wanted.

By the time Nick got back from disposing of our comic collection, we were lying on our stomachs, side by side in front of MTV's Spring Break. I had the novel out and was going through some passages I had high-lighted . . . something I usually never did. As I said, I was a poor, unmotivated student, but Lord of the Flies had excited me, distracted my imagination for a week or so, made me want to live

barefoot and naked on an island, with my own tribe of boys to domi-
nate and lead in savage rituals. I read and reread the parts about Jack
painting his face, smitten with a desire to smear colored muds on my
own face, to be primitive and unknowable and free.

Nick sat on the other side of her, sulking because he didn't want
to share her with me. Nick couldn't talk about the book with us —
he had never read it. Nick had always been in Advanced English
courses, where the assigned reading was Milton and translations of
Dante. Whereas I was pulling Cs in Adventures in English! a course
for the world's future janitors and air conditioner repairmen. We
were the dumb kids, going nowhere, and for our stupidity, we were
rewarded with all the really fun books.

Now and then Angie would stop and check out what was on TV
and ask a provocative question: *do you guys think that girl is totally
hot? Would it be embarrassing to be beaten by a female mud wrestler, or
is that the whole point?* It was never clear who she was talking to, and
usually I answered first, just to fill the silences. Nick acted like his
jaw was wired shut again, and smiled his angry pinched smile when
my answers made her laugh. Once, when she was laughing especially hard, she put a hand on my arm. He sulked about that too.

Angie and I were friends for two years, before the first time we
kissed, in a closet, both of us drunk at a party, with others laughing
and shouting our names through the door. We made love for the first
time three months later, in my room, with the windows open and a
cool breeze that smelled sweetly of pines blowing in on us. After that
first time, she asked what I wanted to do with myself when I grew up.
I said I wanted to learn how to hang-glide. I was eighteen, she was
eighteen. This was an answer that satisfied us both.

Later, not long after she finished nursing school, and we settled
into an apartment together downtown, she asked me again what I
wanted to do. I had spent the summer working as a house painter,
but that was over. I hadn't found another job to replace it yet, and
Angie said I ought to take the time to think about the long-term.

She wanted me to get back into college. I told her I'd think about
it, and while I was thinking, I missed the enrollment period for the
next semester. She said why not learn to be an EMT, and spent several days collecting paperwork for me to fill out, so I could get in the
program: applications, questionnaires, financial aid forms. The pile
of them sat by the fridge, collecting coffee stains, until one of us

threw them out. It wasn't laziness that held me back. I just couldn't bring myself to do it. My brother was studying to be a doctor in Boston. He'd think I was, in some needy way, trying to be like him, an idea that gave me shivers of loathing.

Angie said there had to be something I wanted to do with myself. I told her I wanted to live in Barrow, Alaska, at the edge of the arctic circle, with her, and raise children, and malamuts, and have a garden in a greenhouse: tomatoes, string beans, a plot of mellow weed. We'd earn our living taking tourists dog sledding. We would shun the world of supermarkets, broadband internet and indoor plumbing. We would leave the TV behind. In the winter, the northern lights would paint the sky above us all day long. In the summers, our children would live half-wild, skiing unnamed backcountry hills, feeding playful seals by hand from the dock behind our house.

We had only just set out on the work of being adults, and were in the first stages of making a life with one another. In those days, when I talked about our children feeding seals, Angie would look at me in a way that made me feel both faintly weak and intensely hopeful . . . hopeful about myself and who I might turn out to be. Angie had the too-large eyes of a seal herself, brown, with a ring of brilliant gold around her pupil. She'd stare at me without blinking, listening to me tell it, lips parted, as attentive as a child hearing her favorite bedtime story.

But after my D.U.I., any mention of Alaska would cause her to make faces. Getting arrested cost me my job, too — no great loss, I admit, since I was temping as a pizza delivery man at the time — and Angie was desperate trying to keep up with the bills. She worried all the time, and she did her worrying alone, avoiding me as much as possible, no easy task, considering we shared a three-room apartment.

I brought up Alaska now and then, anyway, trying to draw her back to me, but it only gave her a place to concentrate her anger. She said if I couldn't keep the apartment clean, at home alone all day, what was our lodge going to be like? She saw our children playing amid piles of dogshit, the front porch caving in, rusting snowmobiles and deranged half-breed dogs scattered about the yard. She said hearing me talk about it made her want to scream, it was so pathetic, so disconnected from our lives. She said she was scared I had a problem, alcoholism maybe, or clinical depression. She wanted me to see someone, not that we had the money for that.

None of this explains why she walked out — fled without warning. It wasn't the court case, or my drinking, or my lack of direction. The real reason we split was more terrible than that, so terrible we could never talk about it. If she had brought it up, I would've ridiculed her. And I couldn't bring it up, because it was my policy to pretend it hadn't happened.

I was cooking breakfast for supper one night, bacon and eggs, when Angie arrived home for work. I always liked to have supper ready for her when she got back, part of my plan to show her I was down but not out. I said something about how we were going to have our own pigs up in the Yukon, smoke our own bacon, kill a shoat for Christmas dinner. She said I wasn't funny anymore. It was her tone more than what she said. I sang the song from *Lord of the Flies*, "kill the pig, drain her blood," trying to squeeze a laugh out of what hadn't been funny in the first place, and she said *stop it*, very shrill, *just stop it*. At this particular moment I happened to have a knife in my hand, what I had used to cut open the pack of bacon, and she was leaning with her rump resting against the kitchen counter a few feet away. I had a sudden, vivid picture in my head, imagined turning and slashing the knife across her throat. In my mind I saw her hand fly to her neck, her baby seal eyes springing open in astonishment, saw blood the bright red of cranberry juice gushing down her V-neck sweater.

As this thought occurred to me, I happened to glance at her throat — then at her eyes. And she was staring back at me and she was afraid. She set her glass of orange juice down, very gently, in the sink, and said she wasn't hungry and maybe she needed to lay down. Four days later I went around the corner for bread and milk and she was gone when I got back. She called from her parents to say we needed some time.

It was just a thought. Who doesn't have a thought like that now and then?

When I was two months behind on the rent and my landlord was saying he could get an order to have me thrown out, I moved home myself. My mother was remodeling and I said I wanted to help. I did want to help. I was desperate for something to do. I hadn't worked in four months and had a court date in December.

My mother had knocked down the walls in my old bedroom, pulled out the windows. The holes in the wall were covered with plastic sheeting, and the floor was littered in chunks of plaster. I made a nest for myself in the basement, on a cot across from the washer and dryer. I put my TV on a milk crate at the foot of the bed. I couldn't leave it behind in the apartment, needed it for company.

My mother was no company. The first day I was home, she only spoke to me to tell me I couldn't use her car. If I wanted to get drunk and crash a set of wheels, I could buy my own. Most of her communication was nonverbal. She'd let me know it was time to wake up by stomping around over my head, feet booming through the basement ceiling. She told me I disgusted her by glaring at me over her crowbar, as she pulled boards out of my bedroom floor, yanking them up in a silent fury, as if she wanted to tear away all the evidence of my childhood in her home.

The cellar was unfinished, with a pitted cement floor and a maze of low pipes hanging from the ceiling. At least it had its own bathroom, an incongruously tidy room with a flower-pattern linoleum floor and a bowl of woodland-scented potpourri resting on the tank of the toilet. When I was in there taking a leak, I could shut my eyes and inhale that scent and imagine the wind stirring in the tops of the great pines of northern Alaska.

I woke one night, in my basement cell, to a bitter cold, my breath steaming silver and blue in the light from the TV, which I had left on. I had finished off a couple beers before bed and now I needed to urinate so badly it hurt.

Normally, I slept beneath a large quilt, hand-stitched by my grandmother, but I had spilled Chinese on it and tossed it in the wash, then never got around to drying it. To replace it, I had raided the linen closet, just before bed, gathering up a stack of old comforters from my childhood: a puffy blue bedspread decorated with characters from *The Empire Strikes Back*, a red blanket with fleets of Fokker triplanes soaring across it. None of them, singly, was large enough to cover me, but I had spread the different blankets over my body in overlapping patterns, one for my feet, another for my legs and crotch, a third for my chest.

They had kept me cozy enough to fall asleep, but now were in disarray, and I was huddled for warmth, my knees pulled almost to my chest, my arms wrapped around them, my bare feet sticking into the cold. I couldn't feel my toes, as if they had already been amputated for frostbite.

My head was muddy. I was only half-awake. I needed to pee. I had to get warm. I rose and floated to the bathroom through the dark, the smallest blanket thrown over my shoulders to keep the cold off. I had the sleep-addled idea that I was still balled up to stay warm, with my knees close to my chest, although I was never-the-less moving forward. It was only when I was over the toilet, fumbling with the fly of my boxers, that I happened to look down and saw my knees *were* hitched up, and that my feet weren't touching the floor. They dangled a full foot over the toilet seat.

The room swam around me and I felt momentarily light-headed, not with shock so much as a kind of dreaming wonder. Shock didn't figure into it. I suppose some part of me had been waiting, all that time, to fly again, had almost been expecting it.

Not that what I was doing could really be described as flying. It was more like controlled floating. I was an egg again, tippy and awkward. My arms waved anxiously at my sides. The fingertips of one hand brushed the wall and steadied me a little.

I felt fabric shift across my shoulders and carefully dropped my gaze, as if even a sudden movement of the eyes could send me sprawling to the ground. At the edge of my vision I saw the blue sateen hem of a blanket, and part of a patch, red and yellow. Another wave of dizziness rolled over me and I wobbled in the air. The blanket slipped, just as it had done that day almost fourteen years before, and slid off my shoulders. I dropped in the same instant, clubbed a knee against the side of the toilet, shoved a hand into the bowl, plunging it deep into freezing water.

I sat with the cape spread across my knees, studying it as the first silvery flush of dawn lit the windows high along the basement walls.

The cape was even smaller than I remembered, about the length of a large pillowcase. The red felt lightning bolt was still sewn to the back, although a couple of stitches had popped free, and one corner of the bolt was sticking up. My father's Marine patch was still sewn on, as well, was what I had seen from the corner of my eye: a slash of lightning across a background like fire.

Of course my mother hadn't sent it to the dump to be incinerated. She never got rid of anything, on the theory she might find a use for it later. Hoarding what she had was a mania; not spending money, an obsession. She didn't know anything about home renovation, but it never would've crossed her mind to pay anyone to do the work for her. My bedroom would be torn open to the elements and I would be sleeping in the basement until she was in diapers and I was in charge of changing them. What she thought of as self-reliance was really a kind of white trash mulishness and I had not been home long before it got under my skin, and I had quit helping her out.

The sateen edge of the cape was just long enough for me to tie it around my neck.

I sat on the edge of my cot for a long time, perched with my feet up, like a pigeon on a ledge, and the blanket trailing to the small of my back. The floor was half a foot below, but I stared over the side as if looking at a forty-foot drop. At last, I pushed off.

And hung. Bobbled unsteadily, frontward and backways, but did not fall. My breath got caught behind my diaphragm and it was several moments before I could force myself to exhale, in a great equine snort.

I ignored my mother's wooden-heeled shoes banging overhead at nine in the morning. She tried again at ten, this time opening the door to shout down, *was I ever getting up?* I yelled back that I *was* up. It was true: I was two feet off the ground.

By then I had been flying for hours . . . but again, describing it as flight probably brings to mind the wrong sort of image. You see Superman. Imagine, instead, a man sitting on a magic carpet, with his knees pulled to his chest. Now take away the magic carpet and you'll be close.

I had one speed, which I would call stately. I moved like a float in a parade. All I had to do to glide forward was look forward, and I was going, as if driven by a stream of powerful but invisible gas, the flatulence of the Gods.

For a while, I had trouble turning, but eventually, I learned to change direction in the same way one steers a canoe. As I moved across the room, I'd throw an arm in the air and pull the other in. And effortlessly, I'd veer to the right or left, depending on which metaphorical oar I stuck in the water. Once I got the hang of it, the act of turning became exhilarating, the way I seemed to accelerate into the curves, in a sudden rush that produced a ticklish feeling in the pit of my stomach.

I could rise by leaning back, as if into a recliner. The first time I tried it, I swooped upward so quickly, I bashed a head against a brass pipe, hard enough to make constellations of black dots wheel in front of my eyes. But I only laughed and rubbed at the stinging lump in the center of my forehead.

When I finally quit, at almost noon, I was exhausted, and I lay in bed, my stomach muscles twitching helplessly from the effort it had required to keep my knees hitched up all that time. I had forgotten to eat, and I felt light-headed from low blood sugar. And still, even lying down, under my sheets, in the slowly warming basement, I felt as if I were soaring. I shut my eyes and sailed away into the limitless reaches of sleep.

In the late afternoon, I took the cape off and went upstairs to make bacon sandwiches. The phone rang and I answered automatically. It was my brother.

"Mom tells me you aren't helping upstairs," he said.

"Hi. I'm good. How are you?"

"She also said you sit in the basement all day watching TV."

"That's not all I do," I said. I sounded more defensive than I liked. "If you're so worried about her, why don't you come home and play handyman one of these weekends?"

"When you're third-year premed, you can't just take off whenever you feel like it. I have to schedule my BMs in advance. One day, last week, I was in the ER for ten hours. I should've left, but this old woman came in with heavy vaginal bleeding —" At this, I giggled, a reaction that was met with a long moment of disapproving silence. Then Nick went on, "I stayed at work another hour to make sure she was okay. That's what I want for you. Get you doing something that will lift you up above your own little world."

"I've got things I'm doing."

"What things? For example, what have you done with yourself today?"

"Today — today isn't a normal day. I didn't sleep all night. I've just been — sort of — floating from here to there." I couldn't help it; I giggled again.

He was silent for a while. Then he said, "If you were in total freefall, Eric, do you think you'd even know it?"

I slipped off the edge of the roof like a swimmer sliding from the edge of the pool into the water. My insides churned and my scalp prickled, icy-hot, my whole body clenching up, waiting for freefall. This is how it ends, I thought, and it crossed my mind that the entire morning, all that flying around the basement, had been a delusion, a schizophrenic fantasy, and now I would drop and shatter, gravity asserting its reality. Instead I dipped, then rose. My child's cape fluttered at my shoulders.

While waiting for my mother to go to bed, I had painted my face. I had retreated into the basement bathroom, and used one of her lipsticks to draw an oily red mask, a pair of linked loops, around my eyes. I did not want to be spotted while I was out flying, and if I was, I thought the red circles would distract any potential witnesses from my other features. Besides, it felt good to paint my face, was oddly arousing, the sensation of the lipstick rolling hard and smooth across my skin. When I was done, I stood admiring myself in front of the bathroom mirror for a while. I liked my red mask. It was a simple thing, but made my features strange and unfamiliar. I was curious about this new person staring back at me out of the mirrorglass. About what he wanted. About what he could do.

After my mother closed herself in her bedroom for the night, I had crept upstairs, out the hole in my bedroom wall where the dormer window had been, and onto the roof. A few of the black tar shingles were missing, and others were loose, hanging askew. Something else my mother could try and fix herself in the interest of saving a few nickels. She would be lucky not to slide off the roof and snap her neck. Anything could happen out there where the world touches the sky. No one knew that better than me.

The cold stung my face, numbed my hands. I had sat flexing my fingers for a long time, building up the nerve to overcome a hundred thousand years of evolution, screaming at me that I would die if I went over the edge. Then I was over the edge, and suspended in the clear, frozen air, thirty feet above the lawn.

You want to hear now that I felt a rush of excitement, whooped at the thrill of flight. I didn't. What I felt was something much more subtle. My pulse quickened. I caught my breath for a moment. Then I felt a stillness settling into me, like the stillness of the air. I was drawn completely into myself, concentrating on staying balanced atop the invisible bubble beneath me (which perhaps gives the impression that I could feel something beneath me, some unseen cushion of support; I could not, which was why I was constantly squirming around for balance). Out of instinct, as much as habit, I held my knees up to my chest, and kept my arms out to the side.

The moon was only a little bigger than a quarter full, but bright enough to etch intensely dark, sharp-edged shadows on the ground, and to make the frosty yards below shine as if the grass were blades of chrome.

I glided forward. I did some loops around the leafless crown of a red maple. The dead elm was long gone, had split in two in a windstorm almost eight years before. The top half had come down against the house, a long branch shattering one of my bedroom windows, as if reaching in for me, still trying to kill me.

It was cold, and the chill intensified as I climbed. I didn't care. I wanted to get above everything.

The town was built on the slopes of a valley, a crude black bowl, a-glitter with little lights. I heard a mournful honking in my left ear and my heart gave a lunge. I looked through the inky dark and saw a wild goose, with a liquid black head and a throat of startling emerald, beating its wings and staring curiously back at me. He did not remain by my side for long, but dove, swooped to the south, and was gone.

For a while I didn't know where I was going. I had a nervous moment, when I wasn't sure how I'd get back down without falling eight hundred feet. But when I couldn't bend my fingers anymore, or feel any sensation in my face, I tilted forward slightly and began to sink back to earth, gently descending, in the way I had practiced hour on hour in the basement.

By the time I leveled off over Powell Avenue, I knew where I was headed. I floated three blocks, rising once to clear the wire suspending a stop light, then hung a left and soared on, dreamlike, to Angie's house. She would just be getting off her shift at the hospital.

Only she was almost an hour late. I was sitting on the roof of the garage when she turned into the driveway in the old bronze Civic we had shared, bumper missing and hood battered from where I had crashed it into a dumpster, at the end of my low-speed attempt to evade the police.

Angie was made-up and dressed in her lime colored skirt with tropical flowers printed on it, the one she only wore to staff meetings at the end of the month. It wasn't the end of the month. I sat on the tin roof of the garage and watched her totter to the front door in her heels and let herself in.

Usually she showered when she got home. I didn't have anything else to do.

I slid off the peak of the garage roof, bobbled and rose like a black balloon toward the third floor of her parents' tall, narrow Victorian. Her bedroom was dark. I leaned toward the glass, peering in, looking toward her door and waiting for it to open. But she was already there, and in the next moment she snapped on a lamp, just to the left of the window, on a low dresser. She stared out the window at me and I stared right back, didn't move — couldn't move, was too shocked to make a sound. She regarded me wearily, without interest or surprise. She didn't see me. She couldn't make me out past her own reflection. I wondered if she had ever been able to see me.

I floated outside the window while she stripped her skirt off over her head, and wiggled out of plain girdle underwear. A bathroom adjoined her bedroom, and she considerately left the door open between the two. I watched her shower through the clear glass of the shower cabinet. She showered a long time, lifting her arms to throw her honey-colored hair back, hot water pelting her breasts. I had watched her shower before, but it hadn't been this interesting in a long time. I wished she'd masturbate with the flexible showerhead, something she said she had done as a teenager, but she didn't.

In a while the window steamed over and I couldn't see as clearly. I watched her pink pale form move here and there. Then I heard her voice. She was on the phone. She asked someone why they were studying on a Saturday night. She said she was bored, she wanted to play a game. She pleaded in tones of erotic petulance.

A circle of clear glass appeared in the center of the window and began to expand as the condensation in her room evaporated, giving me a slow reveal. She was in a clinging white halter and a pair of black cotton panties, sitting at a small desk, hair wrapped in a towel. She had hung up the phone, but was playing cribbage on her computer, typing occasionally to send an instant message. She had a glass of white wine. I watched her drink it. In movies, voyeurs watch models prance about in French lingerie, but the banal is kinky enough, lips on a wine glass, the band of simple panties against a white buttock.

When she got offline she seemed happy with herself but restless. She got into bed, switched on her little TV and flipped through the channels. She stopped on the Think! channel to watch seals fucking. One climbed on the back of the other and began humping away, blubber shaking furiously. She looked longingly at the computer.

"Angie," I said.

It seemed to take her a moment to register she had heard anything. Then she sat up and leaned forward, listening to the house. I said her name again. Her eyelashes fluttered nervously. She turned her head to the window almost reluctantly, but again, didn't see me past her reflection . . . until I tapped on the glass.

Her shoulders jumped in a nervous reflex. Her mouth opened in a cry, but she didn't make a sound. After a moment, she came off the bed and approached the window on stiff legs. She stared out. I waved hello. She looked beneath me for the ladder, then lifted her gaze back to my face. She swayed, put her hands on her dresser to steady herself.

"Unlock it," I said.

Her fingers struggled with the locks for a long time. She pulled the window up.

"Oh my God," she said. "Oh my God. Oh my God. How are you doing that?"

"I don't know. Can I come in?"

I eased myself up onto the window sill, turning and shifting, so one arm was in her room, but my legs hung out.

"No," she said. "I don't believe it."

"Yes. Real."

"How?"

"I don't know. Honest." I picked at the edge of the cape. "But I did it once before. A long time back. You know my knee and the scar on my chest? I told you I did all that falling out of a tree, you remember?"

A look of surprise, mingled with sudden understanding, spread across her face. "The branch broke and fell. But you didn't. Not at first. You stayed in the air. You were in your cape and it was like magic and you didn't fall."

She already knew. She already knew and I didn't know how, because I had never told her. I could fly; she was psychic.

"Nicky told me," she said, seeing my confusion. "He said when the tree branch fell, he thought he saw you fly. He said he was so sure, he tried to fly himself and that's what happened to his face. We were talking and he was trying to explain how he wound up with false teeth. He said he was crazy back then. He said you both were."

"When did he tell you about his teeth?" I asked. My brother never got over being insecure about his face, his mouth especially, and he didn't like people to know about the teeth.

She shook her head. "I don't remember."

I turned on the window sill and put my feet up on her dresser.

"Do you want to see what it's like to fly?"

Her eyes were glassy with disbelief. Her mouth was open in a blank, dazed smile. Then she tilted her head to one side and narrowed her eyes.

"How are you doing it?" she asked. "Really."

"It's something about the cape. I don't know what. Magic I guess. When I put it on, I can fly. That's all."

She touched the corner of one of my eyes, and I remembered the mask I had drawn with lipstick. "What about this stuff on your face? What's that do?"

"Makes me feel sexy."

"Holy shit, you're weird. And I lived with you for two years." She was laughing though.

"Do you want to fly?"

I slid the rest of the way into the room, toward her, and hung my legs over the side of the dresser.

"Sit in my lap. I'll ride you around the room."

She looked from my lap to my face, her smile sly and distrustful now. A breeze trickled in through the window behind me, stirring the cape. She hugged herself, and shivered, then glanced down at herself, and noticed she was in her underwear. She shook her head, twisted the towel off her still damp hair.

"Hold on a minute," she said.

She went to her closet and folded back the door and dug in a cubby for sweats. While she was looking, there came a pitiful shriek from the television, and my gaze shifted toward the screen. One seal was biting the neck of another, furiously, while his victim wailed. A narrator said dominant males would use all the natural weapons at their disposal to drive off any rival that might challenge them for access to the females of the herd. The blood looked like a splash of cranberry juice on the ice.

Angie had to clear her throat to get my attention again, and when I glanced at her, her mouth was, for a moment, thin and pinched, the corners crimped downward in a look of irritation. It only took a moment sometimes for me to drift away from myself and into some television program, even something I had no interest in at all. I couldn't help myself. It's like I'm a negative, and the TV is a positive. Together we make a circuit, and nothing outside the circuit matters. It was the same way when I read comics. It's a weakness, I admit, but it darkened my mood to catch her there, judging me.

She tucked a strand of wet hair behind one ear and showed me a quick, elfin grin, tried to pretend she hadn't just been giving me The Look. I leaned back, and she pulled herself up, awkwardly, onto my thighs.

"Why do I think this is some perverted prank to get me in your lap?" she asked. I leaned forward, made ready to push off. She said, "We're going to fall on our a —"

I slipped off the side of the dresser and into the air. I wobbled forward and back and forward again, and she wrapped her arms around my neck and cried out, a happy, laughing, frightened sort of cry.

I'm not particularly strong, but it wasn't like picking her up . . . it was really as if she were sitting on my lap and we were together in an invisible rocking chair. All that had changed was my center of gravity, and now I felt tippy, a canoe with too many people in it.

I floated her around her bed, then up and over it. She screamed-laughed-screamed again.

"This is the craziest —" she said. "Oh my God no one will believe it," she said. "Do you know you're going to be the most famous person in human history?" Then she just stared into my face, her wide eyes shining, the way they had used to when I talked about Alaska.

I made as if to fly back to my perch on the dresser, but when I got to it, I just kept going, ducked my head and carried us right out the open window.

"No! What are you doing? Holy Jesus it's cold!" She was squeezing me so tightly around the neck it was hard to breathe.

I rose toward the slash of silver moon.

"Be cold," I said. "Just for a minute. Isn't it worth it — for this? To fly like this? Like you do in dreams?"

"Yes," she said.

"Isn't this the most incredible thing?"

"Yes."

She shivered furiously, which set off an interesting vibration in her breasts, under the thin shirt. I kept climbing, toward a flotilla of clouds, edged in mercury. I liked the way she clung to me, and I liked the way it felt when she trembled.

"I want to go back," she said.

"Not yet."

My shirt was open a little, and she snuggled into it, her icy nose touching my flesh.

"I've wanted to talk to you," she said. "I wanted to call you to-night. I was thinking about you."

"Who did you call instead?"

"Nobody," she said, and then realized I had been out the window listening. "Hannah. You know. From work."

"Is she studying for something? I heard you ask why she was studying on a Saturday."

"Let's go back."

"Sure."

She buried her face against my chest again. Her nose grazed my scar, a silver slash like the silver slash of the moon. I was still climbing toward the moon. It didn't seem so far away. She fingered the old scar.

"It's unbelievable," she whispered. "Think how lucky you were. A few inches lower and that branch might've gone right through your heart."

"Who said it didn't?" I said, and leaned forward and let her go.

She held onto my neck, kicking, and I had to peel her fingers off, one at a time, before she fell.

Whenever my brother and I played superheroes, he always made me be the bad guy.

Someone has to be.

My brother has been telling me I ought to fly down to Boston one of these nights, so we can do some drinking together. I think he wants to share some big brother advice, tell me I have to pick myself up, have to move on. Maybe he also wants to share some grief. I'm sure he's in grief too.

One of these nights, I think I will . . . fly on down to see him. Show him the cape. See if he'll try it on. See if he wants to take a leap out his fifth-floor window.

He might not want to. Not after what happened last time. He might need some encouragement; a little nudge from little brother.

And who knows? Maybe if he goes out the window in my cape, he will rise instead of fall, float away into the cool, still embrace of the sky.

But I don't think so. It didn't work for him when we were children. Why would it now? Why would it ever?

It's my cape.

# LA PEAU VERTE

## *Caitlín R. Kiernan*

### 1.

In a dusty, antique-littered back room of the loft on St. Mark's Place, room with walls the color of ripe cranberries, Hannah stands naked in front of the towering, mahogany-framed mirror and stares at herself. No — not *her* self any longer, but the new thing that the man and woman have made of her. Three long hours busy with their airbrushes and latex prosthetics, grease paints and powders and spirit gum, their four hands moving as one, roaming excitedly and certainly across her body, hands sure of their purpose. She doesn't remember their names, if, in fact, they ever told their names to her. Maybe they did, and the two glasses of brandy have set the names somewhere just beyond recall. Him tall and thin, her thin but not so very tall, and now they've both gone, leaving her alone. Perhaps their part in this finished; perhaps the man and woman are being paid, and she'll never see either of them again, and she feels a sudden, unexpected pang at the thought, never one for casual intimacies, and they have been both casual and intimate with her body.

The door opens, and the music from the party grows suddenly louder. Nothing she would ever recognize, probably nothing that has a name, even; wild impromptu of drumming hands and flutes, violins and cellos, an incongruent music that is both primitive and drawing-room practiced. The old woman with the mask of peacock feathers and gown of iridescent satin stands in the doorway, watching Hannah. After a moment, she smiles and nods her head slowly, appreciatively.

"Very pretty," she says. "How does it feel?"

"A little strange," Hannah replies and looks at the mirror again. "I've never done anything like this before."

"Haven't you?" the old woman asks her, and Hannah remembers her name, then — Jackie, Jackie something that sounds like Shady or Sadie but isn't either. A sculptor from England, someone said. When she was very young, she knew Picasso, and someone said that, too.

"No," Hannah replies. "I haven't. Are they ready for me now?"

"Fifteen more minutes, give or take. I'll be back to bring you in. Relax. Would you like another brandy?"

*Would I?* Hannah thinks and glances down at the crystal snifter sitting atop an old secretary next to the mirror. It's almost empty now, maybe one last warm amber sip standing between it and empty. She wants another drink, something to burn away the last, lingering dregs of her inhibition and self-doubt, but "No," she tells the woman. "I'm fine."

"Then chill, and I'll see you in fifteen," Jackie Whomever says, smiles again, her disarming, inviting smile of perfect white teeth, and she closes the door, leaving Hannah alone with the green thing watching her from the mirror.

The old Tiffany lamps scattered around the room shed candy puddles of stained-glass light, light as warm as the brandy, warm as the dark chocolate tones of the intricately carved frame holding the tall mirror. She takes one tentative step nearer the glass, and the green thing takes an equally tentative step nearer her. *I'm in there somewhere,* she thinks. *Aren't I?*

Her skin painted too many competing, complementary shades of green to possibly count, one shade bleeding into the next, an infinity of greens that seem to roil and flow around her bare legs, her flat, hard stomach, her breasts. No patch of skin left uncovered, her flesh become a rain-forest canopy, waves on the deepest sea, the shells of beetles and leaves from a thousand gardens, moss and emeralds, jade statues and the brilliant scales of poisonous tropical serpents. Her nails polished a green so deep it might almost be black, instead. The uncomfortable scleral contacts to turn her eyes into the blaze of twin chartreuse stars, and Hannah leans a little closer to the mirror, blinking at those eyes, *with* those eyes, the windows to a soul she doesn't have. A soul of everything vegetable and living, everything growing, soul of sage and pond scum, malachite and verdigris. The fragile translucent wings sprouting from her shoulder blades — at least another thousand greens to consider in those wings alone — and all the many places where they've been painstakingly attached to her skin are hidden so expertly she's no longer sure where the wings end and she begins.

*The one, and the other.*

"I definitely should have asked for another brandy," Hannah says out loud, spilling the words nervously from her ocher, olive, turquoise lips.

Her hair — not *her* hair, but the wig *hiding* her hair — like something parasitic, something growing from the bark of a rotting tree, epiphyte curls across her painted shoulders, spilling down her back between and around the base of the wings. The long tips the man and woman added to her ears so dark that they almost match her nails, and her nipples airbrushed the same lightless, bottomless green, as well. She smiles, and even her teeth have been tinted a matte pea green.

There is a single teardrop of green glass glued firmly between her lichen eyebrows.

*I could get lost in here,* she thinks and immediately wishes she'd thought something else instead.

*Perhaps I already am.*

And then Hannah forces herself to look away from the mirror, reaches for the brandy snifter and the last swallow of her drink. Too much of the night still ahead of her to get freaked out over a costume, too much left to do and way too much money for her to risk getting cold feet now. She finishes the brandy, and the new warmth spreading through her belly is reassuring.

Hannah sets the empty glass back down on the secretary and then looks at herself again. And this time it *is* her self, after all, the familiar lines of her face still visible just beneath the make-up. But it's a damn good illusion. *Whoever the hell's paying for this is certainly getting his money's worth,* she thinks.

Beyond the back room, the music seems to be rising, swelling quickly towards crescendo, the strings racing the flutes, the drums hammering along underneath. The old woman named Jackie will be back for her soon. Hannah takes a deep breath, filling her lungs with air that smells and tastes like dust and old furniture, like the paint on her skin, more faintly of the summer rain falling on the roof of the building. She exhales slowly and stares longingly at the empty snifter.

"Better to keep a clear head," she reminds herself.

*Is that what I have here?* and she laughs, but something about the room or her reflection in the tall mirror turns the sound into little more than a cheerless cough.

And then Hannah stares at the beautiful, impossible green woman staring back at her and waits.

## 2.

"Anything forbidden becomes mysterious," Peter says and picks up his remaining bishop, then sets it back down on the board without making a move. "And mysterious things always become attractive to us, sooner or later. Usually sooner."

"What is that? Some sort of unwritten social law?" Hannah asks him, distracted by the Beethoven that he always insists on whenever they play chess. *Die Geschöpfe des Prometheus* at the moment, and she's pretty sure he only does it to break her concentration.

"No, dear. Just a statement of the fucking obvious."

Peter picks up the black bishop again, and this time he almost uses it to take one of her rooks, then thinks better of it. More than thirty years her senior and the first friend she made after coming to Manhattan, his salt-and-pepper beard and mustache that's mostly salt, his eyes as grey as a winter sky.

"Oh," she says, wishing he'd just take the damn rook and be done with it. Two moves from checkmate, barring an act of divine intervention, and that's another of his games, Delaying the Inevitable. She thinks he probably has a couple of trophies for it stashed away somewhere in his cluttered apartment, chintzy *faux* golden loving cups for his Skill and Excellence in Procrastination.

"Taboo breeds desire. Gluttony breeds disinterest."

"Jesus, I ought to write these things down," she says, and he smirks at her, dangling the bishop teasingly only an inch or so above the chessboard.

"Yes, you really should. My agent could probably sell them to someone or another. *Peter Mulligan's Big Book of Tiresome Truths.* I'm sure it would be more popular than my last novel. It certainly couldn't be *less* —"

"Will you stop it and *move* already? Take the damned rook, and get it over with."

"But it *might* be a mistake," he says and leans back in his chair, mock suspicion on his face, one eyebrow cocked, and he points towards her queen. "It could be a trap. You might be one of those predators that fakes out its quarry by playing dead."

"You have no idea what you're talking about."

"Yes I do. You know what I mean. Those animals, the ones that only *pretend* to be dead. You might be one of those."

"I *might* just get tired of this and go the hell home," she sighs, because he knows that she won't, so she can say whatever she wants.

"Anyway," he says, "it's work, if you want it. It's just a party. Sounds like an easy gig to me."

"I have that thing on Tuesday morning though, and I don't want to be up all night."

"Another shoot with Kellerman?" asks Peter and frowns at her, taking his eyes off the board, tapping at his chin with the bishop's mitre.

"Is there something wrong with that?"

"You hear things, that's all. Well, *I* hear things. I don't think you ever hear anything at all."

"I need the work, Pete. The last time I sold a piece, I think Lincoln was still President. I'll never make as much money painting as I do posing for *other* people's art."

"Poor Hannah," Peter says. He sets the bishop back down beside his king and lights a cigarette. She almost asks him for one, but he thinks she quit three months ago, and it's nice having at least that one thing to lord over him; sometimes it's even useful. "At least you *have* a fallback," he mutters and exhales; the smoke lingers above the board like fog on a battlefield.

"Do you even know who these people are?" she asks and looks impatiently at the clock above his kitchen sink.

"Not first-hand, no. But then they're not exactly my sort. Entirely too, well . . ." and Peter pauses, searching for a word that never comes, so he continues without it. "But the Frenchman who owns the place on St. Mark's, Mr. Ordinaire — excuse me, *Monsieur* Ordinaire — I heard he used to be some sort of anthropologist. I think he might have written a book once."

"Maybe Kellerman would reschedule for the afternoon," Hannah says, talking half to herself.

"You've actually never tasted it?" he asks, picking up the bishop again and waving it ominously towards her side of the board.

"No," she replies, too busy now wondering if the photographer will rearrange his Tuesday schedule on her behalf to be annoyed at Peter's cat and mouse with her rook.

"Dreadful stuff," he says and makes a face like a kid tasting brussels sprouts or Pepto-Bismol for the first time. "Might as well have a big glass of black jelly beans and cheap vodka, if you ask me. *La Fée Verte* my fat ass."

"Your ass isn't fat, you skinny old queen," Hannah scowls playfully, reaching quickly across the table and snatching the bishop from

Peter's hand. He doesn't resist. This isn't the first time she's grown too tired of waiting for him to move to wait any longer. She takes her white rook off the board and sets the black bishop in its place.

"That's suicide, dear," Peter says, shaking his head and frowning. "You know that, don't you?"

"You know those animals that *bore* their prey into submission?"

"No, I don't believe I've ever heard of them before."

"Then maybe you should get out more often."

"Maybe I should," he replies, setting the captured rook down with all the other prisoners he's taken. "So, are you going to do the party? It's a quick grand, you ask me."

"That's easy for you say. You're not the one who'll be getting naked for a bunch of drunken strangers."

"A fact for which we should *all* be forevermore and eternally grateful."

"You have his number?" she asks, giving in, because that's almost a whole month's rent in one night and, after her last show, beggars can't be choosers.

"There's a smart girl," Peter says and takes another drag off his cigarette. "The number's on my desk somewhere. Remind me again before you leave. Your move."

3.

"How old were you when that happened, when your sister died?" the psychologist asks, Dr. Edith Valloton and her smartly-cut hair so black it always makes Hannah think of fresh tar, or old tar gone deadly soft again beneath a summer sun to lay a trap for unwary, crawling things. Someone she sees when the nightmares get bad, which is whenever the painting isn't going well or the modeling jobs aren't coming in or both. Someone she can tell her secrets to who has to *keep* them secret, someone who listens as long as she pays by the hour, the place to turn when faith runs out and priests are just another bad memory to be confessed.

"Almost twelve," Hannah tells her and watches while Edith Valloton scribbles a note on her yellow legal pad.

"Do you remember if you'd begun menstruating yet?"

"Yeah. My periods started right after my eleventh birthday."

"And these dreams, and the stones, this is something you've never told anyone?"

"I tried to tell my mother once."

"She didn't believe you?"

Hannah coughs into her hand and tries not to smile, that bitter, wry smile to give away things she didn't come here to show.

"She didn't even *hear* me," she says.

"Did you try more than once to tell her about the fairies?"

"I don't think so. Mom was always pretty good at letting us know whenever she didn't want to hear what was being said. You learned not to waste your breath."

"Your sister's death, you've said before that it's something she was never able to come to terms with."

"She never tried. Whenever my father tried, or I tried, she treated us like traitors. Like we were the ones who put Judith in her grave. Or like we were the ones *keeping* her there."

"If she couldn't face it, Hannah, then I'm sure it did seem that way to her."

"So, no," Hannah says, annoyed that she's actually paying someone to sympathize with her mother. "No. I guess never really told anyone about it."

"But you think you want to tell me now?" the psychiatrist asks and sips her bottled water, never taking her eyes off Hannah.

"You said to talk about all the nightmares, all the things I think are nightmares. It's the only one that I'm not sure about."

"Not sure if it's a nightmare, or not sure if it's even a dream?"

"Well, I always thought I was awake. For years, it never once occurred to me I might have only been dreaming."

Edith Valloton watches her silently for a moment, her cat-calm, cat-smirk face, unreadable, too well-trained to let whatever's behind those dark eyes slip and show. Too detached to be smug, too concerned to be indifferent. Sometimes Hannah thinks she might be a dyke, but maybe that's only because the friend who recommended her is a lesbian.

"Do you still have the stones?" the psychiatrist asks, finally, and Hannah shrugs out of habit.

"Somewhere, probably. I never throw anything away. They might be up at Dad's place, for all I know. A bunch of my shit's still up there, stuff from when I was a kid."

"But you haven't tried to find them?"

"I'm not sure I *want* to."

"When is the last time you saw them, the last time you can remember having seen them?"

And Hannah has to stop and think, chews intently at a stubby thumbnail and watches the clock on the psychologist's desk, the second hand traveling round and round and round. Seconds gone for pennies, nickels, dimes, and *Hannah, this is the sort of thing you really ought to try to get straight ahead of time,* she thinks in a voice that sounds more like Dr. Valloton's than her own thought-voice. *A waste of money, a waste of time . . .*

"You can't remember?" the psychologist asks and leans a little closer to Hannah.

"I kept them all in an old cigar box. I think my grandfather gave me the box. No, he didn't. No, he gave it to Judith, and then I took it after the accident. I didn't think she'd mind."

"I'd like to see them someday, if you ever come across them again. Wouldn't that help you to know whether it was a dream or not, if the stones are real?"

"Maybe," Hannah mumbles around her thumb. "And maybe not."

"Why do you say that?"

"A thing like that, words scratched onto a handful of stones, it'd be easy for a kid to fake. I might have made them all myself. Or someone else might have made them, someone playing a trick on me. Anyone could have left them there."

"Did people do that often? Play tricks on you?"

"Not that I can recall. No more than usual."

Edith Valloton writes something else on her yellow pad and then checks the clock.

"You said that there were always stones after the dreams. Never before?"

"No, never before. Always after. They were always there the next day, always in the same place."

"At the old well," the psychologist says, like Hannah might have forgotten and needs reminding.

"Yeah, at the old well. Dad was always talking about doing something about it, before the accident, you know. Something besides a couple of old sheets of tin to hide the hole. Afterwards, of course, the county ordered him to have the damned thing filled in."

"Did your mother blame him for the accident, because he never did anything about the well?"

"My mother blamed *everyone.* She blamed him. She blamed

me. She blamed whoever had dug that hole in the first goddamn place. She blamed God for putting water underground so people would dig wells to get at it. Believe me, Mom had blame down to an art."

And again, the long pause, the psychiatrist's measured consideration, quiet moments she plants like seeds to grow ever deeper revelations.

"Hannah, I want you to try to remember the word that was on the first stone you found. Can you do that?"

"That's easy. It was 'follow'."

"And do you also know what was written on the last one, the very last one that you found?"

And this time she has to think, but only for a moment.

"'Fall'," she says. "The last one said 'fall'."

4.

Half a bottle of Mari Mayans borrowed from a friend of Peter's, a goth chick who djs at a club that Hannah's never been to because Hannah doesn't go to clubs. Doesn't dance and has always been more or less indifferent to both music and fashion. The goth chick works days at Trash And Vaudeville on St. Mark's, selling Doc Martens and blue hair dye only a couple of blocks from the address on the card that Peter gave her. The place where the party will be. *La Fête de la Fée Verte*, according to the small white card, the card with the phone number. She's already made the call, has already agreed to be there, seven sharp, seven on the dot, and everything that's expected of her has been explained in detail, twice.

Hannah's sitting on the floor beside her bed, a couple of vanilla-scented candles burning because she feels obligated to make at least half a half-hearted effort at atmosphere. Obligatory show of respect for mystique that doesn't interest her, but she's gone to the trouble to borrow the bottle of liqueur; the bottle passed to her in a brown paper bag at the boutique, anything but inconspicuous, and the girl glared out at her, cautious from beneath lids so heavy with shades of black and purple that Hannah was amazed the girl could open her eyes.

"You're a friend of Peter's?" the girl asked suspiciously.

"Yeah," Hannah replied, accepting the package, feeling vaguely, almost pleasurably illicit. "We're chess buddies."

"A painter," the girl said.

"Most of the time."

"Peter's a cool old guy. He made bail for my boyfriend once, couple of years back."

"Really? Yeah, he's wonderful," and Hannah glanced nervously at the customers browsing the racks of leather handbags and corsets, then at the door and the bright daylight outside.

"You don't have to be so jumpy. It's not illegal to have absinthe. It's not even illegal to drink it. It's only illegal to import it, which you didn't do. So don't sweat it."

Hannah nodded, wondering if the girl was telling the truth, if she knew what she was talking about. "What do I owe you?" she asked.

"Oh, nothing," the girl replied. "You're a friend of Peter's, and, besides, I get it cheap from someone over in Jersey. Just bring back whatever you don't drink."

And now Hannah twists the cap off the bottle, and the smell of anise is so strong, so immediate, she can smell it before she even raises the bottle to her nose. *Black jelly beans*, she thinks, just like Peter said, and that's something else she never cared for. As a little girl, she'd set the black ones aide, and the pink ones, too, saving them for her sister. Her sister had liked the black ones.

She has a wine glass, one from an incomplete set she bought last Christmas, secondhand, and a box of sugar cubes, a decanter filled with filtered tap water, a spoon from her mother's mismatched antique silverware. She pours the absinthe, letting it drip slowly from the bottle until the fluorescent yellow-green liquid has filled the bottom of the glass. Then Hannah balances the spoon over the mouth of the goblet and places one of the sugar cubes in the tarnished bowl of the spoon. She remembers watching Gary Oldman and Winona Ryder doing this in *Dracula*, remembers seeing the movie with a boyfriend who eventually left her for another man, and the memory and all its associations are enough to make her stop and sit staring at the glass for a moment.

"This is so fucking silly," she says, but part of her, the part that feels guilty for taking jobs that pay the bills but have nothing to do with painting, the part that's always busy rationalizing and justifying the way she spends her time, assures her it's a sort of research. A new experience, horizon-broadening something to expand her mind's eye, and, for all she knows, it might lead her art somewhere it needs to go.

"Bullshit," she whispers, frowning down at the entirely uninviting glass of Spanish absinthe. She's been reading, *Absinthe: History in a Bottle* and *Artists and Absinthe*, accounts of Van Gogh and Rimbaud, Oscar Wilde and Paul Marie Verlaine and their various relationships with this foul-smelling liqueur. She's never had much respect for artists who use this or that drug as a crutch and then call it their muse; heroin, cocaine, pot, booze, what-the-hell-ever, all the same shit as far as she's concerned. An excuse, an inability in the artist to hold himself accountable for his *own* art, a lazy cop-out, as useless as the idea of the muse itself. And *this* drug, this drug in particular, so tied up with art and inspiration there's even a Renoir painting decorating the Mari Mayans label, or at least it's something that's supposed to *look* like a Renoir.

*But you've gone to all this trouble, hell, you may as well taste it, at least. Just a* taste, *to satisfy curiosity, to see what all the fuss is about.*

Hannah sets the bottle down and picks up the decanter, pouring water over the spoon, over the sugar cube, and the absinthe louches quickly to an opalescent, milky white-green. Then she puts the decanter back on the floor and stirs the half-dissolved sugar into the glass, sets the spoon aside on a china saucer.

"Enjoy the ride," the goth girl said as Hannah walked out of the shop. "She's a blast."

Hannah raises the glass to her lips, sniffs at it, wrinkling her nose, and the first, hesitant sip is even sweeter and more piquant than she expected, sugar-soft fire when she swallows, a seventy-proof flower blooming warm in her belly. But the taste not nearly as disagreeable as she'd thought it would be, the sudden licorice and alcohol sting, a faint bitterness underneath that she guesses might be the wormwood. The second sip is less of a shock, especially since her tongue seems to have gone slightly numb.

She opens *Absinthe: History in a Bottle* again, opening the book at random, and there's a full-page reproduction of Albert Maignan's *The Green Muse*. Blonde woman with marble skin, golden hair, wrapped in diaphanous folds of olive, her feet hovering weightless above bare floorboards, her hands caressing the forehead of an intoxicated poet. The man is gaunt and seems lost in some ecstasy or revelry or simple delirium, his right hand clawing at his face, the other hand open in what might have been meant as a feeble attempt to ward off the attentions of his unearthly companion. *Or,* Hannah thinks, *perhaps he's reaching for something.* There's a shattered green bottle on the floor at his feet, a full glass of absinthe on his writing desk.

She takes another sip and turns the page.

A photograph, Verlaine drinking absinthe in the Café Procope.

Another, bolder swallow, and the taste is becoming familiar now, almost, *almost* pleasant.

Another page. Jean Béraud's *Le Boulevard, La Nuit.*

When the glass is empty, and the buzz in her head and eyes so gentle, buzz like a stinging insect wrapped in spider silk and honey, Hannah takes another sugar cube from the box and pours another glass.

## 5.

"Fairies.

"'Fairy crosses.'

*"Harper's Weekly*, 50-715:

> That, near the point where the Blue Ridge and the Allegheny Mountains unite, north of Patrick County, Virginia, many little stone crosses have been found.

"A race of tiny beings.

"They crucified cockroaches.

"Exquisite beings — but the cruelty of the exquisite. In their diminutive way they were human beings. They crucified.

"The 'fairy crosses,' we are told in *Harper's Weekly*, range in weight from one-quarter of an ounce to an ounce: but it is said, in the *Scientific American*, 79-395, that some of them are no larger than the head of a pin.

"They have been found in two other states, but all in Virginia are strictly localized on and along Bull Mountain . . .

". . . I suppose they fell there."

— Charles Fort, *The Book of the Damned* (1919)

## 6.

In the dream, which is never the same thing twice, not precisely, Hannah is twelve years old and standing at her bedroom window watching the backyard. It's almost dark, the last rays of twilight, and there are chartreuse fireflies dappling the shadows, already a few stars twinkling in the high, indigo sky, the call of a whippoorwill from the woods nearby.

Another whippoorwill replies.

And the grass is moving. The grass grown so tall because her father never bothers to mow it anymore. It could be wind, only there is no wind; the leaves in the trees are all perfectly, silently still, and no limb swaying, no twig, no leaves rustling in even the stingiest breeze. Only the grass, and *It's probably just a cat,* she thinks, *a cat or a skunk or a raccoon.*

The bedroom has grown very dark, and she wants to turn on a lamp, afraid of the restless grass even though she knows it's only some small animal, awake for the night and hunting, taking a short cut across their backyard. She looks over her shoulder, meaning to ask Judith to please turn on a lamp, but there's only the dark room, Judith's empty bunk, and she remembers it all again. It's always like the very first time she heard, the surprise and disbelief and pain always that fresh, the numbness that follows that absolute.

"Have you seen your sister?" her mother asks from the open bedroom door. There's so much night pooled there that she can't make out anything but her mother's softly glowing eyes the soothing color of amber beads, two cat-slit pupils swollen wide against the gloom.

"No, Mom," Hannah tells her, and there's a smell in the room then like burning leaves.

"She shouldn't be out so late on a school night."

"No, Mom, she shouldn't," and the eleven-year-old Hannah is amazed at the thirty-five-year-old's voice coming from her mouth; the thirty-five-year-old Hannah remembers how clear, how unburdened by time and sorrow, the eleven-year-old Hannah's voice could be.

"You should look for her," her mother says.

"I always do. That comes later."

"Hannah, have you seen your sister?"

Outside, the grass has begun to swirl, rippling round and round upon itself, and there's the faintest green glow dancing a few inches above the ground.

*The fireflies,* she thinks, though she knows it's not the fireflies, the way she knows it's not a cat, or a skunk, or a raccoon making the grass move.

"Your father should have seen to that damned well," her mother mutters, and the burning leaves smell grows a little stronger. "He should have done something about that years ago."

"Yes, Mom, he should have. You should have made him."

"No," her mother replies angrily. "This is not my fault. None of it's my fault."

"No, of course it's not."

"When we bought this place, I told him to see to that well. I *told* him it was dangerous."

"You were right," Hannah says, watching the grass, the softly-pulsing cloud of green light hanging above it. The light is still only about as big as a basketball. Later, it'll get a lot bigger. She can hear the music now, pipes and drums and fiddles, like a song from one of her father's albums of folk music.

"Hannah, have you seen your sister?"

Hannah turns and stares defiantly back at her mother's glowing, accusing eyes.

"That makes three, Mom. Now you have to leave. Sorry, but them's the rules," and her mother does leave, obedient phantom fading slowly away with a sigh, a flicker, a half-second when the darkness seems to bend back upon itself, and she takes the burning leaves smell with her.

The light floating above the backyard grows brighter, reflecting dully off the windowpane, off Hannah's skin and the room's white walls. The music rises to meet its challenge.

Peter's standing beside her now, and she wants to hold his hand, but doesn't, because she's never quite sure if he's supposed to be in this dream.

"I am the Green Fairy," he says, sounding tired and older than he is, sounding sad. "My robe is the color of despair."

"No," she says. "You're only Peter Mulligan. You write books about places you've never been and people who will never be born."

"You shouldn't keep coming here," he whispers, the light from the backyard shining in his grey eyes, tinting them to moss and ivy.

"Nobody else does. Nobody else ever could."

"That doesn't mean —"

But he stops and stares speechlessly at the backyard.

"I should try to find Judith," Hannah says. "She shouldn't be out so late on a school night."

"That painting you did last winter," Peter mumbles, mumbling like he's drunk or only half awake. "The pigeons on your window-sill, looking in."

"That wasn't me. You're thinking of someone else."

"I hated that damned painting. I was glad when you sold it."

"So was I," Hannah says. "I should try to find her now, Peter. It's almost time for dinner."

"I am ruin and sorrow," he whispers.

And now the green light is spinning very fast, throwing off gleaming flecks of itself to take up the dance, to swirl about their mother star, little worlds newborn, universes, and she could hold them all in the palm of her right hand.

"What I need," Peter says, "is blood, red and hot, the palpitating flesh of my victims."

"Jesus, Peter, that's purple even for you," and Hannah reaches out and lets her fingers brush the glass. It's warm, like the spring evening, like her mother's glowing eyes.

"I didn't write it," he says.

"And I never painted pigeons."

She presses her fingers against the glass and isn't surprised when it shatters, explodes, and the sparkling diamond blast is blown inward, tearing her apart, shredding the dream until it's only unconscious, fitful sleep.

7.

"I wasn't in the mood for this," Hannah says and sets the paper saucer with three greasy, uneaten cubes of orange cheese and a couple of Ritz crackers down on one corner of a convenient table. The table is crowded with fliers about other shows, other openings at other galleries. She glances at Peter and then at the long white room and the canvases on the walls.

"I thought it would do you good to get out. You never go anywhere anymore."

"I come to see you."

"My point exactly, dear."

Hannah sips at her plastic cup of warm merlot, wishing she had a beer instead.

"And you said that you liked Perrault's work."

"Yeah," she says. "I'm just not sure I'm up for it tonight. I've been feeling pretty morbid lately, all on my own."

"That's generally what happens to people who swear off sex."

"Peter, I didn't *swear off* anything."

And she follows him on their first slow circuit around the room, small talk with people that she hardly knows or doesn't want to know at all, people who know Peter better than they know her, people whose opinions matter and people whom she wishes she'd never met. She smiles and nods her head, sips her wine, and tries not to look too long at any of the huge, dark canvases spaced out like oil and acrylic windows on a train.

"He's trying to bring us down, down to the very core of those old stories," a woman named Rose tells Peter. She owns a gallery somewhere uptown, the sort of place where Hannah's paintings will never hang. "'Little Red Riding Hood,' 'Snow White,' 'Hansel and Gretel,' all those old fairy tales," Rose says. "It's a very post-Freudian approach."

"Indeed," Peter says. *As if he agrees,* Hannah thinks, *as if he even cares,* when she knows damn well he doesn't.

"How's the new novel coming along?" Rose asks him.

"Like a mouthful of salted thumbtacks," he replies, and she laughs.

Hannah turns and looks at the nearest painting, because it's easier than listening to the woman and Peter pretend to enjoy one another's company. A somber storm of blacks and reds and greys, dappled chaos struggling to resolve itself into images, images stalled at the very edge of perception; she thinks she remembers having seen a photo of this canvas in *Artforum.*

A small beige card on the wall to the right of the painting identifies it as *Night in the Forest.* There isn't a price because none of Perrault's paintings are ever for sale. She's heard rumors that he's turned down millions, tens of millions, but suspects that's all exaggeration and PR. Urban legends for modern artists, and from the other things that she's heard he doesn't need the money, anyway.

Rose says something about the exploration of possibility and fairy tales and children using them to avoid any *real* danger, something that Hannah's pretty sure she's lifted directly from Bruno Bettelheim.

"Me, I was always rooting for the wolf," Peter says, "or the wicked witch or the three bears or whatever. I never much saw the point in rooting for silly girls too thick not to go wandering about alone in the woods."

Hannah laughs softly, laughing to herself, and takes a step back from the painting, squinting at it. A moonless sky pressing cruelly down upon a tangled, writhing forest, a path and something waiting in the shadows, stooped shoulders, ribsy, a calculated smudge of scarlet that could be its eyes. There's no one on the path, but the implication is clear — there will be, soon enough, and the thing crouched beneath the trees is patient.

"Have you seen the stones yet?" Rose asks and no, Peter replies, no we haven't.

"They're a new direction for him," she says. "This is only the second time they've been exhibited."

*If I could paint like that*, Hannah thinks, *I could tell Dr. Valloton to kiss my ass. If I could paint like that, it would be an exorcism.*

And then Rose leads them both to a poorly-lit corner of the gallery, to a series of rusted wire cages, and inside each one is a single stone. Large pebbles or small cobbles, stream-worn slate and granite, and each stone has been crudely engraved with a single word.

The first one reads "follow."

"Peter, I need to go now," Hannah says, unable to look away from the yellow-brown stone, the word tattooed on it, and she doesn't dare let her eyes wander ahead to the next one.

"Are you sick?"

"I need to go, that's all. I need to go *now*."

"If you're not feeling well," the woman named Rose says, trying too hard to be helpful, "there's a rest room in the back."

"No, I'm fine. Really. I just need some air."

And Peter puts an arm protectively around her, reciting his hurried, polite goodbyes to Rose. But Hannah still can't look away from the stone, sitting there behind the wire like a small and vicious animal at the zoo.

"Good luck with the book," Rose says and smiles, and Hannah's beginning to think she *is* going to be sick, that she will have to make a dash for the toilet, after all. A taste like foil in her mouth and her heart like a mallet on dead and frozen beef, adrenaline, the first eager tug of vertigo.

"It was good to meet you, Hannah," the woman says, and Hannah manages to smile, manages to nod her head.

And then Peter leads her quickly back through the crowded gallery, out onto the sidewalk and the warm night spread out along Mercer Street.

8.

"Would you like to talk about that day at the well?" Dr. Valloton asks, and Hannah bites at her chapped lower lip.

"No. Not now," she says. "Not again."

"Are you sure?"

"I've already told you everything I can remember."

"If they'd found her body," the psychiatrist says, "perhaps you and your mother and father would have been able to move on. There could have at least been some sort of closure. There wouldn't have been that lingering hope that maybe someone would find her, that maybe she was alive."

Hannah sighs loudly, looking at the clock for release, but there's still almost half an hour to go.

"Judith fell down the well and drowned," she says.

"But they never found the body."

"No, but they found enough, enough to be sure. She fell down the well. She drowned. It was very deep."

"You said you heard her calling you —"

"I'm not sure," Hannah says, interrupting the psychiatrist before she can say the things she was going to say next, before she can use Hannah's own words against her. "I've never been absolutely sure. I told you that."

"I'm sorry if it seems like I'm pushing," Dr. Valloton says.

"I just don't see any reason to talk about it again."

"Then let's talk about the dream, Hannah. Let's talk about the day you saw the fairies."


9.

The dreams, or the day from which the dreams would arise and, half-forgotten, seek always to return. The dreams or the day itself, the one or the other, it makes very little difference. The mind exists only in a moment, always, a single flickering moment, remembered or actual, dreaming or awake or something between the two, the precious, treacherous illusion of Present floundering in the crack between Past and Future.

The dream of the day — or the day — and the sun is high and small and white, a dazzling July sun coming down in shafts through the tall trees in the woods behind Hannah's house. She's running to catch up with Judith, her sister two years older and her legs grown longer, always leaving Hannah behind. *You can't catch me, slowpoke.*

*You can't even keep up.* Hannah almost trips in a tangle of creeper vines and has to stop long enough to free her left foot.

"Wait up!" she shouts, and Judith doesn't answer. "I want to see. Wait for me!"

The vines try to pull one of Hannah's tennis shoes off and leave bright beads of blood on her ankle. But she's loose again in only a moment, running down the narrow path to catch up, running through the summer sun and the oak-leaf shadows.

"I found something," Judith said to her that morning after breakfast. The two of them sitting on the back porch steps, and "Down in the clearing by the old well," she said.

"What? What did you find?"

"Oh, I don't think I should tell you. No, I *definitely* shouldn't tell you. You might go and tell Mom and Dad. You might spoil everything."

"No, I wouldn't. I wouldn't tell them anything. I wouldn't tell anyone."

"Yes, you would, big mouth."

And, finally, she gave Hannah half her allowance to tell, half to show whatever there was to see. Her sister dug deep down into the pockets of her jeans, and her hand came back up with a shiny black pebble.

"I just gave you a whole dollar to show me a *rock*?"

"No, stupid. *Look* at it," and Hannah held out her hand.

The letters scratched deep into the stone — JVDTH — five crooked letters that almost spelled her sister's name, and Hannah didn't have to pretend not to be impressed.

"Wait for me!" she shouts again, angry now, her voice echoing around the trunks of the old trees and dead leaves crunching beneath her shoes. Starting to guess that the whole thing was a trick after all, just one of Judith's stunts, and her sister's probably watching her from a hiding place right this very second, snickering quietly to herself. Hannah stops running and stands in the center of the path, listening to the murmuring forest sounds around her.

And something faint and lilting that might be music.

"That's not all," Judith said. "But you have to *swear* you won't tell Mom and Dad —"

"I swear."

"If you do tell, well, I *promise* I'll make you wish you hadn't."

"I won't tell anyone *anything.*"

"Give it back," Judith said, and Hannah immediately handed the black stone back to her. "If you *do* tell —"

"I already said I won't. How many times do I have to say I won't tell?"

"Well then," Judith said and led her around to the back of the little tool shed where their father kept his hedge clippers and bags of fertilizer and the old lawnmowers he liked to take apart and try to put back together again.

"This better be *worth* a dollar," Hannah said.

She stands very, very still and listens to the music, growing louder; she thinks it's coming from the clearing up ahead.

"I'm going back home, Judith!" she shouts, not a bluff because suddenly she doesn't care whether or not the thing in the jar was real, and the sun doesn't seem as warm as it did only a moment ago.

And the music keeps getting louder.

And louder.

And Judith took an empty mayonnaise jar out of the empty rabbit hutch behind the tool shed. She held it up to the sun, smiling at whatever was inside.

"Let me see," Hannah said.

"Maybe I should make you give me another dollar first," her sister replied, smirking, not looking away from the jar.

"No way," Hannah said indignantly. "Not a snowball's chance in hell," and she grabbed for the jar, then, but Judith was faster, and her hand closed around nothing at all.

In the woods, Hannah turns and looks back towards home, then turns back towards the clearing again, waiting for her just beyond the trees.

"Judith! This isn't funny! I'm going home right this second!"

Her heart is almost as loud as the music now. Almost. Not quite, but close enough.

Pipes and fiddles, drums and a jingle like tambourines.

And Hannah takes another step towards the clearing, because it's nothing at all but her sister trying to scare her, stupid because it's broad daylight, and Hannah knows these woods like the back of her hand.

Judith unscrewed the lid of the mayonnaise jar and held it out so Hannah could see the small, dry thing curled in a lump at the bottom. Tiny mummy husk of a thing, grey and crumbling in the morning light.

"It's just a damn dead mouse," Hannah said disgustedly. "I gave you a whole dollar to see a rock and a dead mouse in a jar?"

"It's *not* a mouse, stupid. Look closer."

And so she did, bending close enough that she could see the perfect dragonfly wings on its back, transparent, iridescent wings to glimmer faintly in the sun. Hannah squinted and realized that she could see its face, realized that it *had* a face.

"Oh," she said, looking quickly up at her sister, who was grinning triumphantly. "Oh, Judith. Oh my god. What is it?"

"Don't you know?" Judith asked her. "Do I have to tell you everything?"

Hannah picks her way over the deadfall just before the clearing, the place where the path through the woods disappears beneath a jumble of fallen, rotting logs. There was a house back here, her father said, a long, long time ago. Nothing left but a big pile of rocks where the chimney once stood and the well covered over with sheets of rusted corrugated tin. There was a fire, her father said, and everyone in the house died.

On the other side of the deadfall, Hannah takes a deep breath and steps out into the daylight, leaving the tree shadows behind, forfeiting her last chance not to see.

"Isn't it cool," Judith said. "Isn't it the coolest thing you ever seen?"

Someone's pushed aside the sheets of tin, and the well is so dark that even the sun won't go there. And then Hannah sees the wide ring of mushrooms, the perfect circle of toadstools and red caps and spongy brown morels growing round the well. The heat shimmers off the tin, dancing mirage shimmer like the air here is turning to water, and the music is very loud now.

"I found it," Judith whispered, screwing the top back onto the jar as tightly as she could. "I found it, and I'm going to keep it. And you'll keep your mouth shut about it, or I'll never, *ever* show you anything else again."

Hannah looks up from the mushrooms, from the open well, and there are a thousand eyes watching her from the edges of the clearing. Eyes like indigo berries and rubies and drops of honey, gold and silver coins, eyes like fire and ice, eyes like seething dabs of midnight. Eyes filled with hunger beyond imagining, neither good nor evil, neither real nor impossible.

Something the size of a bear, squatting in the shade of a poplar tree, raises its shaggy charcoal head and smiles.

"That's another pretty one," it growls.

And Hannah turns and runs.

10.

"But you *know*, in your soul, what you must have really seen that day," Dr. Valloton says and taps the eraser end of her pencil lightly against her front teeth. There's something almost obscenely earnest in her expression, Hannah thinks, in the steady *tap tap tap* of the pencil against her perfectly-spaced, perfectly white incisors. "You saw your sister fall into the well, or you realized that she just had. You may have heard her calling out for help."

"Maybe I pushed her in," Hannah whispers.

"Is that what you *think* happened?"

"No," Hannah says and rubs at her temples, trying to massage away the first dim throb of an approaching headache. "But, most of the time, I'd rather believe that's what happened."

"Because you *think* it would be easier than what you remember."

"Isn't it? Isn't easier to believe she pissed me off that day, and so I shoved her in? That I made up these crazy stories so I'd never have to feel guilty for what I'd done? Maybe that's what the nightmares are, my conscience trying to fucking force me to come clean."

"And what are the stones, then?"

"Maybe I put them all there myself. Maybe I scratched those words on them myself and hid them there for me to find, because I knew that would make it easier for me to believe. If there was something that real, that tangible, something solid to remind me of the story, that the story is supposed to be the truth."

A long moment of something that's almost silence, just the clock on the desk ticking and the pencil tapping against the psychiatrist's teeth. Hannah rubs harder at her temples, the real pain almost within sight now, waiting for her just a little ways past this moment or the next, vast and absolute, deep purple shot through with veins of red and black. Finally, Dr. Valloton lays her pencil down and takes a deep breath.

"Is this a confession, Hannah?" she asks, and the obscene earnestness is dissolving into something that may be eager anticipation or simple clinical curiosity or only dread. "Did you kill your sister?"

And Hannah shakes her head and shuts her eyes tight.

"Judith fell into the well," she says calmly. "She moved the tin and got too close to the edge. The sheriff showed my parents where a little bit of the ground had collapsed under her weight. She fell into the well, and she drowned."

"Who are you trying so hard to convince? Me or yourself?"

"Do you really think it matters?" Hannah replies, matching a question with a question, tit for tat, and "Yes," Dr. Valloton says. "Yes, I do. You need to know the truth."

"Which one?" Hannah asks, smiling against the pain swelling behind her eyes, and this time the psychiatrist doesn't bother answering, lets her sit silently with her eyes shut until the clock decides her hour's up.

11.

Peter Mulligan picks up a black pawn and moves it ahead two squares; Hannah removes it from the board with a white knight. He isn't even trying today, and that always annoys her.

Peter pretends to be surprised that's he's lost another piece, then pretends to frown and think about his next move while he talks.

"In Russian," he says, "'chernobyl' is the word for wormwood. Did Kellerman give you a hard time?"

"No," Hannah says. "No, he didn't. In fact, he said he'd actually rather do the shoot in the afternoon. So everything's jake, I guess."

"Small miracles," Peter sighs, picking up a rook and setting it back down again. "So you're doing the anthropologist's party?"

"Yeah," she replies. "I'm doing the anthropologist's party."

"*Monsieur* Ordinaire. You think he was born with that name?"

"I think I couldn't give a damn, as long as his check doesn't bounce. A thousand dollars to play dress-up for a few hours. I'd be a fool not to do the damned party."

Peter picks the rook up again and dangles it in the air above the board, teasing her. "Oh, his book," he says. "I remembered the title the other day. But then I forgot it all over again. Anyway, it was something on shamanism and shape-shifters, werewolves and masks, that sort of thing. It sold a lot of copies in '68, then vanished from the face of the earth. You could probably find out something about it online."

Peter sets the rook down and starts to take his hand away.

"Don't," she says. "That'll be check mate."

"You could at least let me *lose* on my own, dear," he scowls, pretending to be insulted.

"Yeah, well, I'm not ready to go home yet." Hannah replies, and

Peter Mulligan goes back to dithering over the chessboard and talking about Monsieur Ordinaire's forgotten book. In a little while, she gets up to refill both their coffee cups, and there's a single black and grey pigeon perched on the kitchen windowsill, staring in at her with its beady piss-yellow eyes. It almost reminds her of something she doesn't want to be reminded of, and so she raps on the glass with her knuckles and frightens it away.

12.

The old woman named Jackie never comes for her. There's a young boy, instead, fourteen or fifteen, sixteen at the most, his nails polished poppy red to match his rouged lips, and he's dressed in peacock feathers and silk. He opens the door and stands there, very still, watching her, waiting wordlessly. Something like awe on his smooth face, and for the first time Hannah doesn't just feel nude, she feels *naked*.

"Are they ready for me now?" she asks him, trying to sound no more than half as nervous as she is, and then turns her head to steal a last glance at the green fairy in the tall mahogany mirror. But the mirror is empty. There's no one there at all, neither her nor the green woman, nothing but the dusty back room full of antiques, the pretty hard-candy lamps, the peeling cranberry wallpaper.

"My Lady," the boy says in a voice like broken crystal shards, and then he curtsies. "The Court is waiting to receive you, at your ready." He steps to one side, to let her pass, and the music from the party grows suddenly very loud, changing tempo, the rhythm assuming a furious speed as a thousand notes and drumbeats tumble and boom and chase one another's tails.

"The mirror," Hannah whispers, pointing at it, at the place where her reflection should be, and when she turns back to the boy there's a young girl standing there, instead, dressed in his feathers and make-up. She could be his twin.

"It's a small thing, My Lady," she says with the boy's sparkling, shattered tongue.

"What's happening?"

"The Court is assembled," the girl child says. "They are all waiting. Don't be afraid, My lady. I will show you the way."

*The path, the path through the woods to the well, the path down the well . . .*

"Do you have a name?" Hannah asks, surprised at the calm in

her voice; all the embarrassment and unease at standing naked before this child, and the one before, the fear at what she didn't see gazing back at her in the looking glass, all of that gone now.

"My name? I'm not such a fool as that, My Lady."

"No, of course not," Hannah replies. "I'm sorry."

"I will show you the way," the child says again. "Never harm, nor spell, nor charm, come our Lady nigh."

"That's very kind of you," Hannah replies. "I was beginning to think that I was lost. But I'm not lost, am I?"

"No, My Lady. You are here."

"Yes. Yes, I *am* here, aren't I?" and the child smiles for her, showing off its sharp crystal teeth. Hannah smiles back, and then she leaves the dusty back room and the mahogany mirror, following the child down a short hallway; the music has filled in all the vacant corners of her skull, the music and the heavy living-dying smells of wildflowers and fallen leaves, rotting stumps and fresh-turned earth. A riotous hothouse cacophony of odors — spring to fall, summer to winter — and she's never tasted air so violently sweet.

*. . . the path down the well, and the still black water at the bottom.*

*Hannah, can you hear me? Hannah?*

*It's so cold down here. I can't see . . .*

At the end of the hall, just past the stairs leading back down to St. Mark's, there's a green door, and the girl opens it.

And all the things in the wide, wide room — the unlikely room that stretches so far away in every direction that it could never be contained in any building, not in a thousand buildings — the scampering, hopping, dancing, spinning, flying, skulking things, each and every one of them stops and stares at her. And Hannah knows that they should frighten her, that she should turn and run from this place. But it's really nothing she hasn't seen before, a long, long time ago, and she steps past the child (who is a boy again) as the wings on her back begin to thrum like the frantic, iridescent wings of bumblebees and hummingbirds, red wasps and hungry dragonflies. Her mouth tastes of anise and wormwood, sugar and hyssop and melissa, and sticky verdant light spills from her skin and pools in the grass and moss at her bare feet.

*Sink or swim, and so easy to imagine the icy black well water closing thickly over her sister's face, filling her mouth, slipping up her nostrils, flooding her belly, as clawed hands dragged her down.*

*And down.*

*And down.*

*And sometimes, Dr. Valloton says, sometimes we spend our entire lives just trying to answer one simple question.*

The music is a hurricane, swallowing her.

My Lady. Lady of the Bottle. *Artemisia absinthium*, Chernobyl, *absinthion*, Lady of Waking Dreaming, Green Lady of Elation and Melancholy.

*I am ruin and sorrow.*

*My robe is the color of despair.*

They bow, *all* of them, and Hannah finally sees the thing waiting for her on its prickling throne of woven branches and bird's nests, the hulking antlered thing with blazing eyes, wolf-jawed hart, the man and the stag, and she bows, in her turn.

# A VERY LITTLE MADNESS GOES A LONG WAY

## M. Rickert

She is a young woman, really, though coming upon her like this, standing at the window staring out at the bright California sun and palm trees, her hair pulled back in an innocuous ponytail, her shoulders slightly hunched, her arms wrapped around herself in a desultory manner, as if hugging someone who has become tiresome, she gives the impression of being a sad old woman.

"I thought you'd be happy here," says her husband, who sits at the edge of the bed unlacing his work shoes, his jogging clothes in a heap beside him and his running shoes on the floor by his feet. He isn't rushing exactly, that would be unkind and he is a kind man, but he does have everything ready to go. He wasn't a runner when they lived in Wisconsin. He smiles in spite of her mood, because he isn't much of a runner now either. Who's he kidding? But he likes the heat on his face, neck and limbs. He likes the vastness of the blue sky, marked irregularly by the palm trees single thrusts like fingers. Take that friggin' Wisconsin winters, he thinks when he jogs down Canal and up Avidio Street. He likes the open feeling, so different from their bedroom where she stares out the window like an old woman.

When he's ready, he resists the temptation to bolt from the room. He walks over to her. Places his hand on her shoulder. She sighs. He tries to think of what to say, searching through the ideas as if they were on note cards. I love you. I'm sorry. Everything will be ok. (But he's finally come to understand it might never be.) We could have another child. (He won't make that mistake again.) I love you. I love you. (Does he? Is that what this emotion is? This rooting next to her when he longs to run out of the room and escape into the vast bright world?) "I love you," he says.

She shrugs. It's very slight but he's almost certain that she shrugs. Yet she leans against him, so perhaps he hasn't interpreted that first inflection of muscles right. "Don't you think," she says, "I mean really, I know what you think, but I can't get them out of my head."

"Melinda," he says. Just that. Just her name. But he says it in such a way that she pulls away from him. He lets her. He stands there for a moment and then he shakes his head. If she were paying attention to him she'd see his reflection in the window, shaking his head. But she doesn't see him standing there and she doesn't see him leave. She doesn't see the palm trees, or the bright blue sky, or the blonde woman across the street bringing groceries into the house, or the man in striped shorts watering his lawn, or the children on bikes in their safety helmets pedaling furiously past as though, on some sub-conscious level, they know what she has brought with her.

Crows. Their sharp black beaks. Beady black eyes. Flap of wings, like the sharp crack of pillowcases and sheets snapped open to make a new bed. For someone else's child. She puts her hands over her eyes and sobs. Her husband, in a white blur she doesn't see, blazes past the window. The children on their bicycles shout at each other. She hears them only vaguely through the harsh cawing of the crows. Thousands and thousands of them. Watching her, with those beady black eyes, devoid.

"What you need to do is get involved in something else for awhile," her best friend, Stella says when she calls. "Have you thought of knitting?"

"I'm going to write about them."

"Who?"

"The crows."

Stella moans. Well, it's not exactly a moan, it's a sigh moan com-bination, that's what Melinda thinks, and she's been noticing that a lot lately, in the people around her. "You know, I've been thinking," Stella says, "of taking a little vacation. Melinda?"

"I know people think I'm nuts now."

"Nobody thinks you're nuts. It's just, listen how 'bout I come out there?"

"That crow spoke to me."

There it is again, that combination moan sigh, perhaps with a small sob or gasp at the end.

"I know you don't believe me. Nobody does. Crows can speak. I just want. . . ." But she doesn't finish the sentence. What she wants is so much. She wants everything. What she's been given is this.

"I'm going to look into some flights, ok? I'll let you know what I find out."

"What? Oh, sure," Melinda says, not really certain what she's agreeing to. All she hears is "flight" and suddenly she is watching them again, thousands and thousands of crows flapping wings and rising only to land swiftly with their cawing sharp cries so loud she can hear them clearly through the closed windows, and all those thousands of miles, and even through time back to that day when she turned from her daughter's bed to stare out the window at those harbingers of death assembled across from the Children's Hospital. No one seemed to notice or understand their significance. Their cold eyes didn't even consider her or the child buried in the clean white sheets and hospital neat folds of a death they came to carry, the same way they picked through the garbage cans, and the lawn, and on one particularly gruesome day which Melinda still remembers by the strange combination of sweat and cold she felt, as they dove and fought over the corpse of one of their own, a dead crow they pulled apart with their sharp beaks and ate, flying into the trees and screaming at each other and her daughter moaned or sighed, she made a sound, Melinda turned to her, and knew, by the beautiful light that emanated there, a shiny bright thing in the dark, what would happen soon and who was to blame.

Later, when the crows fell from the sky, plummeting like rocks and landing in yards and playgrounds, and church parking lots it didn't make her feel better, the way she had thought it would.

Even now, sometimes, she looks to the sky and thinks she sees a black spot hovering above her, destined to spiral down in a swirl of wings and dead weight.

His name is Corvus. His parents, hippies who really did wear flowers in their hair and lived in a bus, had intended to name all their children after birds. He has a sister named Robin and a brother named Jay but he doesn't see or hear from them much. The one he hears from is Melinda, born "just at the edge of my change," as his mother liked to say, during her short second marriage to a carpet salesman from Iowa who died when Melinda was still a baby of something like failure to breathe, or some such malarkey of words, which Corvus can't completely recall. Something stupid like that. Something bureaucratic to get the paperwork through when all it really meant was that they didn't know why he died but he did.

Corvus is the one who flew to the cornfield state to comfort his mother when no one else would and even now Melinda, who is a grown woman with her own life and the sad story of her child's death, seems to confuse him with her father though he doesn't think he looks like anyone's dad with his black leather jacket and his pierced ear and the tattoos of a snake, a naked lady, and on his back right shoulder, a raven, which he'd done out of deference to his name (though ravens and blackbirds, are not the same) years before his kid sister went nuts about crows. So when she calls him from California where they moved to "try to make a fresh start" and says she is going to write a book about crows, "about the things they say and do," he rubs his brow and must have made a sound because she says, "I just wish everyone would quit moaning about me," which causes him to pretend he wasn't moaning at all and act excited and say how he's been thinking of coming out to visit her and that husband of hers, whose name he can never remember. What is it again? Not Jack but something normal and ordinary. Safe.

Is Corvus the only one who realizes the truth about Melinda? She should have changed her name by now to something extraordinary like Universa. He understands why their mother did what she did and gave her a pretty, but basically normal name. But Melinda is a grown woman now. Shouldn't she know the truth? Corvus shakes his head as he begins to sort through piles of black clothes. What's happening to Melinda, Corvus thinks, can best be described by a term used for the poor and unloved. Though Melinda is neither she still suffers from it. "Failure to thrive." She has no idea how extraordinary she is. She's surrounded herself with bland normalcy. Well all right, maybe that's not fair, maybe ordinary people have amazing lives, he wouldn't know, when he sees them, in shopping malls, and coffee shops, or even just driving, they tend to wear the same expression, which is partly how he identifies them, it isn't an expression of much, neither satisfaction, nor despair, and certainly not harmony. It's like a mask they all wear. And Melinda has it too. But the thing is, Corvus thinks as he copies Melinda's new address onto a sheet of paper and tucks it into his wallet, she'll suffocate in that mask, just like her father, like a murder with no witnesses and no blood.

"I can't believe you invited him without talking to me about it first."

"Well, he is my brother."

"He never even remembers my name."

"So, tell him."

"What?"

"It's not like . . . it's not . . . Just tell him."

"I've told him a hundred times."

"You can't possibly. Stella is coming out too. What?"

"I thought we moved here to get away from everyone."

"Not me."

"Where are we going to put them?"

"Stella can sleep in my office and Corvus can sleep on the couch. Ok? Ok?"

The thing he hasn't told her about is the crow. It's just one crow, not thousands and thousands of them. It's one crow and he isn't even certain if it's the same one. How's he supposed to know? They all look alike to him. But this crow, well, he knows this is silly, but he thinks it's following him. He first noticed it back in Wisconsin. When the crows started falling from the sky, suddenly paralyzed from the poison. It wasn't unusual to notice a crow then. Circumstances had sort of created a hyper awareness surrounding them. But this crow always seemed to be looking at him, in that sideways manner of birds. Of course he figured he was imagining it. But then they moved here and he started seeing it again. Just one crow staring at him sideways as he jogged past, watching him when he got into his car in the mornings, standing on the lawn outside the office when he left work. It creeped him out. But he sure wasn't going to tell Melinda, or anyone about it.

Just as he didn't tell anyone about his daughter. People meant well, he knew, but it was nice to not have to deal with sudden kind words and gestures, which, in the end, were woefully inadequate. It was nice to be treated like a regular man and not like someone mortally wounded. That's why he didn't want them coming. Well, ok, and he didn't like either of them very much. They were both strange people. He couldn't understand what Melinda got from them that she couldn't get from him.

Corvus isn't surprised to be directed to the side for a terrorist evaluation. They already have his shoes. He takes off his jacket and belt. Raises his arms and turns for the wand. It's silly, really, how they keep trying to change that day in the past by doing the things now they wish they had done then. Corvus is surprised to feel the tear form and relieved when he's nodded on before it falls, as it does, when he leans over to tie his shoe. How can anyone not have compassion for them? They are so awkward, so earnest, so desperate, and increasingly, so alone. Shut off from the rest of existence, shut off from what would sustain them, by their own fear. He looks at the people waiting in the terminal with him, young families, an old man, some business suit men and women, a kid playing a little computer game, a baby crying, a young girl. When he takes a deep breath he can smell their human scent, marked as it is by the powerful fear motivator, laced with sweat, indigestion, onion, garlic, perfumes and lotions, and that vague odor of love.

Corvus stands in line and follows them into the plane. He knows there is irony in this, but he made a promise years ago and he intends to keep it. Because he's going to break the other one. He's going to tell Melinda what their mother told him.

He turns sideways to move down the narrow aisle. He senses the seated passengers eyeing him suspiciously. As if evil could be measured by black clothes and long hair. Like children, he thinks, who truly believe they can recognize a bad guy. When he gets to his seat number he nods at the bald man who looks up at him, and taking in his size, stands in the aisle to let him through. Corvus scrunches into the window seat. He snaps the buckle shut and closes his eyes until the plane takes off. Then he opens them to look at the clouds. How will he tell her? "We are angels."

"What?" the bald man says.

Corvus looks at him, startled. Had he spoken out loud?

"Were you talking to me?"

Corvus shakes his head.

The man frowns and pretends to read his magazine but Corvus can sense his awareness on him. He readjusts his weight, lowers his seat back, and closes his eyes.

When they land, Corvus gets off the plane, just like the rest of them and while most passengers have noticed him, and marked him in their minds, only one passenger has recognized him as someone who knows exactly what he is, only one passenger follows him.

"It wasn't murder," Stella says rubbing Melinda's back as she weeps while Joe, who Stella assumes is handling all this the best he can, in his own odd way, runs in circles around the house.

"I mean I was filled with hate. That's the thing," Melinda sobs.

"I pretended like it was about reason and logic. But it wasn't. It was just about hate."

"Something had to be done," Stella says, trying to choose her words carefully because the fact is, she'd really been against it all along.

Melinda stops crying. She sits there, staring out the window and biting her fingernail. "Did I tell you one spoke to me?"

"Uh-huh."

"Do you believe me?"

Stella has stood naked in the four directions. She has pledged herself to the earth and the elements. She believes in a lot of things people think are nuts but even she has trouble believing this.

"What did it say?" she asks.

"You don't believe me, do you?"

"Of course I believe you," Stella says, relieved to find this is true. She doesn't add the explanation; I believe you believe it. She doesn't think she needs to.

"Murderer."

"What?"

"That's what the crow said."

She didn't do anything at all for about two weeks after her daughter died. Slept, mostly. Joe had taken time off too. He slept in late and ate the sympathy food people kept sending over; cheesy casseroles, meatloaf, chocolate cake, banana bread, potato salad, and brownies in front of the TV where he muttered invectives at talk shows. Then, one day, he got up right in the middle of a show titled "I'm in love with my mother's husband" or something like that (Melinda could hear it from the bedroom) shut it off, got dressed and went to work. After that the house was very quiet.

Melinda was surprised to find that sleep was like a drug she could always afford. Sure, sometimes she woke up and stared at the flowered border of her walls but if she didn't move around too much, or open her eyes too wide she could sink right back into that place where sometimes she found her daughter still alive.

But one day she woke up to the horrible noise of a crow laughing at her. She got out of bed and walked across the room to the window. The ugly bird was on their lawn. Suddenly, it flew up and perched on top of the swing set. If she had a gun she would have shot it. Instead, she ran out into the yard in her pajamas, shouting. That's when it spoke to her. That single evil word, before it raised those great wings and with one last laugh, flew away. Melinda collapsed, just like the bad witch in the Wizard of Oz, she sank to her knees in her white nightgown and if she could have melted she would have.

When she got up she went into the house, took a shower, put on sweats and a T-shirt, sat down at the kitchen table and began writing letters. To the newspapers, the hospital, the PTA, animal control, the local TV news stations. This city was in danger. Didn't what happened to her daughter prove it? It was an invasion. A possible plague. She started a campaign against the crows. Now, after all this time, she sees her motivation. She can only wonder what got into everyone else. Because the plan was absurd really.

The city council passed the measure with only a vegetarian and a liberal dissenting. They fed them bread laced with poison. That's why birds fell out of the sky the way they did. Suddenly paralyzed, they plummeted to the ground. Their corpses littered sidewalks, parking lots and yards. Once, when Melinda was driving to the post office one plummeted right onto the hood of her car; it's black claws splayed and stiff, its wings spread out like a hard cross.

That night, after Corvus doesn't arrive when he said he would, and Stella is asleep on the futon in Melinda's office and Joe is snoring in their bed, Melinda puts on her sneakers and stands in her front yard. They didn't really have a backyard here, just a deck and a strange tree she hasn't identified yet, spindly-limbed, a fruit tree of some sort. She stands in the front yard and waits for it to happen. After awhile, beneath the white moon glow and the scatter of stars, she begins to rise, she floats up about three or four inches and then, gently, like soft dust, she lands.

She doesn't know what this is all about. She only knows it began happening when things got really bad. She wonders if things are getting really bad again.

Corvus is still alive when the creature removes his jacket, his rings, and the knotted string bracelet Melinda's daughter made for him. He's alive to hear it say, "Clearly a hybrid."

Corvus watches it search through his pockets. When he finds the wallet, he tosses out the money, the credit cards, the driver's license and the library card. He almost tosses the wallet too but then the paper with Melinda's address on it slips out. Suddenly its beady eyes focus on his.

"No," Corvus gasps.

The creature smiles.

Corvus looks down and sees a man splayed, the shape of his limbs at odd angles, but bloodless. Standing beside him is someone wearing Corvus's jacket who turns and looks up at him.

It's like looking at a mirror, only something's not right. The man raises his hand. He is wearing Corvus's rings. He turns and walks away.

Corvus looks down at the body that remains, his eyes ripped out, as though by scavengers. Corvus doesn't have time to mourn. He follows the creature who waves down a taxi and tells the driver Melinda's address.

"Corvus," she says and she opens her arms to hug the creature but she is glowing with a silver sheen, as if she were the moon, it burns him and it takes all his power not to writhe with pain as he walks right past her open arms, pretending he hasn't seen them. He turns at the door to smile at her but everything about her hurts him; even the house contains her glow, even the doorknob.

She stands there, in her nightgown and sneakers, her long hair hanging down, so ordinary looking, so easy, a puzzled expression on her face. Clearly, she has no idea.

"It's not me," Corvus shouts but of course it comes out faint, having to travel all the distance from death to the living.

"Corvus?" she says.

The creature can't help it. He's terrified of her. Even at this distance, he burns. "I've been sick," he says, suddenly remembering humans and their fear of illness.

Melinda frowns.

The creature smiles. He should have a plan, that's the thing. But he doesn't. He's never needed one before. "Let's go inside," he says, though the house burns him too. Buying time, he thinks, is this what that expression means?

When they go inside a man stands there in boxers and a T-shirt. He puts out his hand. But the creature sees her glow there; he slips his hand into the pocket of the leather jacket.

"He's been sick," Melinda says.

Joe nods. To be polite. But the guy is worse than he remembered. There's even a faint odor coming off of him. Like sauerkraut.

"Do you want popcorn?" Melinda can't help it. Whenever she's around Corvus, she's fourteen again. When he used to visit they'd watch the late movie and eat popcorn.

"I think I'll just go to bed," the creature says, trying to form a plan. But he's finding it increasingly difficult to concentrate and he's worried that he'll lose the disguise if he's not careful, which would not be a problem with the man who looks half asleep but he's not sure what would happen with her.

When Melinda brings the creature the sheets and a pillow she looks at his face closely. He looks so different, she thinks, though she can't quite decide why until finally, she sees it. "I never noticed before," she says.

"What?"

"How much you look like a crow."

Behind them, Joe groans.

The creature can't figure out how to get around it, he has to take the pillow and sheets from her or she will just stand there and stare at him, but after he does so he turns away, he is in agony.

"I can help you make it," Melinda says.

"No. I'm going to sit up for awhile."

"I'll stay with you. I'll make popcorn."

"I don't like popcorn," the creature says, remembering the strange feel of it in his mouth, once, years ago when he went to a movie with a young woman who was later found raped and murdered. Not by him, of course. He didn't do petty crime. Right away he knows this might be a mistake. He smiles at her again, that baring of teeth. She just looks at him. He raises his hand in a wave.

She doesn't even try to kiss him goodnight. She is surprised to find that she doesn't really want to. Joe falls asleep right away. But Melinda lies there and tries to figure out what's happening. She has trouble concentrating; her mind keeps drifting back to that night, so long ago. When their mother told them she was an angel.

They tried not to laugh but it was impossible not to. Melinda ended up spitting Dr. Pepper in a spray while tiny white flakes of popcorn flew from Corvus's mouth.

"I'm serious," their mother said.

"I'm sorry, mom. We're sorry," they said.

She stood there in her blaze of red curls and the purple and green kimono and for a minute Melinda thought maybe she was telling the truth, the kimono sleeves sort of looked like wings, and she was the most beautiful mother in the school. Really. Even though she was so old.

Afterwards, the three of them sat on the couch eating popcorn and watching a movie about aliens with long green arms and slits for eyes and the invasion of the world until Melinda fell asleep with her head in her mother's lap, which smelled like dark chocolate. She had the vague impression that Corvus and their mother spoke then, whispering about angels and demons and wings but she was never sure if this was something she actually overheard, or something she dreamed.

It's Saturday and Joe likes to sleep late on the weekend so Melinda gets up and tries to be quiet as she walks across the room. She's tired and she can't shake the feeling she's had, since Corvus arrived, of something not being right.

When she walks past the window they begin cawing. She pulls back the drapes. The room blazes with morning sun and the crows' sharp cries. Hundred of them assembled in her yard, screaming, with their little throats and pointed tongues, the sharp beaks open like her daughter who said, "Mom?"

"Jesus Christ," Joe says, "oh Jesus Christ." He comes to stand behind her and wrap her in his arms but Melinda doesn't move or soften into his embrace. She stands there, frozen stiff as a corpse while the crows scream. With a sob she pushes past Joe and runs out of the room. She wants Corvus. But he isn't in the living room, or the bedroom either, or the kitchen or anywhere in the house.

Stella finds Melinda standing in the living room, staring out the window at the crows. It must be the angle of the sun, Stella thinks, because Melinda is glowing a bright halo of light all around her body and just like that, with the noise of sheets snapping on a clothesline, the crows rise in flight. Melinda turns and Stella gasps at the odd illusion, the glowing woman surrounded by wings.

"Corvus came," Melinda says, "but he's already gone."

"He'll be back," Stella says, though she really has no way of knowing.

"I don't think so," Melinda says, no longer glowing or surrounded by wings.

Joe comes into the room dressed in his jogging clothes. He says good morning to Stella and gives Melinda a kiss on the cheek. "Corvus is gone," she says.

He suppresses a grin. "Probably just went for a walk." But this is absurd. Corvus is not the kind to go for a walk in the California sun. He is more about shadows and dark rooms. If he is gone, sure, it's weird, but also the sort of thing, Joe thinks, that he's always been capable of. He sighs.

"You can go," Melinda says. "Go. Run."

He thinks of asking her if she is sure but he doesn't want to press his luck.

After he leaves, Stella says, "Are you really worried about Corvus?"

"Something strange is happening," Melinda says. "I feel like I'm in *The Birds*."

"In them?"

"You know, that movie."

Joe can't help it; every time he leaves the house he feels like he's escaping a great darkness, he feels like he's running away. He loves the hard concrete beneath his feet, the sun shining on his face and limbs. Hell, he even loves the damn birds. When he's running he feels almost whole again. He can feel his muscles and the sweat on his skin. He feels like a man with a body, instead of the husk he's been. God, he misses her. He misses her too but there's no use trying to talk to Melinda about it because she owns all the sorrow. Well, all right, he thinks as he turns down Avidio Street, that's not fair, but it's been hard enough keeping himself together through all this, and he's not sure how to help her. His feet pound the concrete but he doesn't feel weighted at all, he feels bright, alive, almost winged. He doesn't know what's going to happen to Melinda or to their marriage, but he's already decided, he's going to survive. He's going to learn how to be happy again.

The creature can't believe his luck when her husband runs out of the house like a man making his escape. He watches him and thinks it's just so perfect. He can't destroy her, she's just that powerful, something he understands is both a curse and, he hates to use the word, a blessing, but he can ruin her, oh yes, he can ruin her by ruining everything she loves and believes in.

"Corvus," Joe says, panting and grinning, as if he'd been running to find him. "Melinda was worried about you."

"Come here," the creature says, "I want to show you something."

Joe doesn't know why he's never liked him. That's something the running has helped him with. Afterwards, for fifteen, twenty minutes even, once for almost an hour, he feels like he can love again. As though he drank a witch's potion. This time it's landed on Corvus. Joe follows him down a side street and into a narrow California alley lined with concrete walls, roses and wind chimes.

The creature walks up to Joe who stands there, smiling affably, just for the fun of it, he lets the disguise fall. He watches Joe's face change. Just when he would scream, the creature reaches in, extinguishing the noise, and the light.

"You know what probably happened," Stella says, "they probably ran into each other, went out for coffee together."

Melinda looks at Stella and nods. How can she explain? Evil exists. It stalks her for a reason.

"It's a beautiful day, you should go outside and play."

"I don't wanna."

"Your father and I got you that nice new swing set and you never play on it."

"I hate playing outside."

"Oh, you do not."

"It's buggy. And the grass itches my ankles."

"What are you going to do?"

"I dunno. Sit, I guess."

"I want you to go outside."

"I don't wanna."

"It'll be good for you. You go outside for a while so I can finish my work and then we'll go get ice cream."

"Can't I just stay in the house? I'll be quiet."

"I want you to get some fresh air."

For a while Melinda stood at the window and watched her, lazily swinging and talking to herself. She looked perfectly happy. Safe. But when she came back inside she was probably already dying, though neither of them knew it yet. They went for ice cream. Hers melted so fast she may already have had a fever, "Mom?" she said and Melinda saved her the way she always had, by licking the dripping scoop until it formed a neat round ball and by then she may already have been turning into a spirit.

Melinda remembers the way she looked, all wide eyes shining with fever and light. Though at the time Melinda thought it was just happiness.

Now, Melinda stares out the window. Stella goes into the kitchen, which is brightly lit by the California sun. She tries not to regret coming here. This is to help her friend, after all. But the depression is palpable. In spite of the blue sky and the light, which pours into this little house, Stella feels like she is walking in a thick fog. It presses her body with unwelcome weight. No wonder Joe has taken up running. Stella glances towards the living room. Melinda is still staring out the window. Furtively, she doesn't know why, Stella walks to the front door. She opens it slowly. It makes a slight popping noise but Melinda doesn't seem to notice. Stella opens the door wide. Just as she takes a step towards it, Melinda speaks.

"What?" Stella says.

"I said, where are you going?"

"I just wanted to step outside for a minute. It's so beautiful out. Wanna come?"

"Do you know what's out there?"

Stella looks out the doorway again. She looks at Melinda. "I'll just be a minute."

Melinda doesn't answer.

Stella steps outside and immediately wants to scream or shout. She shuts the door behind her. God, it feels so good to breathe. She doesn't even think about how she's barefoot and wearing boxers and an old T-shirt but if she had thought about it she might have concluded that she's been infected by the California spirit. Melinda, staring out of the window, might have seen what happened to her, except Melinda isn't staring at what exists, but at what she remembers. It takes her a long time to realize Stella isn't coming back either. It's as if, she thinks, they are being swallowed by the light, the beautiful California day. She stands at the window while the neighbors leave their houses in suits and ties, suits and heels, shorts and sandals, carrying briefcases, school bags, coffee mugs, driving SUV's, Volkswagens, skateboards, and bicycles.

"Be careful," Melinda whispers to the glass. No one hears her and really, no one would take her seriously if they did. It's obvious she is someone who isn't all there, something not right about her. And that's what the police think too, when they come by later to tell her they found a body, a jacket, rings, a sheet of paper with her address on it. At first she tells them it's her brother but then they mention the jogging clothes, and she says it's her husband and right away they suspect her of murder, maybe a double homicide.

Then things get really strange. The police officers, the detectives, the coroner, the news reporter, everyone who was at the scene of the crime, though they arrive and leave in separate vehicles, have accidents. Every one of them dies.

When a reporter calls to tell her this, Melinda, who has been crying since she had to identify "the body" suddenly dries up. That's it. She's been crying all day and she cried for months before that and now she's done. Because, at a certain point, she thinks, you have to shut down against all the horror of life.

"Do you have any comment?" the reporter asks.

"The body," she says.

There is a long silence. Melinda isn't sure if he's still there or was ever there. Maybe he's just something she imagined. Maybe everyone was.

"Did you say, 'the body'?"

"The body is heavy," Melinda says.

"The body is heavy?"

"We are . . ."

Again, that silence. Melinda looks out the window and sees the blonde woman arrive home. She gets out of the car and waves to her neighbor, a middle-aged man watering his lawn. He walks over to her and then, in a quick and sudden movement, wraps the garden hose around her neck. She struggles against it, but the man is suddenly amazing in his strength, he pulls the hose tighter, water sprays wildly from the nozzle, the blonde woman kicks but her feet flail in the air, she pulls at the hose, waves her arms in a helpless imitation of its wild gyrations, the stream of water rises and falls, slithering across the blue sky. "My neighbor is strangling my neighbor," Melinda says.

"Right now?"

"Ok. She's dead."

"Did you kill her?"

"No. My neighbor did. Oh, but he's clutching his chest now. A heart attack, I guess."

"Are you saying your neighbors had a fight and killed each other?"

"Uh-oh," Melinda says.

"What now?"

"Children."

"What about the children?"

"Coming down the street. Riding their bicycles."

"Please don't hurt the children."

"What? I would never. Oh, but there they go."

"Where?"

"The car. They're dead."

"Someone hit the children with a car?"

"I suppose. But it didn't look like, wait, here's the driver. She got out of the car. She's covered in blood. She's crying. She's trying to save them. I don't know why. It's obvious, oh, now it's her."

"What?"

Melinda turns away from the window. "Excuse me," she says, "but weren't we talking about something else?"

"The body."

"Oh, that's right. The body is heavy."

"Whose body is heavy? Do you mean your husband's, did you kill him?"

"Kill him?"

"I've done some research. I know about your daughter. Did you kill her as well?"

"It was a mosquito. It bit one of those crows that had it. Then it bit her."

"Yes, well, that's what they said but now, with all that's happened —"

Melinda moves her thumb and presses the button that shuts his voice off. She watches her neighbors running out of their houses, piling into cars with kids, dogs and cats, ferrets, pet pigs, hamsters, while the adults and children talk on cell phones, wave their arms wildly and scream at each other. She hears a helicopter flying overhead and sirens looming nearer. She opens the front door and is assailed by the violent noise, the screams, the terrible noise of the helicopter spiraling down, the sirens veering into sick wails, and she smells the blood metal scent of death. "It's not my fault," she whispers.

It's just like they say, as if a great weight has been lifted from her shoulders. Melinda begins to rise, but this time she doesn't hover, as she always has in the past, she rises higher and higher until she is as high as the palm trees and even higher still.

The creature, shading his eyes against the bright sun, watches her. With a snort he leaves, going in the opposite direction. The mayhem he brought with him, though it remains, does not continue its relentless course. The wounded do not die, but suffer. Crows swoop down and pick at the shiny parts of the dead; watches, rings, silver hair and fillings. A wide-eyed EMT, sloshing through the muck of bloody water, turns off the hose. News crews come and set up their mobile units and food vendors follow. The crows peck at dropped bits of corn dog and discarded fries. The children ride bicycles around the dead, or pick flowers, or go into dark rooms and don't do anything at all. Experts come and say this is recovery. This is the cure.

Melinda soon discovers that she likes to fly so high that she no longer sees anyone, nearer to the sun, unpopulated as it is by human misery. Sometimes she thinks she won't return but she always does. She understands this is the reason for everything. It took her a whole lifetime to learn how to ascend but it doesn't take her long at all to learn how to dive down again. "We are angels," she whispers to the people. Some of them hear her. Some of them don't.

# THERE'S A HOLE IN THE CITY

## Richard Bowes

WEDNESDAY 9/12

On the evening of the day after the towers fell, I was waiting by the barricades on Houston Street and LaGuardia Place for my friend Mags to come up from Soho and have dinner with me. On the skyline, not two miles to the south, the pillars of smoke wavered slightly. But the creepily beautiful weather of September 11 still held and the wind blew in from the north east. In Greenwich Village the air was crisp and clean with just a touch of fall about it.

I'd spent the last day and a half looking at pictures of burning towers. One of the frustrations of that time was that there was so little most of us could do about anything or for anyone.

Downtown streets were empty of all traffic except emergency vehicles. The West and East Villages from Fourteenth Street to Houston were their own separate zone. Pedestrians needed identification proving they lived or worked there in order to enter.

The barricades consisted of blue wooden police horses and a couple of unmarked vans thrown across LaGuardia Place. Behind them were a couple of cops, a few auxiliary police and one or two guys in civilian clothes with I.D.'s of some kind pinned to their shirts. All of them looked tired, subdued by events.

At the barricades was a small crowd, ones like me waiting for friends from neighborhoods to the south, ones without proper identification waiting for confirmation so that they could continue on into Soho, people who just wanted to be outside near other people in those days of sunshine and shock. Once in a while, each of us would look up at the columns of smoke that hung in the downtown sky then look away again.

A family approached a middle aged cop behind the barricade. The group consisted of a man, a woman, a little girl being led by the hand, a child being carried. All were blondish and wore shorts and casual tops. The parents seemed pleasant but serious people in their early thirties, professionals. They could have been tourists. But that day the city was empty of tourists.

The man said something and I heard the cop say loudly, "You want to go where?"

"Down there," the man gestured at the columns. He indicated the children. "We want them to see." It sounded as if he couldn't imagine this appeal not working.

Everyone stared at the family. "No I.D. no passage," said the cop and turned his back on them. The pleasant expressions on the parents' faces faded. They looked indignant, like a maitre d' had lost their reservations. She led one kid, he carried another as they turned west, probably headed for another check point.

"They wanted those little kids to see Ground Zero!" a woman who knew the cop said. "Are they out of their minds?"

"Looters," he replied. "That's my guess." He picked up his walkie-talkie to call the check points ahead of them.

Mags appeared just then, looking a bit frayed. When you've known someone for as long as I've known her, the tendency is not to see the changes, to think you both look about the same as when you were kids.

But kids don't have grey hair and their bodies aren't thick the way bodies get in their late fifties. Their kisses aren't perfunctory. Their conversation doesn't include curt little nods that indicate something is understood.

We walked in the middle of the streets because we could. "Couldn't sleep much last night," I said.

"Because of the quiet," she said. "No planes. I kept listening for them. I haven't been sleeping anyway. I was supposed to be in housing court today. But the courts are shut until further notice."

I said, "Notice how with only the ones who live here allowed in, the South Village is all Italians and hippies?"

"Like 1965 all over again."

She and I had been in contact more in the past few months than we had in a while. Memories of love and indifference that we shared had made close friendship an on and off thing for the last thirty-something years.

Earlier in 2001, at the end of an affair, I'd surrendered a rent stabilized apartment for a cash settlement and bought a tiny co-op in the South Village. Mags lived as she had for years in a run down building on the fringes of Soho.

So we saw each other again. I write, obviously, but she never read anything I publish which bothered me. On the other hand, she worked off and on for various activist leftist foundations and I was mostly uninterested in that.

Mags was in the midst of classic New York work and housing trouble. Currently she was on unemployment and her landlord wanted to get her out of her apartment so he could co-op her building. The money offer he'd made wasn't bad but she wanted things to stay as they were. It struck me that what was youthful about her was that she had never settled into her life, still stood on the edge.

Lots of the Village restaurants weren't opened. The owners couldn't or wouldn't come into the city. Angelina's on Thompson Street was, though, because Angelina lives just a couple of doors down from her place. She was busy serving tables herself since the waiters couldn't get in from where they lived.

Later, I had reason to try and remember. The place was full but very quiet. People murmured to each other as Mags and I did. Nobody I knew was there. In the background Resphigi's Ancient Airs and Dances played.

"Like the Blitz," someone said.

"Never the same again," said a person at another table.

"There isn't even any place to volunteer to help," a third person said.

I don't drink anymore. But Mags, as I remember, had a carafe of wine. Phone service had been spotty but we had managed to exchange bits of what we had seen.

"Mrs. Pirelli," I said. "The Italian lady upstairs from me. I told you she had a heart attack watching the smoke and flames on television. Her son worked in the World Trade Center and she was sure he had burned to death.

"Getting an ambulance wasn't possible yesterday morning. But the guys at that little fire barn around the corner were there. Waiting to be called, I guess. They took her to St. Vincent's in the chief's car. Right about then, her son came up the street, his pinstripe suit with a hole burned in the shoulder, soot on his face, wild eyed. But alive. Today they say she's doing fine."

I waited, spearing clams, twirling linguine. Mags had a deeper and darker story to tell; a dip into the subconscious. Before I'd known her and afterwards, Mags had a few rough brushes with mental disturbance. Back in college where we first met, I envied her that, wished I had something as dramatic to talk about.

"I've been thinking about what happened last night." She'd already told me some of this. "The downstairs bell rang which scared me. But with phone service being bad, it could have been a friend, someone who needed to talk. I looked out the window. The street was empty, dead like I'd never seen it.

"Nothing but papers blowing down the street. You know how every time you see a scrap of paper now you think it's from the Trade Center? For a minute I thought I saw something move but when I looked again there was nothing.

I didn't ring the buzzer, but it seemed someone upstairs did because I heard this noise, a rustling in the hall.

When I went to the door and lifted the spy hole, this figure stood there on the landing. Looking around like she was lost. She wore a dress, long and torn. And a blouse, what I realized was a shirtwaist. Turn-of-the-century clothes. When she turned towards my door, I saw her face. It was bloody, smashed. Like she had taken a big jump or fall. I gasped and then she was gone."

"And you woke up?"

"No, I tried to call you. But the phones were all fucked up. She had fallen but not from a hundred stories. Anyway she wasn't from here and now."

Mags had emptied the carafe. I remember that she'd just ordered a salad and didn't eat that. But Angelina brought a fresh carafe. I told Mags about the family at the barricades.

"There's a hole in the city," said Mags.

That night, after we had parted, I lay in bed watching but not seeing some old movie on TV, avoiding any channel with any kind of news, when the buzzer sounded. I jumped up and went to the view screen. On the empty street downstairs a man, wild eyed, disheveled, glared directly into the camera.

Phone service was not reliable. Cops were not in evidence in the neighborhood right then. I froze and didn't buzz him in. But, as in Mags building, someone else did. I bolted my door, watched at the spy hole, listened to the footsteps, slow, uncertain. When he came into sight on the second floor landing he looked around and said in a hoarse voice, "Hello? Sorry but I can't find my mom's front door key."

Only then did I unlock the door, open it and ask her exhausted son how Mrs. Pirelli was doing.

"Fine," he said. "Getting great treatment. St. Vincent was geared up for thousands of casualties. Instead . . ." he shrugged.

"Anyway, she thanks all of you. Me too."

In fact, I hadn't done much. We said good-night and he shuffled on upstairs to where he was crashing in his mother's place.

THURSDAY 9/13

By September of 2001 I had worked an information desk in the University library for almost thirty years. I live right around the corner from Washington Square and just before 10 A.M. on Thursday, I set out for work. The Moslem-run souvlaki stand across the street was still closed, its owner and workers gone since Tuesday morning. All the little falafel shops in the South Village were shut and dark.

On my way to work I saw a three legged rat running not too quickly down the middle of MacDougal Street. I decided not to think about portents and symbolism.

The big TV's set up in the library atrium still showed the towers falling again and again. But now they also showed workers digging in the flaming wreckage at Ground Zero.

Like the day before, I was the only one in my department who'd made it in. The librarians lived too far away. Even Marco, the student assistant, wasn't around.

Marco lived in a dorm downtown right near the World Trade Center. They'd been evacuated with nothing more than a few books and the clothes they were wearing. Tuesday, he'd been very upset. I'd given him Kleenex, made him take deep breaths, got him to call his mother back in California. I'd even walked him over to the gym where University was putting up the displaced students.

Thursday morning, all of the computer stations around the information desk were occupied. Students sat furiously typing email and devouring incoming messages but the intensity had slackened since 9/11. The girls no longer sniffed and dabbed at tears as they read. The boys didn't jump up and come back from the restrooms red-eyed and saying they had allergies.

I said good-morning and sat down. The kids hadn't spoken much to me in the last few days, had no questions to ask. But all of them from time to time would turn and look to make sure I was still there. If I got up to leave the desk, they'd ask when I was coming back.

Some of the back windows had a downtown view. The pillar of smoke wavered. The wind was changing.

The phone rang. Reception had improved. Most calls went through. When I answered, a voice, tight and tense, blurted out, "Jennie Levine was who I saw. She was nineteen years old in 1911 when the Triangle Shirtwaist Factory burned. She lived in my building with her family ninety years ago. Her spirit found its way home. But the inside of my building has changed so much that she didn't recognize it."

"Hi, Mags," I said. "You want to come up here and have lunch?"

A couple of hours later, we were in a small dining hall normally used by faculty on the west side of the Square. The University, with food on hand and not enough people to eat it, had thrown open its cafeterias and dining halls to anybody with a university identification. We could even bring a friend if we cared to.

Now that I looked, Mags had tension lines around her eyes and hair that could have used some tending. But we were all of us a little ragged in those days of sun and horror. People kept glancing downtown, even if they were inside and not near a window.

The Indian lady who ran the facility greeted us, thanked us for coming. I had a really nice gumbo, fresh avocado salad, a soothing pudding. The place was half empty and conversations again were muted. I told Mags about Mrs. Pirelli's son the night before.

She looked up from her plate, unsmiling, said, "I did not imagine Jennie Levine," and closed that subject.

Afterwards, she and I stood on Washington Place before the University building that had once housed the sweat shop called The Triangle Shirtwaist Factory. At the end of the block, a long convoy of olive green army trucks rolled silently down Broadway.

Mags said, "On the afternoon of March 25 1911, one hundred and forty-six young women burned to death on this site. Fire broke out in a pile of rags. The door to the roof was locked. The fire ladders couldn't reach the eighth floor. The girls burned."

Her voice tightened as she said, "They jumped and were smashed on the sidewalk. Many of them, most of them, lived right around here. In the renovated tenements we live in now. It's like those planes blew a hole in the city and Jennie Levine returned through it."

"Easy, honey. The University has grief counseling available. I think I'm going. You want me to see if I can get you in?" It sounded idiotic even as I said it. We had walked back to the library.

"There are others," she said. "Kids all blackened and bloated and wearing old fashioned clothes. I woke up early this morning and couldn't go back to sleep. I got up and walked around here and over in the East Village."

"Jesus!" I said.

"Geoffrey has come back too. I know it."

"Mags! Don't!" This was something we hadn't talked about in a long time. Once we were three and Geoffrey was the third. He was younger than either of us by a couple of years at a time of life when that still seemed a major difference.

We called him Lord Geoff because he said we were all a bit better than the world around us. We joked that he was our child. A little family cemented by desire and drugs.

The three of us were all so young, just out school and in the city. Then jealousy and the hard realities of addiction began to tear us apart. Each had to find his or her own survival. Mags and I made it. As it turned out, Geoff wasn't built for the long haul. He was twenty-one. We were all just kids, ignorant and reckless.

As I made excuses in my mind Mags gripped my arm. "He'll want to find us," she said. Chilled, I watched her walk away and wondered how long she had been coming apart and why I hadn't noticed.

Back at work, Marco waited for me. He was part Filipino, a bit of a little wise ass who dressed in downtown black. But that was the week before. Today, he was a woebegone refugee in oversized flip-flops, a magenta sweatshirt and gym shorts all of which had been made for someone bigger and more buff.

"How's it going?"

"It sucks! My stuff is all downtown where I don't know if I can ever get it. They have these crates in the gym, toothbrushes, bras, bic razors but never what you need, everything from boxer shorts on out and nothing is ever the right size. I gave my clothes in to be cleaned and they didn't bring them back. Now I look like a clown.

"They have us all sleeping on cots on the basketball courts. I lay there all last night staring up at the ceiling, with a hundred other guys. Some of them snore. One was yelling in his sleep. And I don't want to take a shower with a bunch of guys staring at me."

He told me all this while not looking my way but I understood what he was asking. I expected this was going to be a pain. But, given that I couldn't seem to do much for Mags I thought maybe it would be a distraction to do what I could for someone else.

"You want to take a shower at my place, crash on my couch?"

"Could I, please?"

So I took a break, brought him around the corner to my apartment, put sheets on the daybed. He was in the shower when I went back to work.

That evening when I got home, he woke up. When I went out to take a walk, he tagged along. We stood at the police barricades at Houston Street and Sixth Avenue and watched the traffic coming up from the World Trade Center site. An ambulance with one side smashed and a squad car with its roof crushed were hauled up Sixth Avenue on the back of a huge flatbed truck. NYPD buses were full of guys returning from ground zero, hollow-eyed, filthy.

Crowds of Greenwich Villagers gathered on the sidewalks clapped and cheered, yelled, "We love our firemen! We love our cops!"

The firehouse on Sixth Avenue had taken a lot of casualties when the towers fell. The place was locked and empty. We looked at the flowers and the wreaths on the doors, the signs with faces of the firefighters who hadn't returned and the messages, "To the brave men of these companies who gave their lives defending us."

The plume of smoke downtown rolled in the twilight, buffeted about by shifting winds. The breeze brought with it for the first time the acrid smoke that would be with us for weeks afterwards.

Officials said it was the stench of burning concrete. I believed, as did everyone else, that part of what we breathed was the ashes of the ones who had burned to death that Tuesday.

It started to drizzle. Marco stuck close to me as we walked back. Hip twenty year olds do not normally hang out with guys almost three times their age. This kid was very scared.

Bleecker Street looked semi-abandoned with lots of the stores and restaurants still closed. The ones that were open were mostly empty at nine in the evening.

"If I buy you a six-pack, you promise to drink all of it?" He indicated he would.

At home, Marco asked to use the phone. He called people he knew on campus looking for a spare dorm room and spoke in whispers to a girl named Eloise. In between calls, he worked the computer.

I played a little Lady Day, some Ray Charles, a bit of Haydn, stared at the TV screen. The President had pulled out of his funk and was coming to New York the next day.

In the next room, the phone rang. "No. My name's Marco," I heard him say. "He's letting me stay here." I knew who it was before he came in and whispered, "She asked if I was Lord Geoff."

"Hi, Mags," I said. She was calling from somewhere with walkie- talkie's and sirens in the background.

"Those kids I saw in Astor Place?" she said, her voice clear and crazed. "The ones all burned and drowned. They were on the General Slocum when it caught fire."

"The kids you saw in Astor Place all burned and drowned?" I asked. Then I remembered our conversation earlier.

"On June 15, 1904. The biggest disaster in New York city history. Until now. The East Village was once called Little Germany. Tens of thousands of Germans with their own meeting halls, churches, beer gardens.

"They had a Sunday excursion, mainly for the kids, on a steamship, the General Slocum, a floating fire trap. When it burst into flames there were no lifeboats, the crew and the captain panicked. By the time they got to a dock over a thousand were dead. Burned, drowned. When a hole got blown in the city, they came back looking for their homes."

The connection started to dissolve into static.

"Where are you, Mags?"

"Ground Zero. It smells like burning sulfur. Have you seen Geoffrey yet?" she shouted into her phone.

"Geoffrey is dead, Mags. It's all the horror and tension that's doing this to you. There's no hole. . . ."

"Cops and firemen and brokers all smashed and charred are walking around down here." At that point sirens screamed in the background. Men were yelling. The connection faded.

"Mags, give me your number. Call me back," I yelled. Then there was nothing but static, followed by a weak dial tone. I hung up and waited for the phone to ring again.

After a while, I realized Marco was standing looking at me, slugging down beer. "She saw those kids? I saw them too. Tuesday night I was too jumpy to even lie down on the fucking cot. I snuck out with my friend Terry. We walked around. The kids were there. In old, historical clothes. Covered with mud and seaweed and their faces all black and gone. It's why I couldn't sleep last night."

"You talk to the counselors?" I asked.

He drained the bottle. "Yeah, but they don't want to hear what I wanted to talk about."

"But with me . . ."

"You're crazy. You understand."

The silence outside was broken by a jet engine. We both flinched. No planes had flown over Manhattan since the ones that had smashed the towers on Tuesday morning.

Then I realized what it was. "The Air Force," I said. "Making sure it's safe for Mr. Bush's visit."

"Who's Mags? Who's Lord Geoff?"

So I told him a bit of what had gone on in that strange lost country, the 1960's, the naïveté that lead to meth and junk. I described the wonder of that unknown land, the three way union. "Our problem, I guess, was that instead of a real ménage, each member was obsessed with only one of the others."

"OK," he said. "You're alive. Mags is alive. What happened to Geoff?

"When things were breaking up, Geoff got caught in a drug sweep and was being hauled downtown in the back of a police van. He cut his wrists and bled to death in the dark before anyone noticed."

This did for me, what speaking about the dead kids had maybe done for him. Each of us got to about what bothered him without having to think much about what the other said.

## FRIDAY 9/14

Friday morning two queens walked by with their little dogs as Marco and I came out the door of my building. One said, "There isn't a fresh croissant in the entire Village. It's like the Siege of Paris. We'll all be reduced to eating rats."

I murmured, "He's getting a little ahead of the story. Maybe first he should think about having an English muffin."

"Or eating his yappy dog," said Marco.

At that moment, the authorities opened the East and West Villages, between Fourteenth and Houston Streets, to outside traffic. All the people whose cars had been stranded since Tuesday began to come into the neighborhood and drive them away. Delivery trucks started to appear on the narrow streets.

In the library, the huge TV screens showed the activity at Ground Zero, the preparations for the President's visit. An elevator door opened and revealed a couple of refugee kids in their surplus gym clothes clasped in a passion clinch.

The computers around my information desk were still fully occupied but the tension level had fallen. There was even a question or two about books and data bases. I tried repeatedly to call Mags. All I got was the chilling message on her answering machine.

In a staccato voice, it said, "This is Mags McConnell. There's a hole in the city and I've turned this into a center for information about the victims Jennie Levine and Geoffrey Holbrun. Anyone with information concerning the whereabouts of these two young people, please speak after the beep."

I left a message asking her to call. Then I called every half hour or so hoping she'd pick up. I phoned mutual friends. Some were absent or unavailable. A couple were nursing grief of their own. No one had seen her recently.

That evening in the growing dark, lights flickered in Washington Square. Candles were given out; candles were lighted with matches and bics and wick to wick. Various priests, ministers, rabbis and shamans lead flower-bearing, candlelit congregations down the streets and into the park where they joined the gathering Vigil crowd.

Marco had come by with his friend Terry, a kind of elfin kid who'd also had to stay at the gym. We went to this 9/11 Vigil together. People addressed the crowd, gave impromptu elegies. There were prayers and a few songs. Then by instinct or some plan I hadn't heard about, everyone started to move out of the park and flow in groups through the streets.

We paused at streetlamps that bore signs with pictures of pajama clad families in suburban rec rooms on Christmas mornings. One face would be circled in red and there would be a message like, "This is James Bolton, husband of Susan, father of Jimmy, Anna and Sue, last seen leaving his home in Far Rockaway at 7:30 A.M. on 9/11." This was followed by the name of the company, the floor of the Trade Center tower where he worked, phone and fax numbers, the email address and the words, "If you have any information about where he is, please contact us."

At each sign someone would leave a lighted candle on a tin plate. Someone else would leave flowers.

The door of the little neighborhood Fire Rescue station was open, the truck and command car were gone. The place was manned by retired firefighters with faces like old Irish and Italian character actors. A big picture of a fireman who had died was hung up beside the door. He was young, maybe thirty. He and his wife, or maybe his girlfriend, smiled in front of a ski lodge. The picture was framed with children's drawings of firemen and fire trucks and fires, with condolences and novena cards.

As we walked and the night progressed, the crowd got stretched out. We'd see clumps of candles ahead of us on the streets. It was on Great Jones Street and the Bowery that suddenly there was just the three of us and no traffic to speak of. When I turned to say maybe we should go home, I saw for a moment, a tall guy staggering down the street with his face purple and his eyes bulging out.

Then he was gone. Either Marco or Terry whispered, "Shit, he killed himself." And none of us said anything more.

At some point in the evening, I had said Terry could spend the night in my apartment. He couldn't take his eyes off Marco, though Marco seemed not to notice. On our way home, way east on Bleecker Street, outside a bar that had been old even when I'd hung out there as a kid, I saw the poster.

It was like a dozen others I'd seen that night. Except it was in old-time black and white and showed three kids with lots of hair and bad attitude: Mags and Geoffrey and me.

Geoff's face was circled and under it was written "This is Geoffrey Holbrun, if you have seen him since Tuesday 9/11 please contact . . ." and Mags had left her name and numbers.

Even in the photo, I looked toward Geoffrey who looked towards Mags who looked towards me. I stared for just a moment before going on but I knew that Marco had noticed.

## SATURDAY 9/15

My tiny apartment was a crowded mess Saturday morning. Every towel I owned was wet, every glass and mug was dirty. It smelled like a zoo. There were pizza crusts in the sink and a bag of beer cans at the front door. The night before, none of us had talked about the ghosts. Marco and Terry had seriously discussed whether they would be drafted or would enlist. The idea of them in the army did not make me feel any safer.

Saturday is a work day for me. Getting ready, I reminded myself that this would soon be over. The University had found all the refugee kids dorm rooms on campus.

Then the bell rang and a young lady with a nose ring and bright red ringlets of hair appeared. Eloise was another refugee, though a much better organized one. She had brought bagels and my guests' laundry. Marco seemed delighted to see her.

That morning all the restaurants and bars, the tattoo shops and massage parlors were opening up. Even the Arab falafel shop owners had risked insults and death threats to ride the subways in from Queens and open their doors for business.

At the library, the huge screens in the lobby were being taken down. A couple of students were borrowing books. One or two even had in depth reference questions for me. When I finally worked up the courage to call Mags, all I got was the same message as before.

Marco appeared dressed in his own clothes and clearly feeling better. He hugged me. "You were great to take me in."

"It helped me even more," I told him.

He paused then asked, "That was you on that poster last night wasn't it? You and Mags and Geoffrey?" The kid was a bit uncanny.

When I nodded, he said. "Thanks for talking about that."

I was in a hurry when I went off duty Saturday evening. A friend had called and invited me to an impromptu "Survivors' Party". In the days of the French Revolution, The Terror, that's what they called the soirees at which people danced and drank all night then went out at dawn to see which of their names were on the list of those to be guillotined.

On Sixth Avenue a bakery that had very special cupcakes with devastating frosting was open again. The avenue was clogged with honking, creeping traffic. A huge chunk of Lower Manhattan had been declared open that afternoon and people were able to get the cars that had been stranded down there.

The bakery was across the street from a Catholic church. And that afternoon in that place, a wedding was being held. As I came out with my cupcakes, the bride and groom, not real young, not very glamorous, but obviously happy, came out the door and posed on the steps for pictures.

Traffic was at a standstill. People beeped "Here comes the bride," leaned out their windows, applauded and cheered, all of us relieved to find this ordinary, normal thing taking place.

Then I saw her on the other side of Sixth Avenue. Mags was tramping along, staring straight ahead, a poster with a black and white photo hanging from a string around her neck. The crowd in front of the church parted for her. Mourners were sacred at that moment.

I yelled her name and started to cross the street. But the tie-up had eased, traffic started to flow. I tried to keep pace with her on my side of street. I wanted to invite her to the party. The hosts knew her from way back. But the sidewalks on both sides were crowded. When I did get across Sixth, she was gone.

AFTERMATH

That night I came home from the party and found the place completely cleaned up with a thank you note on the fridge signed by all three kids. And I felt relieved but also lost.

The Survivor party was on the Lower East Side. On my way back, I had gone by the East Village, walked up to Tenth Street between B and C. People were out and about. Bars were doing business. But there was still almost no vehicle traffic and the block was very quiet.

The building where we three had lived in increasing squalor and tension thirty-five years before was refinished, gentrified. I stood across the street looking. Maybe I willed his appearance.

Geoff was there in the corner of my eye, his face dead white, staring up, unblinking, at the light in what had been our windows. I turned toward him and he disappeared. I looked aside and he was there again, so lost and alone, the arms of his jacket soaked in blood.

And I remembered us sitting around with the syringes and all of us making a pledge in blood to stick together as long as we lived. To which Geoff added, "And even after." And I remembered how I had looked at him staring at Mags and knew she was looking at me. Three sides of a triangle.

The next day, Sunday, I went down to Mags' building, wanting very badly to talk to her. I rang the bell again and again. There was no response. I rang the super's apartment.

She was a neighborhood lady, a lesbian around my age. I asked her about Mags.

"She disappeared. Last time anybody saw her was Sunday 9/9. People in the building checked to make sure everyone was OK. No sign of her. I put a tape across her keyhole Wednesday. It's still there."

"I saw her just yesterday."

"Yeah?" She looked skeptical. "Well there's a World Trade Center list of potentially missing persons and her name's on it. You need to talk to them."

This sounded to me like the landlord trying to get rid of her. For the next week, I called Mags a couple of times a day. At some point the answering machine stopped coming on. I checked out her building regularly. No sign of her. I asked Angelina if she remembered the two of us having dinner in her place on Wednesday 9/12.

"I was too busy, staying busy so I wouldn't scream. I remember you and I guess you were with somebody. But no, honey, I don't remember."

Then I asked Marco if he remembered the phone call. And he did but was much too involved by then with Terry and Eloise to be really interested.

Around that time, I saw the couple who had wanted to take their kids down to ground zero. They were walking up Sixth Avenue, the kids cranky and tired, the parents looking disappointed. Like the amusement park had turned out to be a rip-off.

Life closed in around me. A short story collection of mine was being published at that very inopportune moment and I needed to do some publicity work. I began seeing an old lover who'd come back to New York as a consultant for a company that had lost its offices and a big chunk of its staff when the north tower fell.

Mrs. Pirelli did not come home from the hospital, but went to live with her son in Connecticut. I made it a point to go by each of the Arab shops and listen to the owners say how awful they felt about what had happened and smile when they showed me pictures of their kids in Yankee caps and shirts.

It was the next weekend that I saw Mags again. The University had gotten permission for the students to go back to the downtown dorms and get their stuff out. Marco, Terry and Eloise came by the library and asked me to go with them. So I went over to University Transportation and volunteered my services.

Around noon on Sunday 9/23 a couple of dozen kids and I piled into a University bus driven by Roger, a Jamaican guy who has worked for the University for as long as I have.

"The day before 9/11 these kids didn't much want old farts keeping them company," Roger had said to me. "Then they all wanted their daddy." He led a convoy of jitneys and vans down the

FDR drive, then through quiet Sunday streets and then past trucks and construction vehicles.

We stopped at a police check point. A cop looked inside and waved us through.

At the dorm, another cop told the kids they had an hour to get what they could and get out. "Be ready to leave at a moment's notice if we tell you to," he said.

Roger and I as the senior members stayed with the vehicles. The air was filthy. Our eyes watered. A few hundred feet up the street, a cloud of smoke still hovered over the ruins of the World Trade Center. Piles of rubble smoldered. Between the pit and us, was a line of fire trucks and police cars with cherry tops flashing. Behind us the kids hurried out of the dorm carrying boxes. I made them write their names on their boxes and noted in which van the boxes got stowed. I was surprised, touched even, at the number of stuffed animals that were being rescued.

"Over the years we've done some weird things to earn our pensions," I said to Roger.

"Like volunteering to come to the gates of hell?"

As he said that flames sprouted from the rubble. Police and firefighters shouted and began to fall back. A fire department chemical tanker turned around and the crew began unwinding hoses.

Among the uniforms, I saw a civilian, a middle aged woman in a sweater and jeans and carrying a sign. Mags walked towards the flames. I wanted to run to her. I wanted to shout, "Stop her." Then I realized that none of the cops and firefighters seemed aware of her even as she walked right past them.

As she did, I saw another figure, thin, pale in a suede jacket and bell bottom pants. He held out his bloody hands and together they walked through the smoke and flames into the hole in the city.

"Was that them?" Marco had been standing beside me.

I turned to him. Terry was back by the bus watching Marco's every move. Eloise was gazing at Terry.

"Be smarter than we were," I said.

And Marco said, "Sure," with all the confidence in the world.

# NORTHWEST PASSAGE

## *Barbara Roden*

*How then am I so different from the first men through this way?*
*Like them I left a settled life, I threw it all away*
*To seek a Northwest Passage at the call of many men*
*To find there but the road back home again.*
Stan Rogers, Northwest Passage

They vary in detail, the stories, but the broad outline is the same. Someone — hiker, hunter, tourist — goes missing, or is reported overdue, and there is an appeal to the public for information; the police become involved, and search and rescue teams, and there are interviews with friends and relatives, and statements by increasingly grim-faced officials, as the days tick by and hope begins to crack and waver and fade, like colour leaching out of a picture left too long in a window. Then there is the official calling off of the search, and gradually the story fades from sight, leaving family and friends with questions, an endless round of what ifs and how coulds and where dids pursuing each other like restless children.

Occasionally there is a coda, weeks or months or years later, when another hiker or hunter or tourist — more skilled, or perhaps more fortunate — stumbles across evidence and carries the news back, prompting a small piece in the "In Brief" section of the *Vancouver Sun* which is skimmed over by urban readers safe in a place of straight lines and clearly delineated routes. They gaze at the expanse of Stanley Park on their daily commute, and wonder how a person could vanish so easily in a landscape so seemingly benign.

Peggy Malone does not wonder this, nor does she ask herself any questions. She suspects she already knows the answers, and it is safer to keep the questions which prompt them locked away. Sometimes, though, they arise unbidden: when outside her window the breeze rustles the leaves of the maple, the one she asked the Strata Council to cut down, or the wind chimes three doors down are set ringing. Then the questions come back, eagerly, like a dog left on its own too long, and she turns on the television — not the radio, she rarely listens to that now — and turns on the lights and tries, for a time, to forget.

The road was, as back roads in the Interior go, a good one: Len had always ensured that it was graded regularly. Peggy, bumping her way up it in the Jeep, added "get road seen to" to her mental checklist of things to do. She could not let it go another summer; next spring's meltwater would eat away even further at the dirt and rocks, and her sixty-three-year-old bones could do without the added wear and tear.

She followed the twists and turns of the road, threading her way through stands of cottonwood and birch and Ponderosa pine. Here and there the bright yellow of an arrowleaf balsam root flashed into sight beneath the trees, enjoying a brief moment of glory before withering and dying, leaving the silver-grey leaves as the only evidence of its passing. Overhead the sky was clear blue, but the breeze, when she pulled the Jeep in front of the cabin, was cool, a reminder that spring, not summer, held sway.

Peggy opened the rear of the Jeep and began unloading bags of supplies, which seemed, as always, to have proliferated during the drive. There was nothing to be done about it, however; the nearest town was an hour away, and she had long since learned that it was better to err on the side of too much than too little. Even though she was only buying for one now, the old habits died hard, and she usually managed to avoid making the journey more than once every two weeks or so.

She loaded the last of the milk into the fridge, which, like the other appliances and some of the lights, ran off propane; the light switch on the wall near the door had been installed by Len in a fit of whimsy when the cabin was being built, and served no useful purpose, as electricity did not extend up the valley from the highway some miles distant. The radio was battery operated, but seldom used: reception was poor during the day and sporadic at night, with stations alternately competing with each other and then fading away into a buzz of static. Kerosene lanterns and a generator could be used in an emergency, and an airtight fireplace kept the cabin more than warm enough in spring and fall. In winter she stayed with a nephew and his family on Vancouver Island; Len's brother's son, Paul, a good, steady lad who had given up urging his aunt to make the move to the Island permanent when he saw that it did no good. She would move when she was ready, Peggy always replied; she would know when the time came, and as long as she was able to drive and look after herself she was happy with the way things were.

Supplies unloaded, she set the kettle to boiling. A cup of tea would be just the thing, before she went out and did some gardening. It was not gardening in the sense that any of her acquaintances on the Island would understand it, with their immaculate, English-style flowerbeds and neatly edged, emerald green lawns which would not have looked out of place on a golf course; she called it that out of habit. She had learned, early on, that this land was tolerant of imposition only up to a point, and for some years her gardening had been confined to planting a few annuals — marigolds did well — in pots and hanging baskets.

Of course, she now had the grass to cut, and there were the paths to work on. It was Len who had suggested them, the summer before he had died, while watching her struggle to keep the sagebrush and wild grass at bay. The cabin was built on a natural bench, which overlooked the thickly treed valley, and was in turn overlooked by hills, rising relentlessly above until they lost themselves in the mountains behind. On three sides of the cabin the grassland stretched away to the trees, and Peggy had fought with it, trying, with her lawn and her flowers, to impose some sense of order on the landscape. She had resisted the idea of the paths at first, feeling that it would be giving in; but about what, and to whom, she could not have said. Still, she had started them for Len, who had taken comfort, that last summer, in watching her going about her normal tasks, and then she had continued them, partly because she felt she owed it to Len, and partly to fill the hours.

The paths now wound through a large part of the grassy area around the cabin. They were edged with rocks, and there were forks and intersections, and it was possible to walk them for some time without doubling back on oneself; not unlike, thought Peggy, one of those low mazes in which people were meant to think contemplative thoughts as they followed the path. She was not much given to contemplation herself, but keeping the existing paths free of weeds occupied her hands, and she supposed vaguely that it was good for her mind as well.

Now she stood looking at the paths, wondering whether she should do some weeding or check the mower and make sure it was in working order. It might have seized up over the winter; if so, then a good dose of WD-40 should take care of matters. She knew precisely where the tin was — Peggy knew precisely where everything in the cabin was — and was just turning towards the shed where the mower was stored when she heard the unmistakable sound of a vehicle coming up the road.

It was such an unusual sound that she stopped in her tracks and turned to face the gate, which hung open on its support, the only break in the fence of slender pine logs which encircled the property and served to keep out the cattle which occasionally wandered past. The road did not lead anywhere except to the cabin, and visitors were few and far between, for the simple reason that there was almost no one in the area to pay a visit. Peggy stood, waiting expectantly, and after a few moments a ramshackle Volkswagen van swung round the curve and started up the slight incline which levelled off fifty yards inside the gate, not far from the front of the cabin where her own Jeep was parked.

It pulled to a halt just inside the gate, and Peggy watched it. There were two people in the front seat, and for a minute no one made a move to get out; she got the impression that there was an argument going on. Then the passenger door opened, and a boy emerged, waving a tentative hand at her. She nodded her head, and the boy said something to the driver. Again Peggy got the impression that there was a disagreement of some sort; then the driver's door opened slowly, and another boy emerged.

She would have been a fool not to feel a slight sense of apprehension, and Peggy was not a fool. But she prided herself on being able to assess a situation quickly and accurately, and she did not feel any sense of threat. So she stood and waited as they approached her, taking in their appearance: one tall and fair-haired, the other shorter and dark; both in their early twenties, with longish hair and rumpled clothing and a general impression of needing a good square meal or two, but nothing that made her wish that the .202 she kept inside the cabin was close to hand.

The pair stopped a few feet from her, and the fair-haired boy spoke first.

"Hi. We, uh, we were just passing by, and we thought . . ." He trailed off, as if appreciating that "just passing by" was not something easily done in the area. There was a pause. Then he continued, "We heard your Jeep, and were kinda surprised; we didn't think anyone lived up here. So we thought that . . . well, that we'd come by and see who was here, and . . ."

The trickle of words stopped again, and the boy shrugged, helplessly, as if making an appeal. It was clear the other boy was not about to come to his aid, so Peggy picked up the thread.

"Margaret Malone," she said, moving forward, her hand extended. "Call me Peggy."

The fair-haired boy smiled hesitantly, and stuck out his own hand. "Hiya, Peggy. I'm John Carlisle, but everyone calls me Jack."

"Nice to meet you, Jack." Peggy turned to Jack's companion and looked at him evenly. "And you are . . . ?"

There was a pause, as if the boy was weighing the effect of not answering. Jack nudged him, and he said in a low voice, "Robert. Robert Parker."

Something about the way he said it discouraged any thoughts of Bob or Robbie. The conversation ground to a halt again, and once more Peggy took the initiative.

"So, you two boys students?" she asked pleasantly. Jack shook his head and said, "No, why d'you ask?" at the same moment that Robert said sullenly, "We're not boys."

Peggy took a moment to reply. "To answer you first," she said finally, nodding towards Jack, "we sometimes get students up here, from UBC or SFU, studying insects or infestation patterns, so it seemed likely. And to reply to your comment, Robert," she said, looking him directly in the eye, "when you get to my age you start to look at anyone under a certain age as being a boy; I didn't intend it as an insult. If I want to insult someone I don't leave them in any doubt."

Jack gave a sudden smile, which twitched across his face and was gone in an instant. Robert glared at him.

"If you don't mind my asking, what brings you to this neck of the woods? Seems kind of an out of the way spot for two . . . people . . . of your age, especially this time of year."

Nothing.

*Really*, thought Peggy, *was my generation as inarticulate as this when we were young? You'd think they'd never spoken to anyone else before.*

Again it was Jack who broke the silence.

"We're just, well, travelling around, you know? Taking some time out, doing something different, that kind of thing." Seeing the look in Peggy's eyes, he added, "We just wanted to go somewhere we wouldn't be bumping into people, somewhere we could do what we wanted. We've been up here for a few weeks now, staying in an old place we found over there." He pointed an arm in an easterly direction. "It was falling to pieces," he added, as if he was apologising. "No one's lived there for ages, we figured it'd be okay."

Peggy held up a hand. "No problem as far as I'm concerned, if it's the place I think you mean. Used to be a prospector's cabin, but no one's used it for years. You're welcome to it. Last time I hiked over that way was some time ago, and it was a real handyman's special then. You must have done a lot of work to get it fixed up so that you could live in it."

Jack shrugged. "Yeah, but we're used to that. Lots of stuff lying around we could use."

'What do you do about food?"

"We stocked up in town; and there's an old woodstove in the cabin. We don't need a lot; we're used to roughing it."

Peggy eyed them both. "Seems to me you could do with something more than just roughing it in the food line for a couple of days."

"We do okay." It was Robert who spoke, as if challenging Peggy. "We do just fine. We don't want any help."

"I wasn't offering any, just making a comment. Last time I checked it was still a free country."

"Yeah, course it is," Jack said quickly. He glanced at Robert and shook his head; a small gesture, but Peggy noticed it. "Anyway, we heard your Jeep; we were kinda surprised to see someone living up here. We figured it was only a summer place."

"No, I'm up here spring through fall," said Peggy. "Afraid you're stuck with me as your nearest neighbour. Don't worry, I don't play the electric guitar or throw loud parties."

It was a small joke, but Jack smiled again, as if he appreciated Peggy's attempt to lighten the mood. Robert nodded his head in the direction of the van, and Jack's smile vanished.

"Well, we've got to get going," he said obediently. "Nice meeting you, Peggy."

"Nice meeting you two," she said. "If you need anything . . ."

"Thanks, that's really kind of you," said Jack. He seemed about to add something, but Robert cut in.

"Can't think we'll need any help," he said curtly. "C'mon, Jack. Lots to do."

"Yeah, right, lots to do. Thanks again, though, Peggy. See you around."

"Probably. It's a big country, but a small world."

"Hey, that's good." Jack smiled. "Big country, small world."

Robert, who had already climbed into the driver's seat, honked the horn, and Jack turned almost guiltily towards the van. The passenger door had hardly closed before Robert was turning the van around. Jack waved as they passed, and Peggy waved back, but Robert kept his eyes on the road and his hands on the wheel. Within moments they were through the gate, and the curve of the road had swallowed them up.

Over the next few days Peggy replayed this encounter in her head, trying to put her finger on what bothered her. Yes, Robert had been rude — well, brusque, at least — but then a lot of young people were, these days; some old people too. Their story about wanting to see something different; that wasn't unusual, exactly, but Peggy could think of quite a few places which were different but which didn't involve fixing up a dilapidated shack in the middle of nowhere. Yet Jack had said they'd done that sort of thing before, so it was obviously nothing new for them.

Were they runaways? That might explain why they came to check out who was in the cabin. But if they were running away from someone, they would hardly have driven right up to her front door. Drugs crossed her mind; it was almost impossible to pick up the paper or turn on the news without hearing about another marijuana grow-op being raided by police. Most of them were in the city or up the Fraser Valley, but she had heard about such places in the country, too; and didn't they grow marijuana openly in some rural spots, far away from the prying eyes of the police and neighbours? That might explain why Jack had looked so nervous . . . but, when she recalled the conversation, and the way Jack had looked at his friend, she realised that he was not nervous on his own account, he was nervous for, or about, Robert, who had seemed not in the least bit nervous for, or about, anything. He had merely been extremely uncomfortable, as if being in the proximity of someone other than Jack, even for five minutes, made him want to escape. What had Jack said? They wanted to go somewhere they wouldn't be bumping into people.

*Robert must have had a shock when he saw me here*, thought Peggy. *Bet I was the last thing he expected — or wanted — to run into.*

\*      \*      \*

She did not see the pair again for almost three weeks. Once she saw their van at the side of the road as she drove out towards the highway and town, but there was no sign of Jack or Robert, and on another occasion she thought she saw the pair of them far up on the hillside above her, but the sun was in her eyes and she couldn't be sure. She thought once or twice about hiking over to their cabin, which was two miles or so away. There had been a decent trail over there at one time, which she and Len had often walked; but the days were getting hotter, and her legs weren't what they once were, and when she reflected on her likely reception she decided she was better off staying put. If they wanted anything, or needed any help, they knew where to find her.

It was late morning, and Peggy had been clearing a new path. A wind had been gusting out of the northwest; when she stopped work and looked up the hill she could see it before she heard or felt it, sweeping through the trees, bearing down on her, carrying the scent of pine and upland meadows before rushing past and down the hill, setting the wind chimes by the front door tinkling, branches bending and swinging before it as if an unseen giant had passed. Sometimes a smaller eddy seemed to linger behind, puffing up dust on the paths, swirling round and about like something trapped and lost and trying to escape. But Peggy did not think of it like this; at least not then. Those thoughts did not come until later.

She straightened up, one hand flat against her lower back, stretching, and it was then that she saw the boy standing at the edge of the property, by the mouth of the trail leading to the prospector's cabin. She had no idea how long he had been standing there, but she realised that he must have been waiting for her to notice him before he came closer, for as soon as he knew he had been spotted he headed in her direction.

"Hello there," she said. "Jack, isn't it? Haven't seen you for a while; I was beginning to wonder if you'd moved on."

"No, we're still here." He gave a little laugh. "Kind of obvious, I guess."

"A bit. Your friend with you?"

"No."

"I'm not surprised. He didn't seem the dropping-in type."

"No." Jack seemed to feel that something more was needed. "He was a bit pissed off when he found someone was living here. He thought we had the place to ourselves, you see, no one around for miles."

"He likes his solitude, then."

"You could say that."

"Still, it's not as if I'm on your doorstep," said Peggy reasonably, "or, to be strictly accurate, that you're on mine. If your friend doesn't want to run into anyone, he's picked as good a spot as any."

"Yeah, that's what I've been telling him, but I think we'll be heading out before the end of the summer."

"Because of me?"

"Well, no; I mean, sort of, but that's not the whole reason. Robert" — he paused, looking for words — "Robert likes to keep on moving. Restless, I guess you could say. He's always been like that; always wants to see what's over the next hill, around the next corner, always figures there's somewhere better out there."

"Better than what?"

Jack shrugged. "I don't know. He gets somewhere, and he seems happy enough for a while, and then, just when I think 'Right, this is it, this is the place he's been looking for,' off he goes again."

"Do you always go with him?"

"Yeah, usually. We've known each other a long time, since elementary school. His family moved from back east and we wound up in the same grade three class."

"Where was that?"

"Down in Vancouver. Point Grey."

Peggy nodded. Point Grey usually, but not always, meant money, respectability, expectations. She could see Robert, from what little she knew of him, being from, but not of, that world. Jack, though, looked like Point Grey, and she wondered how he had found himself caught up in Robert's orbit.

"He's always been my best friend," the boy said, as if reading her thoughts. "We hung out together. I mean, I had other friends, but Robert just had me. It didn't bother him, though. If he wanted to do something and I couldn't, he'd just go off on his own, no problem. It's like he always knew I'd be there when he needed me."

"Has he always liked the outdoor life?"

Jack nodded. "Yeah, he's always been happiest when he's outside." He shook his head. "I remember this one time I got him to go along with a group of us who were going camping for the weekend. We were all eleven, twelve; our parents didn't mind, they figured there were enough of us that we'd be safe." He paused, remembering. "We rode our bikes from Point Grey out to Sea Island; you know, behind the airport." Peggy nodded. "There used to be a big subdivision out there, years ago, but then they were going to build another runway and the houses got . . . what's the word . . . expropriated, and torn down, and then nothing happened, and it all got pretty wild, the gardens and trees and everything.

"Well, we all had the usual shit . . . I mean stuff; dinky pup tents and old sleeping bags and things, and chocolate bars and pop, but not Robert. He had a tarp, and a plastic sheet, and a blanket, matches, a compass, trail mix, bottled water; he even had an axe. You'd've thought he was on a military exercise, or one of those survival weekends, instead of in the suburbs. We goofed around, and ate, and told stories, and then we crawled into our tents, all except Robert. He'd built a fire, and a lean-to out of branches and the tarp, and he said he'd stay where he was, even when it started to rain. Rain in Vancouver: who'd think it?

"Anyway, when morning came round, we were a pretty miserable bunch of kids; the tents had leaked, and our sleeping bags were soaked, and we'd eaten almost everything we'd brought. And there was Robert, dry as a bone, making a fire out of wood he'd put under cover the night before, with food and water to spare. Made us all look like a bunch of idiots."

"Sounds like a good person to have around you in a place like this."

"Yeah, you could say that." He scuffed the toe of one foot against the dirt, watching puffs of dust swirl up into the air.

"So where is he this morning?"

Jack stopped scuffing and looked up at Peggy. "He went off a couple of hours ago; said he needed to get away for a while, be on his own. He gets like that sometimes. I hung around for a bit by myself and then . . ." His look was almost pleading. "It just got so quiet, you know? You don't realise how quiet it is 'til you're by yourself. Robert doesn't mind; sometimes I think he'd rather be by himself all the time, that he wouldn't even notice if I never came back."

Peggy tried to think of something to say. Jack went back to scuffing the dirt, and a breeze picked up the cloud of dust, swirling it in the direction of the paths. Jack followed the cloud with his eyes, and seemed to notice the paths through the grass for the first time.

"Hey, that's pretty cool." He took a couple of steps forward, and she could see his head moving as he followed the curves of the paths with his eyes. "Bet it would look neat from overhead, like in one of those old Hollywood musicals."

Peggy had not recognized the tension in the situation until it was gone; its sudden disappearance left her feeling slightly off-balance, like an actor momentarily surprised by the unexpected ad-lib of someone else on stage. Jack was still gazing out over the paths.

"Must've taken a long time to do this," he said. "What's it for?"

"Nothing, really." Peggy moved forward so that she was standing beside him. "It was my husband's idea; he said he got tired of watching me trying to control the brush, that I should work with it, not against it."

*If you can't beat 'em, join 'em*, she heard Len's voice say. *And looking at all that* — he had waved his hand towards the expanse of scrub and the hills beyond — *I don't think you're ever going to beat 'em, Peg.*

"If you can't beat them, join them," said Jack, and Peggy started slightly and looked sideways at him. "That's how I feel about Robert sometimes. Can I take a closer look?"

"Go ahead." Peggy looked at her watch. "I'm going to go and make some lunch; nothing fancy, just sandwiches and some fruit, but if you want to stay then you're more than welcome."

"Could I?" he asked eagerly. "I'd really like that. Our cooking's pretty . . . basic."

Peggy, noting Jack's pinched face and pale complexion, could believe it. "I'll go and rustle something up; come in when you're ready."

She stood at the kitchen counter, letting her hands move through the familiar motions of spreading butter and mayonnaise, slicing tomatoes and cucumber, while in her head she went over the conversation with Jack. There were undercurrents she could not fathom, depths she could not chart. She had thought of them as two boys from the city playing at wilderness life, and Jack's words had not dismissed this as a possibility; but there was something else going on, she was sure of it. Were they lovers? Had they had a fight? That could be it, but she did not think so. She could not connect the dark, intense figure she had seen three weeks ago with something as essentially banal as a lovers' tiff.

Through the window she could see Jack moving slowly along one of the paths, his head down as if deep in concentration. He stopped, seemingly aware of her gaze upon him, but instead of turning towards the cabin he looked up at the hillside above, intently, his head cocked a little to one side as if he had heard something. Peggy followed his gaze, but could see nothing on the bare slope, or in the air above; certainly nothing that would inspire such rapt attention.

She stacked the sandwiches on a plate, then sliced some cheese and put it, with some crackers and grapes, on another plate. She wondered what to offer as a drink. Beer would have been the obvious choice, but she had none. Milk or orange juice; or perhaps he'd like a cup of coffee or tea afterwards. . . .

Still pondering beverage choices, she put the plates on the table, then went to the door. Jack had not altered his position; he seemed transfixed by something up on the hill. Peggy looked again, sure that he was watching an animal, but there was nothing to be seen.

She called his name, and he turned to her with a startled look on his face, as if he could not quite remember who she was or how he had got there. Then he shook his head slightly and trotted towards her, like a dog who has heard the rattle of the can opener and knows his supper is ready.

"Sorry it's nothing more elegant," said Peggy, pointing to the table, "but help yourself. Don't be shy."

She soon realized that her words were unnecessary. Jack fell on the meal as if he had not eaten in days, and for some minutes the only sound was him asking if he could have another sandwich. Peggy got up twice to refill his milk glass before finally placing the jug on the table so he could help himself, and watched as the cheese and cracker supply dwindled. Finally Jack drained his glass and sighed contentedly.

"Thanks, Peggy, that was great, really. Didn't know how hungry I was until I saw the food. Guess I wouldn't win any awards for politeness."

Peggy laughed. "That's okay. It's been a long time since I saw someone eat something I'd made with that much pleasure. I'm sorry it wasn't anything more substantial."

Jack looked at his watch. "Geez, is that the time? I better be going; Robert'll be back soon, he'll wonder where I am, and I'll bet you've got things to do."

"Don't worry, my time's my own. Nice watch."

Jack smiled proudly, and held up his wrist so Peggy could see it better. Silver glinted at her. "Swiss Army. My parents gave it to me when I graduated. Keeps perfect time." He sat back in his chair and looked around the cabin. "You live here by yourself? You said something about your husband. Is he . . . ?" He stopped, unsure how to continue the sentence to its natural conclusion, so Peggy did it for him.

". . . dead, yes. Four years ago. Cancer. It was pretty sudden; there was very little the doctors could do."

"I'm sorry."

"That's okay. You didn't know him. He went quite quickly, which is what he wanted. Len was never a great one for lingering."

"So you live up here for most of the year on your own? That's pretty gutsy."

Peggy could not recall having been called gutsy before. "You think so?"

"Yeah, sure. I mean, this place is pretty isolated, and you're . . . well, you're not exactly young." His face went pink. "I don't mean that . . . it just must be tough, that's all, on your own. Don't you ever get lonely?"

"No, there's always something to do. I spend the winter with family on the Island; I get more than enough company then to see me through the rest of the year."

Jack nodded. His eyes continued moving around the cabin, and he spotted the light switch. "Hey, I didn't think you had power up here."

"We don't. That's a bit of a joke, for visitors."

"Bet you don't get too many of those."

"You'd be right. My nephew and his family have been up a couple of times, but not for a while. He doesn't like it much up here; says it makes him uncomfortable. This sort of place isn't for everyone."

Jack nodded. "You've got that right." He looked through the screen door towards the hillside and gestured with his head. "You ever feel that something's up there watching you?"

Peggy considered. "No, not really. An animal sometimes, maybe; but we don't get too many animals up there. Odd, really, you'd think it would be a natural place to spot them." A memory came back to her; Paul, her nephew, on one of his rare visits, standing on the porch looking up at the hills. "My nephew said once it reminded him of a horror movie his sons rented; *The Eyes on the Hill* or something."

"*The Hills Have Eyes*," Jack corrected automatically. "Yeah, I've seen it." He was silent for a moment. "Do you believe that?"

"What — that the hills have eyes? No."

"But don't you feel it?" he persisted. "Like there's something there, watching, waiting, something really old and . . . I don't know, part of this place, guarding it, protecting it, looking for something?"

Peggy couldn't keep the astonishment out of her face and voice. "No, I can honestly say I've never felt that at all." She considered him. "Is that what you think?"

"I don't know." He paused. "There's just something weird about this spot. I mean, we've been in some out of the way places, Robert and me, but nowhere like this. I'll be kind of glad when he decides to move on. I hope it'll be soon."

"I thought you wanted him to settle down somewhere."

"Yeah, I do, but not here."

"Why don't you leave? Robert seems able to fend for himself, and he appears to like this sort of life better than you do. Why do you stay with him?"

"I've always stayed with him."

"But you said that he likes to go off on his own, that you don't think he'd notice if you didn't come back."

Jack looked uncomfortable, like a witness caught by a clever lawyer. "Oh, I just said that 'cause I was pissed off. He'd notice."

"Is he your boyfriend? Is that why you stay?"

Jack looked shocked. "God, no! It's nothing like that. It goes back a long way. . . . Remember I told you about that camping trip out to Sea Island? Well, when I went round to Robert's house to get him his mom was there, fussing, you know, the way moms do, and he was getting kind of impatient, and finally he just said "Bye, mom" really suddenly and went to get his bike, and his mom turned to me and said 'Look after him.' Which was kind of a weird thing to say, 'cause I was only eleven, and Robert wasn't the kind of kid who you'd think needed looking after — well, we found that out next day. But I knew what she meant. She didn't mean he needed looking after 'cause he'd do something stupid, she meant that he needed someone to . . . bring him back, almost, make sure he didn't go off and just keep on going."

"Is that why you stay with him? So he doesn't just keep on going?"

"I guess." His smile was tinged with sadness. "I'm not doing such a great job, am I?"

"You're a long way from Point Grey, if that's what you mean."

"Yeah, and I can't see us making it back anytime soon. Robert wants to keep heading north, up to the Yukon, and then head east."

"What on earth for?"

Jack shrugged. "He does a lot of reading; he's got a box of books in the van, all about explorers and people who go off into the wilderness with just some matches and a rifle and a sack of flour and live off the land. I think that's what he wants to do; go up north and see what's there, see what he can do, what he can find. He loves reading about the Franklin expedition; you know, the one that disappeared when they were searching for the Northwest Passage, and no one knew for years what happened to them. I think he likes the idea of just vanishing, and no one knows where you are, and then you come out when you're ready, and tell people what you've found."

'The Franklin expedition didn't come out."

"Robert figures he can do better than them."

"Well then, you should break it to him that the Northwest Passage was found a long time ago, and tell him he should maybe stick closer to home."

"He doesn't want to find the Northwest Passage; anyway, he says it doesn't really exist, there is no Northwest Passage, not like everyone thought back in Franklin's time."

"And you'll go with him?"

"I suppose so."

"You do have a choice, you know."

"Yeah, like you said, it's a free country. But I kind of feel like I have to go with him, to . . ."

"Look after him?"

"I guess." He shrugged. "It's like there's something out there, waiting for him, and I have to make sure he comes back okay, otherwise he'd just keep on going, and he'd be like those Franklin guys, he'd never come out."

The conversation was interrupted by the unmistakable sound of a vehicle coming up the road towards the cabin. Jack stood up so quickly his chair fell over.

"Shit, it's Robert."

"Probably," Peggy agreed drily. "Don't worry, there's nothing criminal about having lunch with someone."

"No, but . . . Robert can be . . . funny, weird, sometimes. Don't tell him what I said about looking after him, he'd be really pissed off."

"Your secret is safe with me."

They went out on to the porch and watched the van drive up. Robert climbed out and glared at Jack.

"Thought you'd be here," he said, ignoring Peggy. "C'mon, let's go."

"Hello to you too," said Peggy. "You're a friendly sort, aren't you? In my day we'd have considered it bad manners to order a person out from under someone else's roof. Guess times have changed. Or are you just naturally rude?" Robert stared at her, but she gave him no chance to speak. "Jack's here as my guest; he's had a good lunch, which I must say he needed, and you look like you could do with something decent inside you, whatever you might think. So you can either stay here and let me fix you some sandwiches, which I'm more than prepared to do if you're prepared to be civil, or you can climb back into your van and drive away, with or without Jack, but I think that's his decision to make, not yours. He found his way here by himself, and I'd guess he can find his way back if he decides to stay a bit longer."

Robert started to say something; something not very pleasant, if the look that flashed across his face was anything to go by. Then he took a deep breath.

"Yeah, you're right. He can stay if he wants. No problem." He turned towards the van.

"Wait a minute," said Jack, moving off the porch. "Don't go. Peggy said you could stay, she'll fix you some sandwiches. Don't be a jerk. You must be as hungry as me."

"We've got food back at our place," said Robert; but he slowed down. Jack turned and threw a pleading look back at Peggy. *What can I do?* was written on his face.

"Robert. *Robert.*" He stopped, but kept his back turned to Peggy. "If you don't want to stay now, that's fine; maybe this isn't a good time, maybe you've got things to do, I don't know. But why don't you both come back over for supper? I've got some steaks in the fridge that need using up, and I can do salad and baked potatoes. Sound good?"

"What do you say, Robert?" said Jack eagerly. "I'll come with you now, then we both come back later and have supper."

Robert looked at Jack, then at Peggy. She put her hands in front of her, palms out, like a traffic policeman. "No ulterior motive, no strings, just a chance to give you both a good meal and talk to someone other than myself. You'd be doing me a big favour, both of you."

"Yeah," said Robert finally, slowly, "yeah, okay, supper would be great."

"Fine! About six, then."

Robert climbed in the driver's seat, and Jack mouthed *Thanks!* and gave a wave; the sun glinted off the face of his watch, making her blink. He got in the other side, and once more she watched as the van rattled out the gate and round the curve.

"I hope I've done the right thing," she said aloud. "Why can't things be simple?"

The afternoon drew on. Peggy did a bit more work on the paths, clearing some errant weeds. She straightened up at last, and glanced down across the valley below. It was her favourite view, particularly in the late afternoon sun, and she stood admiring it for a few moments, watching the play of light and shade across the trees. The wind, which had been playing fitfully about her all day, had at last died down, and everything was still and calm and clear.

Suddenly she turned and looked up behind her. She could have sworn that she heard someone call her name, but there was no one there; at least no one she could see. Still, the feeling persisted that someone was there; she felt eyes on her, watching.

*The hills have eyes.*

For the first time she realised how exposed she and the cabin were, and how small. Crazy, really, to think that something as essentially puny and inconsequential as a human could try to impose anything of himself on this land. How long had all this been here? How long would it endure after she was gone? *Work with it, not against it*, Len had said. *If you can't beat 'em, join 'em.* But how could you work with something, join with something, that you couldn't understand?

She shook her head. This was the sort of craziness that came from too much living alone. Maybe Paul was right; maybe it was time to start thinking about moving to the Island permanently.

*Or maybe you just need a good hot meal* said a voice inside her head. *Those boys will be here soon; better get going.* She took one last look at the hill, then turned towards the cabin. The wind chimes were ringing faintly as she passed, the only sound in the stillness.

Inside, she turned on the radio; for some reason which she did not want to analyze she found the silence oppressive. The signal was not strong, but the announcer's voice, promising "your favourite good-time oldies," was better than nothing. She started the oven warming and wrapped half a dozen potatoes in foil, to the accompaniment of Simon and Garfunkel's "The Sound of Silence," then started on the salad fixings: lettuce, cucumber, radishes, tomatoes, mushrooms. As she scraped the last of the mushrooms off the board and into the bowl, she glanced out the window, and saw a figure standing on one of the paths, looking back at the hillside. *Jack*, she thought to herself, recognizing the fair hair, and looked at her watch. It was ten past five. *They're early. Must be hungry.*

Simon and Garfunkel gave way to Buddy Holly and "Peggy Sue." The oven pinged, indicating it was up to temperature, and she bundled the potatoes into it. When she returned to the window, the figure was gone.

"C'mon in," she called out, "door's open, make yourselves at home." She put the last of the sliced tomatoes on top of the salad, then realised no one had come in. "Hello?" she called out. "Anyone there?" Buddy Holly warbling about pretty Peggy Sue was the only reply.

Peggy went to the door and looked out. There was no one in sight. The van was not there, and it registered that she had not heard it come up the road. *It's such a nice night, maybe they walked*. She looked to her right, to where the trail they would have taken came out of the woods, but no one was there.

A squawk of static from the radio made her jump. For a moment there was only a low buzzing noise; then Buddy Holly came back on, fighting through the static, for she heard "Peggy" repeated. Another burst of noise, then the signal came through more clearly; only now it was the Beatles, who were halfway through "Help!"

"Interference," she muttered to herself. They often got overlapping channels at night; another station was crossing with the first one. She went outside and looked round the corner of the cabin, but there was no one in sight. When she went back in, "Help!" was ending, and she heard the voice of the announcer. "We've got more good-time oldies coming up after the break," he said, and she realised the radio had been broadcasting the same station all along. They must have got their records, or CDs, or whatever they used now mixed-up, she decided.

She placed the salad on the table and got the steaks out of the fridge. She was beginning to trim the fat away from around the edges when the radio gave another burst of static, then faded away altogether. She flicked the on/off switch, and tried the tuner, but was unable to raise a signal. *Dead batteries*, she thought. *I only replaced them last week; honestly, they don't make things like . . .*

She broke off mid-thought at the sound of a voice calling her name. *Definitely not Buddy Holly this time*, she thought, and walked to the door, ready to call a greeting. What she saw made her freeze in the doorway.

Robert was running towards her across the grass; running wildly, carelessly, frantically even, as if something was on his tracks, calling out her name with all the breath he could muster. In a moment she shook off her fear and began crossing the yard towards him, meeting him near the back of her Jeep. He collapsed on the ground at her feet, and she knelt down beside him as he gasped for breath.

"Robert! Robert, what's wrong? What's happened?"

"Jack," he gasped. "Jack . . . he's gone . . . got to help me . . . just gone . . ."

"Gone! What do you mean? Gone where?"

He was still panting, and she saw that his face was white. He struggled to his knees and swung round so that he could look behind him, in the direction of the blank and staring hillside.

"Don't know . . . we were coming over here . . . walking . . . and then he was gone . . . didn't see him . . ."

"Right." Peggy spoke crisply, calmly. "Just take another deep breath . . . and another . . . that's it, that's better. Now then" — when his breathing had slowed somewhat — "you and Jack were walking over here — why didn't you come in the van?"

"It wouldn't start; battery's dead or something."

"Okay, so you decided to walk, and Jack went on ahead, and you lost sight of him. Well, as mysteries go it's not a hard one; he's already here."

Robert stared at her. "What do you mean, he's already here?" he almost whispered.

"I saw him, over there." Peggy pointed towards the paths. "I looked out the window and there he was."

"Where is he now?"

Peggy frowned. "Well, I don't know; I went outside, but couldn't see him. I thought you'd both come early and were looking around."

"What time was this?"

"Ten past five; I looked at my watch."

"That's impossible," said Robert flatly, in a voice tinged with despair. "At ten past five he'd only just gone missing, and I was looking for him a mile from here. There's no way he could have got here that fast."

Peggy felt as if something was spiralling out of control, and she made a grab at the first thing she could think of. "How do you know exactly when he went missing?"

"I'd just looked at my watch, to see how we were doing for time; then he was gone."

"Maybe there's something wrong with your watch."

Robert shook his head. "It keeps perfect time." He looked down at his left wrist, and Peggy saw him go pale again.

"What the fuck . . ." he whispered, and Peggy bent her head to look.

The face of the digital watch was blank.

Robert began to shiver. "What's going on?" he said, in a voice that was a long way from that of the sullen youth she had seen earlier. "Where's Jack?"

"I don't know; but he can't have gone far. Did you two have a fight about something? Could that be why he went on ahead?"

"But he didn't go on ahead," said Robert, in a voice that sounded perilously close to tears. "That's just it. We were walking along, and he asked what time it was, and I looked at my watch — it was only for a couple of seconds, you know how long it takes to look at a watch — and then he was just . . . gone."

"Could he have . . . I don't know . . . gone off the trail? Gone behind a tree?"

Robert looked at her blankly. "Why would he do that?"

"I don't know!" Peggy took a deep breath. The boy was distraught enough, without her losing control as well. "Playing a joke? Looking at something? Call of nature?"

He shook his head. "No."

"Think! Are you sure you didn't just miss him?"

"I'm positive. There wasn't time for him to go anywhere, not even if he ran like Donovan Bailey. I'd have seen him."

"Okay." Peggy thought for a moment. "You say you were both a mile from here, at ten past five, which is the same time I looked outside and saw Jack here, at my cabin. I'd say that your watch battery was going then, and it wasn't giving you an accurate time, which is how Jack seemed to be in two places at once."

Robert shook his head again. "No." He looked straight at Peggy. His breath was still ragged; he must have run the mile to her cabin. "Jack's gone." Then, more quietly, "What am I going to do?"

Peggy got him inside the cabin and into an armchair, then went back out on the porch. The clock on the radio had died with the batteries, but her old wind-up wristwatch told her it was almost six. *Time for Jack and Robert to be arriving. . . .*

She called out "Jack!" and the sound of her voice in the stillness startled her. She waited a moment, then called again, but the only reply was the tinkle of the wind chimes. She walked round the cabin, not really knowing why; Jack hadn't seemed the kind to play senseless tricks, and she didn't expect to see him, but still she looked, because it seemed the right — the only — thing to do.

She stood at the front of the cabin, looking down over the valley. All those trees; if someone wandered off into them they could disappear forever. She shivered, then shook her head. Jack hadn't disappeared; there had to be an explanation. He and Robert had had a fight; Jack had stormed off, and Robert was too embarrassed to tell her about it. Jack was probably back at their camp by now . . . but that didn't explain how he had been outside the cabin at ten past five. Unless he had come to the cabin as originally planned, then decided he couldn't face Robert, and gone back to their camp by road . . . no, it was all getting too complex. She took a deep breath and walked round the side of the cabin . . . and stopped short at the sight of a figure over on the paths.

Only it wasn't a figure, she realised a split second later; there was no one, nothing, there. She had imagined it, that was all; perhaps that's what she had done earlier, looked up and remembered the image of Jack standing there from before lunch. He hadn't been there at all; Robert was quite right. In which case . . .

"We need to go looking for Jack."

Robert looked up at her as if he did not understand. Peggy resisted the urge to shake him.

"Did you hear me? I said we need to go look for Jack."

"Shouldn't we . . . shouldn't we call the police?"

"Yes; but first we need to go looking for him." She told him about her mistake with the figure. "He was never here at all. So you must have missed him on the path. And he must be injured, or lost, or he'd be here now. So yes, we'll call the police when we get back. Even if we called them now, though, it would be almost dark before they could get here; they wouldn't be able to start a search until daybreak. We're here now; we have the best chance of finding him."

She turned the oven off — *last thing I need now is to come back and find the place burned down* — then gathered together some supplies: two flashlights, a first aid kit, a couple of bottles of water, a sheath knife. She put them in a knapsack, which she handed to Robert. Then she went into her bedroom and got the .202 out from the back of the cupboard. The sight of it seemed to make Robert realise how serious the situation was.

"What do you need that for?"

"There's all sorts of animals out there, and a lot of them start to get active around this time of day. It's their country, not ours, but that doesn't mean I want to become a meal."

"Do you know how to use it?"

Peggy stared at him levelly. "It wouldn't be much use having it around if I couldn't use it. I'm not an Olympic marksman, but if it's within fifty yards of me I can hit it. Let's go.'

They headed out towards the trail, skirting the paths. A little gust of wind was eddying dust along one of them. Peggy was conscious of the hillside above them to their left, and could not shake off the sense that something was watching. What was it Jack had said? *Something there, watching, waiting, something really old . . . part of this place, guarding it, protecting it, looking for something.* No; she had to stop it, stop it now. Thoughts like that were no good. She needed to concentrate.

"Come on, Robert," she called over her shoulder, "let's go. We have a lot of ground to cover, and it'll be dark in another couple of hours. You better go first; it's been a while since I was last through here. Keep yelling Jack's name, and keep your eyes open."

They started along the trail. It was fainter than Peggy remembered, but still distinguishable as such; more than clear enough to act as a guide, even for the most inexperienced eye. They took turns calling, and stared intently about them, looking from side to side, searching for any signs of Jack; but there was nothing, not a trace of his passage, not a hint that he was calling or signalling to them. They stopped every so often to listen, and to give them both a chance to rest; but they only lingered in one place, when Robert indicated that they were at the spot where he had last seen Jack.

"Here," he said, pointing; "I was standing here, and Jack was about fifteen feet in front of me, and then . . . he wasn't."

Peggy looked around, trying to will some sign, some clue into being, but there was nothing that marked the spot out as any different to anywhere else they had passed. Birch and poplar and pines crowded round them, but not so thickly, she thought, that someone could disappear into them and be lost to sight in a matter of seconds. A breeze rustled the branches, and something skittered through the undergrowth; a squirrel, she thought, from the sound. They called, but there was no reply, and searched either side of the trail, but there was no sign of Jack. Without a word they continued on their way.

Robert was still in front, Peggy behind; the trail was not wide enough to allow more than single file passage. *Indian file.* The phrase from her childhood popped unbidden into Peggy's mind, along with the accompanying thought, *I suppose you can't call it that anymore, but Aboriginal file doesn't sound right. Or would it be Native file?* Natives . . . now what did that . . .

"Natives don't like that place." Who had said that? Someone, years before, who she and Len had run into in town, someone who knew the area and was surprised when they told him where they lived. "Natives don't like that place," he had said. "Never have. Don't know why; you can't pin 'em down. Used to be a prospector lived back in there, not far from where you are, I guess, and there was a feeling he was tempting . . . well, fate, I suppose, or the gods, or something. . . . What happened to him? He just up and left one day; disappeared. Some people figured he'd hit it lucky at last and had cleared out with his gold, others said it was cabin fever; whatever happened, it didn't do anything for the place's reputation."

Why had she thought of that now, of all times? She shivered uncontrollably, and was glad that Robert was up ahead and couldn't see her. She hurried to close the distance between them; and although her breath was becoming more ragged, and the ache in her legs more pronounced, she did not stop again until they were at the cabin.

It was much as she remembered it; a low, crudely built structure of weathered pine logs, with a single door and one window in front, and a tin chimney pipe leaning out from the roof at an angle. There was no smoke from the chimney, no movement within or without;

only the sound of the wind, and a far-off crow cawing hoarsely, and their own breath. The dying sun reflected off the one window, creating a momentary illusion of life, but neither one spoke. There was no need. Jack was not here.

They checked the cabin, just to be sure, and the van, sitting uselessly in front, and they called until they were hoarse, but they were merely going through the motions, and Peggy knew it. Robert tried the van again, but the battery was irrevocably dead. Still silent, they turned and headed back the way they had come.

They did not call out now, or search for signs; their one thought, albeit an unspoken one, was to get back to Peggy's before dark. The sun had dipped well below the hills now, and the shadows were lengthening fast, and Peggy found herself keeping her eyes on the trail ahead. Once she thought she heard movement in the trees to their right, and stopped, clutching Robert's arm; but it was only the wind. They continued on their silent way, and did not stop again.

They reached the cabin as the last of the light flickered and died in the western sky. Peggy ached in every joint and muscle in her body, but she lit the propane lamps and put water on to boil for coffee while Robert collapsed into a chair and put his head in his hands. Finally, when she could think of nothing else useful to do with her hands, Peggy sat down opposite him.

"Robert." He looked up at her with tired eyes. "Robert, it's time to phone the police. I'll do it, if you'd like."

"Yeah, that'd be good. Thanks."

She would not have thought that this was the same Robert she had seen earlier in the day. He seemed lost, diminished, and she realised with a start that Jack had been wrong, completely wrong, when he had told her that Robert wouldn't have minded if Jack had gone off and never come back. Something inside Robert compelled him, but Jack, she thought, had always been there, a link with the life he had left behind, and a way back to it. As long as Jack had been with him, Robert would have kept moving; now, without him, Peggy had the feeling that there'd be no Northwest Passage. She wished that Jack could know that, somehow.

She moved to the phone, an old-fashioned one with a dial. She picked up the receiver and listened for a moment, then jiggled the cradle two, three, four times, while the look on her face changed from puzzled to worried to frightened. She replaced the receiver.

"No dial tone."

Robert stared at her. "What do you mean, no dial tone?"

"Just what I said. The line must be down somewhere. We can't call out."

"Great. Just fucking great." Anger mixed with fear flashed across his face, and for a moment he looked like the Robert of old. "What do we do now?"

"We have a cup of coffee and something to eat; then we get in my Jeep and drive to town and tell the police what's happened. After that it's in their hands."

"Shouldn't we go now?"

"Frankly, until I get some coffee into me I won't be in a fit state to drive anywhere, and I'd be surprised if you're any different. And the police won't be able to start a search until morning; another half an hour or so isn't going to make much difference now."

Robert looked at her bleakly. "I guess not," he said finally.

She busied herself with the ritual of making coffee. As she measured and poured, something caught her eye at the window, and she looked up automatically.

A face was staring in at her.

She gave a brief, choked cry, and dropped the teaspoon, which clattered on to the counter. It took her a moment to realise that what she saw was her own reflection, framed in the darkness of the window and what lay beyond. That was all it could be. There was no one out there.

*But she had seen something at the window, out of the corner of her eye, before she looked up.* No; it had been a reflection of something in the room. The cabin was brightly lit, and the windows were acting like mirrors.

From the front of the cabin the wind chimes rang.

Peggy was suddenly conscious of feeling exposed. The little cabin, lights streaming out the windows into the darkness, did not belong here; it was an intruder, and therefore a target. She turned to Robert.

"Close the curtains."

"What?"

She pointed to the picture windows overlooking the valley. "Leave the windows open, but close the curtains."

He did as she asked, while Peggy reached for the blind cord by the kitchen window. The Venetian blinds rattled into place. *That's better,* she thought, and took the coffee in to the living-room.

They sat and sipped, both unconsciously seeking refuge in this ordinary, everyday act. There was silence between them, for there was nothing to be said, or nothing they wanted to say. The wind chimes were louder now, the only sound in the vast expanse around them. The only sound. . . .

A thought which had been at the back of Peggy's mind for some time came into focus then, and she looked up, listening intently. She placed her cup on the table in front of her so hard that coffee sloshed over the side. Robert looked up, startled.

"What . . ." he began, but Peggy held up her hand.

"Listen!" she whispered urgently. Robert looked at her, puzzled. "What do you hear? Tell me. . . ."

Robert tried to concentrate. "Nothing," he said finally. "Just that chiming noise, that's all. Why, did you hear something? Do you think it's . . ."

"Listen. We can hear the chimes, yes, but there's no wind in the trees; we should be able to hear it in the branches, shouldn't we? And the windows are open, but the curtains aren't moving, they're absolutely still. *So why can we hear the wind chimes, if there isn't a wind?*'

Robert stared at her for a moment, uncomprehending. Then he went pale.

"What are you saying?" he asked; but she saw in his eyes that he already knew the answer, or some of it; enough, anyway.

"I'm saying we have to leave," said Peggy, startled by the firmness in her voice. "Now. Don't bother about the lights. Let's *go.*"

She picked up her purse and keys from the shelf where they lay, and moved to the door. She did not want to go out there, did not want to leave the cabin, and it was only with a tremendous effort of will that she put her hand on the knob and pulled open the wooden door, letting a bright trail of light stream out over the rocky ground. She thought she saw something move at the far end of it, something tall and thin, but she did not, would not look, concentrating instead on walking to the driver's door of the Jeep with her eyes on the ground, walking, not running, she would not run. . . .

"Hey!" Robert's voice rang out behind her, and she turned to see him still on the porch, looking, not towards the Jeep, but towards the paths. She followed his gaze, and in the faint light cast by a three-quarter moon could just see a figure standing silent, twenty yards or so from them.

"Jack!" cried Robert, relief flooding his voice. He stepped off the porch and moved towards the figure. "Hey, man, you had us worried! Where've you been? What happened?"

Peggy felt a trickle of ice down her back. "Robert — Robert, come here," she called out, fear making her voice tremble. "Come here now; we have to go."

He stopped and looked back at her. "Can't you see?" he said, puzzled. "It's Jack!" He turned back to the figure. "C'mon, come inside, get something to eat, tell us what happened. You hurt?"

"Robert!" Peggy's voice cracked like a gunshot. "That isn't Jack. Can't you see? *It isn't Jack.*"

"What do you mean? Of course it is! C'mon over here, man, let Peggy take a look at you, you're frightening her. . . ."

All the time Robert had been moving closer to the figure, which remained motionless and silent. Suddenly, when he was only ten feet away from it, he stopped, and she heard him give a strangled cry.

"What the . . . what are you? What's going on?" Then, higher, broken, like a child, "Peggy, what's happening?" He seemed frozen, and Peggy thought for a moment that she would have to go to him, pull him forcibly to the Jeep, and realised that she could not go any closer to that figure. A warning shot, if she had thought to bring the rifle, might have broken the spell, but it was back in the cabin . . . She wrenched open the driver's door and leaned on the horn with all her might.

The sound made her jump, even though she was expecting it, and the effect on Robert was galvanic. He turned and began moving towards the Jeep in a stumbling, shambling run; as he got closer she could hear him sobbing between breaths, ragged, gasping sobs, and she was glad that she had not been close enough to see the figure clearly.

She had dropped the keys twice from fingers that suddenly felt like dry twigs. Now, on the third try, she slammed the key into the ignition and turned it. Nothing. She turned it again. No response. She tried to turn on the headlights, but there was no answering flare of brightness. The battery was dead, and she realised, deep down in a corner of her mind, that she should have expected this.

Robert turned to her, eyes glittering with panic. "C'mon, get it started, let's go! What are you waiting for?"

"The battery's dead." Her chest was heaving as she tried to bite down the panic welling up inside her. Robert began to moan, a low, keening sound, as Peggy forced her mind back. *Think, think,* she told herself. *There's a way to do this, you know there is, you just have to calm down, remember. . . .*

Len's voice sounded in her ear, so clearly that for a moment she thought he was beside her. "It's not difficult," she heard him say, "as long as it's a standard; automatics are trickier." And she remembered; she had asked him, once, what they'd do if the battery went dead, up here with no other car for miles. "We make sure the battery doesn't go dead," he'd said with a laugh, but when she pressed him — she was serious, it could happen, what would they *do?* — he had replied cheerfully, "Not a problem; just put the clutch in, put it in second, let gravity start to work, let out the clutch, and there you go, easy-peasy. Make sure the ignition's on, and just keep driving for a bit; as long as the engine doesn't stop you'll charge the battery back up."

She had no intention of stopping once she got the engine started.

She took a deep breath. The Jeep was parked on the flat, with the downward slope beginning twenty feet away. She would need help.

"Robert." He was still moaning, looking out the passenger window, and Peggy risked a look too. The figure seemed closer. "Robert! Listen to me!" Nothing. She reached out and shook him, and he turned to her, his eyes wide and scared. She hoped he could hear her.

"You need to get out and push the car," she said, slowly and clearly. He started to say something, and she cut him short. "Just do it, Robert. Do it now."

"I can't get out, I can't, I don't . . ."

"You have to. You can do this, Robert, but you have to hurry. Just to the top of the slope. Twenty feet; then you can get back in."

For a moment she thought that he was going to refuse; then, without a word, he opened his door and half-fell, half-scrambled out. Peggy turned the ignition on, pushed in the clutch, put the Jeep in second, and they began to roll, slowly at first, then faster, Robert pushing with all his strength.

It seemed to take hours to cover the short distance; then Peggy felt the car start to pick up momentum, and Robert jumped in, slamming the passenger door. She said under her breath, "Work, please, work," and let out the clutch.

For one brief, terrible second she thought that it wasn't going to work, that she had done something wrong, missed something out.

Then the engine shuddered into life, and she switched on the head-lights, and they were through the gate and round the curve, and the cabin had disappeared behind them, along with everything else that was waiting in the darkness.

They did not speak during the drive to town. Peggy concentrated on the road with a fierceness that made her head ache, glad she had something to think about other than what they had left, while Robert sat huddled down in his seat. She did not ask him what he had seen, and he did not volunteer any information. The only thing she said, as they drew near the police station, was "Keep to the facts. That's all they want to hear. Nothing else. Do you understand?" And Robert, pale, shaking, had nodded.

They told their story, for the first of several times, and answered questions, together and separately. Peggy did not know exactly what they asked Robert; she gathered, from some of the questions di-rected at her, that he was under suspicion, although in the end noth-ing came of this.

Officialdom swung into action, clearly following the procedures and guidelines laid out for just such a situation. Appeals for help were made; search parties were sent out; a spotter plane was em-ployed. There were more questions, although no more answers. Peggy sometimes wondered where they would fit all the pieces she had not told them: eddies of dust and the ringing of chimes on a windless day, someone (not Buddy Holly) calling her name, the figure they had seen outside the cabin, the battery failures, the phone going dead. She imagined the response if she told the police that they should examine local Native legends and the vanishing of a prospector years earlier, or that she had felt that the hillside was watching her, or that Jack had not disappeared at all, he was still there, watching too, that he had only been looking after Robert.

All the searches came to nothing; no further traces of Jack were found. A casual question to one of the volunteers elicited the infor-mation that the phone in the cabin was working perfectly. Peggy herself did not go back; no one expected a sixty-three-year-old woman to participate in the search, and everyone told her they un-derstood why she preferred to stay in a hotel in town. They did not understand, of course, not at all, but Peggy did not try to explain.

Paul came up as soon as he could. He, too, was very understanding, although he was surprised at his aunt's decision to put the property on the market immediately. She was welcome to stay with him and the family for as long as she needed to, that went without saying; but wasn't she being a bit hasty? Yes, it had been a terrible, tragic event, but perhaps she should wait a bit, hold off making a decision . . . she didn't want to do something she would regret. . . .

But Peggy was insistent. If Paul would go with her while she collected some clothing and personal items, she would be grateful; she would arrange with a moving company for everything else to be packed up and put into storage until she had found somewhere to live. She had clearly made up her mind, and although he did not agree with her, Paul did not argue the point any further.

They went up early in the morning, the first day after the search had been called off. Peggy worked quickly, packing up the things she wanted to take with her, while Paul cleared out the food from the fridge and cupboards. When everything had been loaded into his SUV, he went round the cabin, making sure that everything was shut off and locked up, while Peggy waited outside.

Now, in the daylight, with the sun high overhead and birds wheeling against the blue of the sky, everything looked peaceful. A gentle wind ruffled the branches of the trees, and a piece of paper fluttered along — left by one of the searchers, no doubt. It blew across the grass, and landed in the middle of one of the pathways. Out of habit, she walked over to where it lay, picked it up, and put it in her pocket.

She looked up at the hills above her, then back at the cabin, realising that this was the same spot where she had seen . . . or thought she had seen . . . Jack on the afternoon he had disappeared. She shivered slightly, even though the day was hot, and started towards the SUV, anxious to be gone.

It was as she moved away that she saw it, a glint of something metallic at the edge of the path near her foot. She bent down and picked it up. A Swiss Army watch, silver. Although she knew what she would find, she looked at the face. The hands showed ten past five.

When Paul came out and locked the front door, his aunt was already in the SUV. She did not look back as they drove away.

# PROBOSCIS

## *Laird Barron*

### 1.

After the debacle in British Columbia, we decided to crash the Blue-grass festival. Not we — Cruz. Everybody else just shrugged and said yeah, whatever you say, dude. Like always. Cruz was the alpha-alpha of our motley pack.

We followed the handmade signs onto a dirt road and ended up in a muddy pasture with maybe a thousand other cars and beat-to-hell tourist buses. It was a regular extravaganza — pavilions, a massive stage, floodlights. A bit farther out, they'd built a bonfire, and Dead-Heads were writhing among the cinder-streaked shadows with pagan exuberance. The brisk air swirled heavy scents of marijuana and clove, of electricity and sex.

The amplified ukulele music was giving me a migraine. Too many people smashed together, limbs flailing in paroxysms. Too much white light followed by too much darkness. I'd gone a couple beers over my limit because my face was Novocain-numb and I found myself dancing with some sloe-eyed coed who'd fixed her hair in corn rows. Her shirt said MILK.

She was perhaps a bit prettier than the starlet I'd ruined my marriage with way back in the days of yore, but resembled her in a few details. What were the odds? I didn't even attempt to calculate. A drunken man cheek to cheek with a strange woman under the harvest moon was a tricky proposition.

"Lookin' for somebody, or just rubberneckin'?" The girl had to shout over the hi-fi jug band. Her breath was peppermint and whiskey.

"I lost my friends," I shouted back. A sea of bobbing heads beneath a gulf of night sky and none of them belonged to anyone I knew. Six of us had piled out of two cars and now I was alone. Last of the Mohicans.

The girl grinned and patted my cheek. "You ain't got no friends, Ray-bo."

I tried to ask how she came up with that, but she was squirming and pointing over my shoulder.

"My gawd, look at all those stars, will ya?"

Sure enough the stars were on parade; cold, cruel radiation bleeding across improbable distances. I was more interested in the bikers lurking near the stage and the beer garden. Creepy and mean, spoiling for trouble. I guessed Cruz and Hart would be nearby, copping the vibe, as it were.

The girl asked me what I did and I said I was an actor between jobs. Anything she'd seen? No, probably not. Then I asked her and she said something I didn't quite catch. It was either etymologist or entomologist. There was another thing, impossible to hear. She looked so serious I asked her to repeat it.

"Right through your meninges. Sorta like a siphon."

"What?" I said.

"I guess it's a delicacy. They say it don't hurt much, but I say nuts to that."

"A delicacy?"

She made a face. "I'm goin' to the garden. Want a beer?"

"No, thanks." As it was, my legs were ready to fold. The girl smiled, a wistful imp, and kissed me briefly, chastely. She was swallowed into the masses and I didn't see her again.

After a while I staggered to the car and collapsed. I tried to call Sylvia, wanted to reassure her and Carly that I was okay, but my cell wouldn't cooperate. Couldn't raise my watchdog friend, Rob in LA. He'd be going bonkers too. I might as well have been marooned on a desert island. Modern technology, my ass. I watched the windows shift through a foggy spectrum of pink and yellow. Lulled by the monotone thrum, I slept.

Dreamt of wasp nests and wasps. And rare orchids, coronas tilted towards the awesome bulk of clouds. The flowers were a battery of organic radio telescopes receiving a sibilant communiqué just below my threshold of comprehension.

A mosquito pricked me and when I crushed it, blood ran down my finger, hung from my nail.

## 2.

Cruz drove. He said, "I wanna see the Mima Mounds."

Hart said, "Who's Mima?" He rubbed the keloid on his beefy neck.

Bulletproof glass let in light from a blob of moon. I slumped in the tricked-out back seat, where our prisoner would've been if we'd managed to bring him home. I stared at the grille partition, the leg irons and the doors with no handles. A crusty vein traced black tributaries on the floorboard. Someone had scratched R+G and a fanciful depiction of Ronald Reagan's penis. This was an old car. It reeked of cigarette smoke, of stale beer, of a million exhalations.

Nobody asked my opinion. I'd melted into the background smear.

The brutes were smacked out of their gourds on junk they'd picked up on the Canadian side at the festival. Hart had tossed the bag of syringes and miscellaneous garbage off a bridge before we crossed the border. That was where we'd parted ways with the other guys — Leon, Rufus and Donnie. Donnie was the one who had gotten nicked by a stray bullet in Donkey Creek, earned himself bragging rights if nothing else. Jersey boys, the lot; they were going to take the high road home, maybe catch the rodeo in Montana.

Sunrise forged a pale seam above the distant mountains. We were rolling through certified boondocks, thumping across rickety wooden bridges that could've been thrown down around the Civil War. On either side of busted up two-lane blacktop were overgrown fields and hills dense with maples and poplar. Scotch broom reared on lean stalks, fire-yellow heads lolling hungrily. Scotch broom was Washington's rebuttal to kudzu. It was quietly everywhere, feeding in the cracks of the earth.

Road signs floated nearly extinct; letters faded, or bullet-raddled, dimmed by pollen and sap. Occasionally, dirt tracks cut through high grass to farmhouses. Cars passed us head-on, but not often, and usually local rigs — camouflage-green flatbeds with winches and trailers, two-tone pickups, decrepit jeeps. Nothing with out-of-state plates. I started thinking we'd missed a turn somewhere along the line. Not that I would've broached the subject. By then I'd learned to keep my mouth shut and let nature take its course.

"Do you even know where the hell they are?" Hart said Hart was sour about the battle royale at the wharf. He figured it would give the bean counters an excuse to waffle about the payout for Piers' capture. I suspected he was correct.

"The Mima Mounds?"

"Yeah."

"Nope." Cruz rolled down the window, squirted beechnut over his shoulder, contributing another racing streak to the paint job. He twisted the radio dial and conjured Johnny Cash confessing that he'd "shot a man in Reno just to watch him die."

"Real man'd swallow," Hart said. "Like Josey Wales."

My cell beeped and I didn't catch Cruz' rejoinder. It was Carly. She'd seen the bust on the news and was worried, had been trying to reach me. The report mentioned shots-fired and a wounded person, and I said yeah, one of our guys got clipped in the ankle, but he was okay, I was okay and the whole thing was over. We'd bagged the bad guy and all was right with the world. I promised to be home in a couple of days and told her to say hi to her mom. A wave of static drowned the connection.

I hadn't mentioned that the Canadians contemplated jailing us for various legal infractions and inciting mayhem. Her mother's blood pressure was already sky-high over what Sylvia called my, "midlife adventure." Hard to blame her — it was my youthful "adventures" that set the torch to our unhappy marriage.

What Sylvia didn't know, couldn't know, because I lacked the grit to bare my soul at this late stage of our separation, was during the fifteen-martini lunch meeting with Hart, he'd showed me a few pictures to seal the deal. A roster of smiling teenage girls that could've been Carly's schoolmates. Hart explained in graphic detail what the bad man liked to do to these kids. Right there it became less of an adventure and more of a mini-crusade. I'd been an absentee father for fifteen years. Here was my chance to play Lancelot.

Cruz said he was hungry enough to eat the ass-end of a rhino and Hart said stop and buy breakfast at the greasy spoon coming up on the left, materializing as if by sorcery, so they pulled in and parked alongside a rusted-out Pontiac on blocks. Hart remembered to open the door for me that time. One glimpse of the diner's filthy windows and the coils of dogshit sprinkled across the unpaved lot convinced me I wasn't exactly keen on going in for the special.

But I did.

The place was stamped 1950s from the long counter with a row of shiny black swivel stools and the too-small window booths, dingy Formica peeling at the edges of the tables, to the bubble-screen tv wedged high up in a corner alcove. The tv was flickering with grainy black and white images of a talk show I didn't recognize and couldn't hear because the volume was turned way down. Mercifully I didn't see myself during the commercials.

I slouched at the counter and waited for the waitress to notice me. Took a while — she was busy flirting with Hart and Cruz, who'd squeezed themselves into a booth, and of course they wasted no time in regaling her with their latest exploits as hardcase bounty hunters. By now it was purely mechanical; rote bravado. They were pale as sheets and running on fumes of adrenaline and junk. Oh, how I dreaded the next twenty-four to thirty-six hours.

Their story was edited for heroic effect. My private version played a little differently.

We finally caught the desperado and his best girl in the Maple Leaf Country. After a bit of "slap and tickle," as Hart put it, we handed the miscreants over to the Canadians, more or less intact. Well, the Canadians more or less took possession of the pair.

The bad man was named Russell Piers, a convicted rapist and kidnaper who'd cut a nasty swath across the great Pacific Northwest and British Columbia. The girl was Penny Aldon, a runaway, an orphan, the details varied, but she wasn't important, didn't even drive; was along for the thrill, according to the reports. They fled to a river town, were loitering wharf-side, munching on a fish basket from one of six jillion Vietnamese vendors when the team descended.

Piers proved something of a Boy Scout — always prepared. He yanked a pistol from his waistband and started blazing, but one of him versus six of us only works in the movies and he went down under a swarm of blackjacks, tasers and fists. I ran the hand-cam, got the whole jittering mess on film.

The film.

That was on my mind, sneaking around my subconscious like a night prowler. There was a moment during the scrum when a shiver of light distorted the scene, or I had a near-fainting spell, or who knows. The men on the sidewalk snapped and snarled, hyenas bringing down a wounded lion. Foam spattered the lens. I swayed, almost tumbled amid the violence. And Piers looked directly at me. Grinned at me. A big dude, even bigger than the troglodytes clinging to him, he had Cruz in a headlock, was ready to crush bones, to ravage flesh, to feast. A beast all right, with long, greasy hair, powerful hands scarred by prison tattoos, gold in his teeth. Inhuman, definitely. He wasn't a lion, though. I didn't know what kingdom he belonged to.

Somebody cold-cocked Piers behind the ear and he switched off, slumped like a manikin that'd been bowled over by the holiday stampede.

Flutter, flutter and all was right with the world, relatively speaking. Except my bones ached and I was experiencing a not-so-mild wave of paranoia that hung on for hours. Never completely dissipated, even here in the sticks at a godforsaken hole in the wall while my associates preened for an audience of one.

Cruz and Hart had starred on *Cops* and *America's Most Wanted*; they were celebrity experts. Too loud, the three of them honking and squawking, especially my ex brother-in-law. Hart resembled a hog that decided to put on a dirty shirt and steel toe boots and go on its hind legs. Him being high as a kite wasn't helping. Sylvia tried to warn me, she'd known what her brother was about since they were kids knocking around on the wrong side of Des Moines.

I didn't listen. *"C'mon, Sylvie, there's a book in this. Hell, a Movie of the Week!"* Hart was on the inside of a rather seamy yet wholly marketable industry. He had a friend who had a friend who had a general idea where Mad Dog Piers was running. Money in the bank. See you in a few weeks, hold my calls.

"Watcha want, hon?" The waitress, a strapping lady with a tag spelling Victoria, poured translucent coffee into a cup that suggested the dishwasher wasn't quite up to snuff. Like all pro waitresses she pulled off this trick without looking away from my face. "I know you?" And when I politely smiled and reached for the sugar, she kept coming, frowning now as her brain began to labor. "You somebody? An actor or somethin'?"

I shrugged in defeat. "Uh, yeah. I was in a couple tv movies. Small roles. Long time ago."

Her face animated, a craggy talking tree. "Hey! You were on that comedy, one with the blind guy and his seein' eye dog. Only the guy was a con man or somethin', wasn't really blind and his dog was an alien or somethin', a robot, don't recall. Yeah, I remember you. What happened to that show?"

"Cancelled." I glanced longingly through the screen door to our ugly Chevy.

"Ray does shampoo ads," Hart said. He said something to Cruz and they cracked up.

"Milk of magnesia!" Cruz said. "And 'If you suffer from erectile dysfunction, now there's an answer!'" He delivered the last in a passable radio announcer's voice, although I'd heard him do better. He was hoarse.

The sun went behind a cloud, but Victoria still wanted my auto-graph, just in case I made a comeback, or got killed in a sensational fashion and then my signature would be worth something. She even dragged Sven the cook out to shake my hand and he did it with the dedication of a zombie following its mistress's instructions before shambling back to whip up eggs and hash for my comrades.

The coffee tasted like bleach.

The talk show ended and the next program opened with a still shot of a field covered by mossy hummocks and blackberry thickets. The black and white imagery threw me. For a moment I didn't regis-ter the car parked between mounds was familiar. Our boxy Chevy with the driver-side door hanging ajar, mud-encrusted plates, tail-lights blinking SOS.

A grey hand reached from inside, slammed the door. A hand? Or something like a hand? A B-movie prosthesis? Too blurry, too fast to be certain.

Victoria changed the channel to *All My Children*.

### 3.

Hart drove.

Cruz navigated. He tilted a road map, trying to follow the dots and dashes. Victoria had drawled a convoluted set of directions to the Mima Mounds, a one-star tourist attraction about thirty miles over. Cruise on through Poger Rock and head west. Real easy drive if you took the local shortcuts and suchlike.

Not an unreasonable detour; I-5 wasn't far from the site — we could do the tourist bit and still make the Portland night scene. That was Cruz' sales pitch. Kind of funny, really. I wondered at the man's sudden fixation on geological phenomena. He was a NASCAR and *Soldier of Fortune Magazine* type personality. Hart fit the profile too, for that matter. Damned world was turning upside down.

It was getting hot. Cracks in the windshield dazzled and danced.

The boys debated cattle mutilations and the inarguable com-plicity of the Federal government regarding the Grey Question and how the moon landing was fake and remember that flick from the 1970s, *Capricorn One*, goddamned if O.J. wasn't one of the astronauts. Freakin' hilarious.

I unpacked the camera, thumbed the playback button, and relived the Donkey Creek fracas. Penny said to me, "Reduviidea — any of a species of large insects that feed on the blood of prey insects and some mammals. They are considered extremely beneficial by agricultural professionals." Her voice was made of tin and lagged behind her lip movements, like a badly dubbed foreign film. She stood on the periphery of the action, scrawny fingers pleating the wispy fabric of a blue sundress. She was smiling. "The indices of primate emotional thresholds indicate the [*click-click*] process is traumatic. However, point oh-two percent vertebrae harvest corresponds to non-[*click-click*] purposes. As an X haplotype you are a primary source of [*click-click*]. Lucky you!"

"Jesus!" I muttered and dropped the camera on the seat. *Are you talkin' to me?* I stared at too many trees while Robert Deniro did his mirror schtick as a low frequency monologue in the corner of my mind. Unlike Deniro, I'd never carried a gun. The guys wouldn't even loan me a taser.

"What?" Cruz said in a tone that suggested he'd almost jumped out of his skin. He glared through the partition, olive features drained to ash. Giant drops of sweat sparkled and dripped from his broad cheeks. The light wrapped his skull, halo of an angry saint. Withdrawals something fierce, I decided.

I shook my head, waited for the magnifying glass of his displeasure to swing back to the road map. When it was safe I hit the playback button. Same scene on the view panel. This time when Penny entered the frame she pointed at me and intoned in a robust, Slavic accent, "Supercalifragilisticexpialidocious is Latin for a death god of a primitive Mediterranean culture. Their civilization was buried in mudslides caused by unusual seismic activity. If you say it loud enough —" I hit the kill button. My stomach roiled with rancid coffee and incipient motion-sickness.

Third time's a charm, right? I played it back again. The entire sequence was erased. Nothing but deep-space black with jags of silvery light at the edges. In the middle, skimming by so swiftly I had to freeze things to get a clear image, was Piers with his lips nuzzling Cruz' ear, and Cruz' face was corpse-slack. And for an instant, a microsecond, the face was Hart's too; one of those three-dee poster illusions where the object changes depending on the angle. Then, more nothingness, and an odd feedback noise that faded in and out, like Gregorian monks chanting a litany in reverse.

Okay. ABC time.

I'd reviewed the footage shortly after the initial capture in Canada. There was nothing unusual about it. We spent a few hours at the police station answering a series of polite yet penetrating questions. I assumed our cameras would be confiscated, but the inspector simply examined our equipment in the presence of a couple suits from a legal office. Eventually the inspector handed everything back with a stern admonishment to leave dangerous criminals to the authorities. Amen to that.

Had a cop tampered with the camera, doctored it in some way? I wasn't a film-maker, didn't know much more than point and shoot and change the batteries when the little red light started blinking. So, yeah, Horatio, it was possible someone had screwed with the recording. Was that likely? The answer was no — not unless they'd also managed to monkey with the television at the diner. More probable one of my associates had spiked the coffee with a miracle agent and I was hallucinating. Seemed out of character for those greedy bastards, even for the sake of a practical joke on their third wheel — dope was expensive and it wasn't like we were expecting a big payday.

The remaining options weren't very appealing.

My cell whined, a dentist's drill in my shirt pocket. It was Rob Fries from his patio office in Gardena Rob was tall, bulky, pink on top and garbed according to his impression of what Miami vice cops might've worn in a bygone era, such as the '80s. Rob also had the notion he was my agent despite the fact I'd fired him ten years ago after he handed me one too-many scripts for laxative testimonials. I almost broke into tears when I heard his voice on the buzzing line. "Man, am I glad you called!" I said loudly enough to elicit another scowl from Cruz.

"Hola, compadre. What a splash y'all made on page 16. '*American Yahoos Run Amok!*' goes the headline, which is a quote of the Calgary rag. Too bad the stupid bastards let our birds fly the coop. Woulda been better press if they fried 'em. Well, they don't have the death penalty, but you get the point. Even so, I see a major motion picture deal in the works. Mucho dinero, Ray, buddy!"

"Fly the coop? What are you talking about?"

"Uh, you haven't heard? Piers and the broad walked. Hell, they probably beat you outta town."

"You better fill me in." Indigestion was eating the lining of my esophagus.

"Real weird story. Some schmuck from Central Casting accidentally turned 'em loose. The paperwork got misfiled or some-such bullshit. The muckety-mucks are po'd. Blows your mind, don't it?"

"Right," I said in my actor's tone. I fell back on this when my mind was in neutral but etiquette dictated a polite response. Up front, Cruz and Hart were bickering, hadn't caught my exclamation. No way was I going to illuminate them regarding this development — Christ, they'd almost certainly consider pulling a u-turn and speeding back to Canada. The home office would be calling any second now to relay the news; probably had been trying to get through for hours — Hart hated phones, usually kept his stashed in the glovebox.

There was a burst of chittery static. "— returning your call. Keep getting the answering service. You won't believe it — I was having lunch with this chick used to be one of Johnny Carson's secretaries, yeah? And she said her best friend is shacking with an exec who just frickin' adored you in *Clancy & Spot*. Frickin' adored you! I told my gal pal to pass the word you were riding along on this bounty hunter gig, see what shakes loose."

"Oh, thanks, Rob. Which exec?"

"Lemmesee — uh, Harry Buford. Remember him? He floated deals for the *Alpha Team*, some other stuff. Nice as hell. Frickin' adores you, buddy."

"Harry Buford? Looks like the Elephant Man's older, fatter brother, loves pastels and lives in Mexico half the year because he's fond of underage Chicano girls? Did an expose piece on the evils of Hollywood, got himself blackballed? That the guy?"

"Well, yeah. But he's still got an ear to the ground. And he frickin' —"

"Adores me. Got it. Tell your girlfriend we'll all do lunch, or whatever."

"Anywhoo, how you faring with the gorillas?"

"Um, great. We're on our way to see the Mima Mounds."

"What? You on a nature study?"

"Cruz' idea."

"The Mima Mounds. Wow. Never heard of them. Burial grounds, huh?"

"Earth heaves, I guess. They've got them all over the world — Norway, South America, Eastern Washington — I don't know where all. I lost the brochure."

"Cool." The silence hung for a long moment. "Your buddies wanna see some, whatchyacallem —?"

"Glacial deposits."

"They wanna look at some rocks instead of hitting a strip club? No bullshit?"

"Um, yeah."

It was easy to imagine Rob frowning at his flip-flops propped on the patio table while he stirred the ice in his rum and coke and tried to do the math. "Have a swell time, then."

"You do me a favor?"

"Yo, bro'. Hit me."

"Go on the Net and look up X haplotype. Do it right now, if you've got a minute."

"X-whatsis?"

I spelled it and said, "Call me back, okay? If I'm out of area, leave a message with the details."

"Be happy to." There was a pause as he scratched pen to pad. "Some kinda new meds, or what?"

"Or what, I think."

"Uh, huh. Well, I'm just happy the Canucks didn't make you an honorary citizen, eh. I'm dying to hear the scoop."

"I'm dying to dish it. I'm losing my signal, gotta sign off."

He said not to worry, bro', and we disconnected. I worried anyway.

## 3.

Sure enough, Hart's phone rang a bit later and he exploded in a stream of repetitious profanity and dented the dash with his ham hock of a fist. He was still bubbling when we pulled into Poger Rock for gas and fresh directions Cruz, on the other hand, accepted the news of Russell Piers' "early parole" with a Zen detachment demonstrably contrary to his nature.

"Screw it. Let's drink," was his official comment.

Poger Rock was sunk in a hollow about fifteen miles south of the state capitol in Olympia. It wasn't impressive — a dozen or so antiquated buildings moldering along the banks of a shallow creek posted with NO SHOOTING signs. Everything was peeling, rusting or collapsing toward the center of the earth. Only the elementary school loomed incongruously — a utopian brick and tile structure set back and slightly elevated, fresh paint glowing through the alders and dogwoods. Aliens might have landed and dedicated a monument.

Cruz filled up at a mom and pop gas station with the prehistoric pumps that took an eon to dribble forth their fuel. I bought some jerky and a carton of milk with a past-due expiration date to soothe my churning guts. The lady behind the counter had yellowish hair and wore a button with a fuzzy picture of a toddler in a bib. She smiled nervously as she punched keys and furiously smoked a Pall Mall. Didn't recognize me, thank God.

Cruz pushed through the door, setting off the ding-dong alarm. His gaze jumped all over the place and his chambray shirt was molded to his chest as if he'd been doused with a water hose. He crowded past me, trailing the odor of armpit funk and cheap cologne, grunted at the cashier and shoved his credit card across the counter.

I raised my hand to block the sun when I stepped outside. Hart was leaning on the hood. "We're gonna mosey over to the bar for a couple brewskis." He coughed his smoker's cough, spat in the gravel near a broken jar of marmalade. Bees darted among the wreckage.

"What about the Mima Mounds?"

"They ain't goin' anywhere. 'Sides, it ain't time, yet."

"Time?"

Hart's ferret-pink eyes narrowed and he smiled slightly. He finished his cigarette and lighted another from the smoldering butt. "Cruz says it ain't."

"Well, what does that mean? It 'ain't time'?"

"I dunno, Ray-bo. I dunno fuckall. Why'nchya ask Cruz?"

"Okay." I took a long pull of tepid milk while I considered the latest developments in what was becoming the most bizarre road trip of my life. "How are you feeling?"

"Groovy."

"You look like hell." I could still talk to him, after a fashion, when he was separated from Cruz. And I lied, "Sylvia's worried."

"What's she worried about?"

I shrugged, let it hang. Impossible to read his face, his swollen eyes. In truth, I wasn't sure I completely recognized him, this wasted hulk swaying against the car, features glazed into gargoyle contortions.

Hart nodded wisely, suddenly illuminated regarding a great and abiding mystery of the universe. His smile returned.

I glanced back, saw Cruz' murky shadow drifting in the station window.

"Man, what are we doing out here? We could be in Portland by three." What I wanted to say was, let's jump in the car and shag ass for California. Leave Cruz in the middle of the parking lot holding his pecker and swearing eternal vengeance for all I cared.

"Anxious to get going on your book, huh?"

"If there's a book. I'm not much of a writer. I don't even know if we'll get a movie out of this mess."

"Ain't much of an actor, either." He laughed and slapped my shoulder with an iron paw to show he was just kidding. "Hey, lemme tell'ya. Did'ya know Cruz studied geology at UCLA? He did. Real knowledgeable about glaciers an' rocks. All that good shit. Thought he was gonna work for the oil companies up in Alaska. Make some fat stacks. Ah, but you know how it goes, doncha, Ray-bo?"

"He graduated UCLA?" I tried not to sound astonished. It had been the University of Washington for me. The home of medicine, which wasn't my specialty, according to the proctors. Political science and drama were the last exits.

"Football scholarship. Hard hittin' safety with a nasty attitude. They fuckin' grow on trees in the ghetto."

That explained some things. I was inexplicably relieved.

Cruz emerged, cutting a plug of tobacco with his pocket knife. "C'mon, H. I'm parched." And precisely as a cowboy would unhitch his horse to ride across the street, he fired the engine and rumbled the one quarter block to Moony's Tavern and parked in a diagonal slot between a hay truck and a station wagon plastered with anti-Democrat, pro-gun bumper stickers.

Hart asked if I planned on joining them and I replied maybe in a while, I wanted to stretch my legs. The idea of entering that sweltering cavern and bellying up to the bar with the lowlife regulars and mine own dear chums made my stomach even more unhappy.

I grabbed my valise from the car and started walking. I walked along the street, past a row of dented mailboxes, rust-red flags erect; an outboard motor repair shop with a dusty police cruiser in front;

the Poger Rock Grange, which appeared abandoned because its windows were boarded and where they weren't, kids had broken them with rocks and bottles, and maybe the same kids had drawn 666 and other satanic symbols on the whitewashed planks, or maybe real live Satanists did the deed; Bob's Liquor Mart, which was a corrugated shed with bars on the tiny windows; the Laundromat, full of tired women in oversized tee-shirts, and screeching, dirty-faced kids racing among the machinery while an A.M. radio broadcast a Rush Limbaugh rerun; and a trailer loaded with half-rotted firewood for 75 BUCKS! I finally sat on a rickety bench under some trees near the lone stoplight, close enough to hear it clunk through its cycle.

I drew a manila envelope from the valise, spread sloppy typed police reports and disjointed photographs beside me. The breeze stirred and I used a rock for a paper weight.

A whole slew of the pictures featured Russell Piers in various poses, mostly mug shots, although a few had been snapped during more pleasant times. There was even one of him and a younger brother standing in front of the Space Needle. The remaining photos were of Piers' latest girlfriend — Penny Aldon, the girl from Allen Town. Skinny, pimply, mouthful of braces. A flower child with a suitably vacuous smirk.

Something cold and nasty turned over in me as I studied the haphazard data, the disheveled photo collection. I felt the pattern, unwholesome as damp cobwebs against my skin. Felt it, yet couldn't put a name to it, couldn't put my finger on it and my heart began pumping dangerously and I looked away, thought of Carly instead, and how I'd forgotten to call her on her seventh birthday because I was in Spain with some friends at a Lipizzaner exhibition. Except, I hadn't forgotten, I was wired for sound from a snort of primo Colombian blow and the thought of dialing that long string of international numbers was too much for my circuits.

Ancient history, as they say. Those days of fast-living and superstar dreams belonged to another man, and he was welcome to them.

Waiting for cars to drive past so I could count them, I had an epiphany. I realized the shabby buildings were cardboard and the people milling here and there at opportune junctures were macaroni and glue. Dull blue construction paper sky and cotton ball clouds. And I wasn't really who I thought of myself as — I was an ant left over from a picnic raid, awaiting some petulant child god to put his boot down on my pathetic diorama existence.

My cell rang and an iceberg calved in my chest.

"Hey, Ray, you got any Indian in ya?" Rob asked.

I mulled that as a brand new Cadillac convertible paused at the light. A pair of yuppie tourists mildly argued about directions — a man behind the wheel in stylish wraparound shades and a polo shirt, and a woman wearing a floppy, wide-brimmed hat like the Queen Mum favored. They pretended not to notice me. The woman pointed right and they went right, leisurely, up the hill and beyond. "Comanche," I said. Next was a shiny green van loaded with Asian kids. Sign on the door said THE EVERGREEN STATE COLLEGE. It turned right and so did the one that came after. "About one thirty- second. Am I eligible for some reparation money? Did I inherit a casino?"

"Where the hell did the Comanche sneak in?"

"Great grandma. Tough old bird. Didn't like me much. Sent me a straight razor for Christmas. I was nine."

Rob laughed. "Cra-zee. I did a search and came up with a bunch of listings for genetic research. Lemme check this . . ." he shuffled paper close to the receiver, cleared his throat. "Turns out this X haplogroup has to do with mitochondrial DNA, genes passed down on the maternal side — and an X-haplogroup is a specific subdivision or cluster. The university wags are tryin' to use female lineage to trace tribal migrations and so forth. Something like three percent of Native Americans, Europeans and Basque belong to the X-group. Least, according to the stuff I thought looked reputable. Says here there's lots of controversy about its significance. Usual academic crap. Whatch you were after?"

"I don't know. Thanks, though."

"You okay, bud? You sound kinda odd."

"Shucks, Rob, I've been trapped in a car with two redneck psychos for weeks. Might be getting to me, I'll admit."

"Whoa, sorry. Sylvia called and started going on —"

"Everything's hunky-dory, All right?"

"Cool, bro." Rob's tone said nothing was truly cool, but he wasn't in any position to press the issue. There'd be a serious Q&A when I returned, no doubt about it.

Cruz' dad was Basque, wasn't he? Hart was definitely of good, solid German stock only a couple generations removed from the mother land.

Stop me if you've heard this one — a Spaniard, a German and a Comanche walk into a bar —

After we said goodbye, I dialed my ex and got her machine, caught myself and hung up as it was purring. It occurred to me then, what the pattern was, and I stared dumbly down at the fractured portraits of Penny and Piers as their faces were dappled by sunlight falling through a maze of leaves.

I laughed, bitter.

How in God's name had they ever fooled us into thinking they were people at all? The only things missing from this farce were strings and zippers, a boom mike.

I stuffed the photos and the reports into the valise, stood in the weeds at the edge of the asphalt. My blood still pulsed erratically. Shadows began to crawl deep and blue between the buildings and the trees and in the wake of low-gliding cumulus clouds. Moony's Tavern waited, back there in the golden dust, and Cruz' Chevy before it, stolid as a coffin on the altar.

Something was happening, wasn't it? This thing that was happening, had been happening, could it follow me home if I cut and ran? Would it follow me to Sylvia and Carly?

No way to be certain, no way to tell if I had simply fallen off my rocker — maybe the heat had cooked my brain, maybe I was having a long-overdue nervous breakdown. Maybe, shit. The sinister shape of the world contracted around me, gleamed like the curves of a great killing jar. I heard the lid screwing tight in the endless ultraviolet collisions, the white drone of insects.

I turned right and walked up the hill.

4.

About two hours later, a guy in a vintage farm truck stopped. The truck had cruised by me twice, once going toward town, then on the way back. And here it was again. I hesitated; nobody braked for hitchhikers unless the hitcher was a babe in tight jeans.

I thought of Piers and Penny, their expressions in the video, drinking us with their smiling mouths, marking us. And if that was true, we'd been weighed, measured and marked, what was the implication? Piers and Penny were two from among a swarm. Was it open season?

The driver studied me with unsettling intensity, his beady eyes obscured by thick, black-rimmed glasses. He beckoned.

My legs were tired already and the back of my neck itched with sunburn. Also, what did it matter anyway? If I were doing anything besides playing out the hand, I would've gone into Olympia and caught a southbound Greyhound. I climbed aboard.

George was a retired civil engineer. Looked the part — crewcut, angular face like a piece of rock, wore a dress shirt with a row of clipped pens and a tie flung over his shoulder, and polyester slacks. He kept NPR on the radio at a mumble. Gripped the wheel with both gnarled hands.

Seemed familiar — a figure dredged from memories of scientists and engineers of my grandfather's generation. He could've *been* my grandfather. I didn't study him too closely.

George asked me where I was headed. I said Los Angeles and he gave me a glance that said LA was in the opposite direction. I told him I wanted to visit the Mima Mounds — since I was in the neighborhood.

There was a heavy silence. A vast and unfathomable pressure built in the cab. At last George said, "Why, they're only a couple miles farther on. Do you know anything about them?"

I admitted that I didn't and he said he figured as much. He told me the Mounds were declared a national monument back in the '60s; the subject of scholarly debate and wildly inaccurate hypotheses. He hoped I wouldn't be disappointed — they weren't glamorous compared to real natural wonders such as Niagara Falls, the Grand Canyon or the California Redwoods. The preserve was on the order of five hundred acres, but that was nothing. The Mounds had stretched for miles and miles in the old days. The land grabs of the 1890s reduced the phenomenon to a pocket, surrounded it with rundown farms, pastures and cows. The ruins of America's agrarian era.

I said that it would be impossible to disappoint me.

George turned at a wooden marker with a faded white arrow. A nicely paved single lane wound through temperate rain forest for a mile and looped into a parking lot occupied by the Evergreen vans and a few other vehicles. There was a fence with a gate and beyond that, the vague border of a clearing. Official bulletins were posted every six feet, prohibiting dogs, alcohol and firearms.

"Sure you want me to leave you here?"

"I'll be fine."

George rustled, his clothes chitin sloughing. "X marks the spot."

I didn't regard him, my hand frozen on the door handle, more than slightly afraid the door wouldn't open. Time slowed, got stuck in molasses. "I know a secret, George."

"What kind of secret?" George said, too close, as if he'd leaned in tight.

The hairs stiffened on the nape of my neck. I swallowed and closed my eyes. "I saw a picture in a biology textbook. There was this bug, looked exactly like a piece of bark, and it was barely touching a beetle with its nose. The one that resembled bark was what entomologists call an assassin bug and it was draining the beetle dry. Know how? It poked the beetle with a razor sharp beak thingy —"

"A rostrum, you mean."

"Exactly. A rostrum, or a proboscis, depending on the species. Then the assassin bug injected digestive fluids, think hydrochloric acid, and sucked the beetle's insides out."

"How lovely," George said.

"No struggle, no fuss, just a couple bugs sitting on a branch. So I'm staring at this book and thinking the only reason the beetle got caught was because it fell for the old piece of bark trick, and then I realized that's how lots of predatory bugs operate. They camouflage themselves and sneak up on hapless critters to do their thing."

"Isn't that the way of the universe?"

"And I wondered if that theory only applied to insects."

"What do you suppose?"

"I suspect that theory applies to everything."

Zilch from George. Not even the rasp of his breath.

"Bye, George. Thanks for the ride." I pushed hard to open the door and jumped down; moved away without risking a backward glance. My knees were unsteady. After I passed through the gate and approached a bend in the path, I finally had the nerve to check the parking lot. George's truck was gone.

I kept going, almost falling forward.

The trees thinned to reveal the humpbacked plain from the tv picture. Nearby was a concrete bunker shaped like a squat mushroom — a park information kiosk and observation post. It was papered with articles and diagrams under plexiglass. Throngs of brightly-clad Asian kids buzzed around the kiosk, laughing over the wrinkled flyers, pointing cameras and chattering enthusiastically. A shaggy guy in a hemp sweater, presumably the professor, lectured a couple of wind-burned ladies who obviously ran marathons in their spare time. The ladies were enthralled.

I mounted the stairs to the observation platform and scanned the environs. As George predicted, the view wasn't inspiring. The mounds spread beneath my vantage, none greater than five or six feet in height and largely engulfed in blackberry brambles. Collectively, the hillocks formed a dewdrop hemmed by mixed forest, and toward the narrowing end, a dilapidated trailer court, its structures rendered toys by perspective. The paved footpath coiled unto obscurity.

A radio-controlled airplane whirred in the trailer court airspace. The plane's engine throbbed, a shrill metronome. I squinted against the glare, couldn't discern the operator. My skull ached I slumped, hugged the valise to my chest, pressed my cheek against damp concrete, and drowsed. Shoes scraped along the platform. Voices occasionally floated by. Nobody challenged me, my derelict posture. I hadn't thought they would. Who'd dare disturb the wildlife in this remote enclave?

My sluggish daydreams were phantoms of the field, negatives of its buckled hide and stealthy plants, and the whispered words *Eastern Washington*, *South America*, *Norway*. Scientists might speculate about the geological method of the mounds' creation until doomsday. I knew this place and its sisters were unnatural as monoliths hacked from rude stone by primitive hands and stacked like so many dominos in the uninhabited spaces of the globe. What were they? Breeding grounds, feeding grounds, shrines? Or something utterly alien, something utterly incomprehensible to match the blighted fascination that dragged me ever closer and consumed my will to flee.

Hart's call yanked me from the doldrums. He was drunk. "You shoulda stuck around, Ray-bo. We been huntin' everywhere for you. Cruz ain't in a nice mood." The connection was weak, a transmission from the dark side of Pluto. Batteries were dying.

"Where are you?" I rubbed my gummy eyes and stood.

"We're at the goddamned Mounds. Where are *you*?"

I spied a tiny glint of moving metal. The Chevy rolled across the way where the road and the mobile homes intersected. I smiled — Cruz hadn't been looking for me; he'd been trolling around on the wrong side of the park, frustrated because he'd missed the entrance. As I watched, the car slowed and idled in the middle of the road. "I'm here."

The cell phone began to click like a Geiger counter that'd hit the mother lode. Bits of fiddle music pierced the garble.

The car jolted from a savage tromp on the gas and listed ditchward. It accelerated, jounced and bounded into the field, described a haphazard arc in my direction. I had a momentary terror that they'd seen me atop the tower, were coming for me, were planning some unhinged brand of retribution. But no, the distance was too great. I was no more than a speck, if I was anything. Soon, the car lurched behind the slope of intervening hillocks and didn't emerge.

"Hart, are you there?"

The clicking intensified and abruptly chopped off, replaced by smooth, bottomless static. Deep sea squeals and warbles began to filter through. Bees humming. A castrati choir on a gramophone. Giggling. Someone, perhaps Cruz, whispering a Latin prayer. I was grateful when the phone made an electronic protest and expired. I hurled it over the side.

The college crowd had disappeared. Gone too, the professor and his admirers. I might've joined the migration if I hadn't spotted the cab of George's truck mostly hidden by a tree. It was the only rig in the parking lot. I couldn't tell if anyone was behind the wheel.

The sun hung low and fat, reddening as it sank. The breeze had cooled. It plucked at my hair, dried my sweat, chilled me a little. I listened for the roar of the Chevy, buried to the axles in loose dirt, high-centered on a stump; or perhaps they'd abandoned the vehicle. Thus I strained to pick my companions from among the blackberry patches and softly undulating clumps of scotch broom which had invaded this place too.

Quiet.

I went down the stairs and let the path take me. I went as a man in a stupor, my muscles lethargic with dread. The lizard subprocessor in my brain urged me to sprint for the highway, to scuttle into a burrow. It possessed a hint of what waited over the hill, had possibly witnessed this melodrama many times before. I whistled a dirge through clenched teeth and the mounds closed ranks behind me.

Ahead, came the dull clank of a slamming door.

The car was stalled at the foot of a steep slope, its hood buried in a tangle of brush. The windows were dark as a muddy aquarium and festooned with fleshy creepers and algid scum.

I took root a few yards from the car, noting that the engine was dead, yet the vehicle rocked on its springs from some vigorous activity. A rhythmic motion that caused metal to complain. The brake lights stuttered.

Hart's doughy face materialized on the passenger side, bumped against the glass with the dispassion of a pale, exotic fish, and withdrew, descending into a marine trench. His forehead left a starry impact. Someone's palm smacked the rear window, hung there, fingers twitching.

I retreated. Ran, more like. I may have shrieked. Somewhere along the line the valise flew open and its contents spilled — a welter of files, the argyle socks Carly gave me for Father's Day, my toiletries. A handful of photographs pinwheeled in a gust. I dropped the bag. Ungainly, panicked, I didn't get far, tripped and collapsed as the sky blackened and a high-pitched keening erupted from several locations simultaneously. In moments all ambient light had been sucked away; I couldn't see the thorny bush gouging my neck as I wriggled for cover, couldn't make out my own hand before my eyes.

The keening ceased. Peculiar echoes bounced in its wake, gave me the absurd sensation of lying on a sound stage with the kliegs shut off. I received the impression of movement around my hunkered self, although I didn't hear footsteps. I shuddered, pressed my face deeper into musty soil. Ants investigated my pants cuffs.

Cruz called my name from the throat of a distant tunnel. I knew it wasn't him and kept silent. He cursed me and giggled the unpleasant giggle I'd heard on the phone. Hart tried to coax me out, but this imitation was even worse. They went down the entire list and despite everything I was tempted to answer when Carly began crying and hiccupping and begging me to help her, daddy please, in a baby girl voice she hadn't owned for several years. I stuffed my fist in my mouth, held on while the chorus drifted here and there and eventually receded into the buzz and chirr of field life.

The sun flickered on and the world was restored piecemeal — one root, one stump, one hill at a time. My head swam; reminded me of waking from anesthesia.

Dusk was blooming when I crept from the bushes and tasted the air, cocked an ear for predators. The Chevy was there, shimmering in the twilight. Motionless now.

I could've crouched in my blind forever, wild-eyed as a hare run to ground in a ruined shirt and piss-stained slacks. But it was getting cold and I was thirsty, so I slunk across the park at an angle that took me to the road near the trailer court. I went, casting glances over my shoulder for pursuit that never came.

5.

I told a retiree sipping ice tea in a lawn chair that my car had broken down and he let me use his phone to call a taxi. If he witnessed Cruz crash the Chevy into the Mounds, he wasn't saying. The police didn't show while I waited and that said enough about the situation.

The taxi driver was a stolid Samoan who proved not the least bit interested in my frightful appearance or talking. He drove way too fast for comfort, if I'd been in a rational frame of mind, and dropped me at the Greyhound depot in downtown Olympia.

I wandered inside past the rag-tag gaggle of modern gypsies which inevitably haunted these terminals, studied the big board while the ticket agent pursed her lips in distaste. Her expression certified me as one of the unwashed mob.

I picked Seattle at random, bought a ticket. The ticket got me the key to the restroom, where I splashed my welted flesh, combed cat tails from my hair and looked almost human again. Almost. The fluorescent tube crackled and sizzled, threatened to plunge the crummy toilet into darkness, and in the discotheque flashes, my haggard face seemed strange.

The bus arrived an hour late and it was crammed. I shared a seat with a middle-aged woman wearing a shawl and scads of costume jewelry. Her ivory skin was hard and she smelled of chlorine. I didn't imagine she wanted to sit by me, judging from the flare of her nostrils, the crimp of her over-glossed mouth.

Soon the bus was chugging into the wasteland of night and the lights clicked off row by row as passengers succumbed to sleep. Except some guy near the front who left his overhead lamp on to read, and me. I was too exhausted to close my eyes.

I surprised myself by crying.

And the woman surprised me again by murmuring, "Hush, hush, dear. Hush, hush." She patted my trembling shoulder. Her hand lingered.

# HAECKEL'S TALE

## *Clive Barker*

Purrucker died last week, after a long illness. I never much liked the man, but the news of his passing still saddened me. With him gone I am now the last of our little group; there's no one left with whom to talk over the old times. Not that I ever did; at least not with him. We followed such different paths, after Hamburg. He became a physicist, and lived mostly, I think, in Paris. I stayed here in Germany, and worked with Herman Helmholtz, mainly working in the area of mathematics, but occasionally offering my contribution to other disciplines. I do not think I will be remembered when I go. Herman was touched by greatness; I never was. But I found comfort in the cool shadow of his theories. He had a clear mind, a precise mind. He refused to let sentiment or superstition into his view of the world. I learned a good deal from that.

And yet now, as I think back over my life to my early twenties (I'm two years younger than the century, which turns in a month), it is not the times of intellectual triumph that I find myself remembering; it is not Helmholtz's analytical skills, or his gentle detachment.

In truth, it is little more than the slip of a story that's on my mind right now. But it refuses to go away, so I am setting it down here, as a way of clearing it from my mind.

In 1822, I was — along with Purrucker and another eight or so bright young men — the member of an informal club of aspirant intellectuals in Hamburg. We were all of us in that circle learning to be scientists, and being young had great ambition, both for ourselves and for the future of scientific endeavor. Every Sunday we gathered at a coffeehouse on the Reeperbahn, and in a back room that we hired for the purpose, fell to debate on any subject that suited us, as long as we felt the exchanges in some manner advanced our comprehension of the world. We were pompous, no doubt, and very full of ourselves; but our ardor was quite genuine. It was an exciting time. Every week, it seemed, one of us would come to a meeting with some new idea.

It was an evening during the summer — which was, that year,

oppressively hot, even at night — when Ernst Haeckel told us all the story I am about to relate. I remember the circumstances well. At least I think I do. Memory is less exact than it believes itself to be, yes? Well, it scarcely matters. What I remember may as well *be* the truth. After all, there's nobody left to disprove it. What happened was this: toward the end of the evening, when everyone had drunk enough beer to float the German fleet, and the keen edge of intellectual debate had been dulled somewhat (to be honest we were descending into gossip, as we inevitably did after midnight), Eisentrout, who later became a great surgeon, made casual mention of a man called Montesquino. The fellow's name was familiar to us all, though none of us had met him. He had come into the city a month before, and attracted a good deal of attention in society, because he claimed to be a necromancer. He could speak with and even raise the dead, he claimed, and was holding seances in the houses of the rich. He was charging the ladies of the city a small fortune for his services.

The mention of Montesquino's name brought a chorus of slurred opinions from around the room, every one of them unflattering. He was a contemptuous cheat and a sham. He should be sent back to France — from whence he'd come — but not before the skin had been flogged off his back for his impertinence.

The only voice in the room that was not raised against him was that of Ernst Haeckel, who in my opinion was the finest mind amongst us. He sat by the open window — hoping perhaps for some stir of a breeze off the Elbe on this smothering night — with his chin laid against his hand.

"What do you think of all this, Ernst?" I asked him.

"You don't want to know," he said softly.

"Yes we do. Of course we do."

Haeckel looked back at us. "Very well then," he said. "I'll tell you."

His face looked sickly in the candlelight, and I remember thinking — distinctly thinking — that I'd never seen such a look in his eyes as he had at that moment. Whatever thoughts had ventured into his head, they had muddied the clarity of his gaze. He looked fretful.

"Here's what I think," he said. "That we should be careful when we talk about necromancers."

"Careful?" said Purrucker, who was an argumentative man at the best of times, and even more volatile when drunk. "Why should we be *careful* of a little French prick who preys on our women? Good Lord, he's practically stealing from their purses!"

"How so?"

"Because he's telling them he can raise the dead!" Purrucker yelled, banging the table for emphasis.

"And how do we know he cannot?"

"Oh now Haeckel," I said, "you don't believe —"

"I believe the evidence of my eyes, Theodor," Haeckel said to me. "And I saw — once in my life — what I take to be proof that such crafts as this Montesquino professes are real."

The room erupted with laughter and protests. Haeckel sat them out, unmoving. At last, when all our din had subsided, he said: "Do you want to hear what I have to say or don't you?"

"Of *course* we want to hear," said Julius Linneman, who doted on Haeckel; almost girlishly, we used to think.

"Then listen," Haeckel said. "What I'm about to tell you is absolutely true, though by the time I get to the end of it you may not welcome me back into this room, because you may think I am a little crazy. More than a little perhaps."

The softness of his voice, and the haunted look in his eyes, had quieted everyone, even the volatile Purrucker. We all took seats, or lounged against the mantelpiece, and listened. After a moment of introspection, Haeckel began to tell his tale. And as best I remember it, this is what he told us.

"Ten years ago I was at Wittenberg, studying philosophy under Wilhem Hauser. He was a metaphysician, of course; monkish in his ways. He didn't care for the physical world; it didn't touch him, really. And he urged his students to live with the same asceticism as he himself practices. This was of course hard for us. We were very young and full of appetite. But while I was in Wittenberg, and under his watchful eye, I really tried to live as close to his precepts as I could.

"In the spring of my second year under Hauser, I got word that my father — who lived in Luneburg — was seriously ill, and I had to leave my studies and return home. I was a student. I'd spent all my money on books and bread. I couldn't afford the carriage fare. So I had to walk. It was several days' journey, of course, across the empty heath, but I had my meditations to accompany, and I was happy enough. At least for the first half of the journey. Then, out of nowhere there came a terrible rainstorm. I was soaked to the skin, and despite my valiant attempts to put my concern for physical comfort out of my mind, I could not. I was cold and unhappy, and the rarifications of the metaphysical life were very far from my mind.

"On the fourth or fifth evening, sniffling and cursing, I gathered some twigs and made a fire against a little stone wall, hoping to dry myself out before I slept. While I was gathering moss to make a pillow for my head, an old man, his face the very portrait of melancholy, appeared out of the gloom and spoke to me like a prophet.

" 'It would not be wise for you to sleep here tonight,' he said to me.

"I was in no mood to debate the issue with him. I was too fed up. 'I'm not going to move an inch,' I told him. 'This is an open road. I have every right to sleep here if I wish to.'

" 'Of course you do,' the old man said to me. 'I didn't say the right was not yours. I simply said it wasn't wise.'

"I was a little ashamed of my sharpness, to be honest. 'I'm sorry,' I said to him. 'I'm cold and I'm tired and I'm hungry. I meant no insult.'

"The old man said that none was taken. His name, he said, was Walter Wolfram.

"I told him my name, and my situation. He listened, then offered to bring me back to his house, which he said was close by. There I might enjoy a proper fire and some hot potato soup. I did not refuse him, of course. But I did ask him, when I'd risen, why he thought it was unwise for me to sleep in that place.

"He gave me such a sorrowful look. A heartbreaking look, the meaning of which I did not comprehend. Then he said: 'You are a young man, and no doubt you do not fear the workings of the world. But please believe me when I tell you there are nights when it's not good to sleep next to a place where the dead are laid.'

" 'The dead?' I replied, and looked back. In my exhausted state I had not seen what lay on the other side of the stone wall. Now, with the rain clouds cleared and the moon climbing, I could see a large number of graves there, old and new intermingled. Usually such a sight would not have much disturbed me. Hauser had taught us to look coldly on death. It should not, he said, move a man more than the prospect of sunrise, for it is just as certain, and just as unremarkable. It was good advice when heard on a warm afternoon in a classroom in Wittenberg. But here — out in the middle of nowhere, with an old man murmuring his superstitions at my side — I was not so certain it made sense.

"Anyway, Wolfram took me home to his little house, which lay no more than half a mile from the necropolis. There was the fire, as he'd promised. And the soup, as he'd promised. But there also, much to my surprise and delight, his wife, Elise.

"She could not have been more than twenty-two, and easily the most beautiful woman I had ever seen. Wittenberg had its share of beauties, of course. But I don't believe its streets ever boasted a woman as perfect as this. Chestnut hair, all the way down to her tiny waist. Full lips, full hips, full breasts. And such eyes! When they met mine they seemed to consume me.

"I did my best, for decency's sake, to conceal my admiration, but it was hard to do. I wanted to fall down on my knees and declare my undying devotion to her, there and then.

"If Walter noticed any of this, he made no sign. He was anxious about something, I began to realize. He constantly glanced up at the clock on the mantel, and looked toward the door.

"I was glad of his distraction, in truth. It allowed me to talk to Elise, who — though she was reticent at first — grew more animated as the evening proceeded. She kept plying me with wine, and I kept drinking it, until sometime before midnight I fell asleep, right there amongst the dishes I'd eaten from."

At this juncture, somebody in our little assembly — I think it may have been Purrucker — remarked that he hoped this wasn't going to be a story about disappointed love, because he really wasn't in the mood. To which Haeckel replied that the story had absolutely nothing to do with love in any shape or form. It was a simple enough reply, but it did the job: it silenced the man who'd interrupted, and it deepened our sense of foreboding.

The noise from the cafe had by now died almost completely; as had the sounds from the street outside. Hamburg had retired to bed. But we were held there, by the story, and by the look in Ernst Haecker's eyes.

"I awoke a little while later," he went on, "but I was so weary and so heavy with wine, I barely opened my eyes. The door was ajar, and on the threshold stood a man in a dark cloak. He was having a whispered conversation with Walter. There was, I thought, an exchange of money; though I couldn't see clearly. Then the man departed. I got only the merest glimpse of his face, by the light thrown from the fire. It was not the face of a man I would like to quarrel with, I thought. Nor indeed even meet. Narrow eyes, sunk deep in fretful flesh. I was glad he was gone. As Walter closed the door I lay my head back down and almost closed my eyes, preferring that he not know I was awake. I can't tell you exactly why. I just knew that something was going on I was better not becoming involved with.

"Then, as I lay there, listening, I hear a baby crying. Walter called for Elise, instructing her to calm the infant down. I didn't hear her response. Rather, I heard it, I just couldn't make any sense of it. Her voice, which had been soft and sweet when I'd talked with her, now sounded strange. Through the slits of my eyes I could see that she'd gone to the window, and was staring out, her palms pressed flat against the glass.

"Again, Walter told her to attend to the child. Again, she gave him some guttural reply. This time she turned to him, and I saw that she was by no means the same woman as I'd conversed with. She seemed to be in the early stages of some kind of fit. Her color was high, her eyes wild, her lips drawn back from her teeth.

"So much that had seemed, earlier, evidence of her beauty and vitality now looked more like a glimpse of the sickness that was consuming her. She'd glowed too brightly; like someone consumed by a fever, who in that hour when all is at risk seems to burn with a terrible vividness.

"One of her hands went down between her legs and she began to rub herself there, in a most disturbing manner. If you've ever been to a madhouse you've maybe seen some of the kind of behavior she was exhibiting.

"'Patience,' Walter said to her, 'everything's being taken care of. Now go and look after the child.'

"Finally she conceded to his request, and off she went into the next room. Until I'd heard the infant crying I hadn't even realized they had a child, and it seemed odd to me that Elise had not made mention of it. Lying there, feigning sleep, I tried to work out what I should do next. Should I perhaps pretend to wake, and announce to my host that I would not after all be accepting his hospitality? I decided against this course. I would stay where I was. As long as they thought I was asleep they'd ignore me. Or so I hoped.

"The baby's crying had now subsided. Elise's presence had soothed it.

"'Make sure he's had enough before you put him down,' I heard

Walter say to her. 'I don't want him waking and crying for you when you're gone.'

"From this I gathered that she was breast-feeding the child; which fact explained the lovely generosity of her breasts. They were plump with milk. And I must admit, even after the way Elise had looked when she was at the window, I felt a little spasm of envy for the child, suckling at those lovely breasts.

"Then I returned my thoughts to the business of trying to understand what was happening here. Who was the man who'd come to the front door? Elise's lover, perhaps? If so, why was Walter *paying* him? Was it possible that the old man had hired this fellow to satisfy his wife, because he was incapable of doing the job himself? Was Elise's twitching at the window simply erotic anticipation?

"At last, she came out of the infant's room, and very carefully closed the door. There was a whispered exchange between the husband and wife, which I caught no part of, but which set off a new round of questions in my head. Suppose they were conspiring to kill me? I will tell you, my neck felt very naked at that moment . . .

"But I needn't have worried. After a minute they finished their whispering and Elise left the house. Walter, for his part, went to sit by the fire. I heard him pour himself a drink, and down it noisily; then pour himself another. Plainly he was drowning his sorrows; or doing his best. He kept drinking, and muttering to himself while he drank. Presently, the muttering became tearful. Soon he was sobbing.

"I couldn't bear this any longer. I raised my head off the table, and I turned to him.

"'Herr Wolfram,' I said, '. . . what's going on here?'

"He had tears pouring down his face, running into his beard.

"'Oh my friend,' he said, shaking his head, 'I could not begin to explain. This is a night of unutterable sadness.'

"'Would you prefer that I left you to your tears?' I asked him.

"'No,' he said. 'No, I don't want you to go out there right now.'

"I wanted to know why, of course. Was there something he was afraid I'd see?

"I had risen from the table, and now went to him. 'The man who came to the door —'

"Walter's lip curled at my mention of him. 'Who is he?' I asked.

"'His name is Doctor Skal. He's an Englishman of my acquaintance.'

"I waited for further explanation. But when none was forthcoming, I said: 'And a friend of your wife's.'

"'No,' Walter said. 'It's not what you think it is.' He poured himself some more brandy, and drank again. 'You're supposing they're lovers. But they're not. Elise has not the slightest interest in the company of Doctor Skal, believe me. Nor indeed in any visitor to this house.'

"I assumed this remark was a little barb directed at me, and I began to defend myself, but Walter waved my protestations away.

"'Don't concern yourself,' he said. 'I took no offense at the looks you gave my wife. How could you not? She's a very beautiful woman, and I'd be surprised if a young man such as yourself *didn't* try to seduce her. At least in his heart. But let me tell you, my friend: you could never satisfy her.' He let this remark lie for a moment. Then he added: 'Neither, of course, could I. When I married her I was already too old to be a husband to her in the truest sense.'

"'But you have a baby,' I said to him.

"'The boy isn't mine,' Walter replied.

"'So you're raising this infant, even though he isn't yours?'

"'Yes.'

"'Where's the father?'

"'I'm afraid he's dead.'

"'Ah.' This all began to seem very tragic. Elise pregnant, the father dead, and Walter coming to the rescue, saving her from dishonor. That was the story constructed in my head. The only part I could not yet fit into this neat scheme was Doctor Skal, whose cloaked presence at the door had so unsettled me.

"'I know none of this is my business —' I said to Walter.

"'And better keep it that way,' he replied.

"'But I have one more question.'

"'Ask it.'

"'What kind of doctor is this man Skal?'

"'Ah.' Walter set his glass down, and stared into the fire. It had not been fed in a while, and now was little more than a heap of glowing embers. 'The esteemed Doctor Skal is a necromancer. He deals in a science which I do not profess to understand.' He leaned a little closer to the fire, as though talking of the mysterious man had chilled him to the marrow. I felt something similar. I knew very little about the work of a necromancer, but I knew that they dealt with the dead.

"I thought of the graveyard, and of Walter's first words to me:

"'*It would not be wise for you to sleep here tonight.*'

"Suddenly, I understood. I got to my feet, my barely sobered head throbbing. 'I know what's going on here,' I announced. 'You paid Skal so that Elise could speak to the dead! To the man who fathered her baby.' Walter continued to stare into the fire. I came close to him. 'That's it, isn't it? And now Skal's going to play some miserable trick on poor Elise to make her believe she's talking to a spirit.'

"'It's not a trick,' Walter said. For the first time during this grim exchange he looked up at me. 'What Skal does is real, I'm afraid to say. Which is why you should stay in here until it's over and done with. It's nothing you need ever —'

"He broke off at that moment, his thought unfinished, because we heard Elise's voice. It wasn't a word she uttered, it was a sob; and then another, and another, I knew whence they came, of course. Elise was at the graveyard with Skal. In the stillness of the night her voice carried easily.

"'Listen to her,' I said.

"'Better not,' Walter said.

"I ignored him, and went to the door, driven by a kind of morbid fascination. I didn't for a moment believe what Walter had said about the necromancer. Though much else that Hauser had taught me had become hard to believe tonight, I still believed in his teachings on the matter of life and death. The soul, he'd taught us, was certainly immortal. But once it was released from the constraints of flesh and blood, the body had no more significance than a piece of rotted meat. The man or woman who had animated it was gone, to be with those who had already left this life. There was, he insisted, no way to call that spirit back. And nor therefore — though Hauser had never extrapolated this far — was there any validity in the claims of those who said that they could commune with the dead.

"In short, Doctor Skal was a fake: this was my certain belief. And poor distracted Elise was his dupe. God knows what demands he was making of her, to have her sobbing that way! My imagination — having first dwelt on the woman's charms shamelessly, and then decided she was mad — now reinvented her a third time, as Skal's hapless victim, I knew from stories I'd heard in Hamburg what power charlatans like this wielded over vulnerable women. I'd heard of some necromancers who demanded that their seances be held with everyone as naked as Adam, for purity's sake! Others who had so battered the tender hearts of their victims with their ghoulishness that the women had swooned, and been violated in their swoon. I pictured all this happening to Elise. And the louder her sobs and cries became the more certain I was that my worst imaginings were true.

"At last I couldn't bear it any longer, and I stepped out into the darkness to get her.

"Herr Wolfram came after me, and caught hold of my arm. 'Come back into the house!' he demanded. 'For pity's sake, leave this alone *and come back into the house!*'

"Elise was shrieking now. I couldn't have gone back in if my life had depended upon it. I shook myself free of Wolfram's grip and started out for the graveyard. At first I thought he was going to leave me alone, but when I glanced back I saw that though he'd returned into the house he was now emerging again, cradling a musket in his arms. I thought at first he intended to threaten me with it, but instead he said:

"'Take it!' offering the weapon to me.

"'I don't intend to kill anybody!' I said, feeling very heroic and self-righteous now that I was on my way. 'I just want to get Elise out of this damn Englishman's hands.'

"'She won't come, believe me,' Walter said. 'Please take the musket! You're a good fellow. I don't want to see any harm come to you.'

"I ignored him and strode on. Though Walter's age made him wheeze, he did his best to keep up with me. He even managed to talk, though what he said — between my agitated state and his panting — wasn't always easy to grasp.

"'She has a sickness . . . she's had it all her life . . . what did I know? . . . I loved her . . . wanted her to be happy . . .'

"'She doesn't sound very happy right now,' I remarked.

"'It's not what you think . . . it is and it isn't . . . oh God, please come back to the house!'

"'I said no! I don't want her being molested by that man!'

"'You don't understand. We couldn't begin to please her. Neither of us.'

"'So you hire Skal to service her, Jesus!'

"I turned and pushed him hard in the chest, then I picked up my pace. Any last doubts I might have entertained about what was going on in the graveyard were forgotten. All this talk of necromancy was just a morbid veil drawn over the filthy truth of the matter. Poor Elise! Stuck with a broken-down husband, who knew no better way to please than to give her over to an Englishman for an occasional pleasuring. Of all things, an Englishman! As if the English knew anything about making love.

"As I ran, I envisaged what I'd do when I reached the graveyard. I imagined myself hopping over the wall and with a shout racing at Skal, and plucking him off my poor Elise. Then I'd beat him senseless. And when he was laid low, and I'd proved just how heroic a fellow I was, I'd go to the girl, take her in my arms, and show her what a good German does when he wants to make a woman happy.

"Oh, my head was spinning with ideas, right up until the moment that I emerged from the corner of the trees and came in sight of the necropolis . . ."

Here, after several minutes of headlong narration, Haeckel ceased speaking. It was not for dramatic effect, I think. He was simply preparing himself, mentally, for the final stretch of his story. I'm sure that none of us in that room doubted that what lay ahead would not be pleasant. From the beginning this had been a tale overshadowed by the prospect of some horror. None of us spoke; that I do remember. We sat there, in thrall to the persuasions of Haeckel's tale, waiting for him to begin again. We were like children.

After a minute or so, during which time he stared out of the window at the night sky (though seeing, I think, nothing of its beauty) he turned back to us and rewarded our patience.

"The moon was full and white," he said. "It showed me every detail. There were no great, noble tombs in this place, such as you'd see at the Ohlsdorf Cemetery; just coarsely carved headstones and wooden crosses. And in their midst, a kind of ceremony was going on. There were candles set in the grass, their flames steady in the still air. I suppose they made some kind of circle — perhaps ten feet across — in which the necromancer had performed his rituals. Now, however, with his work done, he had retired some distance from this place. He was sitting on a tombstone, smoking a long, Turkish pipe, and watching.

"The subject of his study, of course, was Elise. When I had first laid eyes on her I had guiltily imagined what she would look like stripped of her clothes. Now I had my answer. There she was, lit by the gold of the candle flames and the silver of the moon. Available to my eyes in all her glory.

"But oh God! What she was doing turned every single drop of pleasure I might have taken in her beauty to the bitterest gall.

"Those cries I'd heard — those sobs that had made my heart go out to her — they weren't provoked by the pawings of Doctor Skal, but by the touch of the dead. The dead, raised out of their dirt to pleasure her! She was squatting, and there between her legs was a face, pushed up out of the earth. A man recently buried, to judge by his condition, the flesh still moist on the bone, and the tongue — Jesus, the tongue! — still flicking between his bared teeth.

"If this had been all it would have been enough. But it was not all. The same grotesque genius that had inspired the cadaver between her legs into this resemblance of life, had also brought forth a crop of smaller parts — pieces of the whole, which had wormed their way out of the grave by some means or other. Bony pieces, held together with leathery sinew. A rib cage, crawling around on its elbows; a head, propelled by a whiplash length of stripped spine; several hands, with some fleshless lengths of bone attached. There was a morbid bestiary of these things. And they were all upon her, or waiting their turn to be upon her.

"Nor did she for a moment protest their attentions. Quite the contrary. Having climbed off the corpse that was pleasuring her from below, she rolled over onto her back and invited a dozen of these pieces upon her, like a whore in a fever, and they came, oh God they came, as though they might have out of her the juices that would return them to wholesomeness.

"Walter, by now, had caught up with me. 'I warned you,' he said.

" 'You knew this was happening?'

" 'Of course I knew. I'm afraid it's the only way she's satisfied.'

" 'What is she?' I said to him.

" 'A woman,' Walter replied.

" 'No natural woman would endure *that*,' I said. 'Jesus! Jesus!'

"The sight before me was getting worse by the moment. Elise was up on her knees in the grave dirt now, and a second corpse — stripped of whatever garments he had been buried in — was coupling with her, his motion vigorous, his pleasure intense, to judge by the way he threw back his putrefying head. As for Elise, she was kneading her full tits, directing arcs of milk into the air so that it rained down on the vile menagerie cavorting before her. Her lovers were in ecstasy. They clattered and scampered around in the torrents, as though they were being blessed.

"I took the musket from Walter.

"'Don't hurt her!' he begged. 'She's not to blame.'

"I ignored him, and made my way toward the yard, calling to the necromancer as I did so.

"'Skal! *Skal!'*

"He looked up from his meditations, whatever they were, and seeing the musket I was brandishing, immediately began to protest his innocence. His German wasn't good, but I didn't have any difficulty catching his general drift. He was just doing what he'd been paid to do, he said. He wasn't to blame.

"I clambered over the wall and approached him through the graves, instructing him to get to his feet. He got up, his hands raised in surrender. Plainly he was terrified that I was going to shoot him. But that wasn't my intention. I just wanted to stop this obscenity.

"'Whatever you did to start this, *undo it!'* I told him.

"He shook his head, his eyes wild. I thought perhaps he didn't understand so I repeated the instruction.

"Again, he shook his head. All his composure was gone. He looked like a shabby little cutpurse who'd just been caught in the act. I was right in front of him, and I jabbed the musket in his belly. If he didn't stop this, I told him, I'd shoot him.

"I might have done it too, but for Herr Wolfram, who had clambered over the wall and was approaching his wife, calling her name.

"'Elise . . . please, Elise . . . you should come home . . .'

"I've never in my life heard anything as absurd or as sad as that man calling to his wife. *'You should come home . . .'*

"Of course she didn't listen to him. Didn't *hear* him, probably, in the heat of what she was doing, and what was being done to her.

"But her *lovers* heard. One of the men who'd been raised up whole, and was waiting his turn at the woman, started shambling toward Walter, waving him away. It was a curious thing to see. The corpse trying to shoo the old man off. But Walter wouldn't go. He kept calling to Elise, the tears pouring down his face. Calling to her, calling to her —

"I yelled to him to stay away. He didn't listen to me. I suppose he thought if he got close enough he could maybe catch hold of her arm. But the corpse came at him, still waving its hands, still shooing, and when Walter wouldn't be shooed the thing simply knocked him down. I saw him flail for a moment, and then try to get back up. But the dead — or pieces of the dead — were everywhere in the grass around his feet. And once he was down, they were upon him.

"I told the Englishman to come with me, and I started off across the yard to help Walter. There was only one ball in the musket, so I didn't want to waste it firing from a distance, and maybe missing my target. Besides I wasn't sure what I was going to fire at. The closer I got to the circle in which Elise was crawling around — still being clawed and petted — the more of Skal's unholy handiwork I saw. Whatever spells he'd cast here, they seemed to have raised every last dead thing in the place. The ground was crawling with bits of this and that; fingers, pieces of dried up flesh with locks of hair attached; wormy fragments that were beyond recognition.

"By the time we reached Walter, he'd already lost the fight. The horrors he'd paid to have resurrected — ungrateful things — had torn him open in a hundred places. One of his eyes had been thumbed out, there was a gaping hole in his chest.

"His murderers were still working on him. I batted a few limbs off him with the musket, but there were so many it was only a matter of time, I knew, before they came after me. I turned around to Skal, intending to order him again to bring this abomination to a halt, but he was springing off between the graves. In a sudden surge of rage, I raised the musket and I fired. The felon went down, howling in the grass. I went to him. He was badly wounded, and in great pain, but I was in no mood to help him. He was responsible for all this. Wolfram dead, and Elise still crouching amongst her rotted admirers; all of this was Skal's fault. I had no sympathy for the man.

"'What does it take to make this stop?' I asked him. '*What are the words?*'

"His teeth were chattering. It was hard to make out what he was saying. Finally I understood.

"'When . . . the . . . sun . . . comes up . . .' he said to me.

"'You can't stop it any other way?'

"'No,' he said. 'No . . . other . . . way.'

"Then he died. You can imagine my despair. I could do nothing. There was no way to get to Elise without suffering the same fate as Walter. And anyway, she wouldn't have come. It was an hour from dawn, at least. All I could do was what I did: climb over the wall, and wait. The sounds were horrible. In some ways, worse than the sight. She must have been exhausted by now, but she kept going. Sighing sometimes, sobbing sometimes, moaning sometimes. Not — let me make it perfectly clear — the despairing moan of a woman who understands that she is in the grip of the dead. This was the moan of a deeply pleasured woman; a woman in bliss.

"Just a few minutes before dawn, the sounds subsided. Only when they had died away completely did I look back over the wall. Elise had gone. Her lovers lay around in the ground, exhausted as perhaps only the dead can be. The clouds were lightening in the East. I suppose resurrected flesh has a fear of the light, because as the last stars crept away so did the dead. They crawled back into the earth, and covered themselves with the dirt that had been shoveled down upon their coffins . . ."

Haeckel's voice had become a whisper in these last minutes, and now it trailed away completely. We sat around not looking at one another, each of us deep in thought. If any of us had entertained the notion that Haeckel's tale was some invention, the force of his telling — the whiteness of his skin, the tears that had now and then appeared in his eyes — had thrust such doubts from us, at least for now.

It was Purrucker who spoke first, inevitably. "So you killed a man," he said. "I'm impressed."

Haeckel looked up at him. "I haven't finished my story," he said.

"Jesus . . ." I murmured, ". . . what else is there to tell?"

"If you remember, I'd left all my books, and some gifts I'd brought from Wittenberg for my father, at Herr Wolfram's house. So I made my way back there. I was in a kind of terrified trance, my mind still barely able to grasp what I'd seen.

"When I got to the house I heard somebody singing. A sweet lilting voice it was. I went to the door. My belongings were sitting there on the table where I'd left them. The room was emptying. Praying that I'd go unheard, I entered. As I picked up my philosophy books and my father's gift, the singing stopped.

"I retreated to the door but before I could reach the threshold Elise appeared, with her infant in her arms. The woman looked the worse for her philanderings, no question about that. There were scratches all over her face, and her arms, and on the plump breast at which the baby now sucked. But marked as she was, there was nothing but happiness her eyes. She was sweetly content with her life at that moment.

"I thought perhaps she had no memory of what had happened to her. Maybe the necromancer had put her into some kind of trance, I reasoned; and now she'd woken from it the past was all forgotten.

"I started to explain to her. 'Walter . . .' I said.

"'Yes, I know —' she replied. 'He's dead.' She smiled at me; a May morning smile. 'He was old,' she said, matter-of-factly. 'But he was always kind to me. Old men are the best husbands. As long as you don't want children.'

"My gaze must have gone from her radiant face to the baby at her nipple, because she said:

"'Oh, this isn't Walter's boy.'

"As she spoke she tenderly teased the infant from her breast, and it looked my way. There it was: life-in-death, perfected. Its face was shiny pink, and its limbs fat from its mother's milk, but its sockets were deep as the grave, and its mouth wide, so that its teeth, which were not an infant's teeth, were bared in a perpetual grimace. The dead, it seemed, had given her more than pleasure. I dropped the books, and the gift for my father there on the doorstep. I stumbled back out into the daylight, and I ran — oh God in Heaven, I ran! — afraid to the very depths of my soul. I kept on running until I reached the road. Though I had no desire to venture past the graveyard again, I had no choice: it was the only route I knew, and I did not want to get lost, I wanted to be home. I wanted a church, an altar, piety, prayers.

"It was not a busy thoroughfare by any means, and if anyone had passed along it since daybreak they'd decided to leave the necromancer's body where it lay beside the wall. But the crows were at his face, and foxes at his hands and feet. I crept by without disturbing their feast."

Again, Haeckel halted. This time, he expelled a long, long sigh. "And that, gentlemen, is why I advise you to be careful in your judgments of this man Montesquino."

He rose as he spoke, and went to the door. Of course we all had questions, but none of us spoke then, not then. We let him go. And for my part, gladly. I'd enough of these horrors for one night.

Make of all this what you will. I don't know to this day whether I believe the story or not (though I can't see any reason why Haeckel would have *invented* it. Just as he'd predicted, he was treated very differently after that night; kept at arm's length). The point is that the thing still haunts me; in part, I suppose, *because* I never made up my mind whether I thought it was a falsehood or not. I've sometimes wrondered what part it played in the shaping of my life: if perhaps my cleaving to empiricism — my devotion to Helmholtz's methodologies — was not in some way the consequence of this hour spent in the company of Haeckel's account.

Nor do I think I was alone in my preoccupation with what I heard. Though I saw less and less of the other members of the group as the years went by, on those occasions when we did meet up the conversation would often drift round to that story, and our voices would drop to near-whispers, as though we were embarrassed to be confessing that we even remembered what Haeckel had said.

A couple of members of the group went to some lengths to pluck holes in what they'd heard, I remember; to expose it as nonsense. I think Eisentrout actually claimed he'd retraced Haeckel's journey from Wittenberg to Luneburg, and claimed there was no necropolis along the route. As for Haeckel himself, he treated these attacks upon his veracity with indifference. We had asked him to tell us what he thought of necromancers, and he'd told us. There was nothing more to say on the matter.

And in a way he was right. It was just a story told on a hot night, long ago, when I was still dreaming of what I would become.

And yet now, sitting here at the window, knowing I will never again be strong enough to step outside, and that soon I must join Purrucker and the others in the earth, I find the terror coming back to me; the terror of some convulsive place where death has a beautiful woman in its teeth, and she gives voice to bliss. I have, if you will, fled Haeckel's story over the years; hidden my head under the covers of reason. But here, at the end, I see that there is no asylum to be had from it; or rather, from the terrible suspicion that it contains a clue to the ruling principle of the world.

# LOST

## *Jeff VanderMeer*

"Are you lost?" it says to me in its salt-and-pepper gravelly moan of a voice and for a long moment I can't answer. I'm thinking of how I got here and what it might mean and how to frame an answer and wondering why the answer that came to mind immediately seems caught in my throat like a physical kind of fear, and that line of thought leads to this: remembering the line of color that brought me here: the spray of emerald-velvet-burgundy-chocolate mushrooms suddenly appearing on the old stone wall where yesterday there had been nothing, and me on my way to the university to teach yet another dead-end night class, dusk coming on, but somehow the spray, splay of mushrooms spared that lack of light; something about the way the runnels and patches of exposed understone contrasted with the otherwise gray solidity that brought me out of my thoughts of debt and a problem student named Jenna, who had become my problem, really, and I just

stopped.

right there.

and stared at the tracery of mushrooms, the way they formed such a uniform swoop across that pitted stone, and something about them, something about that glimmer, reminded me of my dead wife and of Jenna — the green was the same as my wife's eyes and that of Jenna's earrings, and I remembered the first time I noticed Jenna's earrings, and how it brought a deep, soundless sob rising out of my chest, my lungs, and I stood there, in front of the whole class, bent over, as if struck by something large and invisible, and how ever since I cannot tell if my fascination with her has to do with that color and my need for companionship or some essential trait in her, and how ironic, how sad, that she misunderstood my reaction and began wearing the earrings every day, until that physical pain inhabiting my body became a dullness, like the ache in an overused muscle, which I hated even as I found myself falling for Jenna . . .

and all of the time.

the whole time.

The light was fading except across the wall, and people in over-coats were walking past in the clear chill, under the embering street-lamps, and I could smell something other than the dankness of the wall as I traced its roughness with my fingers. It must have been a woman's passing perfume, but for a moment I smelled my wife and the emerald color of the mushrooms, the memory of her beneath me, the smell and feel of her — all of this was the same thing, and when I started walking again, I didn't go straight. I didn't head for the ivy-strewn facades of the campus buildings. Instead, I turned

I turned and turned and turned.

turned as if turning meant wrenching my life from a stable orbit.

To the right I turned to follow the scatterings of mushrooms, and I don't know why, if I was just curious or if I'd already been cap-tured in some way, because it wasn't like me. My dad had always said, before he passed from cancer in a very orderly way, that "you have to make a plan and keep to it." He said it to me, my mother, and my estranged sister, and he meant it. Routine was a religion for him, and we made it ours. Set meals. Set appointments. Set activities. I re-member, when I turned eighteen, planning my rebellion, figuring out what I was going to do first and second and last, so I could savor my rebellion even as I . . . planned it. Less satisfying in the execution, the sex quick and lonely and not with someone I loved, the beer and pot putting me to sleep too quickly, waking to a cat licking my face, out cold on someone's sour-smelling lawn.

But I turned the corner, followed the mushroom trail, which moved up and down the wall like a wave, now mirrored on the wall that had sprung up opposite it — and ahead the ache of a dull red sunset, which bathed the mushrooms in a crimson glow, and,

suddenly, it wasn't that night

that place,

but a two-lane road the year before, the lights of our car project-ing through the murk as we drove down a corridor of night. She was driving, and had the pursed lip look of concentration that I loved about her, and which I never told her I loved because I was afraid that if I told her, the expression would become different in some es-sential way, and I never wanted that to happen — never wanted her to be a different person, either, when we made love, staring at her face and seeing that same look of concentration, of being fully en-gaged.

wanted no self-consciousness from her.

wanted her lilting laugh to remain spontaneous.

wanted her.

I wanted her to always preface her questions to me with "Let me ask you a question."

But a look of concentration doesn't mean concentration, and when I said later, in response to the ever-present question, until I had exhausted the gauntlet of friends, family, strangers who didn't know, the ordinary words "car crash," I couldn't help but associate that look with her death, and thus her death with our sex and our conversations and our holidays, and all I really wanted was a way to break that linkage, in almost the same way I wanted the trail of mushrooms to come to an end, because, honestly, where could they possibly lead that would be good for me? Ordinary thoughts, the thoughts we all have: that I was already late for work; that Jenna would miss me or she wouldn't; that this would be my fifth absence this semester and how many did there have to be before they let me go.

My legs didn't seem to have questions, though — they carried me forward. I followed the mushrooms because of the sparkle in Jenna's earrings, the gorgeous color of my wife's eyes. I followed the mushrooms because I can't say my wife's name. If I say her name, if I write her name, I will lose it — the name and my self-control. When I hear her name said, that is enough to conjure up the trail of evidence, the linkage. Unbearable.

The red of the sunset had become as green as . . .

A few people dressed in the outlandish garb I'd become accustomed to on campus pushed past me, and ahead, partially obscured by the lack of light, the spires of an old church or series of churches. Crennelations. A darkness that came from age, inhabiting the corners of the spires. A few circling birds or bats. It reminded me of the vacation my wife and I took to Eastern Europe one year, which made all that was ancient about my university employers look petty and cheap and just-yesterday. She fell asleep in the train from Berlin to Prague. I saw her face, framed by the reflection of the landscape rushing past the window, without lines or care, saw how her arms lay at her sides. She felt secure. She felt safe, I could tell.

Spires, though. I couldn't remember spires anywhere off-campus. I couldn't remember churches. Had I somehow ended up back on campus? It's true I had certain routines that meant I hadn't explored the city as I might have, and my wife to distract me, and then my grief.

Two youths ran by holding flags with symbols on them that I'd never seen before. I saw a man wearing a goat costume. I saw a woman with no legs "walking" on stilts. Fraternities and fraternity jokes came to mind, although there was something too solemn and formal about them. I had lost the thread

of the mushrooms.

no longer followed them.

just walked forward.

randomly.

Bathed in the green light of my wife's death. I turned as if to head back, except where I had come from no longer existed. It was as gone as the swathes of darkness my wife and I left behind us in our little car, headed home from a colleague's party, on the two-lane road at three in the morning.

More people crowded out onto the streets and I came under the weird light of gargoyled lampposts and buildings crowded and hunched in shadow to all sides, cut through by the narrowest of alleys. A festival of some kind, and I was in it or out of it or outside of it but caught up in it and the people kept pouring out of nowhere in their strange clothes and their strange accents and the strange look in their eyes and so I laughed with them and clapped my hands when they clapped their hands, and when the parade came by with animals foreign and fey, when the jugglers and the fire-eaters and the retired soldiers from distant wars, wearing uniforms I'd never seen before, when all of this converged, I tried not to think about it, tried not even to smell the stench of beer in the drains, the stench of vomit, of piss, tried to misread the mischief and malice in the eyes of those whose gaze I met. I realized this might be

a break in the linkage.

a severing of routine.

a way out.

Had I missed how random my world had become since my wife had died? Had my grief obliterated the real world for me?

And so all of these thoughts overwhelmed me when I woke from my hiding place in an alley the next morning, having slept on garbage and filth, to find *it* — wearing a large gray felt hat, small as a child but with the wizened features of something already dead — staring down at me. It had long claws that dragged down below the sleeves of its robes. I could not look it in the face. It swayed back and forth as if in trance, and it said to me, as I looked up at it with a disbelieving smile on my face, "Are you lost?"

And.

I thought about how I had gotten to this point.

I thought about Jenna and I thought about my wife and I realized I didn't love Jenna, that I didn't even really like Jenna, and with that thought came a kind of release and I was back on the two-lane road in the darkness and this time I welcomed it, brought it to me, soaked up those last few miles before she lost control of the car and swerved into the path of oncoming headlights connected to god-knows-what kind of vehicle, the same look of concentration on her face mixed with anger, because I was looking at her not at the road, arguing with her about some stupid point of routine that didn't make any sense to anyone but my father, and I wonder if she saw, in those last moments, some kind of entry to this place, and if she saw something that made her swerve, and it wasn't my fault at all, I wasn't the distraction that killed her.

"Are you lost?" it says to me and I'm more frightened than I've ever been before, even when my wife died in front of me, and I say, "No. I'm not lost. I belong here."

And I do.

# UNBLINKING

## *Ramsey Campbell*

Dignam wasn't sure if the essays he was marking defeated him or the gaze of his neighbour did. Now that the postwoman had delivered to both sides of the road, the man was regarding him across it with what looked unreasonably like accusation. With its unyielding stare and its fixed resentful grimace, Dignam could almost have taken the face for a mask somebody had hung inside the window opposite. It felt as hostile as all the essays he'd graded so far — as their insistence that mental illness could be a gift. He wandered downstairs to see that the post was even less rewarding than he'd assumed: a credit card had sent him the same invitation twice. He was about to bin the duplicate unopened when he realised it was addressed to his neighbour.

His name was Brady, then. How likely was he to welcome the item? Dignam was tempted to throw it away, but it didn't belong to him. He let himself out onto the short path piebald with March frost and fringed with icy spikes of grass. The glazed road was crunchy with frozen winged seeds from Brady's sprawling sycamore. As Dignam stepped between the crumbling stone gateposts under the tree, the man thumped on his window. "Wait there," he shouted and backed into dimness.

Dignam ambled down a path so overgrown it was indistinguishable from the abandoned garden to the front door, which was as scaly as the rest of the exterior. Beside it thick off-white curtains hung inert as paint against the entire interior of a bay window spotted with many rains. He'd started to think Brady had been distracted from claiming his mail when rapid footsteps clumped downstairs and the door was wrenched open with a vicious creak. "I said I was coming," Brady declared, having barely lowered his loose voice.

What had kept him? Not combing his spectacularly uneven greyish hair, nor getting dressed, since he was almost certainly wearing only a dressing-gown stained with egg and toothpaste. This close, his whitish wrinkled puffed-up face more than ever resembled a mask through which his glittering bloodshot eyes peered suspiciously at Dignam. "This is yours," Dignam said. "She delivered it to me by mistake."

"What is it?"

"Just an invitation to take out a credit card, as though there isn't already enough plastic in the world."

"And how would you know how many I've got of those?"

"I've no idea. I meant generally, of course. Me, I've got all I can cope with."

Brady thrust out a hand that involved a smell of stale cloth and turned over the envelope to scrutinise the blank expanse of orange paper before examining the front afresh. OPEN AT ONCE! THIS COULD CHANGE YOUR LIFE! red letters in blue outlines exhorted beneath his address. "Steamed it open, did you?" he enquired.

"Most decidedly not. Why should you —"

"There's where," Brady scoffed, poking a chewed cracked fingernail under the flap. "And you gave yourself away knowing what's inside."

"That's because I received the identical mailing."

"Identical, was it? Had my name on too?"

"Except for that and of course the address. I really must assure you —"

"I'll bet you must." Brady ripped open the envelope and squinted at the picture of a credit card, then stuffed the wad of paper into a dangling pocket. "Teacher, that right?"

"Actually I'm —"

"Don't tell me. A university teacher."

"A lecturer, yes. How did you know?"

"If you don't want everyone knowing you shouldn't let them see you marking papers and thinking what you're thinking about the girls that wrote them."

"They aren't only girls. Plenty of men as well."

Brady looked worse than vindicated. "I think I'll ask you to excuse me," Dignam said, feeling close to trapped by the man's view of him.

He was almost at the pavement when a stout middle-aged woman tramped by. "Watch out for that one, Mrs Vernon," Brady shouted. "Reads other people's letters. He'll be in our houses next."

The woman frowned at Dignam and increased her speed. "Mr Brady," he called for her to overhear, "if you spread that sort of tale I'll be forced to take action."

"Got my name now, have you? I'll be seeing about yours. Get off my property right now with your threats or it'll be me that brings the police."

"I haven't time to argue," Dignam said before he crossed the road to escape the shadow of the tree, a gloom that felt too much like Brady's notion of him. As the man's door shut with a victorious slam, Dignam saw the woman peering back at him while she hurried past the variously bushy gardens to the shop on the corner of the main road. An impulse to head off any rumours sent him after her.

Apart from the counter, the small shop was crammed with shelves laden with groceries. "Here's a newcomer," said the shopkeeper, a woman shorter by a head than Mrs Vernon but compensatively broader.

"Sorry," Dignam felt bound to respond, having passed the shop on his way to work for years. "Just a paper today."

As he made for the counter Mrs Vernon moved aside a little too far for politeness. He rested a hand on the nearest newspaper. "Excuse me, Mrs Vernon, we haven't been introduced . . ."

Her sharp face drew into itself as her lips pressed themselves almost colourless before demanding "Where did you get my name?"

"I heard it just now, if you recall."

"Listening outside, were you? I don't like that, Mrs Timms."

As the shopkeeper opened her pudgy hands in front of her to accept this, Dignam protested "When our friend shouted after you, I meant, of course."

"If you're talking about Mr Brady," Mrs Vernon said, "you didn't sound very friendly."

"Neighbour, then. Would you say he can be a little odd?"

"I wouldn't, and I'm sure you wouldn't either, Mrs Timms."

"I expect you'd rather not speak ill of a customer. He's certainly got an odd idea of me. All I did was take him some post I'd received by mistake."

"Who are you to say he's not right upstairs?" Mrs Vernon apparently saw reason to object. "You're not a doctor."

"I am of psychology, actually. I lecture on it at the university."

"That's no doctor, that's a teacher. How many nutters have you met?"

"Not a great number. If you put it like that," Dignam said in some rebuke, "none."

"Takes one to know one or think someone else is, more like."

Perhaps a cloud had masked the sun, but the growing darkness felt as if his brain was shrinking out of reach of light. "All I wanted to establish was that Mr Brady was mistaken to say I'd tampered with his letter."

"Sounds like everyone's mistaken except you."

"So you won't be going near his house," Mrs Timms advised.

What else had the women been saying about him? As he turned away with as much dignity as he could gather, there seemed to be far too much clutter between him and the door, and in his brain too. "Aren't you buying?" Mrs Timms said.

"I don't think I've laid claim to anything, have I?" He indicated the counter with one upturned hand, only to discover that print from the newspaper he'd leaned on had transferred itself to his palm. MADAM was the solitary word above a report about a brothel, and the latter portion was reversed like an illiterate tattoo on his skin. He slapped a pound coin on the counter hard enough for the shopkeeper to recoil with a timidity he thought melodramatic. "Here's your money. Keep your wares," he said and marched out of the shop.

The clang of the bell above the door spiked the back of his skull. After the dimness the sunlight felt strident too. He closed his eyes to let the flattened sharp-edged world regain some perspective until he realised he must appear to be loitering to overhear what the women said about him. They were silent, having seen him eavesdropping. He narrowed his eyes and stumbled along the road that seemed at best only vaguely imagined. As he widened them to demonstrate how harshly it was present, he wondered if during the entire confrontation Brady could really not have blinked once.

He wasn't doing so now. When Dignam resumed his seat at the desk he was met by a glare as unyielding as the sun that squinted through the branches of the sycamore. "Hope they sting," he muttered, blinking fast, and snatched the next essay off the heap. He recognised Hannah's generously flowing script, and was greeting it with a secret smile until his gaze snagged on the phrase he least hoped to encounter.

She thought schizophrenics had privileged perceptions too, did she? If she was so enamoured of his colleague's ideas, perhaps she should go to bed with Roger Douglas instead of with him. The unworthiness of the idea made Dignam nervous of betraying it to the watcher over the road, an absurd fear but nonetheless one reason why he lowered his head. *Many schizophrenics display insights far beyond the average . . . While it is dangerous to regard mental states as contagious, they can sometimes be shared in part by an observer . . . It requires unusual strength of mind to live with unmedicated schizophrenia . . .* Did Hannah mean to experience it or to be connected with a sufferer? Dignam had taken some satisfaction in inking his query alongside the text when he saw that the next sentence made it clear she'd meant suffering oneself. Too late, he thought, and glanced up to see why the light was flickering.

Brady had retreated from view, but a silent white explosion glared out of the depths of the room — the flash of a bulb. He was photographing Dignam, who heaved his window open as Mrs Vernon passed the house, her coat flapping in a wind. "Watch out for your friend with the camera," he called when she peered nervously towards the rattle of the sash. "Lord knows what he'll do with us now he's taken us."

She didn't look at Brady, despite the finger Dignam stretched forth. She fled onwards as though he'd made an improper approach. While the slam of his window was aimed at Brady, it only spurred her faster. He ducked to Hannah's essay in several kinds of rage. When the light flickered again he felt not merely spied upon but found out. "She's a mature student," he muttered. "She can choose for herself."

Did he imagine Brady could hear? He crouched to give the man a shot or several of his scalp, only to be bring himself too close to the page to read it no matter how hard he stared. Why was he wasting time? He had plenty of essays to mark in his office on the campus, and it was wholly irrational of him not to want to encounter Roger Douglas. He shoved himself away from the desk and twisted to sit with his back to the window as a preamble to quitting the house.

The route to the university led past the corner shop. Any other was absurdly devious. He might have had a word with the proprietor, but she was talking to a bulky man who frowned through the window at Dignam. Did that mean they were discussing him? "Off to work, Mrs Timms," he called, which made her blink.

Five minutes' stroll, but now two minutes' striding, took him along the seasick pavement of the potholed main road to the traffic lights. On his right a hill was piled with concrete tenements whose balconies always reminded him of battlements, though he suspected that he would have felt most beleaguered by living too close to his neighbours; doing so as a student had often brought him within screaming distance of a breakdown. To his left the cross street grew immediately more civilised as it met the campus, and he promised himself that his mind would. There was really no need to look behind him as he crossed the road. It was having a respite from traffic, and certainly nobody was following him.

He hadn't expected the campus to be so busy on a Saturday. Most of the students were bound for the library, though a few small groups were heading for the pub that faced it. Also on that course was a solitary woman in a dark grey suit, whom he would have taken for a lecturer except for her beacon of red hair. Even tied back severely, it was unmistakably Hannah's. She was too distant for him to hail without drawing more attention than he wanted. As she stepped delicately into the pub, he told himself that he deserved a drink.

The moment he crossed the threshold, dimness and uproar fell on him. Although the room was at least twice the size of Mrs Timms' shop, the crowd made it feel even smaller. Blinking let him locate Hannah at the bar. He'd taken a pace towards her when he saw she was talking to Roger Douglas.

Surely they resembled a couple only because they were younger than Dignam, but he would have dodged out of the pub if the other lecturer hadn't caught sight of him. Douglas raised his long lean tanned face, pointing his satyr's beard at him. "Look how psychology brings us all together," he remarked to Hannah.

Hannah turned to recognise Dignam. A smile widened her eyes and then her deceptively prim lips. "Oh, Dr Dignam. I didn't see you were here."

"He wasn't, were you, Terry? He was just behind you."

"Hardly just," Dignam said, having lifted a hand to acknowledge them both.

"So long as we are to our students, hey?"

"I can't imagine why you'd think I wouldn't be. May I buy you whatever you're having, Miss Martin? Just an orange, right you are. I shouldn't think that pint will take you long, Roger. Let me come to the rescue."

Dignam felt expansive and in control once he'd succeeded in coaxing the barmaid over. As she levered out his pint he noticed the book on the bar in front of Douglas: *Visions of Schizophrenia*. "Do you always carry your own book with you? I suppose you feel you need to advertise yourself."

"That's our student's copy that she liked enough to buy."

Dignam was swallowing a rusty mouthful of beer to keep down several retorts, by no means solely aimed at Douglas, when his colleague said "Didn't you have a book in mind once yourself? Will Hannah have a chance to read that too before she leaves us?"

"I'd want to base it on observation. Perhaps I'm less anxious to make a name."

"There's plenty of observation in my book. You should try not just skimming it sometime."

"Observation of yourself when you were taking drugs, you mean."

"Exactly, when I was trying every psychotropic I could lay my hands on, and let me tell you they didn't always look like my hands. No point in being anything but honest, would you agree, Hannah? Nothing good comes of repression."

Dignam was able to hope Douglas had made her uncomfortable until she said "I admired how you didn't hold back."

"Perhaps I shouldn't, then." Dignam saw her face try not to stiffen, though he had no intention of exposing their relationship. "I believe I may have hit upon the subject of my book," he said.

"Do we get to hear?" Douglas urged.

"I've come into contact with a sufferer."

"If you'll accept a word of advice, don't think of them that way. Look on them as an opportunity to share perceptions you might never have otherwise."

"Privileged perceptions, you mean," Dignam said and couldn't resist staring at Hannah.

"They're the ones. Treat yourself to some while you've the chance. They were what you wanted to consult me about, weren't they, Hannah? Forgive me if I don't call you Miss Martin. I like to think of my students as friends."

"I'm sure Miss Martin should be in no doubt as to my regard for her." Shouting this over the hubbub of the bar made Dignam feel walled in by his language. He drained his remaining third of a pint as an excuse to say "I'll see you at my Monday lecture then, Miss Martin."

"If not before, who knows?" Douglas used a finger and thumb to wipe froth from his moustache, a gesture that reminded Dignam of a villain in a melodrama. "Off to continue your observations, Terry?"

"I imagine that should be the case."

Either Dignam left the pub too energetically or his vision had inured itself to the dimness, because he was confronted by an all-embracing glare. Pressing his eyes shut, even with fingers as well as lids, only trapped it. "Are you okay?" someone asked, and he had to insist that he was. Once he was able to distinguish that nobody was spying on him, or at least no longer, he ran across the campus to his office.

There were essays on his desk, but nothing to contain them. While he searched for a carrier, footsteps advanced and hesitated and executed some further movement in the corridor. Their owner must be inspecting pictures on the walls, not deliberately staying out of sight or threatening to appear, but the noises made it harder for Dignam to be sure how empty the room was. His rummaging sent dust like the remnants of chalked words into the lethargically inclined sunlight. The essays weren't so urgent that they couldn't wait, and he was suddenly anxious to be home. No doubt this was how it felt to have an idea for a book, an idea that was eager to reach the page.

Words were scrambling over one another in his head as he emerged into the deserted corridor. In under five minutes he was running past the corner shop. He rammed the key into his lock and sprinted upstairs, to be confronted by the man across the road. The unblinking eyes seemed to tug the expressionless face to meet him, unless his own movement brought it closer. He was resisting the temptation to raise a hand in an ironic greeting when he saw that his palm was still imprinted with a word.

Had Hannah and his rival seen it? He licked the other hand and rubbed the pair together as he sat at the desk, until he began to see himself as Brady must see him, washing himself like an animal or worse. He grabbed a pad out of the desk drawer and seized the nearest pen, the red. *A spies on B because he believes A to be spying on him. A's paranoia narrows the focus of his mind to B or A. Paranoia is a form of focusing that excludes insight and any sense of everything that lies outside the focus. As a substitute for this lack the paranoid mind derives delusions from the subject on which it is focused . . .*

Was this an opening paragraph? It felt more like notes for several or even for a number of chapters. Hannah's unfaithful ideas seemed to be interfering with the clarity he'd thought he was bringing home, and he reached to turn the scattered pages blank side up.

Then his smeared hand faltered. Hadn't he tidied them before leaving the house? Had he failed to notice that he'd left the window raised almost an inch?

His head jerked up, not quite in time to be able to confirm he'd glimpsed a mocking grin across the road. Could someone really have entered the house and opened the window to provide an explanation for any disturbance? The mere thought appeared to send Brady into hiding. When the man thrust his head out of the front door, Dignam wondered if he might be on his way to protest his innocence. Instead Brady stalked along the road, the plastic jackets of three library books glinting dully under his arm. Why should Dignam still feel watched? He frowned at Brady's house and then couldn't stop. A face was peering at him from the gloomy depths of the upstairs room.

He had to lean close enough to the window to coat it with his breath before he understood that he was glimpsing a photograph on the wall. Indeed, there were several, yet he increasingly felt as if he was staring into a mirror. He sat and waited for the sun to crawl far enough to light upon the faces that weren't really watching him. "You're touched all right," he said, though Brady wasn't there to be told. All the faces were so enlarged that they resembled indistinct ghosts, but they weren't quite blurred enough for Dignam not to recognise at least a dozen versions of his own face.

Brady must have developed them while the subject was out of the house. He hadn't shot them all that morning, however. How long had he been spying unobserved? The question troubled Dignam even more than the pictures did. He craned out of the window to no satisfactory effect, then went for a closer look. Before he reached the end of his path the faces had sunk out of view. As he resolved to work while he kept watch for Brady, he saw what the tree had prevented him from noticing. A bunch of keys was dangling from Brady's front door.

Had he left them as a temptation? It seemed more important that it would take him at least an hour to walk to the nearest library and back. Dignam crossed the road and walked once backwards around the sycamore while pretending not to ascertain that he wasn't being watched from any of the houses, and then he strode to Brady's door. The keys were hanging from a mortise lock. He turned that key, then with a deft twist of the rusty Yale admitted himself to the house. In another second the lumbering door shut behind him.

He wished he hadn't been so swift. Before he was embraced by darkness he'd glimpsed a hall papered with newsprint and a millipede fleeing over a ragged tufted brown carpet to huddle, legs and antennae twitching, at the foot of stairs bare except for discoloured splotches. The house smelled of rot and old paper, and was thick with the lack of clarity he thought only ignorance could bring. He was groping to ease the door ajar when his eyes began to take hold of the dimness. He locked the mortise and advanced along the hall.

His first pace felt as if it was sinking into turf or earth. The sound of his next told him why and perhaps explained the underlying rotten odour. He was treading on sycamore seeds that a wind or Brady must have brought into the house. The noise and the sensation put him in mind of trampling insects, one reason why he hurried to the first internal door. Though the pallid plastic doorknob felt sticky as a second-hand lollipop, he turned it back and forth. The door was locked.

He didn't need to open doors to see. Enough illumination seeped through the grubby fanlight above the front door. Any insects in the hall were either lying low among the scattered seeds or dead. At least half a dozen sycamore shoots were growing on or between the uncovered floorboards, but Dignam's attention fastened on the walls. Hardly an inch of them was visible for the newspapers tacked to them and overrun with red ink. A marker pen, if not several, had been used to ring words and link them with lines, some the length of the hall.

"And" was one of the emphasised words; in fact, quite a few. And, and, and, and, and, and, and . . . They felt like threats of a never-ending process. No sense was to be gained from the newspaper photographs either. A man's pointing finger was linked to a woman's hand several yards away, while another wavering line lassoed both a war memorial and the chimney of a mansion. Dignam was trying to imagine a connection when he remembered why he was there: for a closer examination of the pictures of him and then for whatever course of action suggested itself.

A single contact with the banister was enough. The wood was as sticky as the doorknob. He followed his vague jerking shadow to the upper storey, where the dimness felt like the stale smell rendered visible. Only the hollow clatter of his footsteps made it clear that the floor was uncarpeted. He wasn't surprised the front bedroom was locked, but finding that none of the keys fitted threw him.

He crouched to peer through the keyhole. Beyond a dishevelled bed he was just able to identify his own window pinched microscopic, a sight that made his brain feel shrunken. He lurched to his feet and backed across the landing to take a run at the door. Just in time he realised Brady would suspect him. As he shook himself intelligent he elbowed the bathroom door, which swung wide.

A toilet roll squatted on the toilet lid, and the cardboard tubes from perhaps a hundred used rolls were heaped on the cistern. Three seedlings and a sycamore as tall as his waist were rooted in earth several inches deep in the cracked white metal bath. Another stunted infant tree stood in a sink full of earth. He hardly knew why he darted forward to close his fists around all the leaves and crush them to sticky pulp. As he turned away he saw his guiltily gleeful face in the smeary speckled mirror. He started as though he'd caught sight of an intruder. His movement was enough to dislodge a cardboard tube from the top of the pile. Immediately, like lemmings that had found a leader, the rest toppled off the cistern.

He felt as if something had gripped his mouth with claws to manipulate it into one or more of several competing expressions. He couldn't judge from the mirror whether he was grinning or grimacing, unless he was about to be overtaken by quite another look. He stooped to pick up a tube in each hand, then balanced another pair on top of them on the cistern, and a third. He was restoring two more to the pile when the whole array sprawled across the tattered linoleum.

How long had he been in the house? Since he hadn't checked when he'd entered, his watch was useless. He abandoned his asinine task and charged downstairs, then up again to shut the bathroom door. The dimness clung to his mind as he raced down a second time and fumbled the key into the mortise lock. He almost slammed the door behind him, closing it stealthily instead. He thrust the key into the lock and twisted it so hard he bruised his fingers. In no more time than it took him to remember to breathe he was hastening across the road in a flurry of sycamore seeds. He was almost at his gate when Brady turned the corner by the shop.

Could he have seen? All of Dignam was desperate to hide — all except his mind. It kept him leaning nonchalantly on a gatepost while he sorted through remarks. "You read a lot, I see." "Fond of words, Mr Brady?" "I hope you didn't write in those books like you —" His fear that he might utter one or more of these spurred him to blurt "Back from the library, then?"

He thought the unrelenting stare was meant to convict him of fatuousness until Brady demanded "Who told you I was there?"

Too late Dignam realised the man was empty-handed. "I saw you taking your books."

"Better taking them than medicine." Brady smirked without moderating his stare. "Keeping an eye on me, are you? You'll need both and a friend's as well."

"Simply being neighbourly," Dignam said and was suddenly afraid that his face was betraying his escapade, a notion that threatened to distort his lips. "It does no harm to look out for others."

"I'll be looking out for you, that's for sure. Any more observations or am I dismissed?"

Surely he couldn't have been eavesdropping in the dimness of the pub. "Please don't allow me to detain you," Dignam said.

"Don't kid yourself you can stop me."

Dignam thought he'd said the opposite. He was sending a silent gasp of relief after the man's back when he remembered that Brady was about to find the keys. Before Dignam could let him do so by himself, Brady spun around. "Made me forget these, did you?" he yelled past the tree.

"I rather think you did it unaided."

Dignam only spoke, but Brady heard him. "And how did you know?" he shouted louder still.

"You told me."

The silence gave him time to understand that Brady hadn't quite before the man bellowed "What's your next trick going to be? Breaking in to see what you can lecture about? Poison me while you're at it, why don't you."

"Don't talk rot," Dignam shouted for any neighbours to hear and strode to his door. He heard Brady's keys rattle as he took out his own. It seemed crucial that he should be at his window by the time Brady went upstairs. He sprinted for his desk as the door slammed like a lid. A seed crunched underfoot as he reached the stairs. His hand must be sticky, not the banister. He sat panting in his not entirely stable chair and tidied the pages of Hannah's essay, then forgot them as he leaned across them. The room that faced him was empty of faces. The sun showed him a blank wall.

He was staring at the wall as if this might force the images to develop from it when the door let Brady in, and a kitchen chair. He planted it close to the window and sat forward on it, folding his arms, fastening his gaze like twin cameras on his neighbour. Of course he was pretending that he hadn't dashed up to the room before Dignam had reached his. He had needed only to throw the photographs out of sight on the floor. Dignam stood and stretched, but couldn't see them. He felt as if Brady's gaze was weighing him back into the chair to deal with Hannah's thoughts.

Here was the Roger Douglas concept that enraged him most of all: that insanity was somehow magical. She had found more similarities — the ritualistic use of objects, the ambition to alter reality by the power of the mind, the way witches had once been regarded and the mentally ill often were now, a resemblance leading to Dignam's suggestion that before long the insane would be viewed as soothsayers or visionaries. If people were sufficiently irrational to depend on astrology, he often said, why not go to the extreme? She clearly hadn't appreciated his irony. Her conclusion felt like a belated attempt to placate him, and overall the essay seemed designed to mediate between him and Douglas. He was squeezing the red pen so viciously it creaked between his fingers when the phone rang on the corner of his desk.

As he lifted the receiver his gaze couldn't avoid Brady's. He had to rid himself of a grotesque fancy that the man had somehow made the phone go off. "Terry Dignam," he said.

"Terry? Terry," she repeated as if testing her entitlement to use the name. "It's Hannah."

"I gathered that."

"I just wanted to ask if you meant what you said."

"I generally do. It's a peculiarity of mine. Something in particular?"

"I thought you might be saying it so Roger didn't realise, well, you know. Aren't you coming to me for dinner tomorrow?"

"I don't think that's going to be possible," Dignam said, holding Brady's gaze.

"Oh."

The syllable was laden with so much disappointment and self-doubt and accusation that he felt compelled to say "I suppose you could do it here if you liked."

"Only if you want me to."

"I thought I'd made it clear I shouldn't have suggested it otherwise."

"You'll need to tell me where to find you."

"I was about to," he said, and did. He hung up the receiver before informing Brady "You've got what you asked for. There'll be someone else to keep an eye on you."

With an effort he lowered his gaze to the essay. *50%*, he scribbled in the margin. *Some of your ideas will bear developing — decide which.* He looked up in something like triumph to confront an empty room, and was irrational enough to feel relieved until he grasped where Brady might be. The thought seemed to lodge like an infection in his bladder. He waddled wide-legged to the bathroom and drained himself, then returned to his desk. Brady was awaiting him.

His face was an unreadable mask. Even his eyes failed to react to his subject, who felt as if their scrutiny was puppeting him across the room to sit at his desk like a miscreant under the gaze of a teacher. Brady couldn't know that Dignam had been in his house. If Dignam hadn't, the man would believe that he had, but what did that mean? It made Dignam feel embedded in Brady's view of him. He hunched over the next essay, only for a reference to privileged perceptions to swell into his vision as though it had been freshly penned. He shoved the pages aside to concentrate on his own work, his notes, his book. *The subject sits at a window*, he scrawled, which didn't help him deal with the glare he sensed on top of his brain or in it — didn't reduce his awareness of it or give it meaning. He raised his head and met it. If it came to a contest, sanity must win.

He strove to put everything he knew about himself into his eyes. He continued when they began to sting, because it would seem feeble of him to be first to blink. The first time he was forced to, he pinched his thighs between his nails. His leg was aching in too many places to count by the time he observed that night was falling. When he glanced down at the page he couldn't read his own words.

How long did he propose to sit at the window? He was holding Brady still, but that wasn't necessary; the man would never be able to steal into the house. Dignam took the cramp in his guts for hunger. "Time for some of us to eat," he muttered. "Just make sure it's not poisoned."

He was unhappy to find that he couldn't eat much. Half the omelette he made to use up milk he scraped into the bin. He still had several bottles too many from trying to moderate his coffee intake and woo sleep. He finished one and bore another into the front room in case it would soothe the cramp in his innards while he allowed himself some television. There was nothing on the many channels to engage his mind: simplistic quizzes, violence whose lack of apparent effect struck him as close to psychotic, comedy shows accompanied by laughter so inappropriate it seemed crazed. While he gazed at the screen, was Brady gazing at the house? The possibility made his mind feel cramped. As soon as watching had tired him enough he stumbled up to bed.

He didn't recall closing his study door, but he resisted the temptation to peer around it to see if his neighbour was spying, which demonstrated how sane he was, as if he needed proof. Once he was in bed he set about forgetting his tormentor. He shouldn't have given the man a thought; by the time he ceased to feel his eyes he couldn't tell how much of the dark consisted of Brady's fancies about him. Certainly it helped Brady come into the room.

At first he only stared at Dignam and leaned close to show that his eyes were lidless, and then he began to shake his huge wild head. Dignam assumed this expressed disapproval until seeds and insects rained on him. He wasn't sure which dropped into his helplessly gaping mouth as Brady towered over him. The man's head was pressed against the ceiling now; some of the twigs sprouting from his cranium bent with a thin creak and snapped off. He reached up with arms longer than the room was wide and plucked a handful of shoots off the cracked scaly expanse of his forehead. He clamped Dignam's eyes open with two fingers of the other hand before planting the shoots between his victim's lips. With a flabby cry that made him feel less in control of his mouth than ever, Dignam jerked awake. Brady was above him, a looming shape more solid than the dark.

Dignam's gasp felt like taking back his cry. It seemed to suck the contents of his mouth deeper into him. He recoiled against the bars above the pillow, and the metal clashed against the wall as he flung out a hand for the light cord. For a moment his fingers felt entangled by twigs, and then he succeeded in tugging the light on.

He was alone in the room. There were no seeds or insects on or around the bed. Nevertheless he felt poisoned by the dream, which he sensed hovering like the man's oppressive presence, waiting to resume its shape. What stale taste was lingering in Dignam's mouth? When he floundered to the bathroom, gargling seemed to emphasise the taste. He threw his study door open to see if Brady was watching in triumph.

A streetlamp cast a net of shadow from the tree over the house opposite — too much shadow for Dignam to be anything like certain if the window was deserted. Poking his head forth didn't resolve the question. His eyes stung, and a taste like indigestion filled his mouth. He slammed the window and hurried downstairs, wiping his hand on his pyjamas between clutches at the sticky banister.

Two could play at the game Brady had wished on him. He drank half a bottle of milk and eased the metal cap off another, then found the seed that someone had tracked into the hall. He rubbed it between his hands, staining his palms, and crumbled the fragments with his nails into a powder he could sprinkle in the milk. He restored the cap and shook the bottle until it looked full of nothing but innocent milk. Having pulled on a jacket and trousers over his pyjamas, he hid the bottle inside his jacket as he left the house.

What did he intend to do? If Brady was watching, only to remind him he was also being watched. Dignam was beneath the sycamore, whose shadow felt as though innumerable seeds were poised to fall on him, before he could be sure Brady's window was unmanned. He strode as quickly as silence permitted to the man's front door. "Milk-o," he said under his breath. "Special Sunday delivery for Brady." He set the bottle on the step with a clunk far more muted than his heartbeat and allowed his uncontrollable grin to lead him back across the road.

He couldn't sleep now. He had to watch. He almost slammed the front door in his eagerness to dash upstairs and resume his post at the desk. He hadn't missed anything; the bottle was still on the doorstep. Its glimmer put him in mind of a headstone too shrunken by distance to move him. What had he done? Nothing fatal, certainly — nothing as poisonous as Brady's effect on him. Perhaps Brady would see that it was best to call a truce once he understood worse could befall him.

Soon Dignam's eyes felt charred by the dark and by watching. More than once the bottle reared up like a pallid larva or executed a jig from willingness to be discovered. "Gargoyle," he called, "gargoyle," but that failed to summon his adversary. In time the streetlamp grew redundant and eventually, without his noticing, dead. At some point he realised he was visible, and snatched an essay off the heap, not that he could make sense of the words just now. They seemed to underline his view of the house opposite, to suggest only that mattered. Once Brady opened the front door, he was all that did.

He didn't see the milk at first. He advanced to the gate and frowned up and down the street. As he turned back to the house Dignam saw him stiffen. He marched to grab the bottle and tear off the cap before swinging around to display how he was emptying the milk over the wild lawn strewn with seeds. In a few seconds he was at the window, holding up the bottle as evidence.

Evidence of what? He hadn't drunk from it, and he'd thrown away the contents. It would be monstrously unfair of him to accuse a neighbour of poisoning him. If he planned to sit there like a dairy advertisement, that was no reason for Dignam to indulge him. Dignam marked the essays almost faster than he could breathe — *confused thinking, too much identification with your subject, too closely observed for objectivity, too narrowly focused* — and swept the heap aside to work on his book. The solitary sentence on the topmost page brought him back to Brady, who hadn't moved or blinked.

How long was Dignam going to let himself be held there? Usually on Sundays he bought a paper to read in the pub on the campus, but suppose Brady took some crazed revenge while his neighbour was away? For once Dignam would have to patronise the corner shop.

He hadn't reached his gate when Brady emerged, flourishing the bottle. "Didn't kill me yet," he shouted. "Have another go."

"Take it as a warning," Dignam responded barely aloud. As he hurried to the shop he glanced back at every other step to ensure Brady wasn't sneaking towards his house. Had the man mouthed something or gestured to make three youths who were loitering outside the shop snigger at Dignam? A furious glance that screwed an ache into Dignam's neck found Brady turning away to speak to a girl in her teens or younger. As she followed Brady up the path Dignam wondered "Is someone up to no good with that child?"

"Dirty bugger," one youth snarled. The others muttered viciously as Dignam dodged into the shop.

Mrs Vernon and the shopkeeper were waiting for him. "Had a bad night, did you?" Mrs Vernon said.

He felt as if Brady's obsession with him had turned into a plague. "What makes you say that?" he demanded.

"Anybody would, the way you're dressed."

He looked down at himself as a preamble to sarcasm and saw

the pyjama cuffs protruding from his trousers, the pyjama collar sprawling forth from his jacket. As he gaped in search of words, Mrs Timms enquired "What were you saying outside?"

"Your friend Mr Brady has just taken a young girl inside his house."

"That'll be his granddaughter. She visits him on Sundays."

Dignam retreated to the door and surveyed the deserted streets. "Where did those boys go? Have you any idea where they live?"

"Which were those?" said Mrs Timms, and her customer added less gently "We thought you were talking to yourself."

Why were they trying to confuse him? If it was what Brady wanted, let him take the consequences. Dignam bought a newspaper and ran home. Suppose Brady had arranged the diversion to distract him? As soon as he'd secured the door he hunted for telltale seeds and did his best to ascertain whether the banister or any of the door-knobs was stickier than it ought to be.

The news in the paper seemed to belong to a world that had become detached from him. At the end of every sentence, and before long of every phrase, his eyes twitched up to focus on the house across the road. The afternoon, though not the paper, was half finished by the time Brady let the girl out. Dignam sprinted to his gate as Brady sent her on her way with not too much of a hug or a kiss. "Excuse me," Dignam called. "You may want to watch out for some young boys round here."

"Hurry home, Jane." Once she had picked up speed the man said "Maybe that's your kind of thing. It won't do for me."

"I didn't mean it like that."

"Then how do you know what I mean?"

"I'm trying to warn you in case you're in danger," Dignam's unwieldy mouth managed to pronounce. "Some people can get queer notions in their heads."

"You'd be the last person I'd need to tell me, Mr Dignam."

"Where did you get my name?"

"I know everything worth knowing about you, believe me."

If his stare was meant to convey this, Dignam was equal to it. His eyes had only begun to sting when Brady turned his back. "It's Doctor, so there's something you don't know for a start," Dignam said, but he'd blinked. As Brady shut his door Dignam slammed his and ran to his desk.

Sorting paper kept him busy: the news, the essays, the seed of his book. Soon he was beyond telling which was which. Was he watching out for Brady or hoping the youths would teach him manners? Perhaps they were waiting for the dark that sprouted branches against Brady's house. When a solitary figure disentangled itself from the shadows, he thought it was Brady bound for revenge. Once his peeled eyes recognised Hannah he strove to remember why she was there. Of course, she was anxious to learn what he thought of her essay and her.

Perhaps she would assume he was out, since the room was unlit. She met his eyes, however, as she ventured up the path, a plastic bag swinging from each hand. Now he remembered she had undertaken to provide dinner. The prospect kept him at his desk until she'd rung the doorbell twice, at which point he raced down to enquire "Would you mind telling me where you just got those?"

She looked puzzled and a little hurt. "I didn't just get them anywhere. I brought them from home."

"I'm going to watch you prepare the meal, am I?"

"It's made. All we need is a microwave. I know you've got one."

"Which of my neighbours have you been talking to?"

"None of them. I've never even seen one."

"Well, now you have," he said, jabbing all his fingers at the face among the flattened branches.

She gave it rather too perfunctory a look. "Can I come in now, do you think? It's chilly out here."

He was about to say he was too busy for dinner when he wondered if she might report back to Roger Douglas. If his rival heard that Dignam had been behaving oddly, what might he be capable of saying to their colleagues? "Come in by all means," Dignam said loud enough to be heard across the road. "I've nothing to hide."

Once he'd slammed the door behind her Hannah didn't move towards the kitchen until he led the way. He clawed at the light switch and twisted a chair backwards to sit on while he observed her putting the first carton in the microwave. This done, she was so ill at ease that nobody could blame him for enquiring "What's wrong?"

"Have you only just got up?"

"I've been too busy to get dressed. Do you want me to change?"

"You needn't. I've seen worse." Apparently this was a timid joke, perhaps intended to nerve her to say "Busy marking, would that have been?"

"Marking and working on the book I'm not supposed to be up to writing."

"I've never said that and I wouldn't. I know you have it in you." This was plainly the start of the process of asking "Did you finish your marking?"

"Shilly-shally, Hannah, shilly-shally."

"I'm not sure I . . ."

"That's your problem. Try believing in yourself enough to say what you mean. Have I marked your essay? Yes."

"Am I allowed to hear what you thought?"

"It seems to me you're in two minds. Decide which one you're sticking to."

"Can't I take the best from each?"

"They aren't compatible. By the time I'd finished trying to make sense of your essay my head was splitting in half. You're meant to be writing about madness, not driving people mad."

He thought he might have said too much until some of it silenced her. The hush emphasised how little he was eating. Weren't there seeds in the vegetable curry she served as the first course? He did his best to pick forkfuls nowhere near them, which left most of the contents of his plate untouched. "I'm saving myself," he said and felt the choice of words tug at his lips.

At least the silence let him hear any noises in the street. Before he'd finished hacking spicy chicken off its bones and sifting the rice with his fork, he had dashed into the front room twice. The second time Hannah followed, letting him retreat to the kitchen ahead of her and dump most of his plateful in the bin. Did she suspect? He could think of no other reason for her to replenish his plate. "I know you're worried about work," she said, "but it won't help to starve yourself, will it? Anyway, I don't know anyone who thinks you're past it except you."

How many lies were packed into that? "Don't delude yourself you know what I think," he said, and more slyly "I can enjoy your dinner by watching you eat."

She laid her utensils to rest among the bones. "I made it for you."

Suppose she'd eaten precisely enough not to poison herself? He consigned the remains to the bin and stacked the plates in the sink with a clatter that felt as if sections of his skull were grating together. It suddenly seemed crucial that Hannah shouldn't think he was behaving unusually in any way, lest she tell someone at the university. "I hope that doesn't mean you're leaving," he made himself say.

"Not if you don't want me to."

"You know what I want," he said and unzipped his trousers to demonstrate there was no misunderstanding.

Did she stiffen so that she wouldn't recoil? "Not down here, Terry," she protested.

"Indeed not. Up is best."

As he ensured that she preceded him upstairs, his extension raised itself from flopping against his trousers to sway in her direction. From the landing he glimpsed Brady at the window. If he discharged his task with Hannah in the office chair he could keep an eye out for the youths, but she had already switched on the light in the bedroom. When she sat on the edge of the bed he pushed her as flat as the tousled quilt permitted and eased her skirt up.

Her black briefs were slippery silk, which he felt squeaking beneath his nails until they caught in the filigreed edge. He pulled the briefs down far enough that he could insert himself in Hannah as he clambered onto her. At first he wasn't sure if her moans denoted pleasure or discomfort or simply determination to improve her grades, and then he wondered if they were meant to deafen him to sounds outside the house. He was reaching to lean a hand on her mouth and if necessary her nose as well when he heard shouts and a smash of glass across the road.

Dragging himself out of Hannah was more of a release than he was prepared for. Spurts of solidified dimness preceded him into the study. The sensations this entailed were far more remote than the sight of Brady at the window. The man hadn't moved, and there was no sign of the youths. Dignam wiped himself on a sheet of paper, which he flung into the bin as he resumed his seat. He was peering in search of broken glass when Hannah arrived behind him. "Terry," she pleaded, "what are you trying to do?"

He wasn't so easily distracted; he wouldn't even blink. "Are you asking me to believe you don't know?"

"I can't stay if you're going to behave like this."

"Then that solves a good few problems. I'll see you tomorrow in class."

Why was she loitering? She was about to ask for her essay, of course. "Tomorrow," he repeated so loud that it widened his eyes. He didn't let them shrink until he saw her on the stretch of pavement he was able to keep in view without losing sight of Brady. Once she lost shape and vanished from the rim of his vision he felt as if there had never been anyone except himself in the house.

Whatever the sound of breaking glass had signified, it appeared not to have affected Brady. He was staring at Dignam as if his entire being was concentrated in his eyes, but Dignam was equal to him. He wouldn't move or blink until his subject did. If Brady refused to heed his warning, he would bring whatever happened on himself. The gang weren't likely to kill him, after all. He hadn't made Dignam act out Brady's view of him. He never had.

In time Dignam's eyes drooped, and his head. He stretched his eyes wide until they felt on the edge of sprouting from their holes. He roused himself by pinching his thighs and eventually his penis with his nails. He wanted to think his opponent was having to resort to worse, but there wasn't a hint of movement over the road. How could the man sit so inert and never blink? A stealthy dawn had separated the topmost branches from the sky before Dignam was certain something was wrong.

He began to gesture wildly at the figure across the road. He tried to find the grin that had overtaken his face in the other house, and rocked his head from side to side and popped his eyes. When this had no effect he held up the hand that had borrowed a word from the newspaper in the corner shop and stabbed a finger at it. Next he climbed on the desk, trampling the papers, to wave his penis at his tormentor. None of this earned him a reaction. Brady wasn't just still, he was lifeless. Something — surely only his mental condition — must have frightened him to death.

In a moment that felt like stepping over the brink of a nightmare Dignam remembered everything he'd done: the milk, the youths. He leapt off the desk, jarring his ankles, and floundered out of the room. He ought to have checked that Hannah hadn't left the front door unlocked for anyone to sneak in, but it was fastened now. He closed it behind him as gently as his shivering fingers could manage and limped down the path.

Could he still be performing Brady's fantasies about him? What if the man had used the photographs to manipulate him? Just as witches had to let their victims know they were supposed to be under a spell, so Brady had ensured he saw the photographs. Or perhaps the seeds crunching underfoot were the key to it all; perhaps they spread Brady's influence. Dignam was so busy sorting out the truth that he was well across the road before twinges in his penis alerted him that it was exposed to the night air. He was stowing it away when with an outraged shout Brady sprang to his feet and vanished from the window.

What kind of a trick did he think he'd been playing? Dignam folded his arms and challenged the front door. He heard a disarrayed clatter of footsteps at the top of the stairs, and then the noises tumbled over one another. They were brought to an end by a weighty thud in the hall, followed by utter silence.

A nervous grin distorted his mouth as he limped on tiptoe to the door and hauled up the rusty flap of the letterbox. He knelt among the seeds and ducked to the metal slot, and had to lever his eyes wide with fingers and thumbs before he could believe what he was seeing. Brady was upside down, his body on the stairs, his head at an excessive angle in the hall. His accusing glare looked strengthened by its inversion, and seemed to require no effort at all.

Dignam met it as if he might still outstare it, and then he shut the flap and staggered to his feet and fled along the path. How long would Brady take to be discovered? Dignam wanted to be present so that whoever found the corpse would see him at his window and know he couldn't have been responsible. He leaned his elbows on the desk and gripped his head with both hands to keep his eyes trained on the house opposite. The deserted window appeared to be pretending Brady wasn't still obsessed with him. Suppose the man never closed his eyes again, or it no longer mattered if he did, since Dignam's last sight of them was embedded in his mind? The sun was helping parch his own eyes when he realised how he was putting himself at risk. He might be suspected if he behaved unusually in any way — if he didn't go to work.

He grabbed the trampled mass of papers from his desk and stuffed them into a carrier bag he found in the kitchen. At his gate he glanced at Brady's house while pretending to collect seeds, but could see no faces, neither Brady's nor his own. "Just off to work, Mrs Timms," he called into the shop. The stained carrier blundered against him as he limped to the crossroads, where the traffic lights drilled colours into his skull with a piercing buzz. Layers of grey matter piled up on the hill, but he succeeded in leaving their ossification behind as he made his swaying way across the campus. Although it was scattered with students, none of them was heading for

his lecture. He was about to demand an explanation when he realised he was late.

This was no reason for Roger Douglas to have taken the
podium, and why was Hannah on the front row? She gazed up at
Douglas as he said "My experience —"

"My course isn't about yours, Dr Drugless." Dignam limped to
the podium amid a rustling he mistook for general excitement until
he traced it to the carrier bag. "Sorry, that's the last thing I should
call you, isn't it? Thanks for filling in for me. You can stop now."

Douglas grasped himself by the beard or held up a mask. "Are
you sure you're, you'll forgive me, but are you up to this?"

"I could ask what you think you're up to. I believe Miss Martin
thinks I'm still competent to teach, don't you, Miss Martin? And I'm
sure you speak for all your fellow students."

They were certainly all gazing at him in the same way. It could-
n't be pity; it must be sympathy — they were on his side. "Thank
you, Roger," he said, indicating the auditorium with a hand like a
blurred sign.

Douglas stepped down reluctantly but lingered at the back of
the room. If he'd decided he could learn from his colleague, perhaps
there was hope for him. Dignam emptied the carrier onto the lec-
tern, only to find that the pages were stuck together by vegetable
matter. He mustn't let the sight claw at his guts; once the stuff dried
he would be able to separate the essays. "So we've been talking about
experience, have we?" he said, fixing his gaze on the heaps of faces.
"Let's talk about mine, then. My experience . . ."

How could he tell them about Brady? Even mentioning the man
would betray he'd watched him. The thought made everything feel
turned upside down like the eyes he could see on the stairs. "My experience," he said he didn't know how many times while eyes stared
at him. Most of them weren't Brady's, unless they all were. When
had Douglas sneaked out of the room? No doubt he was bringing
someone else to observe the lecture. Dignam had to demonstrate
that he still had plenty to offer, but how? "My experience," he said,
and his gaze lit upon his own handwriting. At once he knew both
what his opening sentence should be and how he could regain control of the lecture. "A man sits in a room," he said in triumph.

It appeared to mean less to his students than to him. He lowered
himself into a chair on the podium and, having tugged his sleeves
over his pyjama cuffs, leaned forward to compose the precarious

stacks of heads with his gaze. "I'm not going to tell you my experience, I'm going to let you observe it for yourselves," he said. "Observe what distinguishes me from a man with a mental problem. Don't look away until you have."

Some of them must have seen almost at once. Others, not only Hannah, apparently found it harder. He wouldn't relax until everyone had finished the assignment. When refusing to blink began to take away his sight, his innards shrank into him, but soon his inability to see whether he was being watched felt more like peace. He heard people leave the auditorium, and others come in, and voices murmuring. He had to be grateful that they were so anxious not to disturb him. When the voices converged on him and hands helped him up, he was content to be led to rest now that he'd carried out the task he was paid for. A solitary thought was enough for him. He need see nothing that he didn't want to see so long as he never blinked.

# REAL PEOPLE SLASH

## *Nick Mamatas*

It was the tediously cyclical nature of the Fourth of July riot that led to my first revelation. I was on a rooftop on Norfolk Street with some comrades and anarchists just a few hours before, watching fireworks explode and them drink because they only had beer and I don't drink beer. The fireworks were bright and loud but far off, on the far end of the tar beach and water tower horizon. Avijut's cologne preceded him by a second as he sauntered up to me in a neatly-pressed purple shirt, his longneck like a girlfriend on his arm.

"So, comrade" he said, rolling his *r*'s, the birdy accent the last remnant of his claim to authenticity. "Doesn't this remind you of the battle of Stalingrad?"

Though he was in the ISO with me and thus was bound to our theories of state capitalism and our related refusal to defend the Soviet Union, Avijut had cut his teeth in about half-a-dozen different Stalinist parties back home in Bangladesh and was still a bit of a tankie. And it was the fifty-year anniversary of the end of the Second World War, so everyone, even the far left, was taking credit for the win.

I tsked at him. "Didn't you read *SW*?" That was *Socialist Worker*, our paper. "We're about resistance movements, not fucking Stalin!" At least it was better than debating Deleuze and Guattari with him. He had never even read Deleuze and Guattari. I was ready to end it early and drop the G-bomb, gulag, but he was interested so I mentioned France and then dived into Greece and ELAS and Stalin's betrayal of them in order to keep the British happy and then this woman whose name I have forgotten — though I remember she was tall and stood like a transgendered rooster when she talked, and she was supposedly an Edison heir who wrote the checks that kept the local anarchist bookstore in what they all unironically called "business" — interrupted to denounce me as a petit nationalist since I'm Greek and told us it was really all about the Spanish Civil War and where was Trotsky then and no POUM didn't count so don't even start and then Marina walked up to us with her boyfriend Roy and offered everyone more beers and smiled apologetically at me for not having anything but tap water for me to drink.

Marina was a comrade, and Roy a sleepy grad student anarchist she had tried to recruit but instead ended up moving in with. She was a short woman with high cheekbones, the kind men liked to talk to, which is why she sold so many SWs on our Saturday afternoon paper sales. Roy stood next to her and ran his fingers through his hair constantly, leaving it to stick up. Throw enough basketballs through a toilet lid and you could have won Roy at a carnival. He mumbled something about sectarianism, which is really all he ever did as far as I could tell. Even the fridge downstairs in the apartment he shared with Marina was covered in the Post-it Notes they left for one another; on them they slowly but surely debated the need for a revolutionary party and also reminded one another to get dishwasher fluid. They never did resolve the party question, and the sink was full of dirty dishes.

The fireworks ended, and the political disagreements over who'd round up and kill whom after the revolution were drowned in El Presidente, so we moved downstairs to the apartment. I found myself by the fridge, smirking, instead of "talking to people," which I put in quotes because talking to people at a party of political sorts meant speaking to anarchists about the ISO and trying to win them over.

"Why aren't you talking to people?" Marina asked me. She opened the fridge slowly, so as not to interrupt my reading, and pulled out a small plastic jar of hummus or something equally noxious and vegetarian that everyone but me would be sure to love as a dip for the crazy blue organic barley chips I didn't like either. I feared for the fate of pretzels and normal potato chips after the revolution. Not really, but I used to tell people that, to test them for humanity.

"I disagree with the perspective; we shouldn't be trying to win rich grad school anarchists. They're committed to their own thing already. See?" I ran my fingers against the curved edges of the aging Post-it Notes.

"Well, disagree with it or not, we all agreed to it," she said.

I rolled my eyes, "I can see why you're not winning Roy over, if that's your argument."

She sniffed at the contents of the container, and her nose twitched dramatically. "This isn't what I thought it was."

I pointed to another Post-it Note; a shopping list. "Did you lose the hummus argument too?"

She smiled and said, "The hummus argument is the most important argument facing the working class today." I laughed because Marina rarely joked, and I wanted to encourage her. In the other room, the phone rang and Roy picked it up. He walked past the kitchen's doorway and into the dark hallway by the apartment door to get away from the chatter and the Brazilian guitar music that filled the book-laden living room. Seconds later he was in the kitchen, grabbing up the empty beer bottles with a wide sweep of his arms and calling out to his friends, "The squatters took back C squat and the cops are attacking." The transgendered rooster sprang to her feet and snatched up the handles to two paper bags of empty bottles outside the kitchen, and behind Roy the entire anarchist contingent left without a word, sneakers and old boots slapping the bowed slabs of marble steps that led down to the building entrance.

"What was that?" said Nathan, swinging into view in the kitchen doorway. "Where did the anarchists go?" His eyes were wide and extra white against flushed bronze skin and recently he had adopted a silly pointed goatee: half Che, half billy goat.

"Oh, they're just very middle-class and eager to recycle stuff," I told him. Nathan almost finished nodding before he got the joke.

"You think they'll use those bottles as weapons?" asked Marina, and then before I could say something sarcastic she said "Everyone in here, please." The anarchists just stormed off, but we were socialists. We needed to vote.

Nathan stepped in, and behind him were Avijut and Delphine, who looked very curious, since she was new and only a contact — she had probably thought the party was a real party.

Do we intervene in the riot? All hands up, the ayes had it. Unanimous. Should we bring leaflets for the next branch meeting? To a riot? It was ridiculous, but it couldn't hurt. All hands up, the ayes had it. Unanimous.

We shuffled behind Marina, who slipped a scarf hanging from a peg by the door around her neck. "All-weather scarf?" I asked.

She pulled the scarf, white fabric decorated with blue, over her mouth and nose to show me, then slipped it back down again with a wink. Intifada kitsch. Marina was Jewish and had taught at some progressive Hebrew daycare center once, so she always made an extra show of solidarity and unconditional but critical support of the Palestinians.

Things moved quickly after that. We didn't arm ourselves except for the leaflet, but Nathan was itching to fight the pigs; he did imitation kung-fu moves and let out Bruce Lee "Whattah!" yelps for five blocks before I called for a stop.

"Don't fuck around," I said. "If this is going to be a riot, we have to be careful."

"Cops are the class enemy," said Nathan, excited.

"Yes, but if we end up beaten up or arrested, it should be on purpose," said Marina. I was glad for her back up. "Stay together, and try to stay in sight of each other if you can't stay close. Talk to people if you can, fight if you have to; try to win people through example, and if you can give 'em a leaflet, give 'em a leaflet." They looked sad, the sheaf of them drooping in her hand as she handed them out. Delphine, the contact, blushed and refused to take any because she didn't "want to be confused for a member."

"But you're coming to the riot?" Nathan asked her. It was love.

"Oh yes," Delphine said. "We riot in France all the time. Students do it every weekend. That's why my parents sent me to grad school in America." She walked on with Marina, the pair of them stylish and invincible thanks to lawyer parents and pockets full of credit cards with balances they'd never have to pay. Behind them Nathan straggled on like a puppy — he had no parents who could help him out of prison, but he also didn't have parents or a job to worry about and so had nothing to lose by spending a few days in central holding in the Tombs.

Avijut and I both let the others walk ahead a bit, then threw our flyers into the trash. On that, we were agreed. We walked on, and when we hit East Thirteenth and Avenue C things started happening very fast.

It was bright, thanks partially to spotlights from the three cop copters circling the block and to the flaming Dumpster. The crowded street was thick with white people, mostly guys in T-shirts but with more than a few women as well. Some had sticks and bottles, but the weapon of choice was drums, some improvised from trash cans, others fairly pricey-looking. One would thump out a beat, and the others would take it up; the drumless stamped their feet or chanted in time, "Whose streets? Our streets!" On the sidewalks, behind linked-together bike racks, stood lines of cops, helmeted and with their riot shields sort of leisurely held up and balanced against the edges of the cordons. They all had plenty of plastic Flexi-Cuffs hanging from their belts, and the extra long, double-thick riot batons at the ready.

The conflict had begun two months ago, when the squatters were evicted following a court battle. Giuliani wasn't going to play nice like the Democrats had, and on May 25th a squad of cops, backed by an armored personnel carrier, smashed through their hasty barricades, battered down their shoddily reinforced doors, and dragged all the squatters out into the street. Barstool meetings for the street kids and CC'ed e-mails among the students had been secretly planning a response ever since. Now, tonight, the squatters had snuck along the rooftops and broken back into their house, then launched a few bottle rockets at the pair of cops who had been stuck with empty-building guard duty. Then they unrolled a banner with the circled N logo of squat defense spray painted on it, and another one that read, "FUCK THE TANK."

They shouted, "Independence Day, pigs!" as they set off their fireworks.

Well, the cops called in for lots and lots of back-up, including the tank that rumbled loudly a few blocks away on Thirteenth and A. I could hear it over the drums, the shouting, the whirlywhip of the copters, and everything else. I could feel it in my shins. It was hot and we all smelled, but I got a chill.

For a second I thought I should take off my shirt, turn it inside out, and put it back on. Marina had given it to me after a British comrade she had been dating left it at her house; it had the logos of the Anti-Nazi League and the TV series Red Dwarf by the shoulders, and was emblazoned with the slogan, "NAZIS ARE SMEGHEADS." The cops, I could tell, were waiting for a signal to kick over the bike racks and charge. They were eyeing us for weak spots — knots of girls and the skinny, crusty kind of punks that would fall right over if nudged with a riot shield. I didn't feel like wearing a bull's-eye. I was also worried that one of the stupider anarchists might take the shirt as a pro-Nazi statement, since the ANL logo was pretty small. It would be difficult to explain the etymology and usage of the word smeghead to a boot. I saw Avijut walk off, gawking like he was at a mall, and had already lost track of everyone else when there was a shout and then a swelling push of limbs. *Charge!*

I linked arms with the people closest me; they were nobody I knew, but they had the look of experience. A long line of us rushed the oncoming shields, and at the last moment we shifted to the left and led with our shoulders, trying to squeeze into the slim spaces between cops, to wedge past the flexible edges of the shields. No pig wants to be caught with a man behind it, not when one arm is strapped to a heavy riot shield and the other is hefting a stick too long for infighting. We hit the wall hard and I stumbled backwards, leaving a lungful of breath where I'd been standing, but enough of us broke through the line to make the cops double-step back and reform. I kept to my feet and moved back to the sidewalk for the stand off. The drumming and chanting began again, and this time the cops charged to hurt, not push, their truncheons held high like knights. We broke and ran down C, screaming and hollering, while some of the drummers shouted "Hold the line! Hold the line!"

I darted to the right edge of Avenue C to avoid a beer bottle someone had tossed over his shoulder while he ran, and managed to walk right into a Snapple bottle instead. Those bastards are thick. You can drop them on the sidewalk and they won't shatter or even chip. My scalp? Not so much. Blood flooded my glasses, which were slipping down my nose from sweat, and my head hurt like failure — a distant, steaming pain.

I stumbled onto the sidewalk, where slow rioters mixed with neighborhood gawkers and tried to blend in. I caught a glimpse of a crowded deli — the Indian brothers who owned the place were plastered against the glass door, holding it shut, and some workers and a few customers peered out over their shoulders. I nudged the door but they held it fast, and then — and I blame the head injury for my thinking this would be a good idea — I pulled a crumpled dollar from my pocket and waved it at the man who held the door shut. "I'm a customer, see?"

His brother reached behind his back and leveled a gun at me through the glass. I put up my hands and stepped back saying sorry sorry sorry like it was falling out of my mouth.

A rioter, a thick woman with a bandana around her head, saw the gun and bellowed "Call the police!"

I pointed up at the sweeping spotlights with one hand and at the triple-thick trotting lines of riot cops coming up behind us with the other and shouted back, "They're already here!" She ran back off into the riot and I cut the corner on East Eleventh.

Halfway down the block a bicyclist tore off the sidewalk and cut me off in the middle of the street. He was black, too large for his bike, sweating like a steam pipe, and too conversational. "Hey, brother," he said. "I gotta ask you something." He held his bike in front of him like a sawhorse to block my way.

I touched my bloody forehead. "What?"

"Wanna buy some?" He reached into the pocket of his shorts and pulled out three small baggies of white powder. "Five dollars."

"No thanks, Officer!" I moved past him, thinking that everyone knows smack is ten bucks a baggie, not five, and slowly made my way across the East Village and into the West, where I lived with two roommates on a fifth-floor walkup railroad apartment. By First Avenue, the riot was muted by several blocks of solid row houses. By the time I reached the Bowery, it was a memory. I got home to West Twelfth Street, a quiet cobblestone block, and rested at each landing on my way up. It was 2:30 AM when I hit my room. It was empty, my roommates either sleeping behind papery plaster walls or still out celebrating independence. I swung, groggy, onto the loft bed's ladder as the floor fell away from me.

Pulling myself up, I lay down on the mattress, my head throbbing and two feet from the ceiling that a previous roommate had decorated with little glow-in-the-dark stars and crescent moons, probably to help shake off the claustrophobia that comes when you try and sleep with your nose scraping plaster. They looked far off and fuzzier than usual thanks to my head, which felt like it was leaking hot lava. Like the ceiling had fallen away, and I was staring into a swirling Van Gogh night.

It was then that I realized my life was being controlled by forces beyond human understanding. Eyes blurred and watery, head cracked wide, I was open to this starry wisdom. The fungous buzzing Mi-Go, peering down from fabled Yuggoth in the darkest corner of this solar system, had turned their blasphemous sensory stalks toward me. It was like that old college freshman thought experiment in reverse: instead of contemplating the possibility that I was the only being with free will on Earth, and everyone else was a shadow play pawn, I realized that I was the pawn. Everyone had free will except for me — a billion billion pincers and points prodded and pushed me from the womb to the slab upon which I finally received this eye-opening communication. Friends, family, powerful strangers in dark suits: they were all real people. Real people, slash alien crustaceans splashing forth from the paranoid inks of Weird Tales.

Every choice I've ever made — grad school in New York, the furious celibacy of a crowded apartment, street fighting nights and days dedicated to the labor theory of value and endless term papers on Maya Deren and the whipcrack of her cinema voodoo — it was all in preparation for my ultimate dissection and the introduction of my cerebrum into the confines of a silvery brain canister to be followed by hyperspatial transport to their blasphemous, necrophagus tenth planet, far beyond Pluto. There was no escape, I knew that now too. There was nothing now but the horror of knowing the true course of history, the Marxist nightmare of an unending cosmic materialism beyond our muscles and machines. I slept then, but not well.

I was up at five, nauseated and dry as sand. I wanted to stay in bed, to stare at the plastic stars and demand more from them, but my status as a no-collar, non-union prole under late capitalism had other plans. Mi-Go or no, I still had to pay my rent, which was now five days late. Soon my roommates would be frowning and threatening me ("How about we just throw your shit down the shaft?"), no matter how impressive the knot on my head was. Luckily, I worked an early morning shift at my bullshit day job, so I had an excuse to be gone before my roomies even woke up. It was part-time and generally enough to pay my bills, provided I stuck to chick peas and rice and held off on cable and electricity till the final notices showed up.

I had no money, so I walked to work in the morning twilight, straight up Eighth Avenue to the McGraw-Hill Building on West Forty-Second. I hadn't changed clothes at all, and I looked bad enough that the morning whores, just coming off from their blowjob nights, didn't even bother with their usual friendly hellos as I walked by.

Nobody who has lived in the city for more than five minutes ever looks up, but I did that morning. The sky was a roiling purple, and heat waves rose like a thousand spectral fingers from the flat roofs of the Village, and Chelsea.

I worked at Video Monitoring Services. My job was to watch the morning news shows and make notes of any businesses or logos that appeared in them, so that the agglomerated information could be marketed and sold to corporate clients. That morning, I saw footage of Marina being shoved into a paddy wagon, of cops perched on rooftops and crowds twisting like snakes on the streets, and sour-faced pigs grunting ballsy talk into their microphones. Now I knew their voices were artificial, the result of alien surgery on vegetable lungs. The inhumanity of television personalities suddenly made sense — their extrahumanity, in fact, full of careful elocutions designed to persuade and opiate. In my cubicle's monitor I saw streets covered in twinkling glass like snow, and a partially caved-in, Snapple-branded fridge from a bodega laying on its side in the middle of Avenue C.

Cyclical. Practice.

Terence Benoit, my supervisor, whose name I've since cannibalized for one of my stories, hovered over me. His jaw chattered like a mandible. "Nick," he said. Then he said it again, to perfect it: "Nick?" I looked at him and slipped my headset off my ears. "Would you like to go home?" It was shaped like a question, and indeed, Terence was shaped like a sawed-off little human. But he wasn't curious, and the question was a false one.

Go home.

"Why?"

"You don't look good at all. You're pale, gray" — not the bright pink of the shelled Mi-Go — "and your shirt is all messed up. Plus, you're covered in puke or something."

I looked down at my lap. So I was. There had been nothing I could stomach at the party, so the vomit crusting on my jeans was light and only sticky. I was still working faster than any of my co-workers, and they were too busy staring at their own monitors and listening to their own headsets to notice my condition, so I wasn't disrupting work that way either. What was he up to?

"You'll still be paid for the day," Benoit said. "It's okay, Nick."

Benoit was a minor phalange of the managerial caste — his life was given toward increasing the exploitation of his subordinates with speed-ups and threats of firing, not to send people home to freshen up. And yet he was standing before me, his sloping remnant of a chin trying to jut out manfully, telling me to go home. As if for my benefit.

I shrugged off my headset, stood up — a bit wobbly, true — and said, "I was in that riot yesterday."

Benoit did an approximation of a shrug, as if his skin was just stretched over an alien exoskeleton; it was a twitch, rendered slow and dubious.

"Thanks for letting me go home," I said.

"You're welcome."

"I'll be back tomorrow."

"Of course you will," he said. "I mean, good." Benoit was one of the few men I've met who was actually shorter than me, but he didn't act the same way I do around taller guys. I stand off to the side, keeping my eyes on their torsos and shoulders, looking down at my own hands and cracking my knuckles — anything to avoid looking up at them like I was a child. Benoit craved this though; he took a step forward and invaded my space, practically resting his jaw against my chest. "Yes, I will see you tomorrow."

"Tomorrow," I said. "Hale and healthy." I touched my head. "And whole. Especially whole."

"Whole," Benoit said, nodding.

Or was it hole?

On the way home, I realized I was hungry and then smelled fresh pizza. Only — was that what really happened? Or did I smell the pizza first, which triggered a series of complex sensory and autonomic responses that just read like hunger? My head throbbed, then stopped when I thought about the throbbing — like the darting look away when a stranger catches you staring on the subway. And that happened to me too, on the train.

I waited for the A, C, or E back downtown because I found a token in my back pocket, and I swear it hadn't been there when I left for work. When it pulled up and I stepped inside, some old woman held the door open and shouted to me that this train, the one I was on, was the wrong one. Three MTA bing-bong notification bells later, a passing subway cop escorted her away. Only she was right; the C started heading even farther uptown. I took it one stop north and hopped off. I walked to the wrong side of the platform and took the wrong C train, which got me back down to the West Village in time for more sleep under the dull daytime stars of my crouching ceiling.

That afternoon, Marina called. She had been unarrested soon after being shoved into the paddy wagon. "And that's totally illegal," she said. "So," I said. "You'd rather have stayed arrested?" She moved on to asking after me, and when I told her about the bottle she suggested I go to the speak-out that night at Tompkins Square Park and tell my story of pig-violence victimization. The anarchists were organizing it, she said, but Roy could get me some time.

"But the anarchists are the ones who threw the bottle at me!"
She had little to say after that.

The second revelation came soon afterward, when I learned that the Mi-Go had not infiltrated just the NYPD, and New York's tiny, far-left groupuscles, but even my own roommates. I had originally moved into the cramped railroad apartment with two women but the leaseholder, Kerry, left to move in with her boyfriend in an attempt to stop breaking up with him every other week, and the other one, Gretchen, left for cheaper digs in the East Village a month later. Kerry found a guy named John, who insisted on being called "Big Gus," to take over the lease. Gus, in turn, found Pablo to fill Gretchen's room. And with Pablo came Andrew, his friend who slept on the floor next to his bed three nights a week. The other four nights were reserved for Pablo's girlfriend, Margarita, who fucked so quietly I once thought Pablo had smothered her with a pillow.

A few nights after the riot, Andrew was staying over and I heard him say, from Pablo's room, "Man, I gotta piss."

Pablo said, "So go piss."

"What about that guy?" He meant me. The place was a railroad, like I said, so to get to the bathroom from Pablo's room you had to walk through my room, and then through the kitchen. Big Gus lived in the room past Pablo's, and he had his own entrance. When he wanted to piss in the middle of the night, he could just walk down the fifth floor hallway to the kitchen entrance. But he never, ever did.

"Nick doesn't care. He's a Communist. He's all about letting people use his stuff. Plus if you gotta go, you gotta go." Pablo giggled like a girl, and Andrew joined him.

"When I was a kid," Andrew said, "I was afraid to go at night. I used to whip it out and piss all over the rug in my room."

"Fucking gross!" The walls were thin, but not that thin. They had been out drinking, I realized in another burst of clarity: loud mouths, and full bladders. It all made sense.

"Yeah, and it got all yellow and crystallized and shit. My mother never knew what was up, even though the whole room smelled like piss."

Pablo said, "Great. Now I have to piss." He got up, opened the door between our rooms, and tried to creep past me with heavy, drunken feet. He stumbled through the dark kitchen and into the bathroom. There, he yanked too hard on the chain light switch, nearly bringing the whole fixture down. It seemed like a drunken accident at the time, but the next morning I figured out that it was nothing less than Pablo's attempt to kill me, all the better to harvest my brain for his alien masters, the Mi-Go. I realized this when I reached for a towel hanging on the shower rod, and became paralyzed by a bolt of blue lightening.

The old bathroom had a tin ceiling. It was once tasteful but had, over the decades, sunk and pooched out like a belly. The shower rod, aluminum, was connected to the tin ceiling by another metal rod. I was soaking wet in the bath and my right foot was placed, through a complex series of minute factors that the Mi-Go had carefully arranged — water temperature and swirl, the design of the old, narrow tub and its alien claw feet, my mood and exhaustion from the night of the riot and the subsequent night of seemingly mindless chatter, the exact position of the bump on my head which partially closed my left eye — directly over the iron drain.

Just above the ceiling a live wire, loosened from the light fixture thanks to Pablo's skillful, late-night yank, had come to rest on the tin. The circuit completed itself with my body, ceiling to rod to arm to leg to drain. My fingers clenched the bar tight in a deadly, involuntary grip, and sparks jumped from filling to filling in my mouth. My brain — I could feel it, rising atop my boiling spine. The crack in my head spread wide as the world around me dilated, flooded with the white light of hell; from across the inky void of space, the Mi-Go reached for my fleshy mind, all too happy to leave my body behind, just an empty skin, burned and pruny and without brain. Who would care? The police, slaves of the Mi-Go themselves? Terence Benoit, who sent me home yesterday in order to further the machinations of his alien masters? I was probably already replaced; turnover was so high that he ran the ad for my exact position in every week's Village Voice.

Somehow, I managed to move my foot from the drain, discovering in the process that every thesis contains within it its own antithesis. As the drain was blocked by my foot, the water that made me so conductive had nowhere to go but into the minute and momentary spaces between flesh and iron, spaces caused not by conscious thought but by my uncontrollable electro-spasms. When enough water rushed under my foot to break the deadly suction and allow me to pull my heel from the drain, I managed to simultaneously regain control of my arm and let go of the shower rod, thus breaking the deadly circuit. My fillings throbbed, the spit in my mouth heated to scalding.

I was on the couch in the kitchen, watching television and waiting, when Big Gus walked in from the hallway to get ready for his Internet date that night, already in his robe, a towel over his shoulders like a boxer before the fight and his clothes, pressed and folded by the Chinese laundry around the corner, held under one arm. I was on the couch because that's all we had, no table and chairs for the kitchen, just the couch and a tiny coffee table. I didn't know anyone in Manhattan who actually had a table in their kitchen. "Hullo," he said, and without waiting for my response he ducked into the bathroom.

I heard a grunt, then the toilet flush, then, a few seconds later, the water in the tub started running. He turned on the showerhead and I raised the volume on the television, only half-ready to accept the truth. My forehead felt like someone had welded a desk safe to it.

Big Gus always hummed in the shower, mostly old AOR hits. It was Bachman-Turner Overdrive tonight. He was taking care of business when I heard a high-pitched squeal — the plaintive screaming of a lobster in a pot, normally beyond the range of human hearing, followed by a massive thump against the bathroom door. The door flew open and Gus fell out, limbs flailing, his belly as white as the underside of fungi from a glacial methane planet, his close-cropped blond hair suddenly frizzled and peachy, the bathroom's hook-lock tearing free from the cheap wood of the door to fly past my head and smack against the far wall.

Gus lay on the kitchen floor, his wet skin smearing and smudging the fine layer of grayish dirt that our linoleum always seemed to attract so easily, without speaking. He didn't even let loose one of the lengthy, Dopplering "fuuuucks" he uttered every time he saw the phone bill, or sports scores on the news, or rain spattering against the window, or any other aspect of human life unknown to the Mi-Go.

I got up and stood over him. "What happened?" I asked innocently. Dazed, he slipped and told me the truth: the trillion year-war against Hastur; Yuggoth long ago stripped of the precious metals it needed to fuel its own fleet of impossible war machines; their mental secret to folding space and the ongoing invasion of Earth; the mining of the Vermont hills and the seizure of certain sensitive brains in shiny, new cylinders; Lovecraft being right, as were all the dreary pastiches that presented the author as a character who stumbled upon the true nature of the world; the morning flapping of rooftop pigeons wasn't the sound of natural birds of all, but of the awkward Mi-Go, still struggling to adapt to our atmosphere; everyone I knew had already been turned, though most of them were as ignorant as plastic pans; and how did I escape the shower, anyway, he asked.

Sheer luck, I told him, the same sheer luck that gave my brain whatever attributes it needed to gain the attention of the Mi-Go. And with that John Gustafson melted into the floor, waxen flesh joining the dirty water and rendering it sizzling at my feet. In the core of the mess writhed what looked like an undercooked pink lobster, with finny wings and a stalk-sprouted mushroom for a head.

In the absence of irrefutable evidence, there is always some doubt, even among true believers. I believed in getting up early on Saturdays to sell socialist newspapers and argue against wars and invasions that even all the New York liberals believed in, such as Haiti, for example, and the Balkans, operations they relished like giggling hyenas breaking bones for marrow, but I always wondered along the way, What if I'm wrong? When I saw the truth in the stars, I wondered then too. Concussions are strange things, after all. But when the less-evil of my two roommates decomposed into pinkish sludge before me, when the kitchen filled with the fecund stink of steaming compost and the dissolved flesh of his man-costume, there was no more room for doubt. I didn't wait for Pablo, I didn't call the cops or my landlord, I just packed my things and left. One of the advantages of puny rooms in tiny Manhattan shares is this: you don't collect a lot of extraneous crap.

I kept the small blanket I used to hang on the back of that kitchen couch. It still smells like rotten orchids.

Ten years passed, and I kept moving around. Just after I left my old place, I found a cramped studio apartment on the Lower East Side, across the street from another quasi-legal squat, ABC No Rio. Every Sunday, after the punk rock matinee, I stepped out onto the pavement and over puddles of punk rock urine to get my groceries and do laundry. My landlords were insane. They demanded the tenants leave cash, not checks, in a red plastic box nailed to the outside of their door. At 5:00 A.M. on the first of every month they showed up, all stomping feet and pounding fists, waking the entire building if even a single tenant didn't leave his or her envelope in the mail drop. Dog shit littered the halls, and most of the other apartment doors, all of them gray steel, were festooned with useless medallions and pictures of the Virgin Mary, superstitious attempts to keep the grasping claws of the Mi-Go away. I lasted in that apartment for eight months despite the rats, the carbon monoxide from the electric heater, the tub in the kitchen that would fill with sewage in the rain, the faulty wiring, and the locked window guards. My landlords held the keys to the window guards, and they refused to give them to me.

Then it was over the river to Jersey City, which had the dual advantages of being extremely close to Manhattan and utterly foreign to any New York City resident. I even dared tell people that I lived in New Jersey and smirked as they marveled at my ability to cross the river with mere rail technology. I lived with a wonderful girl who read tarot cards and counted the seconds till the next minute each time she caught a glance at the clock radio. We never left the house. I started working from home, writing résumés, letters, personal statements, and model term papers for immigrants and ESL students. I'd type up the papers and print them out on a greasy old printer, then walk four blocks down to an office where I'd slip them under the door. Out from under the door would come a small envelope, full of cash and the next day's work.

Everything was great until my girl started manifesting new personalities: sweet children, neurotic men who'd emerge to bite my ears and claw at my chest during sex, that kind of thing. She kept finding The Tower and The Moon in my spreads. Then she left one day, crying and shrieking. The apartment was dead without her. When I started getting junk mail at my new address, I knew it was time to move.

I couldn't trust landlords anymore, not after I caught my last one shoving pennies into the fuse boxes of the building we shared. "They never burn out this way," he told me excitedly when I caught him. "All the power we need will flow." Power needed for what, that was my question, so I got my own place. I also went into business for myself, buying houses and then quickly selling them back to their previous owners, earning money from equity and slovenly tenants who were happy to live in dank basements, ankle-deep in Chinese food and pornography. The children began to avoid my house at Halloween but I got a dog anyway, and I trained her to growl and snap at anyone who didn't smell exactly like me. Some women wonder why I refuse to bathe before sex. For your own good! I tell them, and it's only half a lie. They're safe from my half-mad guard dog, but sometimes I dream that when the Mi-Go come, they will corner a spinster ex with their pincer hands and sterile cylinders by mistake, and leave me be.

I started writing fiction and after a couple of years sold a story. The local weekly paper interviewed me — Jersey City really is two miles and two hundred years away from Manhattan. A local writer is still news. I begged them not to run my picture and they didn't, not until *Northern Gothic* was nominated for a minor literary award, thanks to the intervention of a nameless, faceless Additions Jury of specially selected madmen. I retreated from the world almost entirely, but the dot com thing was on, and homely shut-ins of the day before yesterday became the minor celebrities of the moment. My picture showed up in the Village Voice, then Silicon Alley Reporter and Artbyte. My little checks from writing went up from fifty dollars to three hundred, from three hundred to a thousand — for a moment I dared to dream. I even entered protest politics again, after the victories at Seattle and Genoa. I wore the orange shoes from my week-long stint in prison for civil disobedience as morning slippers for a year, before they disintegrated on my feet.

Then the two towers fell, and the aliens regained the initiative. They missed me though — even supernatural intellects who can navigate the lightless wastes of N'Kai have trouble zeroing in on Jersey City. My backyard became littered with business memos, half-burnt folders, and computer print-outs that had fluttered over the river to Jersey. I kept them in a plastic trash bag and waited for men in dark suits to come and claim them, but they were busy elsewhere planting evidence, imprisoning journalists and discontented foreigners, and undermining the coherence and political efficacy of the "reality-based community." The Mi-Go were sealing off the planet through their endless supply of mindless servitors; they still are. Or maybe it's done already.

The markets for what I laughingly called "non-fiction" dried up, so I redoubled the attention I paid to fiction, hoping that, like Lovecraft who told his story of the Mi-Go based on shadowy reports embedded in the *Brattleboro Reformer* newspaper, I could somehow sneak a few hints about the true nature of the world into the public consciousness.

Last year I moved to California, after one of my houses was inexplicably stripped of all its copper one April night. The police said it was "Gee Dees," which they claimed stood for "juvenile delinquents," who were to have stolen the copper to sell as scrap in order to buy drugs, but I knew that not even the pigs were so stupid as to spell the word "juvenile" with a "G." It was a warning shot, or a slightly misplayed hand by the Mi-Go. Could the precious metal they sought under the Vermont hills seventy-five years ago really be simple copper? I doubt it. They were taunting me.

In Berkeley I lived much as I did before. I never left the house, and I prodded and cajoled my dog to yap at every passer-by and stalled bus she saw from my bedroom window. Let your animals howl all night, for all I care. A friendly word of advice: the Mi-Go fear claw and fang, just as any other crustacean with an easy-to-crush armor plating and a mealy fungal viscera would.

Of course, there aren't any other crustaceans like that . . . that I know of.

No one believed I'd last in California, and I'm not ashamed to admit that they were right. An inexplicable housing bubble, again defying all bourgeois economics, drained my resources. Gangs of liberals in five hundred dollar hippie dresses — a disguise no true human would ever fall for — came to my door to demand I prove my radical credentials by voting for their kill-crazed imperialist candidate, John Kerry. But I never meant for my stay on the West Coast to be permanent. All I wanted was a year of sunshine, golden sunshine clear and pure and warm, without any of the slushy miseries of winter. There'll be winters enough where I'm going: first Brattleboro, Vermont, then, unless I am very fortunate indeed, the caverns of Yuggoth, the dark planet of the Mi-Go where even on the surface our sun registers as nothing but a silver pinprick in the middle of their endless night, like a distant bottle rocket flashing in Manhattan's humid sky.

Yes, I go to Brattleboro, where decades ago the Mi-Go first revealed themselves only to be explained away as the superstitious hallucinations of excitable bumpkins, and the fever dreams of a certain closeted homosexual, slash racist. And it's not because I choose to relocate, either. There are an infinite number of causes for any one effect, and choice has precious little to do with any of them. For what

drove some guy — just out of college, and with zero editorial experience — to start another science fiction webzine, and to solicit this
essay (which he'll label a fiction, and I'll let him, because he pays
more for "lies") from me at 12:09 AM on July 9th, 2005 — ten years
to the day from the revelations in my West Village kitchen? And why
did a grammar school librarian press a volume of Heinlein — and
not a "safer" book — into his hands ten years before that, and how
did she decide to become a librarian, and from whence does a society that needs librarians come about? And from where do our alpha-
bets and pictographs originate, if not the frenzied scratches of our
hominid ancestors who desperately tried to describe their encoun-
ters with the Elder Gods on the bioluminescent, lichen — stained
walls of the twisting caverns they called home? It was a warning, just
like this is not a warning.

And Jeremiah Sturgill's solicitation: the near-promise of quick
money just as I need it to get out of the Bay Area, just as I was sitting
by my computer on a Saturday night, trying to wring out an idea
for a marketable tale — that was the final revelation. This, dear
reader, is it.

What Lovecraft misunderstood, and what I now comprehend
perfectly, is that attempting to warn humanity is futile. Not because
they won't listen to the reason of seeming unreason, not because the
flickering human mind would collapse into babbling madness if it
attempted to correlate the contents of such a warning, but because
there are no human minds left! There are no more people on this
Earth, not even you, gentle reader. And the Mi-Go victory is so complete that you don't even realize you're all play-toy simulacra at the
end of some etheric, tentacular tether. There are no more real people
except for me, Nick Mamatas. The rest of you are all real people
slash fungi from Yuggoth. Your brains have already been seized and
transported, and your braincases filled with sentient muck secreted
from the back of Tsathoggua. Oh yes, everyone has free will but me,
but the free will you have isn't yours. It is of those beyond.

No need to take my word for it. What exists can be perceived, if
not by our senses then by inference, by observing the actual, perceiv-
able impact a presence has on the cosmos. We're still all just matter
in motion after all, no matter how many alien intelligences live
inside twisted dimensions beyond our seeing. But when I said slash,
I meant it. Go to your bathroom. Don't worry, nothing's electrified
there that shouldn't be. Just go to your bathroom, and stare in the

mirror. Look as long as it takes. Soon enough you'll forget your own face, and see yourself for who you really are. Those human features you've been beguiled into thinking you retain will fall away and soon, in color spectra even the most profound synesthesiac could not dream of, you'll perceive the globular masses of sensory stalks that you once called your heads. Your shoulder blades will stretch and tingle, and you will have finally regained your awkward, shell-hard wings. You are the Mi-Go. Every one of you.

And if the sight of your true form drives you insane, the way the true sight of you all drove me insane, then I daresay I wouldn't mind at all if you snatched up a razor blade and took it to your face, to cut through the carapace and the potato meat underneath in a vain attempt to find your sentimental old noses. There'd be nothing for you to find, but at this late date if all I get from this story is five cents a word and a third-hand recounting of the sting of cutting lacerations, I'll take it.

I'm done, and that is why I'm packing up my books and computer again and moving, just days from now, away from Berkeley and up to Brattleboro. A copy editor of my acquaintance, with great fellow-feeling despite her obvious fungal origins, assisted me in finding an apartment. I know that my fate is on Yuggoth, along with all the rest of you, but as I am the last of us I'll go as a man, not as a mass of compressed gray matter inside a steely jar. There are caves in the hills in the north of Windham County, rocky and witch-haunted, and in these caverns are hidden, interior worlds: blue-litten K'n-yan, red-litten Yoth, and black, lightless N'kai. And from there, through twists of crystalline rock, superdense and radioactive, which in their subtle movements slice the subtlest of tears into space-time, I will squeeze through, left shoulder leading like at the '95 riot, and this time I'll make it: I will charge my way through to Yuggoth where, amidst the haphazardly stacked flasks of dead, enslaved humanity that rest upon its black methane shores, I will stand as the last man in the cosmos. To Yuggoth, where I will freeze, crack, and shatter.

# FAIR EXCHANGE

## Michael Marshall Smith

We were in some bloke's house the other night, nicking his stuff, and Bazza calls me over. We've been there twenty minutes already and if it was anyone else I'd tell them to shut up and get on with it, but Baz and I've been thieving together for years and I know he's not going to be wasting my time. So I put the telly by the back door with the rest of the gear (nice little telly, last minute find up in the smaller bedroom) and head back to the front room. I been in there already, of course. First place you look. DVD player, CDs, stereo if it's any good, which isn't often. You'd be amazed how many people have crap stereos. Especially birds — still got some shit plastic midi- system their dad bought them down the High Street in 1987. (Still got LPs, too, half of them. No fucking use to me, are they? I'm not having it away with an armful of things that weigh a ton and aren't as good as CDs: where's the fucking point in that?)

I make my way to Baz's shadow against the curtains, and I see he's going through the drawers in the bureau. Sound tactic if you've got a minute. People always seem to think you won't look in a drawer — *Doh!* — and so in go the cheque books, cash, personal organiser, old mobile phone. Spare set of keys, if you're lucky: which case you bide your time, hope they won't remember the keys were in there, then come back and make it a double feature when the insurance has put back everything you took. They've made it easy for you, haven't they. Pillocks. Anyway, I come up next to Baz, and he presents the drawers. They're empty. Completely and utterly devoid of stuff. No curry menus, no bent-up party photos, no balls of string or rubber bands, no knackered batteries for the telly remote. No dust, even. It's like someone opened the two drawers and sucked everything out with a Hoover.

"Baz, there's nothing there."

"That's what I'm saying."

It's not *that* exciting, don't see Jerry Bruckheimer making a film of it or nothing, but it's odd. I'll grant him that. It's not like the rest of the house is spick and span. There's stuff spilling out of cupboards, kitchen cabinets, old books sitting in piles on the floor. The carpet on the landing upstairs looks like something got spilt there and never cleared up, and the whole place is dusty and smells of mildew or something. And yet these two drawers, perfect for storing stuff — could even have been designed for the purpose, ha ha ha — are completely empty. Why? You'll never know. It's just some private thing. That's one of the weird bits about burglary. It's intimate. It's like being able to see what colour pants everyone is wearing. Actually you could do that too, if you wanted, but that's not what I meant. Not my cup of tea. Not professional, either.

"There was nothing in there at all?"

"Just this," Baz says, and holds something up so I can see it. "It was right at the back."

I took it from him. It's small, about the size and shape of the end of your thumb. Smooth, cold to the touch. "What is it?"

"Dunno," he shrugs. "Marble?"

"Fucking shit marble, Baz. It's not even fucking *round*."

Baz shrugs again and I say "Weird" and then it's time to go. You don't want to be hanging around any longer than necessary. Don't want to be in a burning hurry, either — that's when you can get careless or make too much noise or forget to look both ways as you slip out — but once you've found what you came for, you might as well be somewhere else.

So we go via the kitchen, grab the bin bag full of gear and slip out the back way. Stand outside the door a second, make sure no-one's passing by, then walk out onto the street, calm as you like. Van's just around the corner. We stroll along the pavement, chatting normally, looking like we live in one of the other houses and walk this way every night. Get in the van — bit white fucker, naturally, virtually invisible in London — and off we go.

It's fucking magic, that moment.

The one where you turn the van into the next street and suddenly you're just part of the evening traffic, and you know it's done and you're away and bar a fuck-up with the distribution of the goods it's like it never happened. I always light a fag right then, crack open the window, smell the London air coming in the van. Warm, cold, it's London. Best air in the world.

Weird thing, though. Even though it's not that big a deal, the business with the drawers was still niggling me a few hours later. You do see the odd thing or two in my business — stuff that don't quite make sense. Couple of months ago we doing over a big old house, over Tufnell Park way, and either side of the mantelpiece there's a painting. Two little paintings, obviously done by the same bloke. Signed the same, for a start. Now, there's huge photos all over the mantelpiece, including some wedding ones, and it don't take a genius to work out that these two paintings are of the owners: one of the bloke, and the other of his missus. What's *that* about? For a start, you've already got all the photos. And why get two paintings, one of each of you? If you're going to get a painting done, surely you have the two of you together, looking all lovey-dovey and like you'll never, ever get divorced and stand screaming at each other in some brief's office arguing about bits of furniture you only bought in the first place because they was there and you had the cash burning a hole in your pocket. Maybe that's it — you have the paintings done separate so you can split them when you break up. But if you're already thinking about that, then . . . Whatever. People are just weird. Baz wanted to draw moustaches on the paintings, but I wouldn't let him. They can't have been cheap. So we just did one on the wife.

Anyway, couple of hours in the Junction and everything's peachy. Already shifted most of the electrical goods to blokes we know are either keeping them for themselves or can be trusted to punt them on over the other side of town. Baz and I done a deal and he's going to keep the little telly for his sister's birthday. Couple bits of jewellery Baz found will go to Mr. Pzlowsky, a pro fence I use over in Bow. He don't talk to no-one — can barely understand what the old fucker's saying, anyway — and can be trusted to only rob us short-sighted, not actually blind.

So the only thing left is the little thing I've got in my pocket. I get it out, look at it. Funny thing is, I don't really remember slipping it in there. Like I said, it's small, and it looks like it must be made of glass. It's so shiny, and transparent in parts, that it can't be anything else. But it's got colours and textures in it too — kind of pinks and salmon, and some threads of dark green. And it feels . . . it feels almost wet, even though it had been in my pocket for ages. I suppose it's just some special kind of glass or stone or something.

"Wozzat?"

I look up and see Clive is racking up at the pool table a couple of yards away. "What's what?"

"What you got in your hand, twatface."

I'm not trying to be funny, I don't mind Clive, I'm just surprised he's noticed it from over there.

I hold it up. "Dunno," I said. "What do you think?"

He comes over, chalking up his cue, takes a look. "Dunno," he agrees. "Hold on though, tell you what it looks a bit like."

"What's that?"

"My sister-in-law went on holiday last year. Bali. Over, you know, in Polynesia."

"Polynesia? Where the fuck's that?"

"Dunno," he admitted. "Fucking long flight though, by all accounts. Think they said it was in the South Seas or something. Dunno where that is either. Anyway, she brought our mum back something looked a bit like that. Said it was coral, I think."

"You reckon?"

He leaned forward, looked at it more closely. "Yeah. Could be. Polished up, or something. Tell you what, though. It weren't half as nice as your one. Where'd you get it?"

"Ah," I said. "That would be telling."

He nodded. "You nicked it. Well, I reckon that's worth something, I do."

And he wanders off to the table, where some bloke's waiting for him to break.

"Nice one," I said, and took another look at the thing.

Even though I'm sitting right in the back of the pub, snug into the wood panelling there, this little piece of coral or stone or glass or whatever seems to have a glow about it. Suppose it's catching a glint from the long light over the pool table, but the light coming off it seems like it's almost green. Could be the baize, I suppose, but . . . I dunno. Probably had a Stella too many.

I slipped it back in my pocket. I reckoned Clive was probably right, and it most likely was worth something.

Funny thing, though. I didn't like the idea of getting rid of it.

Next few days just sort of go by. Nothing much going on. Baz had to head East to visit some mate in the London Hospital, so he goes over and does the business with Mr. Pzlowsky. Usually I'd do it because people have been known to take advantage of Bazza, but me and the Pole had words over it a year ago and he plays fair with him now. Fair as he plays with anyone, that is. The handful of jewellery we got from the house with the empty drawers gets us a few hundred quid, which is better than either of us expected. Old silver, apparently. American.

We play pool, we play darts, we watch television. You know how it is. Had a row with me bird, Jackie: she caught sight of the little coral thing (I'd just put it down next to the sink for a minute while I changed trousers) and seemed to think it was for her. Usually I do come back with a little something for the old trout, granted, but on this occasion I hadn't. Pissed me off a bit, to be honest. She just sits at home all evening on her fat arse, doing nothing, and then when I come home she expects I'll have some little present for her. Anyway, whatever. It got sorted out.

Couple days later Baz and I go out on the game again. Nothing mega, just out for a walk, trying back doors, side doors, garden gates, usual kind of stuff. What the coppers call "opportunistic" crime. Actually, we call it that too.

"Fancy a bit of opportunistic, Baz?" I'll say.

He'll neck the last of his pint. "Go on, then. Run out of cash anyway."

We were only out an hour or so, and came back to the pub with maybe three, four hundred quid worth of stuff. Usual bits of jewellery, plus a Palm V, two external hard drives, three phones, wallet full of cash and even a pot of spare change (might as well, plenty of quid coins in there). That's the thing about this business: you've got to know what you're doing. Got to be able to have a quick look at rings and necklaces, and know whether they're worth the nicking. Glance at a small plastic case, realise there's a pricey little personal organiser inside. See things like those portable hard drives, which don't look like anything, and know that if you wipe them clean you can get forty apiece for them in City pubs, more for the ones with more megs or gigs or whatever (it's written on the back). Understand which phones are hard to clone or shift and so not worth the bother. Know that a big old pot of change can be well worth it, and also that if you tip it into a plastic bag it makes a bloody good cosh in case you meet someone on the way out.

The other thing is the mental attitude. I remember having a barney with an old boyfriend of Baz's sister, couple years ago. She'd met him in some wine bar up West and he was a right smartarse, well up himself, fucking student or something it was.

He comes right out and asks me: "How can you do it?"

Not "do," notice, I'd've understood that (and I don't mind giving out some tips): but "can." How *can* I do it? And this from some little wanker who's being put through college by mummy and daddy, who didn't have a lazy girlfriend to support, and who was a right old slowcoach when it came to doing his round at the bar. Annoying thing was, after I'd discussed it with him for a bit (I say "discussed": there was a bit of pushing and shoving at the start), I could sort of see his point.

According to him, it was a matter of attitude. If someone came round and turned me mum's place over, I'd be after their fucking blood. I knew that already, of course, he wasn't teaching me nothing there: I suppose the thing I hadn't really clocked was this mental attitude thing. I know that mum's got some bits and pieces that she'd be right upset if they was nicked. Not even because they're worth much, but just because they mean something to her. From me old man, whatever. If I turn someone's place over, though, I don't know what means what to them. Could be that old ring was a gift from their Gran, whereas to me it's just a tenner from Mr. Pzlowsky if I'm lucky. That tatty organiser could have phone numbers on it they don't have anywhere else. Or maybe it was a big deal that their dad bought them a little telly, it's the first one of their own they've had, and if I nick it then they're always going to be on their second, or third, or tenth.

The point is I don't know all that. I don't know anything about these people and their lives, and I don't really care. To me, they're just fucking cattle, to be honest. What's theirs is mine. Fair enough, maybe it's not a great mental attitude. But that's thieving for you. Nobody said it was a job for Mother Teresa.

Anyway, we're back in the Junction and a few more beers down (haven't even shifted anything on yet, still working through the change pot) when who should walk in the door but the Pole. Mr. Pzlowsky, as I live and breath. He comes in the door, looks around and sees us, and makes his way through the crowd.

Baz and I just stare at him. I've never seen the Pole anywhere except in his shop. Tell the truth, I thought he had no actual legs; just spent the day propped up behind his counter raking in the cash. He's an old bloke, sixties, and he smokes like a chimney and I'm frankly fucking amazed he's made it all the way here.

And also: why?

"I'd like a word with you," he says, when he gets to us.

"Buy us a beer, then," I go.

I'm a bit pissed off at him, truth be known. He's crossing a line. I don't want no one in the pub to know where we shift our gear. As it happens it's just me and Baz there at that moment, but you never know when Clive's going to come in, or any of the others.

He looks at me, then turns right around and goes back to the bar. "Two Stellas," I shout after him, and he just scowls.

Baz and I turn to look at each other. "What's going on?" Baz asks.

"Fucked if I know."

As I watch the Pole at the bar, I'm thinking it through. My first thought is he's come because there's a problem with something we've sold him, he's had the old Bill knocking on his door. But now I'm not sure. If it was grief, he wouldn't be buying us a pint. He'd be in a hurry, and pissed off. "Have to wait and see."

Eventually Mr. Pzlowsky gets back to us with our drinks on a little tray. He sits down at our table, his back to the rest of the pub, and I start to relax. Whatever he's here for, he's playing by the rules. He's drinking neat gin, no ice. Ugh.

"Cheers," I say. "So: what's up?"

He lights one of his weird little cigarettes, coughs. "I have something for you."

"Sounds interesting," I say. "'What?"

He reaches in his jacket pocket and pulls out a brown envelope. Puts it on the table, pushes it across. I pick it up, look inside.

Fifties. Ten of them. Five hundred quid. A "monkey," as they say on television, though no fucker I know does.

"Fuck's this?"

"A bonus," he says, and I can hear Baz's brain fizzing. I can actually hear his thoughts. A bonus from the Pole, he's thinking: What the fuck is going on?

"A bonus, from the Pole?" I say, on his behalf. "What the fuck is going on?"

"This is what it is," he says, speaking quietly and drawing in close. I won't do his accent, but trust me — you have to concentrate. "It is from that jewellery you bring me last week. The silver. The American silver. I have one of my clients in this afternoon, he is the one sometimes buys unusual things, and I decide I will show this silver to him. So I get one of these things out — I always show just one first, you understand, because it can be more expensive that way. He looks at it, and suddenly I am on high alert. This is because I am experienced, see, I know what is what in my trade. I see it in his eyes when he sees the piece: he really wants this thing, yes? I was going to say two hundred to him, maybe two hundred fifty, this is what I think it was worth. But when I see his face, I think a moment, and I say seven hundred fifty! Is a joke, a little bit, but also I think maybe I see what is in his eyes again, and we'll see."

"And?"

"He says "done," just like that, and he asks me if I have some more. I almost fall off my stool, I tell you truthfully."

I nearly fell off my own stool, right there in the pub. Seven hundred and fifty fucking notes! Fuck me!

The Pole, sees my face, laughs. "Yes! And this is just the smallest one, you understand? So I say yes, I have some more, and his eyes are like saucers immediately. In all the time I do this thing, only a very few times do I see this look in a man's face which says "I will pay whatever you want." So I bring them out, one by one. You bring me five of them, you remember. He buys them all."

Baz gapes. "All of them? For seven fifty each?"

The Pole goes all sly, and winks. "At least," he says, and I knew there and then that one of two of them went for a lot more than that. There's quiet for a moment, as we all sip our drinks. I know Baz is trying to do the sums in his head, and not having much luck. I've already done them, and I'm a bit pissed off we didn't realise what we had. Fuck knows what the Pole is thinking.

He finishes his gin in a quick swallow and gets up. "So, thank you, boys. Is a good find. He tell me is turn of the century American silver, from East Coast somewhere, he tell me the name, I forget it, something like Portsmouth, I think. And . . . well, the man says to me that if I find any more of this thing, he will buy it. Straight away. So . . . think of me, okay?"

And he winked again, and shuffled his way out through the crowd until we couldn't see him any more.

"Fuck me," Baz says, when he's gone.

"Fuck me is right," I say. I open the envelope, take out four of the fifties, and give them to him. "There's your half."

"Cheers. Mind you," Baz says, over his beer, "He's still a fucker. How much did all that add up to?"

"Minimum of seven fifty each, that's three grand seven fifty," I said. "But from that fucker's face, I'm thinking he got five, six grand at least. And if he got that off some bloke who knows it's nicked, then in the shops you got to double or treble it. Probably more."

"Sheesh. Still, good for him. He didn't have to see us right."

"Yeah," I said, because he wasn't completely wrong. The Pole could have kept quiet about his windfall. His deal with us was done. "But you know what that cash is really about?

Baz looked at me, shook his head. He's a lovely bloke, don't get me wrong. He's my best mate. But the stuff in his head is mainly just padding to stop his eyeballs falling in. "What it means is," I said, "Is he's very fucking keen to get some more. In fact, probably says he was lying about the seven fifty for the cheapest. He got more. Maybe much more. He got so much dosh for them, in fact, it was worth admitting he did well, and paying us a bonus so we go to him if we find any more."

"Better keep our eyes open, then," Baz said, cheerfully. "More beer?"

"Cheers," I said.

I watched him lurch off to the bar. My hand slipped into my pocket, and I found my cold little friend. The bit of polished stone, coral, glass, whatever. I knew then that Clive had been right. My little piece was probably worth a lot of money. The bits of jewellery had been alright, but nowhere near as pretty as my stone.

I wasn't selling it though, no way. I had got too used to the feel of it in my hand. Twenty, thirty times a day I'd hold it. I liked the way if fitted between my fingers. Longer I had it, better it seemed to fit. Sometimes, if I held it up to my face, I thought I could smell it too. Couldn't put my finger on what it smelled of, but it was nice, comforting. The Pole wasn't getting hold of it. Not Jackie neither.

It was mine.

On the Sunday Baz goes on holiday. He's off to Tenerife for the week. This is fine by me, because I need time to plan.

Now Baz, he thinks we've just got to keep an eye out for this stuff, that it's something like a particular DVD player or whatever. I know different. If it's this fucking valuable, then it's not something we're just going to find in some gaff in Kentish Town, mixed in with all the shit from Ratners or Argos or wherever. This isn't just common-or-garden thieving we're looking at. This is nicking to order, which is a different kind of skill. Happens all the time, of course: you pass the word to the right bloke in the right pub that you want some particular BMW, or a new Mini in cream, and they'll go do the business for you. There's big money in it. Not my area, normally, but this is different. We do alright with the usual gear, but if me and Baz can take some more of this silver to the Pole, we can do very nicely indeed. It's worth making an effort.

So on the Monday night, I'm out on the streets by myself. It's about ten-thirty. I park the van around the corner, and I take a stroll down the street where the house is, the house where we found the stuff. Couldn't remember which one it was at first, but in the end I worked it out. All the other houses in this street, they've been done up. Window sills painted, bricks repointed, new tiles on the path, that kind of thing. Scaffolding on a couple others. Lot of people have moved in recently, the area's coming up. But this particular house, it looks a bit more knackered. I'm thinking the people have been there a while, which makes sense, what with it being so untidy inside. Could be they're foreign. You get that, sometimes. People moved in just after the war or whatever, when it was dirt cheap. House gets passed on to the children, and then bingo, suddenly they're sitting on a gold mine. Could be they're Yanks, even — which would explain the old silver being from the US originally.

I walk past the house and see the curtains are drawn and the lights are on. Lot of people do that when they go out, but if you take lights to mean there's no-one at home, you'll being doing time so fast your feet won't touch the ground. Me, I've never been inside. Not intending to be, either. And I'm not planning on doing the job solo anyhow. It's a big house. It's a two person manoeuvre — not least because it was Baz who picked up the bits of silver in the first place. I don't know where he found them, but it's got to be the first place to look. Quicker you're in and out, the better.

I walk the street one way, then go around the corner and have a fag. Then I walk back past the house. I'm trying to remember the exact layout, because we've been in a few other houses since. I'm glancing across at the front window on the second floor when I see a shape, a shadow on the curtain. I smile to myself, glad I'm not so stupid as to have had a go tonight. And loyal, of course — I want Baz in on it, and he's not back until Sunday.

I slow the pace, keep an eye on this shadow. Never know, it might be a bird with her tits out. Don't see nothing of note, though. Curtains are too tightly drawn, and it's that thing where the light's behind them and they get magnified till they're just some huge blob.

The light goes off, and I realise mostly likely that's the kid just gone to bed. That tells me that room was where the little telly was from, and the whole floor clicks in my head.

I walked back to the van, feeling very professional indeed.

Next night I'm busy, and the one after. Not nicking. The Tuesday was our "anniversary" (or so Jackie says; far as I can see I don't understand why we have them when we're not even fucking engaged, and anyway — anniversary of what? We met at a party, got pissed, shagged in one of the bedrooms on a pile of coats, and that was that). Either way we ended up going up West and having a meal and then getting bladdered at a club. Wednesday night I'm not going fucking anywhere. I felt like shit.

So it's Thursday when I'm outside the house again.

I was there a little earlier, about quarter to nine. You look a bit less suspicious, being out on the street at that time; but on the other hand there's more people around to see you loitering about. I walked past the house first, seeing the curtains are drawn again. Can't work out whether the lights are on full or not: there's still a bit of light in the sky.

I'd actually slowed down, almost stopped, when I heard footsteps coming up the street. I started moving again, sharpish. You don't want the neighbours catching someone staring at a house. There's some right nosey fuckers. They'll call the old Bill quick as you like. Course the Bill won't do much, most of the time, but if they think there's lads scouting for opportunistics then sometimes they'll get someone to drive down the street every now and then, when they're bored.

So I started walking again, and as I look I see there are some people coming up the street towards me. Three of them. Actually, they're still about thirty yards away, which is a surprise. Sounded like they were closer than that. I just walk towards them. I didn't actually whistle — nobody whistles much there days, which I think is a bit of a shame — but I was as casual as you like.

Just as I'm coming up to them, them up to me, the streetlights click on. One of these lights is there just as we're passing each other, and suddenly there's these big shadows thrown across my path. I look across and see there's two of them in front, a man and a woman. The woman's wearing a big floppy hat — must have been to some fancy do — and the bloke happens to be looking across her, towards the street. She's in shadow, he's turned the other way, so I don't see either of their faces, which is fine by me. If I haven't seen theirs then they haven't seen mine, if you know what I mean.

I'm just stepping past them, and I mean around, really, because they're both pretty big, when suddenly someone *was* looking at me.

It was the girl, walking behind them. As I'm passing her, her head turns, and she looks right at me.

I look away quickly, and then they're gone.

All I'm left with is an image of the girl's face, of it slowly turning to look at me. To be honest, she was a bit of a shocker. Not scarred or nothing, just really big-faced. With them eyes look like they're sticking out too far, make you look a bit simple.

But she was young, and I think she smiled.

I walked down to the corner, steady as you like. As I turned around it I glanced back, just quickly. I saw two things. I see the three of them are going into the house. They weren't neighbours, after all. They're the people from the actual house. The people with the jewellery. The people I'm going to be nicking from.

The second thing I notice is that the streetlight we passed isn't lit any more.

I'm a bit unsettled, the next day, to be honest. Don't know why. It isn't like me. Normally I'm a pretty chilled bloke, take things as they come and all that. But I find myself in the pub at lunchtime, which I don't usually do — not on a weekday, anyway, unless it's a Bank Holiday — and by the afternoon I'm pretty lagered up. I sit by myself, in a table at the back, keep knocking them back. Clive pops in about three and I had a couple more with him, but it was quiet. I didn't say much, and in the end he got up and started playing pool with some bloke. It was quite funny actually, some posh wanker in there by mistake, fancied playing for money. Clive reeled him in like a kipper.

So I'm sitting there, thinking, trying to work out why I feel weird. Could be that it's because I've seen the people I'm going to be nicking from. Usually it's not that way. It's just bits of gear, lying around in someone else's house. They're mine to do what I want with. All I see is how much they're worth. Now I know that the jewellery is going to belong to that woman in the hat. And I know that Baz's sister is watching a telly that belonged to the girl who looked at me. Alright, so she was a minger, but it's bad enough being ugly without people nicking your prize possession.

That could be another thing, of course. She'd seen me. No reason for her to think some bloke in the street is the one who turned them over, but I don't like it. Like I didn't like Mr. Pzlowsky being in the Junction. You don't want anyone to be able to make those connections.

I'm thinking that's it, just them having seen me, and I'm beginning to feel bit more relaxed. I've got another pint in front of me, and I've got my stone in my right hand. It's snuggled in there, in my palm, fingers curled around it, and that's helping too. It's like worry beads, or something: I just feel better when it's there.

And then I realise that there's something else on my mind. I want to find that jewellery. But I don't necessarily want to hand it on.

The Pole is still gagging for it, I know. He's rung me twice, asking if I've got any more, and that tells me there's serious money involved. But now I think about it properly, with my stone in my hand and no Baz sitting there next to me, jabbering on, I realise I want the stuff for myself. I didn't actually handle it, the last time. Baz found it, kept it, sold it to the Pole.

If a little bit of stone feels like this one does, though, what would the silver feel like? I don't know — but I want to know.

And that's why, on the Saturday night, I went around there. Alone.

I parked up at five, and walked past once an hour. I walked up, down, on both sides of the street. Unless someone's sitting watching the whole time, I'm just another bloke. Or so I tell myself, anyway. The truth is that I'm just going to do it whatever.

It's a Saturday night. Very least, the young girl is going to go out. Maybe the mum and dad too, out for a meal, to the cinema, whatever. Worst case, I'll just wait until they've all gone to bed, and try the back door. I don't like doing it that way. Avoid it if I can. You never know if you're going to run into some have-a-go-hero who fancies getting his picture in the local paper. Clive had one of those, couple years back. Had to smack the guy for ages before he went down. Didn't do any nicking for three months after that. It puts you right off your stride. Risky, too. Burglary is one thing. Grievous Bodily Harm is something else. The coppers know the score. Bit of nicking is inevitable. The insurance is going to pay anyway, so no-one gets too exercised. But with GBH, they're on your case big time. I didn't want to go into the house with people in it. But by the time I'd walked past if three times, I knew I was going to if I had to.

Then, at half-past seven, the front door opens.

I'm sitting in the van, tucked around the corner, but I can see the house in the rear-view mirror. The front door opens and the girl comes out. She walks to the end of the path, turns left, and goes off up the street.

One down, I think. Now: how many to go?

I tell you, an hour is a long time to wait. It's a long time if you're just sitting there smoking, nothing but a little stone for company, watching a house in the mirror until your neck starts to ache.

At quarter-past eight I see the curtains in the downstairs being drawn. Hello, I thought. It's not dark yet. Nothing happens for another twenty minutes.

Then I see the door opening. Two people come out. She's wearing a big old hat again. It's a bit far away, and I can't see his face, but I see he's got long hair. I see also just how fucking big they are. Fat, but tall too. A real family of beauties, that's for sure.

They fuck around at the door for a while, and then they walk up the path, and they turn right too.

Bingo. Fucking bingo. I've had a result.

I give them fifteen minutes. Long enough to get on the bus or down the tube, long enough that they won't suddenly turn up again because one of them forgot their phone or wallet. Also, enough for the light to go just a little bit more, so it's going to be a bit darker, and I won't stick out so much.

Then I get out of the van, and walk over to the house. First thing I do is walk straight down the front path, give a little ring on the door. Okay, so I've only seen three of them before, but you never know. Could be another kid, or some old dear. I ring it a couple of times. Nothing happens.

So then I go around the side, the way we got in last time. It's a bit of a squeeze, past three big old bins. Fuck knows what was in them — smelt fucking terrible. Round the back there's the second door. Last time it was unlocked, but I'm not reckoning on that kind of luck twice. Certainly not after it got them burgled. I try it, and sure enough, it didn't budge.

So I get myself up close to the glass panel in the door, and look through the dusty little panes. Some people, soon as they get burgled, they'll have a system put in. Bolting the stable door. It's why you've got to be careful if you find some keys the first time and go back a couple weeks later. Can't see any sign of wires.

So I take the old T-shirt out of my pocket, wrap it around my fist. One quick thump.

It makes a noise, of course. But London is noisy. I wait to see if anybody's light goes on. I can be back out on the street and away in literally seconds.

Nothing happens. No lights. No-one shouts "Oi!"

I reach my hand in through the window and would you fucking believe it: they've only left the key in the lock. I love people, I really do. They're so fucking *stupid*. Two seconds later, I'm inside.

Now's here the point I wish Baz is with me. He's not bright, but he's got a good memory for places. He'd remember exactly where he'd found everything. I don't have a clue, but I've got a hunch.

The bureau with the empty drawer. The place where I got my stone. Well, Baz found it, of course. But it's mine now.

I walk through the kitchen without a second glance. Did it properly last time. The main light's on in the living room, and I can see it's even more untidy than last time. The sofa is covered in all kinds of shit. Old books, bits of clothes. A big old map. Looks *very* old, in fact, and I make a mental note to take that when I go. Could be the Pole's contact would be interested in that too.

I stand in front of the bureau. My heart is going like a fucking jackhammer. Partly it's doing a job by myself. Mainly I just really, really want to find something. I want the jewellery. More even than that, I want another stone.

I look through the drawers. One by one. Methodical. I take everything out, look through it carefully. There's nothing. I'm pissed off, getting jittery. I've always known it might be that there just isn't any more of the stuff. But now I'm getting afraid.

In the end I go to the drawer I know is empty, and I pull it out. It's still empty. I'm about to shove it closed again, when I notice something. A smell. I look around the room, but at first I can't tell what's making it. Could be a plate with some old food on it, I think, lost under a pile of books somewhere. Then I realise it's coming from the drawer. I don't know how to describe it, but it's definitely there. It's not strong, but . . .

Then I get it, I think. It's air. It's a different kind of air. It's not like London. It's like . . . the sea. Sea air, like you'd get down on the front in some pissy little town on the coast, the kind people don't go to any more and didn't have much to recommend it in the first place. Some little town or village with old stone buildings, cobbled streets, thatched roofs. A place where there's lots of shadows, maybe a big old deserted factory or something on a hill overlooking the town;

where you hear odd footsteps down narrow streets and alleys in the dark afternoons and when the birds cry out in the night the sound is stretched and cramped and echoes as if it is bouncing off things you cannot see.

That kind of place. A place like that.

I lean down to the drawer, stick my nose in, give it another good sniff. No doubt about it — the smell's definitely coming from inside. I don't like it. I don't like it at all. So I slam it shut.

And that's when I realise.

When the drawer bangs closed, I hear a little noise. Not just the slam, but something else.

Slowly, I pull it back out again. I put my hand inside, and feel towards the back. My arm won't go in as far as it should.

The drawer's got a false back.

I pull it and pull it, but I can't get it to come out. So I get the screwdriver out of my back pocket and slip it inside. I angle my hand around and get the tip into the join right at the back. I'm feeling hot, and starting to sweat. Fucking tricky to get any pull on it, but I give it a good yank.

There's a splintering sound, and my hand whacks into the other side. I let go of the screwdriver and feel with my fingers. An inch of the wooden back has come away. There's something behind it, for sure. A little space. I can tell because my fingertips feel a little cold, as if there's a breeze coming from in there. Can't be, of course, but it tells me what I need to know.

Something's behind there. Could be the jewellery I came for. Could be even better. Could be another stone. Another stone that smells like the sea. So I get the screwdriver in position again. Get it good and tight against the side, and got ready to give it an almighty pull.

And that's when I feel the soft breath on the back of my neck, and her hands coming gently around my waist; and one of the others turning off the lights.

It *is* just a question of attitude, it turns out. The student tosser had it right. It's all a matter of how you see the people you're doing over, whether you think about them at all, or if you just see what you can get from them. What you *need*.

I gave them Baz, on the Sunday night. They didn't make me watch, but I heard. An hour later there was just a stain on the carpet, like the one we'd seen upstairs. They gave me another one of the stones, even prettier than the one I had before. It's beautiful.

Fair exchange is no robbery. I'm giving them Jackie next.

# THIS HAND, WAVING

## *Simon Owens*

For an even fifty dollars the father got the undertaker to give up his son's hand. The undertaker delivered the hand in a box full of ice. He stuffed the body's arm in the pocket so at the viewing it looked like the boy was searching for some loose change and nobody thought any differently. Even the dead don't want to walk around penniless and this little boy was no different.

The mother found her husband alone in their room with the hand between his own, the little boy's fingers spread out on his knee, the fingernails sharp and jagged where they had been bitten just days before. "I hope," she said quietly, "you have a reason for having that here and not in the ground with the rest of him." She stood there in the doorway, the sunlight streaming in from the kitchen trying to claw its way around her black dress.

He had his reasons. His first reason was to shake hands. There were dinner parties and meetings and elevators. There were other men with little boys toting behind them, their shirts tucked in their pants, their eyes wide and open and not dead. When someone would go to shake the father's hand, they'd meet something cold and soft and small, something insubstantial. They'd look down to their fists and see themselves holding a little boy's hand, neatly severed at the wrist, its owner holding on lightly just below the palm. "This is my son's hand," the father would say softly. "I see," they would say. They would give one more shake and return their own hands to their pockets, their fingers closing in on themselves in repulsive resentment. How dare this man show me death, how dare he let it come so close, let its filth touch the living in such a casual way.

"Do not shake his hand," they'd tell their coworkers. Do not shake his hand or you will be shaking hands with death, its inanimate structures, its filaments, its subtle hiding places in all of our lives.

This is human loss. This is his son lying in a hospital bed, his skin yellow. Here is his X-ray torn into myriad shadows with the help of the light, the dark, the dots of white. The doctor says, he says, "There is severe liver failure, his blood is quickly becoming poisoned. The skin color has changed dramatically in the last twenty-four hours."

This is his living room, its chairs filled, people walking across its carpeted floor. This is the phone, each ear poised, ready for it to ring. On the other end somewhere is a dead body, another little boy whose parents will sign away his liver, if only they will sign away their son's liver so that this other boy shall live.

Here is waiting. Here is the brevity which links each moment to the next, this brevity that is waiting. Here is the clock's face and with each tick the poison in their son's blood thickens.

And here is the end, poised between some last glance and leaving the room to visit the snack machine in the lobby. Here is the lifeless body in the bed upon return, the rage at the components of coincidence and the absence of goodbyes.

Here are words, their sentences, their misgivings. Here are five fingers held in the palm of the father's hand, and it is in this instance when he decides to keep them, to hold them here above the ground, as if to hold his hand from the other side of death.


His second reason was to remember. We are peculiar. Substance adds memories, triggers synapses leading from one cell to another, dots connecting on a chronological basis of time. The father held the severed hand, playing with the fingers. He slept with it at night, a teddy curled up underneath his pillow.

Consider the fingers. The skin soft and pale. On the index finger lay a small scar. A cut which had been stitched. The father remembered his son reaching up with his glass only to have it shatter on the table, the individual shards lodging into the child's hand, the blood leaking out, his face shocked into silence for a moment before he screamed.

Consider the palm. Smooth and ready, curved. He held this hand when crossing the street. He let these fingers curl around his own in infancy, the hand not much bigger than the father's thumb.

Consider the wrist, what little was still left. A dull pinkness spread out to pale skin. A small vein snaked its way into the hand, a rogue tunnel leading back into its nerves.

It sat on his mantle piece during the day. They'd serve tea under its watch, its index finger pointed out slightly, the hand propped almost as if the muscles were tense. Others would enter and watch the hand. "How's your little boy?" they'd say and then pause. Oh yes, their little boy was dead, but there was something about the hand that made his presence known, gave it some permanence in this household. Others did not like the hand in the living room. The dead should stay dead, they thought, and the hand seemed confused, lost, torn away from its home.

"He's fine," the father would reply. He'd stand up and place the hand in his own. He'd use it to wave to them, back and forth, a lazy wave to say hello. The guests would watch the hand for a few moments, unsure of what to do, before hesitantly raising their hands and waving in return.

"There now," the father would say at night, his pajamas on, his wife already lying down beside him. "Goodnight," he'd say to the hand and lie back, switching off the light and staring at the ceiling. The hand was a silhouette in the darkness, moving up and down on his chest. The man's fingers would move along its veins, searching for some semblance of pulse. After awhile, the search would give into sleep, where the father would enter the hospital room over and over again, his boy still alive, still holding on to say goodbye.

This man is not himself. There were years leading up to this. There were years after the death. The death is the starting point, and now the man feels his life has begun with his son's death, every year before a kind of timeless void.

This mother is not herself. Her husband has become something apart from her, a separate entity. She finds the hand has become a sort of barrier between them. He has fallen in love with the hand, and in this essence he does not love his wife.

She finds the hand one day on the kitchen counter. Upstairs, she knows her husband sleeps. The hand, as always, seems to point, telling her something with its inanimate gestures. This is not her son's hand, she thinks, her son is dead, this hand is not dead, sitting here somehow still connected to the living.

There are knives in the drawers. Steak knives and butter knives and even a butcher knife sitting on the rack near the sink. She imagines herself with the knife in her hand, holding her son's fingers up slightly, cutting into them. The bone would resist at first, but she'd be persistent and continue to cut.

She'd start with the index finger and move on, slicing it into tiny pieces, turning to each finger and doing the same, until they were nothing but hubs. Then, she'd open up the palm, peeling away the flesh, slicing into veins and muscle. The process would be slow, patient, the knife coming away every few seconds to wipe the little bit of congealed blood off on a towel.

When she was done, there would be little pieces of flesh on the cutting board. There would be only small portions of blood. Without a heart, there is nothing from which to pump, to flow. She would scoop the pieces into a pile together, flesh placed upon flesh, and only then would she be able to cry. Her son has been in the ground for three weeks now, but this hand is a link, a leftover remnant. How can one mourn something that isn't truly gone?

She never slices into the hand. It is too late for goodbyes.

His third reason for keeping the hand was to forget.

Curious that, keeping a keepsake to forget. He did, though, every day he forgot his son a little more. With this hand, there were new memories flooding in. Through age, the son's personality changed. No longer was his son a little boy, but rather in three years he'd grown into an adolescent, independent and intelligent, conversational. In time, he stopped saying, "this is my son's hand," and simply told the person "this is my son." His son, different from the son all those years ago, a separate person entirely.

The mother, of course, watched these actions with growing concern. She did not appreciate what her son had become, a bodiless entity who sat there pointing. By now, the severed hand had grown stiff with age, leathered, the fingers frozen into a perpetual accusation. "I should be dead with the rest of me," that index finger said, "we should not face each other in the morning or lie beside each other at night."

The father lost his job. His coworkers were tired of seeing death every day, passing it in the hallway, the thought of it lingering in their offices. Together, they conspired against him, and like Caesar, he fell. He packed all his things in a little brown box and sat the hand on top, letting the finger point at all of them as he walked out.

This night, the mother was once again left in the kitchen, her husband asleep, the hand splayed out before her. In the passing years, the fingernails had grown longer, the skin thicker, but curiously it had not begun to decay. In most aspects, it was still her son's hand, her dead little boy.

Knives were everywhere, but she no longer held any notion of slicing it to pieces, scooping everything up and burying it with the rest of him. By now, he had become a permanent fixture in their home. There were nights when she was almost glad he was here, when lying awake at night and listening to her husband's snores. When he was here it was like he'd never gone, and each passing day was another day when she didn't have to say goodbye.

There were times when she could not imagine this. There were times when she sat across watching him, his face intact, his stare blank. There were times when it seemed he had never died, only stayed there silently watching her from across the kitchen. "You and me are not the same," she imagined him thinking, "You are still here while I am gone." The hand was her defense. "You are still here," she'd reply. "With me."

She picked up the hand now and held it in her own. It was cold and stiff. "Do you blame me for not mourning you?" she asked.

"No," the hand seemed to say, a brief sense of warmth pulsing once. Upstairs, her husband continued to sleep.

No, not at all.

# THE CALL OF FARTHER SHORES

## *David Niall Wilson*

The barber shop in Cedar Falls was more than just a gathering spot for tired old men with nothing better to do than to trim the few remaining wisps of gray from their temples and pass on the latest fish stories. Brown's small shop sported two chairs, three barbers, off and on, the memorabilia of dozens of lives. Terry Brown was the sixth generation of Browns to run the small shop. His father had come back from the war, honored and decorated, just in time to take the reigns from Jeremiah Brown, who'd cut hair in Cedar Falls for nearly forty years. There were sighs of relief when that torch was passed. Morc than a few heads of hair had borne the mark of a slight palsy and unattended cataracts, but it hadn't been enough to keep them away.

Jeremy stood on the steps, taking in the changes time and weather had etched across the face of the old building. He hadn't stepped foot in Cedar Falls in nearly ten years, but he remembered the last time he'd mounted the steps to Brown's Barber shop with a clarity that ran like cold rain down his spine. Small details surfaced, details with more clarity than those he could have brought to mind from the breakfast barely cool in his stomach. The aroma of his father's cigarette-scented flannel shirt, the rustle of leaves, rolling and scurrying down the sidewalks as he'd stepped up onto the curb. Cars had been larger in those days, and Jeremy smaller. The scents of gas and oil had carried on the wind, blending with wood-smoke and the acrid scent of burning leaves.

There had been chairs outside the shop in those days, metal chairs that bounced if you hit them just right, and leaned back nearly to the sidewalk behind if you had the proper size and age. They were usually full, pulled close in beside the sand-filled ashtray and flanked by a Thermos cooler.

Now anti-smoking laws and open-container fines had ended all that, and what remained of the chairs themselves were deep scrapes in the wooden planks of the Main Street boardwalk. Jeremy hesitated outside the door. The exterior changes had done nothing to still the *presence* of the place. He closed his eyes, and years melted away in an instant.

There were animals of all sorts lining the walls, some heads, fish so large they seemed surreal and improbable to a young boy whose fishing experience extended to Bluegill and catfish. There were the heads of deer, a bear, a wild pig, and in the corner, Jeremy's favorite, a stuffed mongoose poised in eternal battle with a coiled, moth-eaten snake. There were tools of unknown use and origin, black and white photos so yellowed and dusty you had to stand with your nose pressed to the glass of their frames to make out the images. Squat figures in black pants, black shoes and white shirts, standing in front of buildings that only peripherally resembled the city streets Jeremy had walked as a child.

And the wooden figurehead. Jeremy stood, leaning against the frame of the doorway, and shook as the memory of that worm-eaten chunk of wood invaded and took over. Dark wood, so dark it seemed soaked with sea-water, damp and rotting, the thing had glittered with coat after coat of varnish. Jeremy's father had told him it was to fight off the rot, but Jeremy had never believed it. The varnish — so thick it clogged the lines of the original sculpture — had seemed more a prison, holding that rot *in* so it couldn't escape and infect those standing too near.

It was a woman, or had been, at some point in history. Carved from a single log, long angular features, huge, mournful eyes that stretched down and down to high cheekbones and a slender, pointed nose — almost Roman, he'd heard others say. You could tell the woman the piece had been modeled after had been beautiful. Even the ravages of the ocean, the weather, and the years hadn't been able to mask it. There was an eerie sense of something hovering just beneath the surface of the wood, staring back at you if you studied it too closely and watching you move about the room if you pretended not to notice. Always.

In his pocket, sharp page folds pressing through the worn denim of his jeans to scrape his thigh, was the letter that had dragged him home. The type had smeared from sweat, too many folds, and too many readings. The return address was one he'd never seen before, and would likely never see again. Probst and Palmer, Attorneys at law. The address wasn't local to Cedar Falls. Jeremy's father had left him with two standard rules. Never do business with friends, and even if you break rule number one, never do business in your own back yard. The less people knew about what lay behind your smile, or your frown, the less likely they were to be able to find a chink in your armor and take you down.

Jeremy had never understood who in Cedar Falls would want to take him down, or his father, for that matter, but he understood the rules. Probst and Palmer's offices were in Kingston, 100 miles to the north, and Jeremy had stopped through on his way to pick up paperwork, and keys. His father had left things in good order. The house was paid for, the taxes good for the year and the insurance caught up both on the property, and the ancient Chevrolet sedan he'd left behind.

All of it was ordered and neat, empty and far too bizarre to be handled all at once. Jeremy had driven to the house, parked out front and stared at the door and the windows for about fifteen minutes, then driven away. He knew he should have gone in, checked the place over and unpacked. There were more papers to sign, and the utility companies would have to be notified that services should be restored. Jeremy knew, but he just couldn't face it.

So here he was, head against the wooden frame of Brown's Barber Shop, sweat trickling under the flannel collar of his shirt as he fought for balance against suddenly weak knees and a whirling panorama of memory and pain. He didn't need a haircut, but he very suddenly needed to sit down, so Jeremy twisted away from the wall and slipped inside with a deep breath.

There were two bright overhead lamps, one swinging over each chair on a single stainless steel chain and funneled toward the floor by aluminum shades. The edges of each were yellowed and dusty, and Jeremy wondered, just for a moment, if some of that stain wasn't tobacco from his father's cigars.

Some things hadn't changed at all, except in perspective. The once-giant sailfish, while still huge, seemed possible through adult eyes, the mongoose and snake seedy and dusty rather than mysterious and dark.

The room was empty, and though the lights were on, there was a sensation of — emptiness. Deep, dark emptiness that matched the hollow ache in the pit of Jeremy's gut. He stepped in and let the door swing closed behind him with a squeak.

For a moment, he just stood there, taking in the room, the scent of old leather chairs and hair tonic, the slightly acrid scent of oil burned in the gears of Chrome and Bakelite clippers that should have been retired in the sixties. Whispered voices from his past spoke of presidents and congressmen long dead, bake sales and sea stories. Dust motes danced beneath the hanging lamps, and Jeremy turned to the wall at the back, taking a step deeper into the gloom.

She was there, just as he remembered. There were a few more photographs lining the wall to either side, some in color, which didn't fit his memory at all, but Jeremy's gaze was focused. The wood seemed to grow from the wall, curving and taking shape slowly as it built up to the deep-set holes that were her eyes. Long, flowing hair, deeply etched into the wood, each line darker in the center and lightening as it neared the surface of the wood. The longer Jeremy stared the more real she became, the room fading around her until all he could see was a woman, gazing back at him in quiet desperation. He stepped closer, one foot hesitantly sliding through the dust, then the other. Just as he reached out his hand to trace her cheek with one finger a voice cut through the shadows.

"Can I help you?"

Jeremy spun, eyes wide and his mouth dropping open. The man who'd spoken leaned against the second barber chair on one elbow, watching Jeremy with interest. The cheeks had grown heavier, and wrinkles lined the skin beneath his eyes, but Jeremy recognized Terry Brown instantly. It had to be Terry. He was the spitting image of his Father, and in that instant the echo of Jeremy's father's voice, and the scent of smoke and leather nearly overwhelmed him.

"I . . ." his words caught in his throat for a second, then he turned, stepped forward and offered his hand shakily. "I'm Jeremy Lyons," he said. "I used to come here with my father."

In that moment, the other man's face shifted through a series of emotions, surprise, a deep, impressive smile — a quick flash of insight, and ended in a sympathetic frown. "Jack Lyons' boy?"

Jeremy nodded. "The last time you cut my hair," he said softly, "was for my high school graduation."

"Flat top," Terry nodded, "high and tight, just like always."

Jeremy turned back to the wooden woman mounted on the wall for just a second, then stepped away and walked toward the barber's chair, extending his hand.

"I'm guessing you aren't here for a trim?"

Jeremy grinned wryly. "I don't know why I'm here, exactly. I went by the house, just wasn't quite ready for it. When I came back into town, it just seemed natural. I don't know how many afternoons and evenings I spent in here, reading — drawing — listening. Guess I thought it would be a little more like home than that empty house."

"Not a lot of action these days," Terry smiled. "I get busy about one or so, but by three or four it thins out. Only a few old-timers remember the way things were, and mostly they come around on the weekends. Not a one of them has needed a real haircut in years, but they come, and they pay, regular as clockwork."

Jeremy smiled. "Just like always."

The two laughed comfortably, and Terry moved away from the chair toward the front door.

"Let me lock up," he said. "I've got a few bottles of beer in back. No one waiting up for either of us."

Jeremy almost bowed out. He had no right imposing his depression on someone else. The more he thought about it, the less sense it made that he'd come to the old barber shop at all. It was a place to get your hair cut, and all the magic, if there'd truly been any, had long departed. He turned, caught sight of the figurehead on the wall, and frowned.

Jeremy had never been in the back room of Brown's Barber Shop. He'd seen his father disappear through those doors countless times, but he'd never been allowed past the entrance. Even now, as Terry slipped in ahead of him and flicked on the dim light, he hesitated. It was like violating his father's will beyond the grave.

"We had to move most of the social activities back here as the years passed," Terry said conversationally, pulling open an aged refrigerator and grabbing two long-necks from the frosty interior. "Health inspectors were cracking down, mothers dragging their children in where father's had always done so before, complaining about the cigarette smoke and threatening to close us down.

"Hell," Terry chuckled, plopping into one of the old leather chairs lining the wall of the back room and twisting the top off his beer, "we even had animal rights activists protesting the animals on the walls."

"I don't know how you survived it all," Jeremy said, shaking his head and taking a seat a few feet away. "I don't know how you stayed here at all."

"Well, the staying is in my blood," Terry smiled. "Been a Brown in this shop almost as long as there's been a Cedar Falls. Wouldn't want to be the one to break a streak like that. The rest was easier than it seemed. They opened a new shop in the mall out Whitewall way. It's got a big clown chair for the kids and a play room with Nintendo. That left us to the regulars and the few too lazy to drive that far. It's enough for a living, and that's all a man can rightly ask of life, I think."

Jeremy thought about that for a moment, taking a long pull from the beer bottle.

"I wish I could have thought that way," he said at last. "I wish I'd been happy to come here every week, get a trim and hear the old stories. I wish I could have been more like my father — at least a little. I feel like it's all been lost, and all I have to show for the years is an empty house and dreams I have no one to share with."

"Never married, huh?" Terry turned away for a moment, then took another long drink, draining his bottle and rising for a second, glancing at Jeremy, who shook his head. "I never settled either. Never could find anyone I felt comfortable with, not after Dad passed on. There's been a couple of times I thought I might be on the right track, but . . ." he shrugged and opened his second beer. "Some men are meant to be alone."

Jeremy nodded.

"I miss those days, sometimes," he said softly. "I miss the stories. I miss hearing old Mulligan talk about catching that Marlin out there. I knew, even then, that he never set foot on the deck of a fishing boat in his life, but the words were magic. It wasn't the truth, but the story, you know?"

Terry nodded. "I do. Don't get much of that any more. Mulligan passed on about seven years ago, Billy Jensen shortly after that. Mostly they come and talk about those who've died, now, and wait for their own turn."

"There's one story I never heard," Jeremy said suddenly. "I know there's a story, because my father used to let bits and pieces slip. That figurehead on the wall out there, the woman. He said your father brought her back from the war. . ."

Terry grew suddenly stiff, and for a moment Jeremy thought the man would chase him out of the shop and lock the doors behind him forever. Tension rippled through the air and tingled along the hairs on Jeremy's arm. His hand shook, and he forced it to steady.

"Some stories are best left to the dead and their memory," Terry muttered, downing his second beer and rising quickly.

"Did I say something wrong?" Jeremy asked quickly, taken aback by the sudden reaction his words had brought.

"Not at all," Brown said brusquely, "but it's getting late. I know you need to get settled in. Maybe you could stop in during regular hours for a trim."

Jeremy sat, stunned, staring at the bigger man and trying to figure out whether he was kidding. There was no humor in the barber's slate-gray eyes, so Jeremy rose slowly, downing the beer and handing over the empty bottle.

"Nice to see you again, then," he said, turning. "Nice to be back."

Terry's features trembled, as if he were fighting some inner battle. Maybe he wanted to say something, take something back, but in the end, he held to his silence, only nodding as Jeremy slipped out of that forbidden room and into the shadowed barber shop once again. Jeremy glanced at the wall, and in the darkness, shadow cloaking the carved wood, it seemed a woman stood, watching him. He could have sworn her eyes glittered brightly and that a slender arm reached out — fingers beckoning.

Then Brown was at his side, ushering him toward the door with a firm hand on his back, mumbling something about the good old days. The air was cool, and the streets were deserted. Jeremy stood on the walk outside in confusion, then shrugged and turned to the road, and his car. Might as well get to some memories of his own.

The old home was full of stale air and dim memory. Jeremy had had vague ideas of cleaning up, arranging things and putting them back in order, but he should have known that his father would leave no such satisfaction. Everything was in its place. A very light sheen of dust coated everything, but beneath it the floors gleamed. The glass glittered — even the silver had only the faintest tinge of tarnish. The power was alive and waiting. There was a yellow note, hanging from the knob of the front door, to let him know they'd stopped and cut it on. "Just as his father had asked."

Jeremy's room was much as he'd left it last visit home. He'd been in his senior year of college, and the remnants of that time littered the desk and the walls. His bed was turned down, as if expecting him. Too much. Jeremy closed the door on that particular set of nightmares and moved down the hall. He pushed and the door to his parent's room swung open easily, hinges oiled. No sound. There had never been a sound. Jeremy had listened and listened, but he'd never been able to tell when they came and went. The room beckoned, dark and — inviting. It was a strange, exhilarating invitation, but an invitation nonetheless. For the first time since driving into the tiny, dirt-water town, Jeremy felt as if he were home.

The switch beside the door didn't operate a ceiling fixture as he'd expected. A single, dim light pooled yellow illumination over the floor from the dresser to his right. Rather than cutting the deeper shadows, the lamp's glow accentuated them. The bed was an expansive darkness, flanked by low-slung night-stands of still-darker wood. The windows were hung with heavy drapes of indeterminate color, pulled tight across closed blinds.

Odd shapes hung from the walls, and a huge old mirror glittered across the back of the dresser. Jeremy stared at that mirror. He couldn't make out anything in the silvered surface, but he stood, still and quiet, and watched the reflected glow of the lamp.

His mother had sat there, right in front of that mirror, brushing her long hair for hours. Jeremy had never actually set foot in his parent's room, but he'd watched her from the doorway, when she didn't know he was looking. He wondered if a part of her might be captured there. If he stared long enough, would her face appear? Would he feel the soft stroke of the brush through his hair? And where had his father been when . . .

Shaking his head, Jeremy turned from the mirror quickly. Again, too much.

Moving to the bed, he laid his suitcase out and unsnapped it quickly. He needed to get his mind out of the past. There were a lot of things to accomplish, clearing out the house, gathering his parents papers and belongings, the lawyers. All of it loomed over him like the specter of his father, leering and poking, tugging him first one direction, then another, and the last thing he needed in the midst of it all was more illusion and memory. Illusions and memories had haunted him for too many years.

Before he could think of his father's accusing gaze, he opened the drawers of the old dresser and shoved his clothes hurriedly inside. It was nearly comical, the way the finality of the gesture washed through him in a wave of sudden relief. He was in. The dresser was his, not his father's, not a thing he would be punished for violating. The room — the house — everything in it — was his.

With a sigh he pushed the drawer shut and turned, seating himself on the edge of the bed. The woman stared down at him, smoother than he remembered, and darker, her hair seeming to drip from the polished wood surface.

Jeremy grew very still. His heart pulsed, slowing with his breath painfully until it felt as if it might stop altogether. The moment was identical to a hundred acid-tripping moments in his youth, pulsing with the neon-beat of bar-lights and the sultry back-beat of strip clubs, pounding with the rhythms of a thousand songs. Still and silent.

Beside the window, sliding out from the edge of the heavy curtains, was the wooden figurehead from the barber shop. He knew it couldn't be the same one. He had just seen it — had reached out his hand and touched it — but the sensation it was there — that it was real and identical and *watching* him was undeniable.

Mesmerized, Jeremy rose, stepping forward. He heard the soft echo of Terry's words in his ear. "Some stories are best left to the dead, and their memory," but the words flitted through his mind and away, as if whispered across a great distance.

Jeremy reached out one hand, letting his fingers come to rest on the smooth, polished wood, and his stomach lurched. The scent of hair tonic and musty leather assaulted his senses violently. His vision blurred, then focused. The wall had changed. Lengthened. For just an instant, the floor pitched beneath his feet, and he clutched the wooden carving tightly for support.

"No," he whispered.

Everything had shifted, and the pungent scent of tobacco smoke hung in the air. To his left, dim, yellow light flickered, and he could hear the scrape of feet, the groan and squeal of old springs as heavy bodies settled into aged chairs. The shadow-forms of dead, mounted animals surrounded him, glass-eye stares too-high. As if he were shorter. As if he were younger.

As if time had rewound its tape.

A heavy cough, then laughter, deep and guttural. Jeremy's heart lurched. He knew that cough, and that laugh. He pressed into the wall, nearly collapsing, and closed his eyes so tightly that they squeezed shut on the heavy smoke, burning and tingling. He thought about the bed behind him. He thought about the door, still ajar, less than three feet away, and the hallway beyond. He thought about his father's liquor cabinet, and with a sudden shove he pushed away from the wall and spun.

His knee banged into something hard, and he cried out. His eyes opened to shadows, flickering, and a huge, dark shape silhouetted against yellowed light.

"Who is it?"

The words hung in the smoky air, mocking Jeremy's sanity.

Jeremy held his breath, pressing back to the wall.

"That you boy?"

Jeremy tried to remain silent, but it was too much. That voice, a voice he'd been conditioned from birth to obey, was irresistible.

"Dad?"

The world shifted again. Jeremy felt his mind whirl, saw the lights shift and heard heavy footsteps approaching like the beating of primal drums, timed with his heartbeat. He knew he was falling, but somehow he couldn't react to it. Strong arms clasped him under his arms, hands too large, covering his shoulders, fingers gripping and lifting.

Then — mercifully — it was dark.

Jeremy woke next to the scent and cool caress of leather. He was curled in a chair. How was that possible? A single chair, club-style with brown leather and metal rivets. Voices droned, the sound shifting and growing more clear with each beat of his heart. He smelled smoke, thick in the air above him, and he saw that a single dim bulb hung from a bare wire in the center of the room.

Jeremy curled tighter. He wanted to know what was being said, to put it into perspective before he sat up. It was all a mistake, obviously. He shouldn't be there. Not like this, not small and vulnerable, shivering in a chair shrouded in shadow, but alone and brooding in his father's room. It would all fade if he sat up. He would be passed out across that bed, nothing on the wall behind him at all. Nothing but a mirror to stare into that would stare back and mock his meaningless life — that would show him the younger face of the father he'd lost.

"She's hung there nearly ten years," a deep, guttural voice cut through Jeremy's thoughts. "Hung her there myself. The nail is a square one; drew it by hand from the very wood of that ship."

There were murmurs, but no words, in reply, and the voice continued until an image twisted into shape in Jeremy's mind. It was Terry, but not exactly Terry. It was an aged, too-squat Terry with a beard gone half-grey down the center and gnarled, liver-spotted hands. It was a Terry two generations back, when the barber shop had been so much more than a barber shop, and the back room had been sacred.

"She'd ridden the waves so long it took a good hour's work just to wipe away the salt scum that held her to the prow. She was bolted down, of course, but those bolts had long since surrendered to salt and wind. They crumbled like dust when I tried to pry them loose. For all that, it was no easy task. That ship clung to her like a lover, green mossy slime stretching like some god-forsaken glue. Two more days and she'd have dined with Davey Jones himself. The plan was to scuttle her over the far side of the reef, where her bones could blend with the coral and not be a hazard."

"Seems a shame," a softer voice replied, floating out from the far corner of the room. "I mean, that ship was a beauty. Shame to see her go down."

The silence that followed grew heavy, and despite the ludicrous notion of cowering in a chair much too big to be real, Jeremy felt himself shiver as the weight of it settled over the room. Someone coughed, and a glass hit the table with a heavy clunk.

"Maybe you should have let her go, too." The words echoed. Jeremy recognized his father's voice. For some reason this was more comforting than disturbing in that moment.

There was a quick, grating sound as a chair pushed away from the table. Heavy footsteps followed, and then Terry Brown's grand-father's rough voice continued, as though no other words had been spoken.

"I couldn't bear to see her go. Not that way. Not after all I knew. She didn't belong to the sea, not then, not ever, though the barnacles and the weather had done their best to disguise her as one of their own." He paused again, then added more softly. "I couldn't send her back to him. Not that."

"Tell us," the soft voice Jeremy didn't recognize cut in. "Tell us again."

Jeremy dared to uncoil his small frame slightly, peeking just over the arm of the old leather chair. He saw a tall, broad-shouldered man with his back to the table, one hand gently caressing the cheek of the figurehead on the wall. The woman's eyes returned that gaze

302 | THE CALL OF FARTHER SHORES

with more emotion than was possible, and Jeremy ducked back into the tentative safety of the chair.

"They said she was beautiful," the elder Brown's voice rose, a practiced story-teller practicing his art, "so beautiful that men would travel miles just for the chance to see her face, or hear her voice. They say she had the beauty that starts wars, or ends a dynasty. They say . . . she was loved . . ."

Jeremy felt the world shift again and he started from the leather seat. His balance failed, and he teetered to the side, clutching at the arm of the chair. It wasn't there. He grabbed an armful of air and toppled, crying out softly and striking the floor hard. His senses reeled, and he felt the soft brush of something on his cheek. The acrid scent of mothballs filled his nostrils and he coughed violently, rolling to his back.

The silence of his parent's room surrounded him. The ceiling, lowered tiles he remembered his father laying in place, one at a time on the rickety, dangling framework that held them suspended over the room, shimmered.

"Makes the room look longer and wider."

Jeremy heard the voice clearly. His father's voice. Staring at the tiles, the room in the back of the barber shop fading from his mind slowly, he could still hear the words as clearly as the day they'd first been spoken. He remembered the skeptical frown in his mother's eyes, and the silent nod. He remembered thinking that the tiles did nothing but make the room short, and squat. He remembered saying nothing.

Rising slowly, he reached to the bed for support and levered himself to his feet. The wall was bare. Nothing. Not even a photograph, or a gilt-framed mirror to fill the space. The mirror he might have understood, because then the face he'd touched could have been his own.

On the night stand beside the bed, a framed photograph of his parents watched him.

"Not this time, old man," Jeremy whispered.

He grabbed the pillows from the head of the bed and yanked free the down comforter, heading for the hall. Moments later, without a backward glance, he slipped through the doorway into his old room. He didn't flip on the light. He sprawled out over the bed and wrapped himself in the comforter, sliding his head between two down pillows and closing his eyes, drifting off to sleep before the dreams could descend and trap him in that netherworld between rest and reality.

Autumn in Cedar Falls was a quiet time. Things were ending, and beginning, school in session and the football season in full swing. Churches were gearing up for the final bake sale before Thanksgiving, and the road crews were oiling and winterizing their equipment for the annual war with the weather. Despite the comfortable familiarity of it all, Jeremy couldn't shake the cold knot of ice free from his chest.

He could still hear his father's voice, and every time he closed his eyes, the scents of leather and tobacco permeated his world. He drove straight through the center of town, skipping the market and passing the "General Store," still in operation despite the competition of the new Super Walmart down by the highway. There was only one place he was likely to get his answers.

He parked right out front of the barber shop, waiting until the dust had settled before he stepped out and closed the door behind himself. There was no light inside, but he knew Terry was open. The barber shop had always been open — Jeremy couldn't remember a time when it had not been. Of course, most of those memories were of visits with his father, and there was no clarity of time, or space. Jeremy had been more of an accessory than a companion, brought along because it was what father's in Cedar Falls did.

Now there was no father, and the town was slowly dying around the edges. So little remained of what had seemed so huge and imposing those many years in the past that the town hung against the sky like a tattered and torn postcard. Not many people were up and about on a Saturday morning, at least not in town. There were a couple of kids playing in the park out front of the Post Office, and just before Jeremy reached the barber shop door, a police cruiser rolled slowly past behind him, moving on to other pockets of inactivity en-route to the diner by Route 12.

Jeremy wondered fleetingly why he hadn't noticed the general decline the day before. Everything had seemed so — quaint. So rural and down-home comfortable. Now it looked like a too-old prop in a bad horror movie. The buildings leaned, ready to fall over backward at the slightest provocation, nothing more than propped up plywood silhouettes.

The barber shop was dark. Even more so than before, and

though the door was open, there was no sign that Terry was open for business. There was no sign of any activity at all, in fact. Dust covered the chairs and the walls were dingy. Jeremy released the door and it swung to with a squeal of old metal in need of oil. The only illumination came through the slats of the blinds to his rear, and from beneath the crack of the door to the back. From there a soft, yellowish light trickled, slipping to puddle just beyond the base of the door, which was closed.

"Terry?" Jeremy didn't call out too loudly. Something held him back. There was no answer.

He called out again, a bit more insistently, and stepped closer to the door in back. "Terry? Are you there?"

Nothing again, and moments later he stood, ear to the wooden frame of the door, trying to press his eye to the crack that was releasing the light. The sound of feet shuffling reached him, and the soft murmur of voices.

Hesitantly, Jeremy reached out and rapped on the door. At first he thought no one had heard him, and he was hovering between the desire to knock louder, pounding until they let him in and told him what the hell was going on when the door swung wide. The floor beneath him lurched sickeningly, tumbling him forward, and Jeremy reached out with a cry drowned quickly in the roar of . . .

Waves. Crashing, rolling high above and tumbling toward him, foam-tipped and peppering face and eyes with hard, stinging salt-slaps of spray. His stumble brought him up abruptly against a wooden rail, and he clutched the slimy surface tightly as his chest slammed into the solid wood and his knees threatened to buckle from the impact.

The water hit then, and everything else disappeared. Jeremy pressed himself tightly to the wood, clutching with his hands and gripping with his knees, fighting the crushing weight of the cold, relentless pull of the seawater as it pounded, then receded with a sickening, sucking sound over the side and the world tilted backward as quickly as it had leaned forward. Closing his eyes, Jeremy clung more tightly still to the rail, fingers slipping and groping along the wet-slick wood for purchase and feet threatening to slip off behind him and down.

For an eternity of deafening sound and flashing lightning, he hung nearly perpendicular to the sea, then he rushed back the other way, compressed tightly to the wooden rail and his breath left him.

Voices cried out, nearly lost in the gale, and Jeremy's mind swam with the words, trying to order them so they made sense, trying to find the courage to release the rail, turn, and step back through the door and into the barber shop — the world.

The same world that chose that moment to lurch again, not so violently this time, and Jeremy felt the ship turning beneath him — felt the prow coming about, just in time, slicing the next of the monstrous waves that had threatened moments before to wash him from the deck into a sea of insanity. The voices grew clearer, and Jeremy risked releasing the rail with one hand to brush the soaked hair from his eyes.

It was dark, too dark to make out anything much more than the length of his arm from his face, but the lightning flashes gave a strobed pseudo-light just visible through the stinging salt. Jeremy could make out the prow of the ship, dropping down with a stomach-stealing lurch to shimmy at the base of a huge swelling wave, then rising, so high that only the sky and the angry face of the storm, creased in deep green, blue-black and silver by the searing crackles of lightning, filled his vision. There was a shape, solid and unmoving, like a body leading the ship through the storm. A woman. Droplets of water washed back and off, giving the illusion of silver hair in each lightning burst.

From behind, strong fingers gripped suddenly beneath Jeremy's arms, and he was jerked from the rail and hauled up and back. The ship was no more steady than before, but the danger of slipping side to side had passed, and moments later Jeremy crashed to the wall of what must have been the ship's cabin.

"Get inside!" The words screamed through his eardrums, blocking out the storm, just for an instant, and Jeremy turned, wild-eyed. Terry stood there — not Terry — taller with similar features. The man's hair waved wildly about his head and his eyes smoldered with barely controlled anger — and strength.

"Get below, damn you!" The man repeated, cuffing Jeremy on the side of the head. "I've not enough men to make it without you."

Other hands groped from the shadowed doorway of the cabin and Jeremy was jerked inside, just as another wave crashed across the deck and threatened to drag him back to the railing, or further. As he tumbled backward into the shadows, Jeremy caught a last lightning flash. The woman's figure stared out over the waves stoically.

His foot caught on the top stair, and he tumbled, ignoring the loud cursing of whoever it was that had dragged him to safety. He felt the contact as the two of them slammed into the wall, then continued back and down, banging one knee painfully and twisting mid-air to try and get his hands beneath him. There was nothing. Nothing but shadow, and as he passed to darkness, he felt damp wood as his hands struck first, chin following in a jarring tangle of tar-soaked hemp and salt-soaked planks. The darkness that followed was sudden, and complete.

Jeremy returned to consciousness amid the scents of leather and tobacco. His head pounded painfully, and his eyes refused to focus. The room was adrift in smoke — tobacco smoke, pungent and overpowering. He coughed, hand rising to cover his mouth and body convulsing until he bent nearly double from the effort to draw clean air into his lungs. His eyes stung, and he could barely focus through the pain, so he closed them tightly.

"Quite a tumble."

The words hung in the air, making no sense coming from the direction and voice that they did. Jeremy brushed his fingers gingerly over the growing knot on his head and forced his eyes open once more.

He was in the back room of the barber shop. The old refrigerator hummed too-loudly against the wall. Terry sat across the table from him, an open beer resting between cupped palms.

"I was wrong," Terry went on. "Been here by myself so long, I'd started to think things would come full-circle and end. Seemed right. Now I see she's been callin' you back all along."

"She?" Jeremy coughed the word out, making it a question.

Terry just watched him, raising his beer and taking a long drink.

"You know who I mean," he said at last. "Now I have a story — *the* story. You just sit there and try to concentrate."

Terry rose slowly, moving to the refrigerator and drawing forth a second cold beer, which he carried across the room and placed in front of Jeremy on the table. The barber untwisted the cap with a quick jerk of his wrist and left the bottle to stand, tiny wisps of steam rising from the neck to remind Jeremy of the ship — the waves. The throbbing in his head subsided to a dull ache, and he rose, moving the leather chair he was leaning back in closer to the table and grabbing the beer tightly. He raised the cold glass to press against his temple for a moment, then took a drink and met Terry's gaze.

"Tell me."

"It started in Scotland," Terry began slowly. His eyes, and his voice, took on a distance and a depth they'd not seemed to possess previously. "None of our fathers were even gleams in their own father's eyes at the time, but one thing was the same. The ocean. Even then, when women waited by the fires and wars were fought hand to hand, enemies staring one another in the eye and defying death, she called to us. There was one who answered.

"Angus was his name, and he took to the sea so young they say he was sailing from near the day he was born. The son of a son of a sea captain, bred to the ocean — the far shore. Born with the burning need to see what lay beyond the next wave. Angus Griswold belonged to the sea.

"Until he met her," Terry stopped, nodding toward the door, and the barber shop beyond — the woman hanging on the wall — the world that seemed so distant Jeremy could scarcely grant it credence.

"She was the daughter of a merchant he met in his travels. Angus wasn't one to settle in one place, but the day he met her, he found that an anchor had been cast that would not dislodge. She was beautiful. Beyond anything he'd seen, rivaling even the blue of the deepest lagoons and the scent of the islands after a storm, she drew him. At night, on the deck of his ship, he would think of her, writing letters long into the night, only to crumple them and toss them aside in anger, drowning his imagination in rum and dark thoughts, until even his men began to talk.

"He returned to Scotland, soon after, and erected a keep overlooking the waves, tall and strong of stone dragged from the very edge of the sea. All that time, he kept her face in his heart. He wrote more letters, and eventually, a few of them weren't crumpled. He sent the first, then the second, and when she replied to his third, he wrote again, until at last he found himself before her father, a tall, thin man with piercing eyes. You've seen those eyes, mirrored in the countenance of his daughter.

"They were wed, soon after, and settled into that keep. That prison."

"Prison?" Jeremy asked, finally finding the courage and

strength to take the beer in a shaky hand and draw deep. "You said it was a keep."

"It was that," Terry said softly. "It kept him from his other love — his oldest love. It kept him from the sea while holding it out before him like a carrot dangled before an ass. She loved him, Jeremy. She loved him with all her heart, mind — soul. She loved him, and in the end, it wasn't enough.

"Ten years to the day after he brought her home, Angus bought a boat. He told her it would be for short trips — jaunts up the coast and back, but she knew. In his eyes, the waves danced, and the sun set over shores with unknown lines.

"He sailed within the year."

"Sailors have always sailed away," Jeremy said, lifting his eyes to meet the barber's. "They come home."

"Not Angus," Terry shook his head and sipped his beer. "Not that time.

"He was gone a year before she began to really worry, sending letters home to her father, who was less than sympathetic. He'd received her dowry, and she was aging — still beautiful, but not of marrying age, and still married, in any case, to Angus. The year stretched into another, and another — ten years, Jeremy. She lived alone in that keep for ten years, spending the money Angus had amassed in a life of sailing and trade, and pining for the one thing that had drawn her to the ocean's side. The one thing she couldn't have.

"Every night she watched at the balcony outside her room until the sun set and the moon rose high above the waves. Every night she prayed. Some say, near the end, when the loneliness had started to make her crazy, that she prayed to others than the God we know. There were books found in her towers, books none could place, or translate — some written by hand, others printed in far away lands. Angus must have brought them home, but it was obvious that his lover was the one to find their use.

"Then one day, the ship returned."

"You said he never came back."

"And he did not. The ship came back. Most of his men came back. Angus died of a fever, wasted him away to nothing in the cabin of that ship. They buried him at sea, but before he died, he set them to bring his boat home. To bring her the treasures and secrets of the world he'd found. To tell her he loved her.

"None of it mattered. They pulled in and she flew to that shore a woman possessed, to find no man, but only wealth. Only salt-soaked board and men too-long away from home. Only more loneliness washed ashore.

"They brought it all to her, and she held a feast such as had not been seen in those parts since Angus himself was alive. They drowned themselves in the food they'd missed and the local girls, washed it all down with barrels of wine. She watched, smiling all the while as if she was sharing their good humor.

"When they woke, every man-jack was locked in that ballroom. She'd had men come in during the night and bar the doors with stout planks. They were left to rot with what remained of the food, and the wine, even the women who'd joined them. They carried on and wailed at her, even tried to set the place on fire. None of it worked. They were trapped, and she was going to go and let them stay, leave and never come back."

Jeremy shuddered, casting a glance at the door — toward what lay beyond. "What happened?" he asked softly.

"That night, she stood on her balcony as always," Terry replied. "As she stood, staring into the waves, he came to her. Moss was matted and woven into the long hairs of his beard, and his eyes were half-eaten by fish, but he came, staggering from the waves. She just watched him come, no effort to help him, or to hinder. She watched as he staggered to the walls of the keep and beat his rotting hands against the stone walls.

"Let them go," he cried. "Let them go, my love. I've come back."

"No one knows for certain if she listened," Terry said at last. "She released the men the next day, giving them back enough of what they'd brought her to build a new ship. She made certain that everything was perfect — every board, every sail — hand-picked. And she sent for an artist. A young man, some say a Eunuch. He brought the wood with him from Egypt, a solid block of it, taking up half his cart. As the ship was built, the man worked."

"She sailed with that ship?" Jeremy asked, breaking the silence.

"No. She died. She died, alone in her tower, leaning on the wall that overlooked the waves below, but the work was finished, and when they saw what she'd commissioned, the work the eunuch had left, the men would not leave her behind."

Both men stared at the doorway now. Beyond it, they could feel the draw of the wood, dark and curving tightly to the wall behind, eyes sockets of something darker than shadow. In their heads, a voice, calling out softly.

"Your great grandfather found that ship," Jeremy breathed. "He brought her here."

Terry rose, turning toward the refrigerator again without a word, and the lights flickered, suddenly, threatened to die, then steadied. They were dimmer, their radiance more yellow, and Jeremy staggered half to his feet, bracing himself on the arms of the chair as the floor lurched sickeningly.

"Damn," Terry cursed. He turned back, a brown-necked bottle in his hand. Tipping it up, he took a long swig and strode across the deck to where Jeremy now stood, wild-eyed and staring at the doorway, now a stairway once more. Beyond the walls, the waves crashed, and Terry — not Terry — handed over the bottle with a wild-eyed stare.

"We can't let her go down," the man whispered softly, almost plaintively. "We must keep her afloat. She . . . she loves me."

Jeremy took the bottle, turned to the stairs, and staggered through — into the clear night air beneath the stars. His car stood just to his right, and the moon was bright and full. He downed the beer in a single gulp and fell heavily over the hood of his car. In the shadows behind him, he felt the weight of eyes, and the call of farther shores.

It was good to be home.

# CONTRIBUTORS

After working a variety of jobs, and writing in his spare time, **JOE R. LANSDALE** became a full-time writer in 1981 and has practiced his craft ever since. He is the author of over 200 short stories, articles, and essays, as well as twenty novels and several short-story collections. He has edited or coedited (some with his wife Karen Lansdale) seven anthologies — five fiction, two nonfiction. He is well-known for his series/suspense adventures, several of which have been optioned for film, including *Mucho Mojo*. Joe has also scripted teleplays for the Emmy-award winning *Batman* series. He has scripted comics, including the award winning DC Comics *Jonah Hex* series, and also *It Crawls*, the comic that revived the Lone Ranger. He even had his own comic series at Dark Horse.

Joe is a member of the Texas Institute of Letters. He's won several awards for his work, including the Edgar Award for best novels, six Bram Stokers, the British Fantasy Award, the American Mystery award, the Horror Critics Award, and many other awards and recognitions.

**JACK CADY** worked as a truck driver intermittently until his late 30s and for a time ran his own landscape construction business. Following four years with the Coast Guard in Maine, he earned a bachelor's degree at the University of Louisville in 1961. In 1965, he received the *Atlantic Monthly*'s Atlantic First Award for the short story "The Burning." During the course of his career, he would go on to win some of the most prestigious awards in the science fiction, fantasy and horror fields. A former teacher at the Pacific Lutheran University in Tacoma, Washington, Cady penned the superb novels: *The Well*, *Singleton*, *The Jonah Watch*, *McDowell's Ghost*, *The Man Who Could Make Things Vanish*, *Dark Dreaming* (writing as Pat Franklin), *Embrace of the Wolf* (writing as Pat Franklin), *Inagehi*, *Street: A Novel*, *The Off Season*, *The Hauntings of Hood Canal*; the collections *The Burning & Other Stories*, *Tattoo & Other Stories*, *The Sons of Noah & Other Stories*, *The Night We Buried Road Dog*, *Ghostland & Ghosts of Yesterday*, and the nonfiction book *The American Writer: Shaping A Nation's Mind*. Sadly, Jack passed away in January 2004.

**HOLLY PHILLIPS** is the author of *In the Palace of Repose* and *The Burning Girl* (Prime Books, 2006). She lives and writes in the mountains of western Canada.

Of her story, Holly writes: "'The Other Grace' was inspired by a fascination for the connection between memory and identity: would I still be me even if I couldn't remember who I was? It was also a story that was bounced from magazine to magazine before finding its first home in the collection *In the Palace of Repose*. Like a lot of my stories, it was apparently too long and too odd for the literary markets, and not quite odd enough for the genre ones."

**NICHOLAS ROYLE** was born in Manchester in 1963. He is the author of five novels — *Counterparts*, *Saxophone Dreams*, *The Matter of the Heart*, *The Director's Cut* and *Antwerp* — in addition to more than one hundred short stories. Widely published as a journalist, he has also edited twelve anthologies and has won the British Fantasy Award three times. Forthcoming in October 2006 is his first collection of short stories, *Mortality*. More information on his work can be found at <www.nicholasroyle.com>.

The author writes: "I don't know how long it's meant to be after you move into a house before it feels like it's yours. Particularly old houses. Most British towns and cities have limited stocks of Edwardian and Victorian houses, with more people after them than there are houses to go around. This is good for estate agents and those looking to sell, but for househunters it's a like a bad dream. Which sometimes turns into a nightmare only after you get your house and you move in."

**JOE HILL**'s first book, *20TH Century Ghosts*, a collection of his stories, was released last year, and received a starred review in *Publishers Weekly*. He is the past winner of the Ray Bradbury Fellowship, the A.E. Coppard Long Fiction Prize, and the William Crawford Award for outstanding new fantasy writer. His first novel, *Heart-Shaped Box*, will be released in 2007 by William Morrow.

"A couple years ago I lucked into the writing assignment of my childhood dreams, when I was offered the chance to script an eleven-page story for *Spider-Man Unlimited*. I don't know if what I wrote was anything all that special, but I had the good fortune to be paired with Seth Fisher, a gifted young illustrator. Seth's talent was completely idiosyncratic. His panels were crowded with grotesque fools, bobble-headed dimwits, rubbery, perverted-looking monsters, and pot-bellied, slacker superheroes. Seth made me look good.

We became pals in short order and I had a head full of all the stories we were going to tell together. 'The Cape' was one of them. When I wrote it, I was imagining it as Seth might have drawn it, something I won't get a chance to see now. I'm grateful, though, for the too-short time I had to be his friend. So here's one for Seth Fisher, 1972 – 2006, artist, husband, son and daddy."

CAITLÍN R. KIERNAN's short fiction has been collected in *Tales of Pain and Wonder, From Weird and Distant Shores, Wrong Things* (with Poppy Z. Brite), and, most recently, *To Charles Fort, With Love* and *Alabaster*, and has been selected for *The Year's Best Fantasy and Horror, The Mammoth Book of Best New Horror*, and *The Year's Best Science Fiction*. She is also the author of seven novels, including *Silk, Threshold, Low Red Moon, Murder of Angels, The Five of Cups*, and *Daughter of Hounds* (the latter to be released early in 2007). A number of her shorter works, such as *The Dry Salvages* and *In the Garden of Poisonous Flowers*, have been released by Subterranean Press. Trained as a vertebrate paleontologist and evolutionary biologist, her scientific papers have appeared in the *Journal of Vertebrate Paleontology, Journal of Paleontology*, and a number of other academic publications. Currently, Caitlín lives in Atlanta with her partner, Kathryn (a dollmaker and photographer), and her eighty-four year old cat, Sophie.

Caitlín spends far too much time on her online journal, which you may read at <http://greygirlbeast.livejournal.com>. "La Peau Verte," written in the winter of 2003, was composed entirely under the influence of Mari Mayans absinthe.

MARY RICKERT grew up in Fredonia, Wisconsin. When she was eighteen she moved to California where she worked at Disneyland. She still has fond memories of selling balloons there at night and learning to boogie board during the day. Sometimes she would go to the beach early in the morning, before anyone else was there, sit in the lifeguard's tower and write poetry. After many years (and through the sort of "odd series of events" that describe much of her life) she got a job as a kindergarten teacher in a small private school for gifted children. She worked there for almost a decade, then left to pursue her life as a writer.

Because the position of writer is for many years one of apprenticeship, she worked at a series of odd jobs, bookshop clerk, personnel clerk, hotel night auditor, and coffee shop clerk before settling into her current position as a nanny. There are, of course, mysterious gaps in this account, and that is where all the truly interesting stuff happened.

She has had many stories published by *The Magazine of Fantasy & Science Fiction*. A few of those stories have been reprinted in Year's Best anthologies.

**RICHARD BOWES** has lived in New York City since 1966 doing the usual jumble of things. Over the last twenty years he has published five novels, the most recent of which is *From the Files of the Time Rangers* (Golden Gryphon 2005), a couple of dozen short stories in *The Magazine of Fantasy & Science Fiction*, *Sci Fiction* and elsewhere, and won a World Fantasy and a Lambda Award.

Recent and upcoming appearances include a short fiction collection *Streetcar Dreams and other Midnight Fancies* (PS Publications 2006) and stories in *The Nebula Awards Showcase 2005*, *Postscripts 3*, *Electric Velocipede* and *The Coyote Road*, *So Fey* and *Salon Fantastique* anthologies.

**BARBARA RODEN** was born in Vancouver, British Columbia in 1963, and has been reading ghost stories since the age of seven. With her husband, Christopher, she co-founded and runs the World Fantasy Award-winning Ash-Tree Press, and is co-editor of the World Fantasy Award-nominated journal *All Hallows*. "Northwest Passage" originally appeared in the Ash-Tree Press anthology *Acquainted With the Night*, which won a World Fantasy Award for Best Anthology; the story was nominated for Best Short Story. Although the exact setting of the story is not specified in the tale, it is based on a real place, a cabin called The Lookout, which perches above a valley some miles southwest of Ashcroft, B.C., where the author lives. The tale was inspired by such works as Margaret Atwood's "Death by Landscape" and Algernon Blackwood's "The Wendigo," and also by the author's fascination with those people who feel a need to distance themselves from society and go in search of an elusive something which even they cannot define, often — as in the case of Sir John Franklin's quest for the Northwest Passage — with disastrous results."

**CLIVE BARKER** is the best-selling author of twenty books, including the *New York Times* best-seller *Abarat*. He is also an acclaimed artist, film producer, and director. Mr. Barker lives in California with his partner, the photographer David Armstrong, and their daughter, Nicole. They share their house with five dogs, sixty fish, nine rats, innumerable wild geekoes, five cockatiels, an African gray parrot called Smokey, and a yellow-headed Amazon parrot called Malingo.

**LAIRD BARRON** was born in Alaska, where he raised and trained huskies for many years. Three-time Iditarod finisher and lifelong outdoorsman, he migrated to the Pacific Northwest in the mid 90s and began to concentrate on writing poetry and fiction. He counts Charles Simic, Mark Strand, Roger Zelazny, Martin Cruz Smith and Cormac McCarthy among his influences.

His award-nominated work has appeared in *Sci Fiction*, *The Magazine of Fantasy & Science Fiction* and been reprinted in *The Year's Best Fantasy & Horror* and *Year's Best Fantasy 6*. Mr. Barron currently resides in Olympia, Washington and is hard at work on many projects, including a novel and his first collection of short fiction.

The author writes: "'Proboscis' was inspired in part by a few long, cold autumn days spent wandering amid the Mima Mounds, a weird, mysterious geological holdover from ancient times. All but five hundred or so acres of the once sprawling prairie lie hidden by a patchwork of farmsteads and country back roads; nonetheless, its existence has palpably influenced the folklore of Little Rock, Washington and environs. The origins of the Mima Mounds remain a subject of controversy and conjecture."

**JEFF VANDERMEER** is a two-time winner of the World Fantasy Award, and has made the year's best lists of *Publishers Weekly*, *The San Francisco Chronicle*, *The Los Angeles Weekly*, *Publishers' News*, and Amazon.com. His fiction has been shortlisted for *Best American Short Stories* and appeared in several year's best anthologies. Books by VanderMeer are forthcoming from Bantam, Pan Macmillan, and Tor. He currently lives in Tallahassee, Florida, with his wife, Ann. He is 37 years old.

He writes: "'Lost' arose out of a lot of readers emailing me and saying that they sometimes felt like my imaginary city of Ambergris was really a part of the real world. It also arose out of being in a melancholy mood and trying to imagine the thing that would most destroy my life and putting it down on paper. I think this piece is very close thematically to 'In the Hours After Death' in *City of Saints and Madmen*."

The *Oxford Companion to English Literature* describes **RAMSEY CAMPBELL** as "Britain's most respected living horror writer." He has been given more awards than any other writer in the field, including the Grand Master Award of the World Horror Convention and the Lifetime Achievement Award of the Horror Writers Association. Among his novels are *The Face That Must Die, Incarnate, Midnight Sun, The Count of Eleven, Silent Children, The Darkest Part of the Woods, The Overnight*, and *Secret Stories*. Forthcoming are *The Grin of the Dark* and *Spanked by Nuns*. His collections include *Waking Nightmares, Alone with the Horrors, Ghosts and Grisly Things* and *Told by the Dead*, and his non-fiction is collected as *Ramsey Campbell, Probably*. His novels *The Nameless* and *Pact of the Fathers* have been filmed in Spain.

Ramsey Campbell lives on Merseyside with his wife Jenny. He reviews films and DVDs weekly for BBC Radio Merseyside. His pleasures include classical music, good food and wine, and whatever's in that pipe. His web site is: <www.ramseycampbell.com>.

**NICK MAMATAS** is the author of the Lovecraftian Beat road novel *Move Under Ground*, which was nominated for the Bram Stoker and International Horror Guild Awards. *Under My Roof*, a novel of neighborhood nuclear superiority, will be released in 2006.

Of his story, he writes: "'Real People Slash' is a memoir of some years of the life of the author. The inclusion of a single false claim renders the memoir fiction. Try to guess which one it is; you may be pleasantly surprised."

He lives in Vermont.

**MICHAEL MARSHALL (SMITH)** is a novelist and screenwriter. His first novel, *Only Forward*, won the August Derleth and Philip K. Dick awards. *Spares* and *One of Us* were optioned for film by DreamWorks and Warner Brothers. *The Straw Men* and *The Lonely Dead* were international bestsellers. He is a three-time winner of the BFS Award for short fiction, and his stories are collected in two volumes — *What you Make It* and *More Tomorrow and Other Stories* (which won the international Horror Guild Award). His latest novel, *Blood of Angels*, is available in paperback now.

He lives in North London with his wife Paula, a son and two cats.

**SIMON OWENS** is a twenty-one-year-old college student living in Pennsylvania. He has sold short fiction to a variety of venues, including *Flesh & Blood, Chizine, The Book of Dark Wisdom*, and *Flytrap*. He also dabbles in non-genre work and creative nonfiction and hopes to pursue it more in the future. He wrote the beginning of "This Hand, Waving" when attending Tobias Buckell's Writing Jam, a weekend getaway for neo-pro writers. A good friend read the first few paragraphs and badgered him to finish it for months before he finally did.

**DAVID NIALL WILSON** has been writing professionally since the mid 1980s. He has sold twelve novels to date, including *This is My Blood*, and *Deep Blue*, and the trilogy *The Grails Covenant*. His novella, *Roll Them Bones*, was a finalist for the Bram Stoker Award in long fiction. David won the Bram Stoker Award for poetry for his part in the three-way collection *The Gossamer Eye*, written with Rain Graves and Mark McLaughlin. He has over a hundred and thirty published short stories in markets as diverse as *Cavalier Magazine*, *Cemetery Dance Magazine* and anthologies such as *Robert Bloch's Psychos, Deathport, Murder Most Delicious*, and *The Daw Year's Best Horror, XIX*. His work has been collected three times in the volumes *The Fall of the House of Escher & Other Illusions, The Subtle Ties That Bind*, and *Spinning Webs & Telling Lies*. His screenplay, *Godhead*, written in collaboration with creator/director Rosanna Jeran, is in pre-production in 2005. Wilson is a former president of the Horror Writer's Association and an active member of the ITW, HWA and SFWA.

**JOHN GREGORY BETANCOURT** is the best-selling author of thirty-seven fantasy and science fiction books, as well as the editor of *Adventure Tales* and *Cat Tales* magazines. He also co-edits *Weird Tales* magazine (with George Scithers and Darrell Schweitzer). More information can be found on John and his various endeavors at <www.wildsidepress.com>.

**SEAN WALLACE** has worked full-time for Wildside Press, for both its book and magazine divisions, since 2001. In between editing the award-winning Prime Books imprint, issues of *Fantasy Magazine*, and the *Best New Fantasy* anthology series, he occasionally plays a mean game of racquetball. He currently resides in Maryland with his fiancée, Jennifer.

# COPYRIGHTS